D0886755

THE LOEB CLASSICAL LIBRARY

FOUNDED BY JAMES LOEB 1911

EDITED BY

JEFFREY HENDERSON

EDITOR EMERITUS

G. P. GOOLD

VIRGIL

II

LCL 64

VIRGIL

AENEID VII-XII
APPENDIX VERGILIANA

WITH AN ENGLISH TRANSLATION BY

H. RUSHTON FAIRCLOUGH

REVISED BY G. P. GOOLD

HARVARD UNIVERSITY PRESS
CAMBRIDGE, MASSACHUSETTS
LONDON, ENGLAND
2000

LOEB CLASSICAL LIBRARY® is a registered trademark
of the President and Fellows of Harvard College

ISBN 0-674-99586-4

CONTENTS

AENEID

VII–XII

LIBER VII

MPR   Tu quoque litoribus nostris, Aeneïa nutrix,
      aeternam moriens famam, Caieta, dedisti;
      et nunc servat honos sedem tuus, ossaque nomen
      Hesperia in magna, si qua est ea gloria, signat.
FMPR   At pius exsequiis Aeneas rite solutis,
6   aggere composito tumuli, postquam alta quierunt
      aequora, tendit iter velis portumque relinquit.
      aspirant aurae in noctem nec candida cursus
      luna negat, splendet tremulo sub lumine pontus.
10   proxima Circaeae raduntur litora terrae,
      dives inaccessos ubi Solis filia lucos
      adsiduo resonat cantu, tectisque superbis
      urit odoratam nocturna in lumina cedrum
      arguto tenuis percurrens pectine telas.
15   hinc exaudiri gemitus iraeque leonum
      vincla recusantum et sera sub nocte rudentum,
      saetigerique sues atque in praesepibus ursi
      saevire ac formae magnorum ululare luporum,
      quos hominum ex facie dea saeva potentibus herbis
20   induerat Circe in vultus ac terga ferarum.

      [4] signat *R*: signant *MP*

BOOK VII

You, too,[1] Caieta, nurse of Aeneas, have by your death given eternal fame to our shores; and still your honour guards your resting place, and in great Hesperia, if that be glory, your name marks your dust!

Now good Aeneas, when the last rites were duly paid and the funeral mound was raised, as soon as the high seas were stilled, sails forth on his way and leaves the haven. Breezes blow on into the night, and the Moon, shining bright, smiles on their voyage; the sea glitters beneath her dancing beams. The next shores they skirt are those of Circe's realm,[2] where the wealthy daughter of the Sun thrills the untrodden groves with ceaseless song and in her proud palace burns fragrant cedar to illuminate the night, while she drives her shrill shuttle through the fine web. From these shores could be heard the angry growls of lions chafing at their bonds and roaring in midnight hours, the raging of bristly boars and caged bears, and huge wolfish shapes howling. These were they whom, robbing them of their human form with potent herbs, Circe, cruel goddess, had clothed in the features and frames of beasts. But so

[1] As well as Misenus (6.234) and Palinurus (6.381). Caieta gave her name to Gaeta and the Gulf of Gaeta.

[2] Circeii, a promontory of Latium, but once an island, is identified by Virgil with Homer's island of Aeaea, the home of Circe.

3

quae ne monstra pii paterentur talia Troes
delati in portus neu litora dira subirent,
Neptunus ventis implevit vela secundis,
atque fugam dedit et praeter vada fervida vexit.
25   Iamque rubescebat radiis mare et aethere ab alto
Aurora in roseis fulgebat lutea bigis,
cum venti posuere omnisque repente resedit
flatus, et in lento luctantur marmore tonsae.
atque hic Aeneas ingentem ex aequore lucum
30   prospicit. hunc inter fluvio Tiberinus amoeno
verticibus rapidis et multa flavus harena
in mare prorumpit. variae circumque supraque
adsuetae ripis volucres et fluminis alveo
aethera mulcebant cantu lucoque volabant.
35   flectere iter sociis terraeque advertere proras
imperat et laetus fluvio succedit opaco.
    Nunc age, qui reges, Erato, quae tempora, rerum
quis Latio antiquo fuerit status, advena classem
cum primum Ausoniis exercitus appulit oris,
40   expediam, et primae revocabo exordia pugnae.
tu vatem, tu, diva, mone. dicam horrida bella,
dicam·acies actosque animis in funera reges,
Tyrrhenamque manum totamque sub arma coactam
Hesperiam. maior rerum mihi nascitur ordo,
45   maius opus moveo.
                Rex arva Latinus et urbes
iam senior longa placidas in pace regebat.
hunc Fauno et nympha genitum Laurente Marica

---

[37] tempora, rerum *punctuated by Peerlkamp*: t. r., *codd.*

that the pious of Troy should not suffer so monstrous a fate on entering the harbour and setting foot on the accursed shore, Neptune filled their sails with favouring winds, giving them flight, and bore them past the seething shallows.

Now the sea was reddening with the rays of dawn, and from heaven's height the goddess of Dawn on her rosy chariot shone in saffron light, when the winds dropped and suddenly every breeze sank; the oars toil slowly against the marble smoothness of the water. At this moment Aeneas, looking from the sea, beholds a mighty forest. Through its midst the Tiber's lovely stream leaps forth to sea in swirling eddies with his burden of golden sand. Around and above, birds of many a kind that haunt the river's banks and channel were thrilling heaven with their song and flying in the grove. He bids his comrades change their course and turn their prows to land, and joyfully enters the shady river.

Awake now, Erato[3]! Who were the kings, what were the times, what the state of affairs in ancient Latium, when first that foreign army landed on Ausonia's shore—this will I unfold; and the prelude of the opening strife will I recall. And you, goddess, prompt your bard! I will tell of grim wars, will tell of battle array, and princes in their valour rushing upon death—of Tyrrhenian bands, and all Hesperia mustered in arms. Greater is the story that opens before me; greater is the task that I attempt.

King Latinus, now old, ruled over lands and towns in the calm of a long peace. He was sprung of Faunus, we are told, and the Laurentine nymph, Marica. Faunus' sire was

[3] Erato, invoked as the Muse of Love (as by Apollonius in *Argonautica* 3.1) in view of the entrance of Lavinia into the story. See F. A. Todd, *Classical Review* 45 (1931) 216ff.

accipimus; Fauno Picus pater, isque parentem
te, Saturne, refert, tu sanguinis ultimus auctor.
50 filius huic fato divum prolesque virilis
nulla fuit, primaque oriens erepta iuventa est.
sola domum et tantas servabat filia sedes
iam matura viro, iam plenis nubilis annis.
multi illam magno e Latio totaque petebant
55 Ausonia; petit ante alios pulcherrimus omnis
Turnus, avis atavisque potens, quem regia coniunx
adiungi generum miro properabat amore;
sed variis portenta deum terroribus obstant.
MPR laurus erat tecti medio in penetralibus altis
60 sacra comam multosque metu servata per annos,
quam pater inventam, primas cum conderet arces,
ipse ferebatur Phoebo sacrasse Latinus,
Laurentisque ab ea nomen posuisse colonis.
huius apes summum densae (mirabile dictu)
65 stridore ingenti liquidum trans aethera vectae
obsedere apicem, et pedibus per mutua nexis
examen subitum ramo frondente pependit.
continuo vates "externum cernimus" inquit
"adventare virum et partis petere agmen easdem
70 partibus ex isdem et summa dominarier arce."
praeterea, castis adolet dum altaria taedis,
et iuxta genitorem astat Lavinia virgo,
visa (nefas) longis comprendere crinibus ignem
atque omnem ornatum flamma crepitante cremari,
75 regalisque accensa comas, accensa coronam
insignem gemmis; tum fumida lumine fulvo
involvi ac totis Volcanum spargere tectis.
id vero horrendum ac visu mirabile ferri:
namque fore inlustrem fama fatisque canebant

Picus, and he boasts you, Saturn, as his father; you are the first founder of the line. By Heaven's decree his son, his male descent, was no more, but had been cut off in the spring of early youth. Alone, to preserve the house and noble home, was a daughter, now ripe for a husband, now of full age to be a bride. Many wooed her from wide Latium and all Ausonia, yet handsomest above all other wooers was Turnus, of long and lofty ancestry, whom the queen mother yearned with wondrous passion to unite to her as son. But divine portents, with manifold alarms, bar the way. In the midst of the palace, in the high inner courts, stood a laurel of sacred foliage, preserved in awe through many years, which lord Latinus himself was said to have founded and dedicated to Phoebus, when he built his first towers; and from it he gave his settlers their name Laurentes. In the top of this tree, wondrous to tell, settled a dense swarm of bees, borne with loud humming across the liquid air, and with feet intertwined hung in sudden swarm from the leafy bough. At once the prophet cries: "I see a stranger draw near; from the selfsame quarter a troop seeks the same quarter, and reigns in the topmost citadel!" Moreover, while with hallowed torch he kindles the altars, and at her father's side stands the maiden Lavinia, she was seen (O horror!) to catch fire in her long tresses, and burn with crackling flame in all her headgear, her queenly hair ablaze, ablaze her jewelled coronal; then wreathed in smoke and yellow glare, she scattered fire throughout the palace. That indeed was noised abroad as an awful and wondrous vision; for she, they foretold, would herself be

80　ipsam, sed populo magnum portendere bellum.
　　　At rex sollicitus monstris oracula Fauni,
　　fatidici genitoris, adit lucosque sub alta
　　consulit Albunea, nemorum quae maxima sacro
　　fonte sonat saevamque exhalat opaca mephitim.
85　hinc Italae gentes omnisque Oenotria tellus
　　in dubiis responsa petunt; huc dona sacerdos
　　cum tulit et caesarum ovium sub nocte silenti
　　pellibus incubuit stratis somnosque petivit,
　　multa modis simulacra videt volitantia miris
90　et varias audit voces fruiturque deorum
　　conloquio atque imis Acheronta adfatur Avern is.
　　hic et tum pater ipse petens responsa Latinus
　　centum lanigeras mactabat rite bidentis,
　　atque harum effultus tergo stratisque iacebat
95　velleribus: subita ex alto vox reddita luco est:
　　"ne pete conubiis natam sociare Latinis,
　　o mea progenies, thalamis neu crede paratis;
　　externi venient generi, qui sanguine nostrum
　　nomen in astra ferant, quorumque a stirpe nepotes
100　omnia sub pedibus, qua sol utrumque recurrens
　　aspicit Oceanum, vertique regique videbunt."
　　haec responsa patris Fauni monitusque silenti
　　nocte datos non ipse suo premit ore Latinus,
　　sed circum late volitans iam Fama per urbes
105　Ausonias tulerat, cum Laomedontia pubes
　　gramineo ripae religavit ab aggere classem.

---

4 Albunea is here identified with the forest. Situated at or near Lavinium, this must be different from the Albunea of Horace, *Odes* 1.7.12, which is a cascade at Tibur.

glorious in fame and fortune, yet to her people she boded a mighty war.

But the king, troubled by the portent, visits the oracle of Faunus, his prophetic sire, and consults the groves beneath high Albunea, which, mightiest of forests,[4] echoes with hallowed fountain, and breathes forth from her darkness a deadly vapour. From this place the tribes of Italy and all the Oenotrian land seek responses in days of doubt; to it the priestess brings the offerings , and as she lies under the silent night on the outspread fleeces of slaughtered sheep and woos slumber, she sees many phantoms flitting in wondrous wise, hears many voices, holds converse with the gods, and speaks with Acheron in lowest Avernus. Here then, also, King Latinus himself, seeking an answer, duly slaughtered a hundred woolly sheep, and lay couched on their hides and outspread fleeces. Suddenly a voice came from the deep grove: "Seek not, my son, to ally your daughter in Latin wedlock, and put no faith in the bridal chamber that is ready at hand. Strangers shall come, to be your sons, whose blood shall exalt our name to the stars, and the children of whose race shall behold, where the circling sun looks on each ocean,[5] the whole world roll obedient beneath their feet." This answer of his father Faunus, and the warning he gave in the silent night, Latinus keeps not shut within his own lips; but Rumour, flitting far and wide, had already borne the tidings through the Ausonian cities when the sons of Laomedon moored their ships to the river's grassy bank.

[5] I.e. in East and West; the Ocean being conceived as flowing round the earth.

    Aeneas primique duces et pulcher Iulus
corpora sub ramis deponunt arboris altae,
instituuntque dapes et adorea liba per herbam
110   subiciunt epulis (sic Iuppiter ipse monebat)
et Cereale solum pomis agrestibus augent.
consumptis hic forte aliis, ut vertere morsus
exiguam in Cererem penuria adegit edendi,
et violare manu malisque audacibus orbem
115   fatalis crusti patulis nec parcere quadris:
"heus, etiam mensas consumimus?" inquit Iulus,
nec plura, adludens. ea vox audita laborum
prima tulit finem, primamque loquentis ab ore
eripuit pater ac stupefactus numine pressit.
120   continuo "salve fatis mihi debita tellus
vosque" ait "o fidi Troiae salvete penates:
hic domus, haec patria est. genitor mihi talia namque
(nunc repeto) Anchises fatorum arcana reliquit:
'cum te, nate, fames ignota ad litora vectum
125   accisis coget dapibus consumere mensas,
tum sperare domos defessus, ibique memento
prima locare manu molirique aggere tecta.'
haec erat illa fames, haec nos suprema manebat
exitiis positura modum . . .
130   quare agite et primo laeti cum lumine solis
quae loca, quive habeant homines, ubi moenia gentis,
vestigemus et a portu diversa petamus.
nunc pateras libate Iovi precibusque vocate
Anchisen genitorem, et vina reponite mensis."

[110] ipse *MPR*: ille *M²*, *known to Servius*

Aeneas, his chief captains, and fair Iülus lay their limbs to rest under the boughs of a high tree, and spread the feast; they place cakes of meal on the grass beneath the food—Jove himself inspired them—and they crown the wheaten base with fruits of the field. Here, haply, when the rest was consumed, and the scantness of fare drove them to turn their teeth upon the thin cakes—to profane with hand and daring jaw the fateful circles of crust, and spare not the broad loaves:[6] "Oh, look! we are eating our tables too!" said Iülus in jest; and said no more. That cry, when heard, first brought an end of toil; and as it first fell from the speaker's lips, his father caught it up and checked his utterance, awestruck at Heaven's will. Straightway, "Hail," he cries, "land destined as my due! and hail to you, faithful gods of Troy! Here is our home, here our country! For my father Anchises[7]—now I recall it—bequeathed me this secret of fate: 'My son, when you are carried to an unknown shore and hunger compels you, as food fails, to eat your tables, then in your weariness hope for a home, and there be mindful first to set up your dwellings with your hand and bank them with a mound.' This was that hunger foretold, this the last strait awaiting us, that was to set an end to our deadly woes! . . . Come then, and gladly with the sun's first beams let us explore what lands these are, what people here dwell, where is the city of the nation, and from the harbour let us explore in different directions. Now pour your cups to Jove, and call in prayer on my sire Anchises, and set the wine again upon the board."

[6] The round cakes were scored by crossed lines into four quarters (*quadrae*).   [7] Cf. 3.255, where, however, the prophecy is uttered by Celaeno, not by Anchises.

135 Sic deinde effatus frondenti tempora ramo
implicat et geniumque loci primamque deorum
Tellurem Nymphasque et adhuc ignota precatur
flumina, tum Noctem Noctisque orientia signa
Idaeumque Iovem Phrygiamque ex ordine matrem
140 invocat, et duplicis caeloque Ereboque parentis.
hic pater omnipotens ter caelo clarus ab alto
intonuit, radiisque ardentem lucis et auro
ipse manu quatiens ostendit ab aethere nubem.
diditur hic subito Troiana per agmina rumor
145 advenisse diem quo debita moenia condant.
certatim instaurant epulas atque omine magno
crateras laeti statuunt et vina coronant.
    Postera cum prima lustrabat lampade terras
orta dies, urbem et finis et litora gentis
150 diversi explorant: haec fontis stagna Numici,
hunc Thybrim fluvium, hic fortis habitare Latinos.
tum satus Anchisa delectos ordine ab omni
centum oratores augusta ad moenia regis
ire iubet, ramis velatos Palladis omnis,
155 donaque ferre viro pacemque exposcere Teucris.
haud mora, festinant iussi rapidisque feruntur
passibus. ipse humili designat moenia fossa
moliturque locum, primasque in litore sedes
castrorum in morem pinnis atque aggere cingit.
160 iamque iter emensi turris ac tecta Latini
ardua cernebant iuvenes muroque subibant.
ante urbem pueri et primaevo flore iuventus
exercentur equis domitantque in pulvere currus,

160 Latini *M²(late)*: Latinorum *MPR*

So speaking, he straightway wreaths his temples with leafy bough and prays to the genius of the place, and Earth, first of gods; to the nymphs and the rivers yet unknown; then to Night and Night's rising signs, and to Jove of Ida and the Phrygian Mother, each in order, and his two parents, in heaven and in the underworld. At this, the almighty Father thundered thrice from a clear sky, and showed forth from heaven a cloud ablaze with shafts of golden light, brandishing it in his own hand. Then suddenly through the Trojan band runs the rumour that the day has come to found their promised city. Emulously they renew the feast, and cheered by the mighty omen set on the bowls and wreathe the wine.

On the morrow, when the risen day was lighting the earth with her earliest torch, by separate ways they search out the city[8] and boundaries and coasts of the nation. This, they learn, is the pool of Numicius' fount; this the Tiber river; here dwell the brave Latins. Then Anchises' son commands a hundred envoys, chosen from every rank, to go to the king's stately city, all shadowed by the boughs of Pallas, to bear gifts to the hero, and crave peace for the Trojans. They linger not, but hasten at his bidding and move with rapid steps. Aeneas himself marks out his walls with a shallow trench, toils over the ground, and encircles this first settlement on the coast, after the fashion of a camp, with mound and battlements. And now his men had traversed their way; they were in sight of the towers and steep roofs of Latinus, and drew near to the wall. Outside the city, boys and youths in their early bloom practise horsemanship, or break in teams amid the dust, or bend

---

[8] Lavinium.

aut acris tendunt arcus aut lenta lacertis
165 spicula contorquent, cursuque ictuque lacessunt:
cum praevectus equo longaevi regis ad auris
nuntius ingentis ignota in veste reportat
advenisse viros. ille intra tecta vocari
imperat et solio medius consedit avito.
170   Tectum augustum, ingens, centum sublime columnis
urbe fuit summa, Laurentis regia Pici,
horrendum silvis et religione parentum.
hic sceptra accipere et primos attollere fascis
regibus omen erat; hoc illis curia templum,
175 hae sacris sedes epulis; hic ariete caeso
perpetuis soliti patres considere mensis.
quin etiam veterum effigies ex ordine avorum
antiqua e cedro, Italusque paterque Sabinus
FMPR vitisator curvam servans sub imagine falcem,
180 Saturnusque senex Ianique bifrontis imago
vestibulo astabant, aliique ab origine reges,
Martiaque ob patriam pugnando vulnera passi.
multaque praeterea sacris in postibus arma,
captivi pendent currus curvaeque secures
185 et cristae capitum et portarum ingentia claustra
spiculaque clipeique ereptaque rostra carinis.
ipse Quirinali lituo parvaque sedebat
succinctus trabea laevaque ancile gerebat
Picus, equum domitor, quem capta cupidine coniunx
190 aurea percussum virga versumque venenis
fecit avem Circe sparsitque coloribus alas.

---

[182] Martiaque *PR*: Martia qui *FM*

---

[9] Quirinus (i.e. Romulus) was Rome's first augur, and as such

eager bows, or hurl with their arms tough darts, and challenge each other to race or box—when, galloping up, a messenger brings word to the aged monarch's ears that mighty men are come in unknown attire. The king bids them be summoned into the halls, and takes his seat in the midst on his ancestral throne.

Stately and vast, towering with a hundred columns, his house crowned the city, once the palace of Laurentian Picus, awe-inspiring with its grove and the reverence of generations. Here it was auspicious for kings to receive the sceptre, and first uplift the fasces; this shrine was their senate house, this the scene of their holy feasts; here, after slaughter of rams, the elders were wont to sit down at the long line of tables. There, too, in order are images of their forefathers of long ago, carved of old cedar—Italus and father Sabinus, planter of the vine, guarding in his image the curved pruning hook, and aged Saturn, and the likeness of two-faced Janus—all standing in the vestibule; and other kings from the beginning, and men who had suffered wounds of war, fighting for their fatherland. Many arms, moreover, hang on the sacred doors, captive chariots, curved axes, helmet crests and massive bars of city gates; javelins and shields and beaks wrenched from ships. There sat one, holding the Quirinal staff[9] and girded in his robe of state, his left hand bearing the sacred shield—Picus, tamer of steeds, whom his bride Circe, smitten with love's longing, struck with her golden rod, and with drugs changed into a bird with plumes of dappled hue.

carried the augur's badges of office—the *lituus,* or curved staff, and the *ancile,* or sacred shield—while he wore the purple striped toga, or *trabea.*

Tali intus templo divum patriaque Latinus
sede sedens Teucros ad sese in tecta vocavit,
atque haec ingressis placido prior edidit ore:
195 "dicite, Dardanidae (neque enim nescimus et urbem
et genus, auditique advertitis aequore cursum),
quid petitis? quae causa rates aut cuius egentis
litus ad Ausonium tot per vada caerula vexit?
sive errore viae seu tempestatibus acti,
200 qualia multa mari nautae patiuntur in alto,
fluminis intrastis ripas portuque sedetis,
ne fugite hospitium, neve ignorate Latinos
Saturni gentem haud vinclo nec legibus aequam,
sponte sua veterisque dei se more tenentem.
205 atque equidem memini (fama est obscurior annis)
Auruncos ita ferre senes, his ortus ut agris
Dardanus Idaeas Phrygiae penetrarit ad urbes
Threiciamque Samum, quae nunc Samothracia fertur.
hinc illum Corythi Tyrrhena ab sede profectum
210 aurea nunc solio stellantis regia caeli
accipit et numerum divorum altaribus auget."
Dixerat, et dicta Ilioneus sic voce secutus:
"rex, genus egregium Fauni, nec fluctibus actos
atra subegit hiems vestris succedere terris,
215 nec sidus regione viae litusve fefellit:
consilio hanc omnes animisque volentibus urbem
adferimur pulsi regnis, quae maxima quondam
extremo veniens sol aspiciebat Olympo.
ab Iove principium generis, Iove Dardana pubes
220 gaudet avo, rex ipse Iovis de gente suprema:

[207] penetrarit *R*: penetravit *FMP*

Such was the temple of the gods in which Latinus, seated on the throne of his fathers, summoned the Teucrians to his presence in the halls, and as they entered greeted them thus with gentle countenance: "Tell, sons of Dardanus—for your city and race we know, and not unheard of is your journey over the deep—what do you seek? What cause, or what need, has borne you to the Ausonian shore over so many dark-blue waters? Whether straying from your course, or driven by storms (for such things sailors often suffer on the high seas), you have entered the river banks and lie in haven, shun not our welcome, and be not unaware that the Latins are Saturn's race, righteous not by bond or laws, but self-controlled of their own free will and by the custom of their ancient god. And in truth I remember, though time has dimmed the tale, that Auruncan elders told how in this land Dardanus was born,[10] and hence passed to the towns of Phrygian Ida and Thracian Samos, that men now call Samothrace. It was from here, from the Tuscan home of Corythus, he came, and now the golden palace of the starry sky admits him to a throne, and he increases the number of altars of the gods."

He ceased, and Ilioneus followed thus: "O King, illustrious seed of Faunus, no black storm has tossed us on the waves and driven us to seek shelter in your lands, nor has star or shore misled us in our course. Of set purpose and with willing hearts do we draw near to this city of yours, exiled from a realm once the greatest that the sun beheld as he journeyed from the uttermost heaven. From Jove[11] is the origin of our race; in Jove, their ancestor, the sons of Dardanus glory; of Jove's supreme race is our king himself,

---

[10] Cf. 3.167.   [11] Jupiter was the father of Dardanus.

Troïus Aeneas tua nos ad limina misit.
quanta per Idaeos saevis effusa Mycenis
tempestas ierit campos, quibus actus uterque
Europae atque Asiae fatis concurrerit orbis,
225 audiit et si quem tellus extrema refuso
summovet Oceano et si quem extenta plagarum
quattuor in medio dirimit plaga solis iniqui.
diluvio ex illo tot vasta per aequora vecti
dis sedem exiguam patriis litusque rogamus
230 innocuum et cunctis undamque auramque patentem.
non erimus regno indecores, nec vestra feretur
fama levis tantique abolescet gratia facti,
nec Troiam Ausonios gremio excepisse pigebit.
fata per Aeneae iuro dextramque potentem,
235 sive fide seu quis bello est expertus et armis:
multi nos populi, multae (ne temne, quod ultro
praeferimus manibus vittas ac verba precantia)
et petiere sibi et voluere adiungere gentes;
sed nos fata deum vestras exquirere terras
240 imperiis egere suis. hinc Dardanus ortus,
huc repetit iussisque ingentibus urget Apollo
Tyrrhenum ad Thybrim et fontis vada sacra Numici.
dat tibi praeterea fortunae parva prioris
munera, reliquias Troia ex ardente receptas.
245 hoc pater Anchises auro libabat ad aras,
hoc Priami gestamen erat cum iura vocatis
more daret populis, sceptrumque sacerque tiaras
FMPRV Iliadumque labor vestes . . ."

Trojan Aeneas, who has sent us to your doors. How fierce the storm that burst from cruel Mycenae and passed over the plains of Ida; how, driven by fate, the two worlds of Europe and Asia clashed—this has come to the ears of all whom the farthest land where Ocean is flung back keeps far away, and of all whom the zone of the tyrannous sun, stretched in the middle of the four, severs from us.[12] From that deluge we have sailed over many waste seas, and now crave a scant home for our country's gods, a harmless landing place, and air and water free to all. We shall be no shame to the realm, nor shall your renown be lightly told or the grace of such a deed grow faint, nor shall Ausonia repent of having welcomed Troy to her breast. By the fortunes of Aeneas I swear, and by his right hand, found strong when any tested it for loyalty or in war and arms: many are the peoples, many the nations—scorn us not, that of ourselves we proffer garlands with our hands and address to you words of suppliance—who have sought us for themselves and craved our alliance; but the will of heaven has forced us by its behests to seek out your shores. From here Dardanus came forth, hither Apollo calls us back and with high decrees urges us to Tuscan Tiber and the sacred waters of the Numician spring. Further, to you our king offers these poor tokens of his former fortune—relics snatched from burning Troy. With this gold did his father Anchises pour libation at the altars; this was Priam's array when after his wont he gave laws to the assembled nations—the sceptre, the sacred diadem, and the robes wrought by Ilium's daughters. . . ."

[12] Those who dwell farthest away on Atlantic shores, and those beyond the tropics, alike have heard.

Talibus Ilionei dictis defixa Latinus
250 obtutu tenet ora soloque immobilis haeret,
intentos volvens oculos. nec purpura regem
picta movet nec sceptra movent Priameïa tantum
quantum in conubio natae thalamoque moratur,
et veteris Fauni volvit sub pectore sortem:
255 hunc illum fatis externa ab sede profectum
portendi generum paribusque in regna vocari
auspiciis, huic progeniem virtute futuram
egregiam et totum quae viribus occupet orbem.
tandem laetus ait: "di nostra incepta secundent
260 auguriumque suum! dabitur, Troiane, quod optas.
munera nec sperno: non vobis rege Latino
divitis uber agri Troiaeve opulentia deerit.
ipse modo Aeneas, nostri si tanta cupido est,
si iungi hospitio properat sociusque vocari,
265 adveniat, vultus neve exhorrescat amicos:
pars mihi pacis erit dextram tetigisse tyranni.
vos contra regi mea nunc mandata referte:
est mihi nata, viro gentis quam iungere nostrae
non patrio ex adyto sortes, non plurima caelo
270 monstra sinunt; generos externis adfore ab oris,
hoc Latio restare canunt, qui sanguine nostrum
nomen in astra ferant. hunc illum poscere fata
et reor et, si quid veri mens augurat, opto."
FMPR   Haec effatus equos numero pater eligit omni
275 (stabant ter centum nitidi in praesepibus altis);
omnibus extemplo Teucris iubet ordine duci
FMR instratos ostro alipedes pictisque tapetis
(aurea pectoribus demissa monilia pendent,

264 sociusque *MP*: sociusve *FRV*

At these words of Ilioneus Latinus holds his face fixed in steady gaze downward, moving his eyes in deep thought. Nor is it so much that the embroidered purple or the sceptre of Priam moves the king, as that he broods over his daughter's wedlock and bridal bed, and revolves in his breast the oracle of ancient Faunus. "This," he thought, "must be he who, coming from a stranger's home, is predestined by the fates as my son, and called to sovereignty with equal power; his must be the offspring, glorious in valour, whose might is to master all the world." At last, in gladness, he speaks: "May the gods prosper our intent and their own prophecy! Trojan, your wish shall be granted; nor do I spurn your gifts. While Latinus is king, you shall not lack the bounty of a fruitful soil, nor Troy's abundance. Only let Aeneas, if so he longs for us, if he is eager to join us in amity and be called our ally, let him come in person and shrink not from friendly eyes. To me it shall be a term of the peace to have touched your sovereign's hand! Now in turn take back to the king my answer: I have a daughter whom oracles from my father's shrine and countless prodigies from heaven do not allow me to unite to a bridegroom of our race; sons shall come from shores of strangers—such destiny, they foretell, awaits Latium—whose blood shall exalt our name to the stars. That this is he on whom fate calls, I both think, and, if my soul forebodes aught of truth, I wish it too."

With these words the old king picks out horses from all his number—three hundred stood sleek in their high stalls. At once for all the Teucrians in order he commands them to be led forth, fleet of foot and caparisoned with purple and embroidered housings. Golden are the chains that hang low from their breasts, of gold are their trap-

21

tecti auro fulvum mandunt sub dentibus aurum),
280 absenti Aeneae currum geminosque iugalis
semine ab aetherio spirantis naribus ignem,
illorum de gente patri quos daedala Circe
supposita de matre nothos furata creavit.
talibus Aeneadae donis dictisque Latini
285 sublimes in equis redeunt pacemque reportant.
    Ecce autem Inachiis sese referebat ab Argis
saeva Iovis coniunx aurasque invecta tenebat,
et laetum Aenean classemque ex aethere longe
Dardaniam Siculo prospexit ab usque Pachyno.
290 moliri iam tecta videt, iam fidere terrae,
deseruisse rates: stetit acri fixa dolore.
tum quassans caput haec effundit pectore dicta:
"heu stirpem invisam et fatis contraria nostris
fata Phrygum! num Sigeis occumbere campis,
295 num capti potuere capi? num incensa cremavit
Troia viros? medias acies mediosque per ignis
invenere viam. at, credo, mea numina tandem
fessa iacent, odiis aut exsaturata quievi.
quin etiam patria excussos infesta per undas
300 ausa sequi et profugis toto me opponere ponto.
absumptae in Teucros vires caelique marisque.
quid Syrtes aut Scylla mihi, quid vasta Charybdis
profuit? optato conduntur Thybridis alveo
securi pelagi atque mei. Mars perdere gentem
305 immanem Lapithum valuit, concessit in iras
ipse deum antiquam genitor Calydona Dianae,

---

[13] Circe was daughter of the Sun. His horses were immortal;
her mare was mortal.

[14] The wild boar ravaged Calydon because King Oeneus failed
to sacrifice to Diana.

pings, and yellow gold they champ with their teeth. For the absent Aeneas he chooses a chariot and twin coursers of ethereal seed, breathing fire from their nostrils, and sprung from the stock of those steeds which cunning Circe, stealing them from her sire, bred bastard from the mare she had mated.[13] With such words and gifts from Latinus, the sons of Aeneas, mounted on their horses, return carrying back peace.

But the fierce wife of Jove was coming back from Argos, city of Inachus, holding her airy flight; and from the sky afar, all the way from Sicilian Pachynus, she espied the rejoicing Aeneas and his Dardan fleet. She sees them already building a home, already trusting in the land, their ships deserted. She stopped, pierced with sharp grief; then, shaking her head, pours forth from her breast these words: "Ah! hated race, and Phrygian fates that cross my own! Could they not have perished on the Sigean plains? Captured, could they not have suffered captivity? Did the fires of Troy consume them? No! through the midst of armies, through the midst of flames, they have found a way. But I think my power at last lies outworn; or my wrath is sated, and I rest! Nay more, when they were hurled forth from their country, with my vengeance I dared to follow the exiles through the waves and confront them over all the deep: against the Teucrians has been spent all the power of sea and sky. Yet what have the Syrtes availed me, or Scylla, what yawning Charybdis? They find shelter in Tiber's longed-for channel, heedless of ocean and of me. Mars could destroy the Lapiths' giant race; the very father of the gods yielded ancient Calydon to Diana's wrath,[14]

quod scelus aut Lapithas tantum aut Calydona merentem?
ast ego, magna Iovis coniunx, nil linquere inausum
quae potui infelix, quae memet in omnia verti,
310 vincor ab Aenea. quod si mea numina non sunt
magna satis, dubitem haud equidem implorare quod
        usquam est:
flectere si nequeo superos, Acheronta movebo.
non dabitur regnis, esto, prohibere Latinis,
atque immota manet fatis Lavinia coniunx:
315 at trahere atque moras tantis licet addere rebus,
at licet amborum populos exscindere regum.
hac gener atque socer coeant mercede suorum:
sanguine Troiano et Rutulo dotabere, virgo,
et Bellona manet te pronuba. nec face tantum
320 Cisseis praegnas ignis enixa iugalis;
quin idem Veneri partus suus et Paris alter,
funestaeque iterum recidiva in Pergama taedae."
    Haec ubi dicta dedit, terras horrenda petivit;
luctificam Allecto dirarum ab sede dearum
325 infernisque ciet tenebris, cui tristia bella
FMRV iraeque insidiaeque et crimina noxia cordi.
odit et ipse pater Pluton, odere sorores
Tartareae monstrum: tot sese vertit in ora,
tam saevae facies, tot pullulat atra colubris.
MRV quam Iuno his acuit verbis ac talia fatur:
331 "hunc mihi da proprium, virgo sata Nocte, laborem,

---

307 Lapithas M^2: Lapithis $FM\gamma R$ | Calydona $F^2M^2\gamma$: Calydo F:
Calydone MR | merentem $FM^2\gamma$: merentes M: merente R

---

[15] This verse was chosen by Sigmund Freud as the epigraph
for his *Interpretation of Dreams*.

though for what heinous sin did Lapiths or Calydon merit such penalty? But I, Jove's mighty consort, who have endured, poor wretch, to leave nothing undared, who have turned myself to every shift, I am worsted by Aeneas! But if my powers are not strong enough, surely I need not be slow to seek help wherever it may be; if Heaven I cannot bend, then Hell I will arouse![15] Not mine will it be—I grant it—to keep him from the crown of Latium, and by fate Lavinia abides immovably his bride; yet to put off the hour and to bring delay to such great issues—that I may do; I may yet uproot the nations of both kings. At such price of their people's lives may father and son-in-law be united! Blood of Trojan and Rutulian shall be your dower, maiden, and Bellona awaits you as your bridal matron. Nor was it only Cisseus' daughter who conceived a firebrand and gave birth to nuptial flames.[16] No, Venus has the like in her own child, a second Paris, another funeral torch for reborn Troy."

When she had uttered these words, with awful countenance she came to earth, and calls baleful Allecto from the home of the Dread Goddesses and the infernal shades—Allecto, whose heart is set on gloomy wars, passions, plots, and baneful crimes. Hateful is the monster even to her sire Pluto, hateful to her Tartarean sisters; so many are the forms she assumes, so savage their aspect, so thick her black sprouting vipers.[17] Her Juno inflames with these words, speaking thus: "Grant me, maiden daughter

[16] Hecuba, before bearing Paris, dreamed that she would give birth to a firebrand.

[17] The Furies are commonly represented with snakes for hair.

hanc operam, ne noster honos infractave cedat
fama loco, neu conubiis ambire Latinum
Aeneadae possint Italosve obsidere finis.
335 tu potes unanimos armare in proelia fratres
atque odiis versare domos, tu verbera tectis
funereasque inferre faces, tibi nomina mille,
mille nocendi artes. fecundum concute pectus,
disice compositam pacem, sere crimina belli;
340 arma velit poscatque simul rapiatque iuventus."
    Exim Gorgoneis Allecto infecta venenis
principio Latium et Laurentis tecta tyranni
celsa petit, tacitumque obsedit limen Amatae,
quam super adventu Teucrum Turnique hymenaeis
345 femineae ardentem curaeque iraeque coquebant.
huic dea caeruleis unum de crinibus anguem
conicit, inque sinum praecordia ad intima subdit,
quo furibunda domum monstro permisceat omnem.
ille inter vestis et levia pectora lapsus
350 volvitur attactu nullo, fallitque furentem
vipeream inspirans animam; fit tortile collo
MR aurum ingens coluber, fit longae taenia vittae
innectitque comas et membris lubricus errat.
ac dum prima lues udo sublapsa veneno
355 pertemptat sensus atque ossibus implicat ignem
necdum animus toto percepit pectore flammam,
mollius et solito matrum de more locuta est,
multa super natae lacrimans Phrygiisque hymenaeis:
"exsulibusne datur ducenda Lavinia Teucris,
360 o genitor, nec te miseret nataeque tuique?
nec matris miseret, quam primo Aquilone relinquet

<hr>

358 natae *Mγ*: nata *R*

of Night, this service, a boon all my own, that my honour and glory not yield overmastered, and that the sons of Aeneas be not able to cajole Latinus with wedlock or beset the borders of Italy. You can arm for strife brothers of one soul, and overturn homes with hate; you can bring under the roof the lash and funeral torch; you have a thousand names, a thousand means of ill. Rouse your fertile bosom, shatter the pact of peace, sow seeds of wicked war! In the same hour let the men crave, demand, and seize the sword!"

At this Allecto, steeped in Gorgonian venom, first seeks Latium and the high halls of the Laurentine king, and sits down before the silent threshold of Amata, who, with a woman's distress, a woman's passion, was seething with frenzy over the Teucrian's coming and Turnus' marriage. On her the goddess flings a snake from her dusky tresses, and thrusts it into her bosom, into her inmost heart, that maddened by the pest she may embroil all the house. Gliding between her raiment and smooth breasts, it winds its way unfelt and, unseen by the frenzied woman, breathes into her its viperous breath. The huge snake becomes the collar of twisted gold about her neck, becomes the festoon of the long fillet, entwines itself into her hair, and slides smoothly over her limbs. And while first the taint, stealing on in fluent poison, thrills her senses and wraps her bones with fire, and her soul has not yet caught the flame throughout her breast, softly, and as mothers are wont, she spoke, shedding many a tear over her daughter's and the Phrygian's wedlock: "Is it to exiled Teucrians Lavinia is given as wife, O father? And have you no pity on your daughter and yourself? Have you no pity on her mother, whom with the first North Wind the faithless

27

perfidus alta petens abducta virgine praedo?
an non sic Phrygius penetrat Lacedaemona pastor,
Ledaeamque Helenam Troianas vexit ad urbes?
365 quid tua sancta fides? quid cura antiqua tuorum
et consanguineo totiens data dextera Turno?
si gener externa petitur de gente Latinis,
idque sedet, Faunique premunt te iussa parentis,
omnem equidem sceptris terram quae libera nostris
370 dissidet externam reor et sic dicere divos.
et Turno, si prima domus repetatur origo,
Inachus Acrisiusque patres mediaeque Mycenae."
   His ubi nequiquam dictis experta Latinum
contra stare videt, penitusque in viscera lapsum
375 serpentis furiale malum totamque pererrat,
tum vero infelix ingentibus excita monstris
immensam sine more furit lymphata per urbem.
ceu quondam torto volitans sub verbere turbo,
quem pueri magno in gyro vacua atria circum
380 intenti ludo exercent—ille actus habena
curvatis fertur spatiis; stupet inscia supra
impubesque manus mirata volubile buxum;
dant animos plagae: non cursu segnior illo
per medias urbes agitur populosque ferocis.
385 quin etiam in silvas, simulato numine Bacchi,
maius adorta nefas maioremque orsa furorem
evolat et natam frondosis montibus abdit,
quo thalamum eripiat Teucris taedasque moretur,

363 an non *M*: at non γ*R*

18 Paris was brought up as a shepherd on Mount Ida.
19 Turnus was descended from the kings of Argos through the

pirate will desert, steering for the deep with the maid as
booty? Or was it not thus that the Phrygian shepherd[18] en-
tered Lacedaemon and bore off Leda's Helen to Trojan
towns? What of your solemn pledge? What of your old love
for your own, and the hand so often pledged to Turnus,
your kinsman? If a son-in-law of foreign stock is sought for
Latins, and if that is fixed, and the commands of your sire
Faunus weigh upon you, then I hold that every land, free
and separate from our rule, is strange, and that such is the
word of the gods. Turnus, too, if the first origin of his house
be traced back, has ancestry in Inachus and Acrisius and
mid-most Mycenae."[19]

When, after trying in vain with words, she sees Latinus
stand firm against her—when the serpent's maddening
venom has glided deep into her veins and courses through
her whole frame—then, indeed, the luckless queen, stung
by monstrous horrors, in wild frenzy rages from end to end
of the city. As at times a top, spinning under the twisted
lash, which boys intent on the game drive in a great cir-
cle through an empty court—urged by the whip it speeds
on round after round; the ignorant childish throng hang
over it in wonder, marvelling at the whirling boxwood; the
blows give it life: so, no slacker in her course, is she driven
through the midst of cities and proud peoples. Nay more,
feigning the spirit of Bacchus, essaying a greater sin and
launching a greater madness, she flies forth to the forest,
and hides her daughter in the leafy mountains, in order
by this means to rob the Teucrians of their marriage and

daughter of Acrisius, Danaë, who came to Italy, founded Ardea,
and married Pilumnus. Mycenae is regarded as in the centre of
Greece.

euhoe Bacche fremens, solum te virgine dignum
390 vociferans: etenim mollis tibi sumere thyrsos,
te lustrare choro, sacrum tibi pascere crinem.
fama volat, furiisque accensas pectore matres
idem omnis simul ardor agit nova quaerere tecta.
deseruere domos, ventis dant colla comasque;
395 ast aliae tremulis ululatibus aethera complent
pampineasque gerunt incinctae pellibus hastas.
ipsa inter medias flagrantem fervida pinum
sustinet ac natae Turnique canit hymenaeos
sanguineam torquens aciem, torvumque repente
400 clamat: "io matres, audite, ubi quaeque, Latinae:
si qua piis animis manet infelicis Amatae
gratia, si iuris materni cura remordet,
solvite crinalis vittas, capite orgia mecum."
MRV talem inter silvas, inter deserta ferarum
405 reginam Allecto stimulis agit undique Bacchi.
   Postquam visa satis primos acuisse furores
consiliumque omnemque domum vertisse Latini,
protinus hinc fuscis tristis dea tollitur alis
audacis Rutuli ad muros, quam dicitur urbem
410 Acrisionaeis Danaë fundasse colonis
praecipiti delata Noto. locus Ardea quondam
dictus avis, et nunc magnum manet Ardea nomen,
sed fortuna fuit. tectis hic Turnus in altis
iam mediam nigra carpebat nocte quietem.
415 Allecto torvam faciem et furialia membra
exuit, in vultus sese transformat anilis
et frontem obscenam rugis arat, induit albos
cum vitta crinis, tum ramum innectit olivae;

---

[20] Cf. 372 and note.

delay the nuptial torch. "Evoe Bacchus!" she shrieks. "You alone," she shouts, "are worthy of the maiden! It is for you, in truth, she takes up the waving thyrsus, to you she pays honour in the dance, for you she grows her sacred tresses." Fame flies abroad, and the matrons, their breasts kindled with fury, are driven on, all by the same frenzy, to seek new dwellings. They have left their homes, and bare their necks and hair to the winds, while some fill the sky with tremulous cries and, clad in fawn skins, carry vine-bound spears. Herself in their midst, the frenzied queen uplifts a blazing brand of pine and sings the marriage song of her daughter and Turnus, rolling her blood-shot eyes; then of a sudden she fiercely shouts: "Ho! mothers of Latium, give ear, wherever you are! If in your loyal hearts still lives affection for unhappy Amata, if care for a mother's rights stings your souls, loose the fillets from your hair, join the revels with me!" So fares it with the queen, as amid woods, amid wild beasts' coverts, Allecto drives her far and wide with Bacchic goad.

As soon as she deemed that she had whetted enough the first shafts of frenzy, and had overturned Latinus' purpose and all his household, forthwith the gloomy goddess flies hence on dusky wings to the walls of the bold Rutulian, the city which Danaë, they say, borne thither by the headlong South Wind, built with her Acrisian settlers.[20] The place was once called Ardea by our forebears, and still Ardea stands, a mighty name, but its fortune is fled. Here in his high palace Turnus, at dead of night, was deep in sleep. Allecto puts off her grim features and fiendish limbs, transforms herself into the appearance of an old dame, furrows her loathly brow with wrinkles, assumes hoary locks and a fillet, next entwines them with an olive

fit Calybe Iunonis anus templique sacerdos,
420 et iuveni ante oculos his se cum vocibus offert:
"Turne, tot incassum fusos patiere labores,
et tua Dardaniis transcribi sceptra colonis?
rex tibi coniugium et quaesitas sanguine dotes
abnegat, externusque in regnum quaeritur heres.
425 i nunc, ingratis offer te, inrise, periclis;
Tyrrhenas, i, sterne acies, tege pace Latinos.
haec adeo tibi me, placida cum nocte iaceres,
FMRV ipsa palam fari omnipotens Saturnia iussit.
quare age et armari pubem portisque moveri
FMR laetus in arva para, et Phrygios qui flumine pulchro
431 consedere duces pictasque exure carinas.
caelestum vis magna iubet. rex ipse Latinus,
ni dare coniugium et dicto parere fatetur,
sentiat et tandem Turnum experiatur in armis."
435   Hic iuvenis vatem inridens sic orsa vicissim
ore refert: "classis invectas Thybridis undam
non, ut rere, meas effugit nuntius auris;
ne tantos mihi finge metus. nec regia Iuno
immemor est nostri . . .
440 sed te victa situ verique effeta senectus,
o mater, curis nequiquam exercet, et arma
regum inter falsa vatem formidine ludit.
cura tibi divum effigies et templa tueri;
bella viri pacemque gerent quîs bella gerenda."
445   Talibus Allecto dictis exarsit in iras.
at iuveni oranti subitus tremor occupat artus,
deriguere oculi: tot Erinys sibilat hydris
tantaque se facies aperit; tum flammea torquens

---

430 arva *Peerlkamp*: arma *FMγR*

spray; she becomes Calybe, aged priestess of Juno and her temple, and with these words presents herself to the young man's eyes: "Turnus, will you endure all these labours spent in vain, and sceptre transferred to Dardan settlers? The king denies you your bride and the dowry your blood has won, and a stranger is sought as heir to your throne. So go now, confront thankless perils, scorned as you are: go, lay low the Tuscan ranks; shield the Latins with peace. This it was that Saturn's almighty daughter in person bade me say to you as you were lying in the stillness of night. Rise then, and gladly make ready the arming of your men, and their march from the gates into the fields. Burn the Phrygian chiefs, who are anchored in our fair stream, burn their painted ships. The mighty force of the gods commands. Let King Latinus himself, unless he consents to give you your bride and stand by his word, know of it, and at last make proof of Turnus as a foe."

Now the youth, mocking the seer, thus in turn takes up the speech: "That a fleet has entered Tiber's waters, the news has not, as you suppose, escaped my ear—feign not for me such terrors; and Queen Juno does not forget me . . . But you, mother, old age, enfeebled by decay and barren of truth, frets with vain distress, and amid the feuds of kings mocks your prophetic soul with false alarms. Your charge it is to keep the gods' images and temples; war and peace men shall wield, whose work war is."

At these words Allecto blazed forth in fury. But even as the young man spoke, a sudden tremor seized his limbs, and his eyes set in fear; so many are the Fury's hissing snakes, so monstrous the countenance that reveals itself.

lumina cunctantem et quaerentem dicere plura
450 reppulit, et geminos erexit crinibus anguis,
verberaque insonuit rabidoque haec addidit ore:
"en ego victa situ, quam veri effeta senectus
arma inter regum falsa formidine ludit.
respice ad haec: adsum dirarum ab sede sororum,
455 bella manu letumque gero . . ."
    Sic effata facem iuveni coniecit et atro
lumine fumantis fixit sub pectore taedas.
olli somnum ingens rumpit pavor, ossaque et artus
perfundit toto proruptus corpore sudor.
460 arma amens fremit, arma toro tectisque requirit;
saevit amor ferri et scelerata insania belli,
ira super: magno veluti cum flamma sonore
virgea suggeritur costis undantis aëni
exsultantque aestu latices, furit intus aquai
465 fumidus atque alte spumis exuberat amnis,
nec iam se capit unda, volat vapor ater ad auras.
ergo iter ad regem polluta pace Latinum
indicit primis iuvenum et iubet arma parari,
tutari Italiam, detrudere finibus hostem;
MR se satis ambobus Teucrisque venire Latinisque.
471 haec ubi dicta dedit divosque in vota vocavit,
certatim sese Rutuli exhortantur in arma.
hunc decus egregium formae movet atque iuventae,
hunc atavi reges, hunc claris dextera factis.
475   Dum Turnus Rutulos animis audacibus implet,
Allecto in Teucros Stygiis se concitat alis,

---

459 perfundit *FγR*: -fudit *M* | proruptus *MR*: prae- *Fγ*
464 aquai *M, Servius*: aquae vis *FR, Macrobius*: aquae γ (vis *add.* γ²)

34

Then, rolling her flaming eyes, she thrust him back, as he faltered and sought to say more, reared two snakes from her tresses, sounded her whip, and spoke further with rabid lips: "Behold me, enfeebled by decay, whom old age, barren of truth, amid the feuds of kings, mocks with vain alarm! Look on this! I am come from the home of the Dread Sisters, and in my hand I bear war and death . . ."

So saying, she hurled at the youth a torch, and fixed in his breast the brand, smoking with lurid light. A monstrous terror broke his sleep, and the sweat, bursting from all his frame, drenched bone and limb. For arms he madly shrieks; arms he seeks in couch and chamber; lust of the sword rages in him, the accursed frenzy of war, and resentment crowning all: just as when flaming sticks, loud crackling, are heaped under the sides of a billowing cauldron, and the waters dance with the heat; within seethes the liquid flood, steaming and bubbling up high with foam; and now the wave contains itself no longer, and the black smoke soars aloft. Therefore, profaning peace, he orders his chief warriors to march upon Latinus, and bids arms be made ready. "Defend Italy," he cries, "drive the foe from her borders; I come, a match for both Teucrians and Latins." When thus he spoke, and called the gods to hear his vows, the Rutuli vie in exhorting one another to arms. One is moved by the peerless beauty of his form and youth, one by his royal ancestry, another by the glorious deeds of his hand.

While Turnus fills the Rutuli with daring courage, Allecto on Stygian wing speeds toward the Trojans, with

arte nova, speculata locum, quo litore pulcher
insidiis cursuque feras agitabat Iulus.
hic subitam canibus rabiem Cocytia virgo
480 obicit et noto naris contingit odore,
ut cervum ardentes agerent; quae prima laborum
MRV causa fuit belloque animos accendit agrestis.
cervus erat forma praestanti et cornibus ingens,
Tyrrhidae pueri quem matris ab ubere raptum
485 nutribant Tyrrhusque pater, cui regia parent
FMRV armenta et late custodia credita campi.
adsuetum imperiis soror omni Silvia cura
mollibus intexens ornabat cornua sertis,
pectebatque ferum puroque in fonte lavabat.
490 ille manum patiens mensaeque adsuetus erili
errabat silvis rursusque ad limina nota
ipse domum sera quamvis se nocte ferebat.
    Hunc procul errantem rabidae venantis Iuli
commovere canes, fluvio cum forte secundo
495 deflueret ripaque aestus viridante levaret.
ipse etiam eximiae laudis succensus amore
Ascanius curvo derexit spicula cornu;
nec dextrae erranti deus afuit, actaque multo
perque uterum sonitu perque ilia venit harundo.
500 saucius at quadripes nota intra tecta refugit
successitque gemens stabulis, questuque cruentus
atque imploranti similis tectum omne replebat.
Silvia prima soror palmis percussa lacertos
auxilium vocat et duros conclamat agrestis.
505 olli (pestis enim tacitis latet aspera silvis)
improvisi adsunt, hic torre armatus obusto,

---

486 late $F^2\gamma$: lati *FMR*   497 derexit *FγRV*: direxit F^2M

new wiles spying out the place, where, on the shore, fair Iülus was hunting wild beasts with nets and steeds. Here the hellish maid flings upon his hounds a sudden frenzy, and touches their nostrils with the well-known scent, so that in hot haste they course a stag. This was the first source of ill; this first kindled the rustic spirit to war. There was a stag of wondrous beauty and mighty antlers, which, torn from its mother's breast, the sons of Tyrrhus nurtured, and Tyrrhus, their sire, controller of the royal herds and charged with care of pastures near and far. Their sister Silvia had trained it to obey, and with constant love she adorned it, twining its horns with soft garlands, combing the wild thing's coat, and bathing it in the crystal spring. Tame to handling and accustomed to food from its master, it roved the woods, and of its own accord went home again to the well-known door, however late the night.

While far afield the stag was straying, the maddened hounds of the huntsman Iülus started it, as by chance it swam down stream and cooled its heat on the grassy bank. Ascanius himself, too, fired with longing for chiefest honour, aimed a shaft from his bent bow, and the goddess did not fail his faltering hand; the reed whistled as it sped, and pierced belly and flank alike. But the wounded creature fled under the familiar roof, and moaning crept into its stall, where, bleeding and suppliant-like, it filled all the house with its plaints. First Silvia the sister, beating her arms with her hands, calls for help and summons the hardy country folk. They—for the fell fiend lurks in the silent woods—came unlooked for, armed one with seared brand,

502 replebat $M\gamma V^2$: replevit RV (F def.)

stipitis hic gravidi nodis; quod cuique repertum
FMR rimanti telum ira facit. vocat agmina Tyrrhus,
quadrifidam quercum cuneis ut forte coactis
MR scindebat rapta spirans immane securi.
511   At saeva e speculis tempus dea nacta nocendi
ardua tecta petit stabuli et de culmine summo
pastorale canit signum cornuque recurvo
Tartaream intendit vocem, qua protinus omne
515 contremuit nemus et silvae insonuere profundae;
audiit et Triviae longe lacus, audiit amnis
sulpurea Nar albus aqua fontesque Velini,
et trepidae matres pressere ad pectora natos.
tum vero ad vocem celeres, qua bucina signum
520 dira dedit, raptis concurrunt undique telis
indomiti agricolae, nec non et Troïa pubes
Ascanio auxilium castris effundit apertis.
derexere acies. non iam certamine agresti
stipitibus duris agitur sudibusve praeustis,
525 sed ferro ancipiti decernunt atraque late
horrescit strictis seges ensibus, aeraque fulgent
sole lacessita et lucem sub nubila iactant:
fluctus uti primo coepit cum albescere vento,
paulatim sese tollit mare et altius undas
530 erigit, inde imo consurgit ad aethera fundo.
hic iuvenis primam ante aciem stridente sagitta,
natorum Tyrrhi fuerat qui maximus, Almo,
sternitur; haesit enim sub gutture vulnus et udae
vocis iter tenuemque inclusit sanguine vitam.

    [528] vento γ: ponto *MR*

one with heavy-knotted stick; what each can find in his
quest, wrath makes a weapon. Tyrrhus summons his bands,
snatching up an axe and breathing savage rage—for then
by chance he was cleaving an oak in four with inward
driven wedges.

But the cruel goddess, espying from her watchtower
the moment of mischief, seeks the steep farm roof, and
from the topmost ridge sounds the shepherds' call, and
on the twisted horn strains her hellish voice, at which at
once every grove trembled and the woods echoed to their
depths. It was heard by Trivia's lake afar,[21] heard by Nar
with his white sulphurous water, and by the springs of
Velinus; and startled mothers clasped their children to
their breasts. Then indeed, hurrying to the sound, with
which the dread clarion gave the signal, the wild husband-
men snatch up their weapons and gather from all sides; no
less do the Trojan youth pour through the camp's open
gates to help Ascanius. The lines are ranged: now they do
not contend in rustic quarrel with heavy clubs or seared
stakes, but with two-edged steel they try the issue; far and
wide bristles a dark harvest of drawn swords, while brass
shines at the challenge of the sun and flings its light to the
clouds: as when a billow begins to whiten under the wind's
first breath, little by little the sea swells and lifts its waves
higher, till at last it rises to heaven from its lowest depths.
Here in the front rank, young Almo, who had been eldest
of Tyrrhus' sons, is laid low by a whistling arrow; for the
wound was fixed beneath his throat, choking with blood
the path of liquid speech and the slender breath. Around

[21] The famous and beautiful Lago di Nemi, beside which was a
grove of Diana.

535 corpora multa virum circa seniorque Galaesus,
dum paci medium se offert, iustissimus unus
qui fuit Ausoniisque olim ditissimus arvis:
quinque greges illi balantum, quina redibant
armenta, et terram centum vertebat aratris.

540 Atque ea per campos aequo dum Marte geruntur,
promissi dea facta potens, ubi sanguine bellum
imbuit et primae commisit funera pugnae,
deserit Hesperiam et caeli conversa per auras
Iunonem victrix adfatur voce superba:

545 "en, perfecta tibi bello discordia tristi;
dic in amicitiam coeant et foedera iungant.
quandoquidem Ausonio respersi sanguine Teucros,
hoc etiam his addam, tua si mihi certa voluntas:
finitimas in bella feram rumoribus urbes,

550 accendamque animos insani Martis amore
undique ut auxilio veniant; spargam arma per agros."
tum contra Iuno: "terrorum et fraudis abunde est:
stant belli causae, pugnatur comminus armis,
quae fors prima dedit sanguis novus imbuit arma.

555 talia coniugia et talis celebrent hymenaeos
egregium Veneris genus et rex ipse Latinus.
te super aetherias errare licentius auras
haud pater ille velit, summi regnator Olympi.
cede locis. ego, si qua super fortuna laborum est,

560 ipsa regam." talis dederat Saturnia voces;
illa autem attollit stridentis anguibus alas
Cocytique petit sedem supera ardua linquens.
est locus Italiae medio sub montibus altis,
nobilis et fama multis memoratus in oris,

543 conversa *M*: convexa *M²γR* (4.451)

him lie many dead, and among them old Galaesus, slain as he throws himself between to plead for peace—he who was of all men most righteous and once wealthiest in Ausonia's fields; for him five flocks bleated, five herds came back from pasture, and a hundred ploughs turned the soil.

While thus over the plains they fight in even warfare, the goddess, her promise fulfilled, when once she has stained with blood and opened with death the first encounter, quits Hesperia, and turning away through the air of heaven, addresses Juno in haughty tones of triumph: "Lo, at your will, discord is ripened into gloomy war. Bid them unite in friendship and join alliance, seeing that I have sprinkled the Teucrians with Ausonian blood. Moreover, this I will add, if I am assured of your wish: with rumours I will draw bordering towns to battle, and will kindle their minds with lust of maddening war, that from all sides they may come to aid; I will sow the land with arms." Then Juno, in answer: "Enough of alarms and treachery; the causes of war are established; man with man they fight in arms, and the arms that chance first gave are now stained with fresh blood. Let this be the alliance, this the bridal they solemnize—this peerless son of Venus, and this great king Latinus! That you should roam too freely in the upper air, the mighty sire, sovereign of high Olympus, did not wish. Leave this place. Whatever issue of sorrow is still to come I will deal with myself." So spoke Saturn's daughter; but the other raises her serpent-hissing pinions and, leaving the heights above, seeks her home in Cocytus. There is a place in the heart of Italy, beneath high hills, renowned and famed in many lands, the Vale of Amsanctus. On either

---

[562] supera γ: super *MR* (6.787)

565 Amsancti valles; densis hunc frondibus atrum
urget utrimque latus nemoris, medioque fragosus
dat sonitum saxis et torto vertice torrens.
hic specus horrendum et saevi spiracula Ditis
monstrantur, ruptoque ingens Acheronte vorago
570 pestiferas aperit fauces, quîs condita Erinys,
invisum numen, terras caelumque levabat.
    Nec minus interea extremam Saturnia bello
imponit regina manum. ruit omnis in urbem
pastorum ex acie numerus, caesosque reportant
575 Almonem puerum foedatique ora Galaesi,
implorantque deos obtestanturque Latinum.
Turnus adest medioque in crimine caedis et igni
terrorem ingeminat: Teucros in regna vocari,
stirpem admisceri Phrygiam, se limine pelli.
580 tum quorum attonitae Baccho nemora avia matres
insultant thiasis (neque enim leve nomen Amatae)
undique collecti coeunt Martemque fatigant.
ilicet infandum cuncti contra omina bellum,
contra fata deum perverso numine poscunt.
585 certatim regis circumstant tecta Latini;
MRV ille velut pelago rupes immota resistit,
ut pelagi rupes magno veniente fragore,
quae sese multis circum latrantibus undis
mole tenet; scopuli nequiquam et spumea circum
590 saxa fremunt laterique inlisa refunditur alga.
verum ubi nulla datur caecum exsuperare potestas
consilium, et saevae nutu Iunonis eunt res,
multa deos aurasque pater testatus inanis
FMRV "frangimur heu fatis" inquit "ferimurque procella!

570 condita *R*: condit *M*γ

hand a fringe of forest, dark with dense leafage, hems it in, and in the centre a roaring torrent resounds over the rocks in swirling eddies. Here is shown an awful cavern, and a breathing place of savage Dis; and a vast gorge, from which Acheron bursts forth, opens its pestilential jaws. In these the Fury, abhorred deity, hid, relieving earth and heaven.

No less, meanwhile, does Saturn's royal daughter put a final hand to the war. From the battlefield there pours into the city the whole company of shepherds, bearing back the slain—the boy Almo, and Galaesus with mangled face— calling on the gods and adjuring Latinus. Turnus is there, and amid the outcry at the slaughter, and fire of passion, he redoubles their terror: "Teucrians are called to reign; a Phrygian stock mingles its taint; I am spurned from the door!" Then they, whose matrons, frenzied by Bacchus, tread the pathless woods in dancing bands (for of no light weight is Amata's name), draw together from every side, and importune the War God. Straightway, one and all, despite the omens, despite the oracles of gods, with perverse will clamour for unholy war. With emulous zeal they swarm round Latinus' palace. He, like an unmoved ocean cliff, resists; like an ocean cliff, which, when a great crash comes, stands steadfast in its bulk amid many howling waves; in vain the crags and foaming rocks roar about, and the seaweed, dashed upon its sides, is whirled back. But when no power is given him to quell their blind resolve, and all goes as cruel Juno wills, then with many an appeal to the gods and the voiceless skies, "Alas!" the father cries, "we are shattered by fate, and swept away by the storm!

586–615 *omitted by M, but inserted by an ancient hand*
593 testatus V: testatur *MγR*

595 ipsi has sacrilego pendetis sanguine poenas,
o miseri. te, Turne, nefas, te triste manebit
supplicium, votisque deos venerabere seris.
nam mihi parta quies, omnisque in limine portus
funere felici spolior." nec plura locutus
600 saepsit se tectis rerumque reliquit habenas.

Mos erat Hesperio in Latio, quem protinus urbes
Albanae coluere sacrum, nunc maxima rerum
Roma colit, cum prima movent in proelia Martem,
sive Getis inferre manu lacrimabile bellum
605 Hyrcanisve Arabisve parant, seu tendere ad Indos
Auroramque sequi Parthosque reposcere signa:
sunt geminae Belli portae (sic nomine dicunt)
religione sacrae et saevi formidine Martis;
centum aerei claudunt vectes aeternaque ferri
610 robora, nec custos absistit limine Ianus.
has, ubi certa sedet patribus sententia pugnae,
FMR ipse Quirinali trabea cinctuque Gabino
insignis reserat stridentia limina consul,
ipse vocat pugnas; sequitur tum cetera pubes,
615 aereaque adsensu conspirant cornua rauco.
hoc et tum Aeneadis indicere bella Latinus
more iubebatur tristisque recludere portas.
abstinuit tactu pater aversusque refugit
foeda ministeria, et caecis se condidit umbris.
620 tum regina deum caelo delapsa morantis
impulit ipsa manu portas, et cardine verso

---

22 Used of the East generally.

23 The Temple of Janus was opened in time of war, and closed
in peace.

24 Cf. line 187 above, with note. The "Gabine cincture" refers

You yourselves, my wretched children, with your impious blood shall pay the price of this! The guilt and its bitter punishment shall await you, Turnus, and too late with vows shall you supplicate the gods. As for me, my rest is assured, but having reached the harbour gate I am totally robbed of the happiness I might have had in death." And saying no more he shut himself in the palace, and let drop the reins of rule.

A custom there was in Hesperian Latium, which thenceforth the Alban cities held holy, as now does Rome, mistress of the world, when they first rouse the war god to battle, be it Getae or Arabs or Hyrcanians against whom their hands prepare to carry tearful war, or to march on India's sons[22] and pursue the Dawn, and reclaim their standards from the Parthian: there are twin gates[23] of War (so men call them), hallowed by religious awe and the terrors of fierce Mars; a hundred brazen bolts close them, and the eternal strength of iron, and Janus their guardian never quits the threshold. Here, when the sentence of the Fathers is firmly fixed on war, the Consul, arrayed in Quirinal robe[24] and Gabine cincture, with his own hand unbars the grating portals, with his own lips calls forth war; then the rest of the warriors take up the cry, and brazen horns blare out their hoarse accord. In this manner then, too, Latinus was bidden to proclaim war on the sons of Aeneas, and to unclose the grim gates. But the father withheld his hand, shrank back from the hateful office, and hid himself in blind darkness. Then the queen of the gods, gliding from the sky, with her own hand drove in the lingering doors,

to a special way of wearing the toga, one part of which was folded round the waist, leaving the arm free.

Belli ferratos rumpit Saturnia postis.
ardet inexcita Ausonia atque immobilis ante;
pars pedes ire parat campis, pars arduus altis
625 pulverulentus equis furit; omnes arma requirunt.
pars levis clipeos et spicula lucida tergent
arvina pingui subiguntque in cote securis;
signaque ferre iuvat sonitusque audire tubarum.
quinque adeo magnae positis incudibus urbes
630 tela novant, Atina potens Tiburque superbum,
Ardea Crustumerique et turrigerae Antemnae.
tegmina tuta cavant capitum flectuntque salignas
umbonum cratis; alii thoracas aënos
aut levis ocreas lento ducunt argento;
635 vomeris huc et falcis honos, huc omnis aratri
cessit amor; recoquunt patrios fornacibus ensis.
classica iamque sonant, it bello tessera signum;
hic galeam tectis trepidus rapit, ille trementis
ad iuga cogit equos, clipeumque auroque trilicem
640 loricam induitur fidoque accingitur ense.

    Pandite nunc Helicona, deae, cantusque movete,
qui bello exciti reges, quae quemque secutae
complerint campos acies, quibus Itala iam tum
floruerit terra alma viris, quibus arserit armis;
FMPR et meministis enim, divae, et memorare potestis;
646 ad nos vix tenuis famae perlabitur aura.
MPR   Primus init bellum Tyrrhenis asper ab oris
contemptor divum Mezentius agminaque armat.
filius huic iuxta Lausus, quo pulchrior alter
650 non fuit excepto Laurentis corpore Turni;
Lausus, equum domitor debellatorque ferarum,

---

638 trementis *FMγR* (*G*.3.84): frementis *c* (12.82)

and on their turning hinges Saturn's daughter burst open the iron-bound gates of war. All ablaze is Ausonia, which before was sluggish and unmoved. Some make ready to march over the plains on foot, some, mounted on high steeds, storm amid clouds of dust: all cry out for arms. Some with rich fat burnish shields smooth and javelins bright, and whet axes on the stone; they joy to bear the standards, and hear the trumpet call. And five mighty cities set up anvils and forge new weapons—strong Atina and proud Tibur, Ardea and Crustumeri and turreted Antemnae. They hollow helmets to guard the head, and weave the wicker frame of shields; others beat out breastplates of bronze, or polished greaves from pliant silver. To this is come all pride in share and sickle, all passion for the plough; they retemper in the furnace their fathers' swords. And now the clarion sounds; the password goes forth, the sign for war. One in wild haste snatches a helmet from his home; another harnesses his quivering steeds to the yoke, dons his shield and coat of mail, triple-linked with gold, and girds on his trusty sword.

Now fling Helicon wide open, goddesses, and set on foot poetic strains, telling what kings were roused to war; what embattled hosts followed each one, filling the plain; with what manhood even then did kindly Italy bloom; what armed forces kindled her to flame. For you, divine sisters, have both remembrance and power to relate, while to us is scarce wafted some scant breath of fame.

First into the war comes the ferocious king from Tuscan coasts, Mezentius, scorner of the gods, and arrays his bands. At his side stands his son Lausus, whom none surpassed in beauty of physique save Laurentine Turnus. Lausus, tamer of horses, vanquisher of beasts, leads from

ducit Agyllina nequiquam ex urbe secutos
mille viros, dignus patriis qui laetior esset
imperiis et cui pater haud Mezentius esset.
655 Post hos insignem palma per gramina currum
victoresque ostentat equos satus Hercule pulchro
pulcher Aventinus, clipeoque insigne paternum
centum anguis cinctamque gerit serpentibus Hydram;
collis Aventini silva quem Rhea sacerdos
660 furtivum partu sub luminis edidit oras,
mixta deo mulier, postquam Laurentia victor
Geryone exstincto Tirynthius attigit arva,
Tyrrhenoque boves in flumine lavit Hiberas.
MPRV pila manu saevosque gerunt in bella dolones,
665 et tereti pugnant mucrone veruque Sabello.
ipse pedes, tegimen torquens immane leonis,
terribili impexum saeta cum dentibus albis
indutus capiti, sic regia tecta subibat,
horridus Herculeoque umeros innexus amictu.
670 Tum gemini fratres Tiburtia moenia linquunt,
fratris Tiburti dictam cognomine gentem,
Catillusque acerque Coras, Argiva iuventus,
et primam ante aciem densa inter tela feruntur:
ceu duo nubigenae cum vertice montis ab alto
675 descendunt Centauri Homolen Othrymque nivalem
linquentes cursu rapido; dat euntibus ingens
silva locum et magno cedunt virgulta fragore.
Nec Praenestinae fundator defuit urbis,
Volcano genitum pecora inter agrestia regem

671 cognomine *MRV*: de nomine *P* (1.563)

Agylla's town a thousand men, that followed him in vain,[25] a son worthy to be happier in a father's rule, a father other than Mezentius!

After these, Aventinus, handsome son of handsome Hercules, displays on the grass his palm-crowned chariot and victorious steeds, and on his shield bears his father's blazon—a hundred snakes and the Hydra, girt with serpents. Him, in the wood of the Aventine hill, the priestess Rhea bore in secret birth into the borders of light— a woman mated with a god—when the conquering Tirynthian, having slain Geryon, reached the Laurentian fields and bathed his Iberian oxen in the Tuscan stream.[26] In their hands the men carry to battle javelins and grim pikes, and fight with the tapering sword and Sabellian dart. Himself he marched on foot, swinging a huge lion's skin, unkempt with terrifying mane, its white teeth crowning his head; in such guise he entered the royal halls, a fearful sight, the garb of Hercules covering his shoulders.

Next twin brothers leave the walls of Tibur and the folk called after the name of their brother Tiburtus—Catillus and valiant Coras, Argive youths. On they come in the forefront of battle among the thronging spears, as when the cloud-born Centaurs descend from a lofty mountain peak, leaving Homole or snowy Othrys in rapid race; the mighty forest yields before them as they go, and the thickets give way with a loud crash.

Nor was the founder of Praeneste's city absent, Caeculus, the king who, as every age has believed, was born to Vulcan among the royal herds, and found upon

---

[25] Because they could not save him from his fate.
[26] The Tiber.

680 inventumque focis omnis quem credidit aetas,
Caeculus. hunc legio late comitatur agrestis:
quique altum Praeneste viri quique arva Gabinae
Iunonis gelidumque Anienem et roscida rivis
Hernica saxa colunt, quos, dives Anagnia, pascis,
685 quos, Amasene pater. non illis omnibus arma
nec clipei currusve sonant; pars maxima glandes
liventis plumbi spargit, pars spicula gestat
bina manu, fulvosque lupi de pelle galeros
tegmen habent capiti; vestigia nuda sinistri
MPR instituere pedis, crudus tegit altera pero.
691   At Messapus, equum domitor, Neptunia proles,
quem neque fas igni cuiquam nec sternere ferro,
iam pridem resides populos desuetaque bello
agmina in arma vocat subito ferrumque retractat.
695 hi Fescenninas acies Aequosque Faliscos,
hi Soractis habent arces Flaviniaque arva
et Cimini cum monte lacum lucosque Capenos.
ibant aequati numero regemque canebant:
ceu quondam nivei liquida inter nubila cycni
700 cum sese e pastu referunt et longa canoros
dant per colla modos, sonat amnis et Asia longe
pulsa palus . . .
nec quisquam aeratas acies examine tanto
misceri putet, aëriam sed gurgite ab alto
705 urgeri volucrum raucarum ad litora nubem.
   Ecce Sabinorum prisco de sanguine magnum

> 684 pascis V: pascit MPR
> 691 = 9.523, 12.128
> 703 examine χ: ex agmine MPR

the hearth. With him marches, spreading far around, a troop levied among the fields, warriors dwelling in steep Praeneste, in the ploughlands of Juno who guards Gabii, by cool Anio and among Hernican rocks bedewed by streams; they whom you nurture, rich Anagnia, and you, father Amasenus. Not all of these have armour or shields, or rattling chariots. Mostly they shower bullets of dull lead; some wield two darts in the hand, and have for headgear tawny caps of wolf skin. Bare is the left foot as they plant their steps; a boot of rawhide shields the other.

But Messapus, tamer of horses, the seed of Neptune, whom none may lay low with fire or steel, suddenly calls to arms tribes long inert and troops unused to war, and again grasps the sword. These hold the ranks of Fescennium and of Aequi Falisci; these Soracte's heights and Flavinian fields, Ciminus' lake and hill and the groves of Capena. In dressed lines they marched and sang their king: as snowy swans among the moist clouds, when they return from feeding, and from their long throats utter their tuneful strains; the river echoes, and the Asian mead, struck from afar[27] . . . Nor would one think that mail-clad ranks were massed in that vast swarm, but that high in the air a cloud of hoarse-voiced birds was pressing shoreward from the deep gulf.

See! Clausus,[28] of the ancient Sabine blood, leading a

[27] Referring to the valley of the Caÿster in Lydia.

[28] Cf. Livy 2.16, where we learn that the Claudian tribe was founded by Attus Clausus, who seceded from the Sabines in 506 B.C. and was received as a citizen in Rome. Virgil, however, refers the founding of the Claudian *gens* to the earlier day when Romulus formed a treaty with the Sabines under Titus Tatius.

agmen agens Clausus magnique ipse agminis instar,
Claudia nunc a quo diffunditur et tribus et gens
per Latium, postquam in partem data Roma Sabinis.
710 una ingens Amiterna cohors priscique Quirites,
Ereti manus omnis oliviferaeque Mutuscae;
qui Nomentum urbem, qui Rosea rura Velini,
qui Tetricae horrentis rupes montemque Severum
Casperiamque colunt Forulosque et flumen Himellae
715 qui Tiberim Fabarimque bibunt, quos frigida misit
Nursia, et Ortinae classes populique Latini,
quosque secans infaustum interluit Allia nomen:
quam multi Libyco volvuntur marmore fluctus
saevus ubi Orion hibernis conditur undis,
720 vel cum sole novo densae torrentur aristae
aut Hermi campo aut Lyciae flaventibus arvis.
scuta sonant pulsuque pedum conterrita tellus.

    Hinc Agamemnonius, Troiani nominis hostis,
curru iungit Halaesus equos Turnoque ferocis
725 mille rapit populos, vertunt felicia Baccho
Massica qui rastris, et quos de collibus altis
Aurunci misere patres Sidicinaque iuxta
aequora, quique Cales linquunt amnisque vadosi
accola Volturni, pariterque Saticulus asper
730 Oscorumque manus. teretes sunt aclydes illis
tela, sed haec lento mos est aptare flagello.
laevas caetra tegit, falcati comminus enses.

    Nec tu carminibus nostris indictus abibis,
Oebale, quem generasse Telon Sebethide nympha
735 fertur, Teleboum Capreas cum regna teneret,
iam senior; patriis sed non et filius arvis

---

[29] The inhabitants of Cures.

mighty host, and equal to a mighty host himself; from whom now through Latium spreads the Claudian tribe and clan, since Rome was shared with the Sabines. With him came Amiternum's vast cohort, and the ancient Quirites,[29] the whole band of Eretum and olive-bearing Mutusca; those who dwell in Nomentum's city and the Rosean country by Velinus, on Tetrica's rugged crags and Mount Severus, in Casperia and Foruli, and by Himella's stream; those who drink of Tiber and Fabaris, those whom cold Nursia sent, the Ortine squadrons, the Latin peoples, and those whom Allia, ill-boding name, severs with its flood; as many as the waves that roll on the Libyan main, when fierce Orion sinks in the wintry waves; or thick as the corn ears that are scorched by the early sun in the plain of Hermus or the yellow fields of Lycia. The bucklers clang, and the earth trembles under the tramping feet.

Next, Agamemnon's son, foe of the Trojan name, Halaesus, yokes his steeds to the car, and in Turnus' cause sweeps along a thousand warlike tribes, men who turn with mattocks the wine-rich Massic lands; whom Auruncan fathers sent from their high hills, and the Sidicine plains hard by; those who leave Cales, and the dweller by Volturnus' shallow river, and by their side the rough Saticulan and the Oscan bands. Shapely javelins are their weapons, but it is their way to fit these with a pliant thong. A shield protects their left side; their curved swords are for close combat.

Nor will you, Oebalus, pass unhonoured in our songs— you whom, it is said, the nymph Sebethis bore to Telon, when he reigned over Teleboan Capreae, now stricken in years; but, not content with his ancestral fields, his son

contentus late iam tum dicione premebat
Sarrastis populos et quae rigat aequora Sarnus,
quique Rufras Batulumque tenent atque arva Celemnae,
741 Teutonico ritu soliti torquere cateias;
740 et quos maliferae despectant moenia Abellae,
tegmina quis capitum raptus de subere cortex
aerataeque micant peltae, micat aereus ensis.
    Et te montosae misere in proelia Nersae,
745 Ufens, insignem fama et felicibus armis,
horrida praecipue cui gens adsuetaque multo
venatu nemorum, duris Aequicula glaebis.
armati terram exercent semperque recentis
convectare iuvat praedas et vivere rapto.
750   Quin et Marruvia venit de gente sacerdos
fronde super galeam et felici comptus oliva
Archippi regis missu, fortissimus Umbro,
vipereo generi et graviter spirantibus hydris
spargere qui somnos cantuque manuque solebat,
755 mulcebatque iras et morsus arte levabat.
sed non Dardaniae medicari cuspidis ictum
evaluit neque eum iuvere in vulnera cantus
somniferi et Marsis quaesitae montibus herbae.
te nemus Angitiae, vitrea te Fucinus unda,
760 te liquidi flevere lacus . . .
    Ibat et Hippolyti proles pulcherrima bello,
Virbius, insignem quem mater Aricia misit,
eductum Egeriae lucis umentia circum

737 premebat *R*: tenebat *MP* (1.632)
741 *before* 740 *Courtney*
740 Abellae *"alii" Servius*: Bellae *MPR*
757 vulnera *M²P*: -e *MR*

54

even then held sway far and wide over the Sarrastian tribes, and the plains watered by Sarnus, those who dwell in Rufrae and Batulum and Celemna's fields, wont to hurl their darts in Teuton fashion,[30] and those on whom look down the battlements of Abella, rich in apples, men whose headgear was bark stripped from the cork tree; bronze flash their shields, their sword flashes bronze.

You too, Ufens, mountainous Nersae sent forth to battle, of noble fame and success in arms—whose clan, on the rough Aequian clods, was rugged above all others, and inured to hard hunting in the woods. In arms they till the earth, and it is ever their joy to bear away fresh booty, and to live on plunder.

As well, from the Marruvian race, sent by King Archippus, there came a priest, his helmet decked with leaves of the fruitful olive, most valiant Umbro, who with charm and touch was wont to shed slumber on the viperous brood and water snakes of baneful breath, soothing their wrath and curing their bites by his skill.[31] But he availed not to heal the stroke of the Dardan spearpoint, nor against wounds did slumbrous charms aid him, or herbs culled on Marsian hills. For you Angitia's grove wept, for you Fucinus' glassy wave, for you the limpid lakes! . . .

Likewise went to war Hippolytus' son, Virbius, most fair, whom his mother Aricia sent forth in his glory. In Egeria's groves he was reared round the marshy shores,

---

[30] The *cateia* is a throwing weapon intended, like the *aclys* (730), to return to the thrower. Servius says this was done by a line attached, Isidore (*Origines* 18.7.7) makes it a boomerang.

[31] The Marsians were skilled in magic and incantations.

litora, pinguis ubi et placabilis ara Dianae.
765　namque ferunt fama Hippolytum, postquam arte novercae
occiderit patriasque explerit sanguine poenas
turbatis distractus equis, ad sidera rursus
aetheria et superas caeli venisse sub auras,
Paeonîs revocatum herbis et amore Dianae.
770　tum pater omnipotens aliquem indignatus ab umbris
mortalem infernis ad lumina surgere vitae,
ipse repertorem medicinae talis et artis
fulmine Phoebigenam Stygias detrusit ad undas.
at Trivia Hippolytum secretis alma recondit
775　sedibus et nymphae Egeriae nemorique relegat,
solus ubi in silvis Italis ignobilis aevum
exigeret versoque ubi nomine Virbius esset.
unde etiam templo Triviae lucisque sacratis
cornipedes arcentur equi, quod litore currum
780　et iuvenem monstris pavidi effudere marinis.
filius ardentis haud setius aequore campi
exercebat equos curruque in bella ruebat.
　　Ipse inter primos praestanti corpore Turnus
vertitur arma tenens et toto vertice supra est.
785　cui triplici crinita iuba galea alta Chimaeram
sustinet Aetnaeos efflantem faucibus ignis;
tam magis illa fremens et tristibus effera flammis
quam magis effuso crudescunt sanguine pugnae.
at levem clipeum sublatis cornibus Io
790　auro insignibat, iam saetis obsita, iam bos,
argumentum ingens, et custos virginis Argus,

769 Paeonis *M*2: Paeoniis MR
773 Phoebigenam *P*: Poenigenam *MR*

where stands Diana's altar, rich and gracious. For they tell that Hippolytus—when he fell by his stepmother's arts, and satisfied his father's vengeance with his blood, torn asunder by frightened steeds—came again to the starry firmament and heaven's upper air, recalled by the Healer's herbs and Diana's love. Then the Father omnipotent, angered that any mortal should rise from the nether shades to the light of life, himself with his thunder hurled down to the Stygian waters the finder of such healing craft, the one born of Phoebus.[32] But Trivia, kindly goddess, hides Hippolytus in a secret dwelling, and sends him away to the nymph Egeria and her grove, that there alone, amid Italian woods, he might live out his inglorious days, and take the altered name of Virbius. For this reason, too, hoofed horses are kept far from Trivia's temple and hallowed groves, that they, frightened by ocean monsters, strewed chariot and youth along the shore. None the less, his son was driving his fiery steeds on the level plain, and hastened to war in his chariot.

Among the foremost moves Turnus himself, of wondrous frame, holding sword in hand, and by a whole head overtopping all. His lofty helmet, crested with triple plume, bears a Chimaera, breathing from her jaws Aetnean fires, raging the more, and the madder with baleful flames, the more blood is shed and the fiercer waxes the fight. But on his polished shield Io with uplifted horns was emblazoned in gold[33]—Io, wondrous device, already covered with bristles, already a heifer—and Argus, the

---

[32] Aesculapius, son of Apollo (the Healer).

[33] A figure of Io, wrought in gold, formed the device on the iron shield.

caelataque amnem fundens pater Inachus urna.
insequitur nimbus peditum clipeataque totis
agmina densentur campis, Argivaque pubes
795 Auruncaeque manus, Rutuli veteresque Sicani,
et Sacranae acies et picti scuta Labici;
qui saltus, Tiberine, tuos sacrumque Numici
litus arant Rutulosque exercent vomere collis
Circaeumque iugum, quîs Iuppiter Anxurus arvis
800 praesidet et viridi gaudens Feronia luco;
qua Saturae iacet atra palus gelidusque per imas
quaerit iter vallis atque in mare conditur Ufens.
   Hos super advenit Volsca de gente Camilla
agmen agens equitum et florentis aere catervas,
805 bellatrix, non illa colo calathisve Minervae
femineas adsueta manus, sed proelia virgo
dura pati cursuque pedum praevertere ventos.
illa vel intactae segetis per summa volaret
gramina nec teneras cursu laesisset aristas,
810 vel mare per medium fluctu suspensa tumenti
ferret iter celeris nec tingeret aequore plantas.
illam omnis tectis agrisque effusa iuventus
turbaque miratur matrum et prospectat euntem,
attonitis inhians animis ut regius ostro
815 velet honos levis umeros, ut fibula crinem
auro internectat, Lyciam ut gerat ipsa pharetram
et pastoralem praefixa cuspide myrtum.

814 inhians *MR*: haesere *P* (5.529)

maiden's warder, and father Inachus pouring his stream from an embossed urn.[34] Behind him comes a cloud of infantry, and shielded columns throng all the plain, Argive manhood and Auruncan troops, Rutulians and old Sicanians, the Sacranian lines and Labicians with painted bucklers; those who till your glades, Tiber, and Numicius' sacred shore, whose ploughshare moves the Rutulian hills and Circe's ridge;[35] over whose fields Jupiter of Anxur reigns, and Feronia rejoicing in her greenwood; where Satura's black marsh lies, and cold Ufens winds his way through the valley depths and sinks into the sea.

To crown the array comes Camilla, of Volscian race, leading her troop of horse, and squadrons gay with brass— a warrior maid, never having trained her woman's hands to Minerva's distaff or basket of wool, but hardy to bear the brunt of battle and in speed of foot to outstrip the winds. She might have flown over the topmost blades of unmown corn, and not bruised the tender ears in her course; or sped her way over mid sea, poised above the swelling wave, and not dipped her swift feet in the flood. All the youth, streaming from house and field, and thronging matrons marvel, and gaze at her as she goes; agape with wonder at how the glory of royal purple drapes her smooth shoulders, how the clasp entwines her hair with gold, how her own hands bear a Lycian quiver and the pastoral myrtle tipped with steel.

[34] The river Inachus is represented by a figure of the river god, pouring water from an urn.

[35] Cf. line 10 above.

LIBER VIII

MPR Ut belli signum Laurenti Turnus ab arce
extulit et rauco strepuerunt cornua cantu,
utque acris concussit equos utque impulit arma,
extemplo turbati animi, simul omne tumultu
5 coniurat trepido Latium saevitque iuventus
effera. ductores primi Messapus et Ufens
contemptorque deum Mezentius undique cogunt
auxilia et latos vastant cultoribus agros.
mittitur et magni Venulus Diomedis ad urbem
10 qui petat auxilium, et Latio consistere Teucros,
advectum Aenean classi victosque penatis
inferre et fatis regem se dicere posci
edoceat, multasque viro se adiungere gentis
MPRV Dardanio et late Latio increbrescere nomen:
15 quid struat his coeptis, quem, si fortuna sequatur,
eventum pugnae cupiat, manifestius ipsi
quam Turno regi aut regi apparere Latino.
  Talia per Latium. quae Laomedontius heros
cuncta videns magno curarum fluctuat aestu,
20 atque animum nunc huc celerem nunc dividit illuc
in partisque rapit varias perque omnia versat:

10 consistere *MPR*: considere (6.67) *P*[2]
20,21 = 4.285,286

BOOK VIII

When Turnus raised up the flag of war from the Laurentine citadel and the horns rang with their hoarse notes, when he roused his fiery steeds and clashed his arms, straightway men's hearts were troubled; all Latium at once swears allegiance in eager uprising, and her sons rage madly. The chief captains, Messapus and Ufens, with Mezentius, scorner of the gods, from all sides muster forces and strip the wide fields of farmers. Venulus too is sent to mighty Diomedes' city[1] to seek aid, and announce that Teucrians are settling in Latium; that Aeneas is come with his fleet, bringing in his vanquished gods, and proclaiming himself a king summoned by Fate; that many tribes are joining the Dardan hero and his name spreads far and wide in Latium. What end he compasses with these beginnings, what outcome of the feud he craves, should Fortune attend him, would be more clearly seen by Diomedes himself than by King Turnus or King Latinus.[2]

Thus it was in Latium. The hero of Laomedon's line, seeing it all, tosses on a mighty sea of troubles; and now this way, now that he swiftly throws his mind, casting it in diverse ways, and turning it to every shift; as when in

[1] Argyripa or Arpi, in Apulia, near the modern Foggia (cf. *Aen.* 11.246–250).   [2] Knowing the Trojans as he did, Diomedes could best judge their plans and aspirations.

sicut aquae tremulum labris ubi lumen aënis
sole repercussum aut radiantis imagine lunae
omnia pervolitat late loca, iamque sub auras
25   erigitur summique ferit laquearia tecti.
     Nox erat et terras animalia fessa per omnis
alituum pecudumque genus sopor altus habebat,
cum pater in ripa gelidique sub aetheris axe
Aeneas, tristi turbatus pectora bello,
30   procubuit seramque dedit per membra quietem.
huic deus ipse loci fluvio Tiberinus amoeno
populeas inter senior se attollere frondes
visus (eum tenuis glauco velabat amictu
carbasus, et crinis umbrosa tegebat harundo),
35   tum sic adfari et curas his demere dictis:
     "O sate gente deum, Troianam ex hostibus urbem
qui revehis nobis aeternaque Pergama servas,
exspectate solo Laurenti arvisque Latinis,
hic tibi certa domus, certi (ne absiste) penates.
MPR neu belli terrere minis; tumor omnis et irae
41   concessere deum . . .
iamque tibi, ne vana putes haec fingere somnum,
litoreis ingens inventa sub ilicibus sus
triginta capitum fetus enixa iacebit,
45   alba solo recubans, albi circum ubera nati.
hic locus urbis erit, requies ea certa laborum,
ex quo ter denis urbem redeuntibus annis
Ascanius clari condet cognominis Albam.
haud incerta cano. nunc qua ratione quod instat
50   expedias victor, paucis (adverte) docebo.
Arcades his oris, genus a Pallante profectum,

43–46 = 3.390–393   46 *om. MP: given by R*

bronze bowls a flickering light from water, flung back by
the sun or the moon's glittering form, flits far and wide over
all things, and now mounts high and smites the fretted ceil-
ing of the roof high above.

It was night, and over all lands deep sleep held wearied
creatures, birds and beasts alike, when father Aeneas, his
heart troubled by woeful war, lay down on the bank under
the vault of the cold sky, and let sleep at last steal over his
limbs. He dreamed that before him the very god of the
place, Tiberinus of the pleasant stream, raised his aged
head amid the poplar leaves; fine linen draped him in a
mantle of grey, and shady reeds crowned his hair. Then
thus he spoke to him, and with these words took away his
cares:

"Seed of a race divine, you who from foemen's hands
bring back to us our Trojan city,[3] and preserve her towers
for ever, you who have been long looked for on Laurentine
ground and Latin fields, here your home is sure—draw not
back—and sure are your gods! Be not scared by threats of
war; all the swelling wrath of Heaven has abated. . . . Even
now, lest you deem these words the idle feigning of sleep,
you will find a huge sow lying under the oaks on the shore,
just delivered of a litter of thirty young, a white mother re-
clining on the ground—white, too, the young about her
teats. *Here shall be the city's site, here a sure rest from your
toils.* By this token in thirty revolving years Ascanius will
found a city, Alba of glorious name. Not doubtful is my
prophecy. Now in what way you can make your way trium-
phant through this present ill, in few words—pay heed—I
will explain. On these coasts Arcadians, a race sprung from

---

[3] Dardanus came from Italy.

qui regem Euandrum comites, qui signa secuti,
delegere locum et posuere in montibus urbem
Pallantis proavi de nomine Pallanteum.
55 hi bellum adsidue ducunt cum gente Latina;
hos castris adhibe socios et foedera iunge.
ipse ego te ripis et recto flumine ducam,
adversum remis superes subvectus ut amnem.
surge age, nate dea, primisque cadentibus astris
60 Iunoni fer rite preces, iramque minasque
supplicibus supera votis. mihi victor honorem
persolves. ego sum pleno quem flumine cernis
stringentem ripas et pinguia culta secantem,
caeruleus Thybris, caelo gratissimus amnis.
65 hic mihi magna domus; celsis caput urbibus exit."
    Dixit, deinde lacu fluvius se condidit alto
ima petens; nox Aenean somnusque reliquit.
surgit et aetherii spectans orientia solis
lumina rite cavis undam de flumine palmis
70 sustinet ac talis effundit ad aethera voces:
FMPR "Nymphae, Laurentes Nymphae, genus amnibus unde est,
tuque, o Thybri tuo genitor cum flumine sancto,
accipite Aenean et tandem arcete periclis.
quo te cumque lacus miserantem incommoda nostra
75 fonte tenet, quocumque solo pulcherrimus exis,
semper honore meo, semper celebrabere donis
corniger Hesperidum fluvius regnator aquarum.
adsis o tantum et propius tua numina firmes."
sic memorat, geminasque legit de classe biremis
80 remigioque aptat, socios simul instruit armis.

56 foedera *MP*: foedere *R*   65 magna *MR*: certa (39) *P*
75 tenet *MP*: tenent *FR*

Pallas, who were the company of King Evander and fol-
lowed his banner, have chosen a site and set their city on
the hills, from their forefather Pallas called Pallanteum.
They wage war ceaselessly with the Latin race; them you
must take to your camp as allies, and join with them in
league. I myself will guide you along the banks straight up
the stream, that so, impelled by your oars, you may over-
come the opposing current. Up, arise, goddess-born, and,
as the stars first set, duly offer prayers to Juno, and with
suppliant vows vanquish her wrath and her threats. To me
you will pay your tribute when victorious. I am he whom
you see grazing my banks with full flood and cleaving the
rich tilth—the blue Tiber, river best beloved of Heaven.
Here is my mighty home; among lofty cities flows forth my
fountainhead."

So spoke the River, then plunged into his deep pool,
seeking the lowest depths; night and sleep left Aeneas. He
arises and, gazing toward the eastern beams of the celes-
tial sun, uplifts water from the stream in his hollow palms
as use ordains, and pours forth to Heaven this prayer:
"O Nymphs, Laurentine Nymphs, from whom rivers have
their being, and you, father Tiber, you and your hallowed
stream—receive Aeneas, and at last shield him from per-
ils. In whatever spring your water contains you as you pity
our travails, from whatever soil you flow forth in all your
beauty, ever with my offerings, ever with my gifts, you will
be graced, horned stream, lord of Hesperian waters. Only
be with me, and confirm your will with your presence." So
he speaks, and choosing two galleys from his fleet mans
them with crews, and at once equips his comrades with
arms.

Ecce autem subitum atque oculis mirabile monstrum,
candida per silvam cum fetu concolor albo
procubuit viridique in litore conspicitur sus;
quam pius Aeneas tibi enim, tibi, maxima Iuno,
85 mactat sacra ferens et cum grege sistit ad aram.
Thybris ea fluvium, quam longa est, nocte tumentem
leniit, et tacita refluens ita substitit unda,
mitis ut in morem stagni placidaeque paludis
sterneret aequor aquis, remo ut luctamen abesset.
90 ergo iter inceptum celerant rumore secundo:
labitur uncta vadis abies; mirantur et undae,
miratur nemus insuetum fulgentia longe
FMPRV scuta virum fluvio pictasque innare carinas.
olli remigio noctemque diemque fatigant
95 et longos superant flexus, variisque teguntur
arboribus, viridisque secant placido aequore silvas.
sol medium caeli conscenderat igneus orbem
cum muros arcemque procul ac rara domorum
MPRV tecta vident, quae nunc Romana potentia caelo
100 aequavit, tum res inopes Euandrus habebat.
ocius advertunt proras urbique propinquant.
Forte die sollemnem illo rex Arcas honorem
Amphitryoniadae magno divisque ferebat
ante urbem in luco. Pallas huic filius una,
105 una omnes iuvenum primi pauperque senatus
tura dabant, tepidusque cruor fumabat ad aras.
ut celsas videre rates atque inter opacum

90 celerant *FMP*: peragunt (6.384) *R, Macrobius*

But lo! a portent, sudden and wondrous to see. Gleaming white through the wood, of one colour with her milk-white brood, there lay outstretched on the green bank before their eyes a sow; good Aeneas offers her in sacrifice to you, indeed to you, most mighty Juno, and sets her with her young before your altar. All that night long Tiber calmed his swelling flood, and flowing back with silent wave so halted that like a gentle pool or quiet mere he smoothed his watery plain, so that the oars might know no struggle. Therefore with cheering cries they speed the voyage they have begun; over the waters glides the well-pitched pine; in wonder the waves, in wonder the woods unused to such a sight, view the far-gleaming shields of warriors and the painted hulls floating on the stream. They with their rowing give night and day no rest, pass the long bends, are shaded with diverse trees, and cleave the green woods on the calm surface.[4] The fiery sun had scaled the mid arch of heaven, when at a distance they see walls and a citadel, and scattered rooftops which today Roman might has exalted to heaven, but then Evander ruled, a scant domain. Quickly they turn the prows to land and draw near the town.

It chanced that on that day the Arcadian king was paying wonted homage to Amphitryon's mighty son[5] and the gods in a grove before the city. With him his son Pallas, with him all the foremost of his people and his humble senate were offering incense, and the warm blood smoked at the altars. When they saw the high ships, saw them gliding

---

[4] Thus Servius, who rightly supposes that Virgil refers to the reflected woods.   [5] Hercules. Virgil doubtless has in mind the rites connected with the Ara Maxima in the Forum Boarium.

adlabi nemus et tacitos incumbere remis,
terrentur visu subito cunctique relictis
110 consurgunt mensis. audax quos rumpere Pallas
sacra vetat raptoque volat telo obvius ipse,
et procul e tumulo: "iuvenes, quae causa subegit
ignotas temptare vias? quo tenditis?" inquit.
"qui genus? unde domo? pacemne huc fertis an arma?"
115 tum pater Aeneas puppi sic fatur ab alta
paciferaeque manu ramum praetendit olivae:
"Troiugenas ac tela vides inimica Latinis,
quos illi bello profugos egere superbo.
MPR Euandrum petimus. ferte haec et dicite lectos
120 Dardaniae venisse duces socia arma rogantis."
obstipuit tanto percussus nomine Pallas:
"egredere o quicumque es" ait "coramque parentem
adloquere ac nostris succede penatibus hospes."
excepitque manu dextramque amplexus inhaesit;
125 progressi subeunt luco fluviumque relinquunt.
    Tum regem Aeneas dictis adfatur amicis:
"optime Graiugenum, cui me Fortuna precari
et vitta comptos voluit praetendere ramos,
non equidem extimui Danaum quod ductor et Arcas
130 quodque a stirpe fores geminis coniunctus Atridis;
sed mea me virtus et sancta oracula divum
cognatique patres, tua terris didita fama,
coniunxere tibi et fatis egere volentem.
Dardanus, Iliacae primus pater urbis et auctor,
135 Electra, ut Grai perhibent, Atlantide cretus,
advehitur Teucros; Electram maximus Atlas
edidit, aetherios umero qui sustinet orbis.

108 tacitos *MPR*: tacitis *Servius*   115 fatur *MRV*: fatus *P*

up between the shady woods and noiselessly plying their oars, they are alarmed by the sudden sight, and rise up as one, quitting the feast. But Pallas, undaunted, forbids them to break off the rites and, seizing his spear, flies to meet the strangers himself, and from a mound at a distance cries: "Warriors, what cause has driven you to try unknown paths? Where are you heading? Of what race are you? From what home? Is it peace or war you bring hither?" Then father Aeneas speaks thus from the high stern, holding out in his hand a branch of peaceful olive: "You see men of Trojan stock and arms hostile to Latins—men whom they have driven to flight by insolent warfare. We seek Evander; bear this message, and say that chosen captains of Dardania are come, suing for alliance in arms." Pallas was astounded, struck by that mighty name. "Come forth," he cries, "whoever you are; speak to my father face to face, and come as a guest beneath our roof!" And with a grasp of welcome he caught and clung to his hand. Advancing, they enter the grove and leave the river.

Then with friendly words Aeneas addresses the king: "Noblest of the sons of Greece, to whom Fortune has willed that I make my prayer, and offer boughs decked with fillets, I was not afraid that you were a Danaan chief, an Arcadian and linked by blood with the twin sons of Atreus; but my own worth and Heaven's holy oracles, our ancestral kinship, and your fame that has spread through the world, have bound me to you, and led me here as Fate's willing follower. Dardanus, first father and founder of Ilium's city, born (as Greeks relate) of Atlantean Electra, came to the Teucrians; Electra was begotten of mightiest Atlas, who on his shoulders sustains the heavenly spheres.

vobis Mercurius pater est, quem candida Maia
Cyllenae gelido conceptum vertice fudit;
140   at Maiam, auditis si quicquam credimus, Atlas,
idem Atlas generat caeli qui sidera tollit.
sic genus amborum scindit se sanguine ab uno.
his fretus non legatos neque prima per artem
temptamenta tui pepigi; me, me ipse meumque
145   obieci caput et supplex ad limina veni.
gens eadem, quae te, crudeli Daunia bello
insequitur; nos si pellant nihil afore credunt
quin omnem Hesperiam penitus sua sub iuga mittant,
et mare quod supra teneant quodque adluit infra.
150   accipe daque fidem. sunt nobis fortia bello
pectora, sunt animi et rebus spectata iuventus."
    Dixerat Aeneas. ille os oculosque loquentis
iamdudum et totum lustrabat lumine corpus.
tum sic pauca refert: "ut te, fortissime Teucrum,
155   accipio agnoscoque libens! ut verba parentis
et vocem Anchisae magni vultumque recordor!
nam memini Hesionae visentem regna sororis
Laomedontiaden Priamum Salamina petentem
protinus Arcadiae gelidos invisere finis.
160   tum mihi prima genas vestibat flore iuventas,
mirabarque duces Teucros, mirabar et ipsum
Laomedontiaden; sed cunctis altior ibat
Anchises. mihi mens iuvenali ardebat amore
compellare virum et dextrae coniungere dextram;
165   accessi et cupidus Phenei sub moenia duxi.
ille mihi insignem pharetram Lyciasque sagittas
discedens chlamydemque auro dedit intertextam,

---

167 intertextam *MP*2: intertexto *PR, known to Servius*

Your ancestor is Mercury, whom fair Maia conceived and bore on Cyllene's cold peak; but Maia, if we have any trust in tales we have heard, is child of Atlas, the same Atlas who holds up the starry heavens; so the lineage of us both branches from one blood. Relying on this, no embassy did I plan, no crafty overtures to you; myself I have brought— myself and my own life—and am come a suppliant to your doors. The same Daunian race pursues us, as you, in cruel war; if they drive us forth, they deem that nothing will keep them from laying all Hesperia utterly beneath their yoke, and from holding the seas that wash her above and below.[6] Take and give friendship; we have hearts valiant in war, high souls and manhood tried in action."

Aeneas finished speaking. As he spoke, Evander's gaze had long scanned his face and eyes, and all his form; then thus briefly he replies: "Bravest of the Teucrians, how gladly I receive and recognize you! How I recall your father's words, and the voice and features of great Anchises! For I remember how Priam, Laomedon's son, when on his way to Salamis he came to see the realm of his sister Hesione, passed on to visit Arcadia's cold borders. In those days early youth clothed my cheeks with bloom, and I wondered at the chiefs of Troy, wondered at their prince, Laomedon's son; but towering above all walked Anchises. My heart burned with youthful ardour to speak to him and clasp hand in hand; I drew near, and led him eagerly to Pheneus' city. When he left, he gave me a glorious quiver with Lycian shafts, a scarf woven with gold, and a pair of

6 The Adriatic and Tuscan seas.

frenaque bina meus quae nunc habet aurea Pallas.
ergo et quam petitis iuncta est mihi foedere dextra,
170 et lux cum primum terris se crastina reddet,
auxilio laetos dimittam opibusque iuvabo.
interea sacra haec, quando huc venistis amici,
annua, quae differre nefas, celebrate faventes
nobiscum, et iam nunc sociorum adsuescite mensis."
175   Haec ubi dicta, dapes iubet et sublata reponi
pocula gramineoque viros locat ipse sedili,
praecipuumque toro et villosi pelle leonis
accipit Aenean solioque invitat acerno.
tum lecti iuvenes certatim araeque sacerdos
180 viscera tosta ferunt taurorum, onerantque canistris
dona laboratae Cereris, Bacchumque ministrant.
vescitur Aeneas simul et Troiana iuventus
perpetui tergo bovis et lustralibus extis.
     Postquam exempta fames et amor compressus edendi,
185 rex Euandrus ait: "non haec sollemnia nobis,
has ex more dapes, hanc tanti numinis aram
vana superstitio veterumque ignara deorum
imposuit: saevis, hospes Troiane, periclis
servati facimus meritosque novamus honores.
190 iam primum saxis suspensam hanc aspice rupem,
disiectae procul ut moles desertaque montis
stat domus et scopuli ingentem traxere ruinam.
hic spelunca fuit vasto summota recessu,
semihominis Caci facies quam dira tenebat
195 solis inaccessam radiis; semperque recenti
caede tepebat humus, foribusque adfixa superbis
ora virum tristi pendebant pallida tabo.

194 tenebat *M*2: tegebat *MPR*

golden bits that now my Pallas possesses. Therefore, the hand you seek I join with you in league and, when first tomorrow's dawn revisits earth, I will send you hence cheered by an escort, and will aid you with our stores. Meanwhile, since you are come hither as friends, this yearly festival, which we may not defer, graciously solemnize with us, and even now become familiar with your comrades' board."

This said, he orders the repast and cups, by now removed, to be replaced, and with his own hand ranges the guests on the grassy seat, and chief in honour he welcomes Aeneas to the cushion of a shaggy lion's hide, and invites him to a maple throne. Then chosen youths, and the priest of the altar, in emulous haste bring roast flesh of bulls, pile on baskets the gifts of Ceres, fashioned well, and serve the wine of Bacchus. Aeneas and with him the warriors of Troy feast on the long chine of an ox and the sacrificial meat.

When hunger was banished and the desire of food stayed, King Evander spoke: "These solemn rites, this wonted feast, this altar of a mighty Presence—it is no idle superstition, ignorant of the gods of old, that has laid them on us. Saved from cruel perils, Trojan guest, we celebrate the rites, and repeat the worship due. Now first look at this rocky overhanging cliff, how the masses are scattered afar, how the mountain dwelling stands desolate, and the crags have toppled down in mighty ruin. Here once was a cave, receding to unfathomed depth, never visited by the sun's rays, where dwelt the awful shape of half-human Cacus; and ever the ground reeked with fresh blood, and, nailed to its proud doors, faces of men hung pallid in ghastly de-

huic monstro Volcanus erat pater: illius atros
ore vomens ignis magna se mole ferebat.
200 attulit et nobis aliquando optantibus aetas
auxilium adventumque dei. nam maximus ultor
tergemini nece Geryonae spoliisque superbus
Alcides aderat taurosque hac victor agebat
ingentis, vallemque boves amnemque tenebant.
205 at furiis Caci mens effera, ne quid inausum
aut intractatum scelerisve dolive fuisset,
quattuor a stabulis praestanti corpore tauros
avertit, totidem forma superante iuvencas.
atque hos, ne qua forent pedibus vestigia rectis,
210 cauda in speluncam tractos versisque viarum
indiciis raptor saxo occultabat opaco;
quaerenti nulla ad speluncam signa ferebant.
interea, cum iam stabulis saturata moveret
Amphitryoniades armenta abitumque pararet,
215 discessu mugire boves atque omne querelis
impleri nemus et colles clamore relinqui.
reddidit una boum vocem vastoque sub antro
mugiit et Caci spem custodita fefellit.
hic vero Alcidae furiis exarserat atro
220 felle dolor: rapit arma manu nodisque gravatum
robur, et aërii cursu petit ardua montis.
tum primum nostri Cacum videre timentem
turbatumque oculis; fugit ilicet ocior Euro
speluncamque petit, pedibus timor addidit alas.
225 Ut sese inclusit ruptisque immane catenis
deiecit saxum, ferro quod et arte paterna

---

205 furiis *PR*: furis *M*   211 raptor *Wakefield*: raptos *MPR*
212 quaerenti *MP*: quaerentes *R*

cay. This monster's father was Vulcan; his were the black
fires he belched forth, as he moved with massive bulk. In
due course, time brought the help and presence of a god.
For to us, too, in our need, the mightiest of avengers, glo-
rying in the slaughter and spoils of triple Geryon, Hercules
came, and this way drove his huge bulls in triumph, and his
oxen filled vale and riverside. But Cacus, his wits wild with
frenzy, that no crime or craft might prove to be left un-
dared or untried, drove from their stalls four bulls of sur-
passing form, and as many heifers of peerless beauty. And
that there might be no tracks pointing forward, the
rustler dragged them by the tail into his cave, and, with the
signs of their course thus turned backwards, the thief hid
them in the rocky darkness: anyone who sought them
could find no marks leading to the cave. Meanwhile, when
Amphitryon's son was now moving the well-fed herds from
their stalls and making ready to set out, the cattle lowed as
they went; all the grove they fill with their plaint, and with
clamour quit the hills. One heifer returned the cry, lowed
from the high cave's depths, and from her prison baffled
the hopes of Cacus. At this the wrath of Alcides furiously
blazed forth with black gall; seizing in hand his weapons
and heavily knotted club, he seeks with speed the crest of
the steep mountain. Then first our people saw Cacus afraid
and with trouble in his eyes; in a twinkling he flees swifter
than the East Wind and seeks his cave; fear lends wings to
his feet.

Just as he shut himself in and, bursting the chains,
dropped the giant rock suspended in iron by his father's

---

[221] et aerii *PR*: aetherii *M*

[223] oculis *MPR*: oculi χ, *known to Servius*

pendebat, fultosque emuniit obice postis,
ecce furens animis aderat Tirynthius omnemque
accessum lustrans huc ora ferebat et illuc,
230 dentibus infrendens. ter totum fervidus ira
lustrat Aventini montem, ter saxea temptat
limina nequiquam, ter fessus valle resedit.
stabat acuta silex praecisis undique saxis
speluncae dorso insurgens, altissima visu,
235 dirarum nidis domus opportuna volucrum.
hanc, ut prona iugo laevum incumbebat ad amnem,
dexter in adversum nitens concussit et imis
avulsam solvit radicibus, inde repente
impulit; impulsu quo maximus intonat aether,
240 dissultant ripae refluitque exterritus amnis.
at specus et Caci detecta apparuit ingens
regia, et umbrosae penitus patuere cavernae,
non secus ac si qua penitus vi terra dehiscens
infernas reseret sedes et regna recludat
245 pallida, dis invisa, superque immane barathrum
cernatur, trepident immisso lumine Manes.
ergo insperata deprensum luce repente
inclusumque cavo saxo atque insueta rudentem
desuper Alcides telis premit, omniaque arma
250 advocat et ramis vastisque molaribus instat.
ille autem, neque enim fuga iam super ulla pericli,
faucibus ingentem fumum (mirabile dictu)
evomit involvitque domum caligine caeca
prospectum eripiens oculis, glomeratque sub antro
255 fumiferam noctem commixtis igne tenebris.

---

239 intonat *MP*: insonat (7.515) *R*   244 reseret *M*: -at *PR*
246 trepident *MP*: trepidantque *R*

craft and with its barrier blocked the firm-stayed entrance, there was the Tirynthian in a frenzy of wrath; scanning every approach, he turned his face this way and that, gnashing his teeth. Three times, hot with rage, he traverses the whole Aventine Mount; three times he tries the stony portals in vain; three times he sinks down exhausted in the valley. There stood a pointed rock of flint, cut sheer away all around, rising above the cavern's ridge, and very tall to see, fit home for the nestlings of foul birds. This, as it leaned sloping with its ridge to the river on the left, he shook, straining against it from the right and, wrenching it from its lowest roots, tore it loose; then suddenly he thrust it forth; with that thrust the mighty heaven thunders, the banks leap apart, and the terrified river recoils. But the den of Cacus and his huge palace stood revealed and, deep below, the darkling cave lay open: just as if, through some force, the earth, gaping open deep below, were to unlock the infernal abodes and disclose the pallid realms abhorred by the gods, and from above the vast abyss be seen, and the ghosts tremble at the inrushing light. On him, then, caught suddenly by unexpected daylight, pent up in the hollow rock and bellowing as never before, Alcides hurls missiles from above, calling all weapons to his aid, and rains upon him boughs and giant millstones. He, meanwhile, since now no other escape from peril was left, belches from his throat dense smoke, wondrous to tell, and veils the dwelling in blinding darkness, blotting all view from the eyes, and rolling up in the cave's depth smoke-laden night, its blackness mingled with flame. In his fury

---

[247] luce *MP*: in luce *R*

non tulit Alcides animis, seque ipse per ignem
praecipiti iecit saltu, qua plurimus undam
fumus agit nebulaque ingens specus aestuat atra.
hic Cacum in tenebris incendia vana vomentem
260 corripit in nodum complexus, et angit inhaerens
elisos oculos et siccum sanguine guttur.
panditur extemplo foribus domus atra revulsis
abstractaeque boves abiurataeque rapinae
caelo ostenduntur, pedibusque informe cadaver
265 protrahitur. nequeunt expleri corda tuendo
terribilis oculos, vultum villosaque saetis
pectora semiferi atque exstinctos faucibus ignis.
ex illo celebratus honos laetique minores
servavere diem, primusque Potitius auctor
270 et domus Herculei custos Pinaria sacri
hanc aram luco statuit, quae Maxima semper
dicetur nobis et erit quae maxima semper.
quare agite, o iuvenes, tantarum in munere laudum
cingite fronde comas et pocula porgite dextris,
275 communemque vocate deum et date vina volentes."
dixerat, Herculea bicolor cum populus umbra
velavitque comas foliisque innexa pependit,
et sacer implevit dextram scyphus. ocius omnes
in mensam laeti libant divosque precantur.
280 Devexo interea propior fit Vesper Olympo.
iamque sacerdotes primusque Potitius ibant
pellibus in morem cincti, flammasque ferebant.
instaurant epulas et mensae grata secundae

---

257 iecit *MR*: iniecit *P*
261 elisos *MPR*: elidens *"multi" says Servius*, χ
262 atra *MR*: alta (*G*.2.461) *P*

Alcides did not tolerate this: headlong he dashed through the flame, where the smoke rolls its wave thickest, and through the mighty cave the mist surges black. Here, as Cacus in the darkness vomits forth unavailing fires, he seizes him in a knot-like embrace and, close entwined, throttles him till the eyes burst forth and the throat is drained of blood. At once the doors are torn off and the dark den laid bare; the stolen oxen and the theft he had denied are shown to heaven, and the hideous carcase is dragged forth by the feet. Men cannot sate their hearts with gazing on the terrible eyes, the face, and shaggy bristling chest of the brutish creature, and the quenched fires of his throat. From that time has this rite been solemnized and joyous posterity has kept the day—Potitius foremost, founder of the rite, and the Pinarian house, custodian of the worship of Hercules. He himself set in the grove this altar, which shall always be called Mightiest by us, and mightiest it shall always be. Come then, warriors, and, in honour of deeds so glorious, wreath your hair with leaves, and stretch forth the cup in your hands; call on our common god, and with a will pour forth the wine." He had no sooner spoken than the variegated poplar veiled his hair with the shade dear to Hercules, hanging down with a festoon of leaves, and the sacred goblet charged his hand. Speedily all pour glad libation on the board, and offer prayer to the gods.

Meanwhile, evening draws nearer down heaven's slope, and now the priests went forth, Potitius at their head, girt with skins after their fashion, and bearing torches. They renew the banquet and bring the welcome offerings of a

dona ferunt cumulantque oneratis lancibus aras.
285 tum Salii ad cantus incensa altaria circum
populeis adsunt evincti tempora ramis,
hic iuvenum chorus, ille senum, qui carmine laudes
Herculeas et facta ferunt: ut prima novercae
monstra manu geminosque premens eliserit anguis,
290 ut bello egregias idem disiecerit urbes,
Troiamque Oechaliamque, ut duros mille labores
rege sub Eurystheo fatis Iunonis iniquae
pertulerit. "tu nubigenas, invicte, bimembris
Hylaeumque Pholumque manu, tu Cresia mactas
295 prodigia et vastum Nemeae sub rupe leonem.
te Stygii tremuere lacus, te ianitor Orci
ossa super recubans antro semesa cruento;
nec te ullae facies, non terruit ipse Typhoeus
arduus arma tenens; non te rationis egentem
300 Lernaeus turba capitum circumstetit anguis.
salve, vera Iovis proles, decus addite divis,
et nos et tua dexter adi pede sacra secundo."
talia carminibus celebrant; super omnia Caci
speluncam adiciunt spirantemque ignibus ipsum.
305 consonat omne nemus strepitu collesque resultant.
    Exim se cuncti divinis rebus ad urbem
perfectis referunt. ibat rex obsitus aevo,
et comitem Aenean iuxta natumque tenebat
ingrediens varioque viam sermone levabat.
310 miratur facilisque oculos fert omnia circum
Aeneas, capiturque locis et singula laetus

295 Nemeae *P*: Nemea *R*: Nemaea *M*

second repast, and heap the altars with laden platters. Then the Salii come to sing round the kindled altars, their brows bound with poplar boughs—one band of youths, the other of old men—and these in song extol the glories and deeds of Hercules: how first he strangled in his grip the twin serpents, the monsters of his stepmother;[7] how likewise in war he dashed down peerless cities, Troy and Oechalia; how under King Eurystheus he bore a thousand grievous toils by the doom of cruel Juno. "You, unconquered one, you with your hand are slayer of the cloudborn creatures of double shape, Hylaeus and Pholus, the monsters of Crete, and the huge lion beneath Nemea's rock. Before you the Stygian lakes trembled; before you, the warder of Hell as he lay on half-gnawn bones in his bloody cave; no shape daunted you, no, not Typhoeus himself, towering aloft in arms; your wits did not fail you when Lerna's snake encompassed you with its swarm of heads. Hail, true seed of Jove, to the gods an added glory! Graciously with favouring foot visit us and your rites!" Such are their hymns of praise; and they crown all with the tale of Cacus' cavern, and the fire-breathing monster himself. All the woodland rings with the clamour, and the hills resound.

Then, the sacred rites completed, all return to the city. There walked the king, worn-out with years, and as he moved along he kept Aeneas and his son at his side as companions, relieving the way with varied talk. Aeneas marvels as he turns his ready eyes all around, is charmed with the

---

[7] Juno, who in jealousy sent two snakes to kill Hercules in his cradle, and through whose craftiness Hercules had to serve Eurystheus for twelve years.

exquiritque auditque virum monumenta priorum.
tum rex Euandrus Romanae conditor arcis:
"haec nemora indigenae Fauni Nymphaeque tenebant
315 gensque virum truncis et duro robore nata,
quîs neque mos neque cultus erat, nec iungere tauros
aut componere opes norant aut parcere parto,
sed rami atque asper victu venatus alebat.
primus ab aetherio venit Saturnus Olympo
320 arma Iovis fugiens et regnis exsul ademptis.
is genus indocile ac dispersum montibus altis
composuit legesque dedit, Latiumque vocari
maluit, his quoniam latuisset tutus in oris.
aurea quae perhibent illo sub rege fuere
325 saecula: sic placida populos in pace regebat,
deterior donec paulatim ac decolor aetas
et belli rabies et amor successit habendi.
tum manus Ausonia et gentes venere Sicanae,
saepius et nomen posuit Saturnia tellus;
330 tum reges asperque immani corpore Thybris,
a quo post Itali fluvium cognomine Thybrim
diximus; amisit verum vetus Albula nomen.
me pulsum patria pelagique extrema sequentem
Fortuna omnipotens et ineluctabile fatum
335 his posuere locis, matrisque egere tremenda
Carmentis nymphae monita et deus auctor Apollo."
    Vix ea dicta, dehinc progressus monstrat et aram
et Carmentalem Romani nomine portam

---

338 Romani *MP*: Romano *R*

---

8 Cf. Homer, *Odyssey* 19.163, where Penelope says to the
disguised Odysseus: "Tell me of your stock, from which you come,

scene, and joyfully seeks and learns, one by one, the stories of the men of old. Then King Evander, founder of Rome's citadel: "In these woodlands the native Fauns and Nymphs once dwelt, and a race of men sprung from trunks of trees and hardy oak,[8] who had no rule or art of life, and knew not how to yoke the ox or to lay up stores, or to husband their gains; but tree branches nurtured them and the huntsman's savage fare. First from heavenly Olympus came Saturn, fleeing from the weapons of Jove and exiled from his lost realm. He gathered together the unruly race, scattered over mountain heights, and gave them laws, and chose that the land be called Latium, since in these borders he had found a safe hiding place.[9] Under his reign were the golden ages men tell of: in such perfect peace he ruled the nations; till little by little there crept in a race of worse sort and duller hue, the frenzy of war, and the passion for gain. Then came the Ausonian host and the Sicanian tribes, and often the land of Saturn laid aside her name.[10] Then kings arose, and fierce Thybris with giant bulk, from whose name we Italians have since called our river Tiber; the ancient river Albula has lost her true name. As for me, exiled from my country and seeking the very limits of the sea, almighty Fortune and inevitable Fate planted me on this soil; and the dread warnings of my mother, the nymph Carmentis, and Apollo's divine warrant, drove me here."

Scarce had he finished when he advances and points out the altar and the Carmental Gate, as the Romans call

---

for you are not sprung of oak or rock, as told in olden tales."

[9] Evidently deriving *Latium* from *latere* "to hide."

[10] Cf. Ausonia, Hesperia, Oenotria, Italia.

quam memorant, nymphae priscum Carmentis honorem,
340   vatis fatidicae, cecinit quae prima futuros
Aeneadas magnos et nobile Pallanteum.
hinc lucum ingentem, quem Romulus acer asylum
rettulit, et gelida monstrat sub rupe Lupercal
Parrhasio dictum Panos de more Lycaei.
345   nec non et sacri monstrat nemus Argileti
testaturque locum et letum docet hospitis Argi.
hinc ad Tarpeiam sedem et Capitolia ducit
aurea nunc, olim silvestribus horrida dumis.
iam tum religio pavidos terrebat agrestis
350   dira loci, iam tum silvam saxumque tremebant.
"hoc nemus, hunc" inquit "frondoso vertice collem
(quis deus incertum est) habitat deus; Arcades ipsum
credunt se vidisse Iovem, cum saepe nigrantem
aegida concuteret dextra nimbosque cieret.
355   haec duo praeterea disiectis oppida muris,
reliquias veterumque vides monumenta virorum.
hanc Ianus pater, hanc Saturnus condidit arcem;
Ianiculum huic, illi fuerat Saturnia nomen."
    Talibus inter se dictis ad tecta subibant
360   pauperis Euandri, passimque armenta videbant
Romanoque foro et lautis mugire Carinis.
ut ventum ad sedes, "haec" inquit "limina victor
Alcides subiit, haec illum regia cepit.

---

341 nobile *M*: nomine *R*: nobine *P* (*conflation of variants*)
357 arcem *MP*: urbem (*1.5*) *R*
361 lautis *PR*: latis *M* | Carinis *MP*: cavernis *R*

---

11 A parenthesis of Virgil's, not to be attributed to Evander.
12 The Argiletum gets its name from *argilla*, white clay, proba-

it, ancient tribute to the Nymph Carmentis, soothsaying prophetess, who first foretold the greatness of Aeneas' sons, and the glory of Pallanteum. Next he shows him a vast grove, where[11] valiant Romulus restored an asylum, and, beneath a chill rock, the Lupercal, bearing in Arcadian fashion the name of Lycaean Pan. He shows too the wood of holy Argiletum, and calls the place to witness, and tells of the death of Argus his guest.[12] From here he leads him to the Tarpeian house, and the Capitol—golden now, then bristling with woodland thickets. Even then the dread sanctity of the region awed the trembling rustics; even then they shuddered at the forest and the rock. "This grove," he cries, "this hill with its leafy crown—though we know not what god it is—is yet a god's home; my Arcadians believe they have looked on Jove himself, when as often happens, his right hand has shaken the darkening aegis and summoned the storm clouds. Moreover, in these two towns with their walls overthrown you see the relics and memorials of men of old. This fort father Janus built, that Saturn; Janiculum was this called, that Saturnia."[13]

So talking to each other, they came to the house of humble Evander, and saw cattle all about, lowing in the Roman Forum and in the fashionable Carinae. When they reached his dwelling, he cries: "These portals victorious Alcides stooped to enter; this mansion had room for him.

bly designating the potters' quarter. But popular etymology derived it from *Argi letum* and invented the story that one Argus plotted to dethrone Evander, but was detected and killed.

[13] Cf. Cato, *Origines*: *Saturnia olim, ubi nunc Capitolium.* The fort of Janus was the Janiculum, on the right bank of the Tiber.

aude, hospes, contemnere opes et te quoque dignum
365 finge deo, rebusque veni non asper egenis."
dixit, et angusti subter fastigia tecti
ingentem Aenean duxit stratisque locavit
effultum foliis et pelle Libystidis ursae:
nox ruit et fuscis tellurem amplectitur alis.
370   At Venus haud animo nequiquam exterrita mater
Laurentumque minis et duro mota tumultu
Volcanum adloquitur, thalamoque haec coniugis aureo
incipit et dictis divinum aspirat amorem:
"dum bello Argolici vastabant Pergama reges
375 debita casurasque inimicis ignibus arces,
non ullum auxilium miseris, non arma rogavi
artis opisque tuae, nec te, carissime coniunx,
incassumve tuos volui exercere labores,
quamvis et Priami deberem plurima natis,
380 et durum Aeneae flevissem saepe laborem.
nunc Iovis imperiis Rutulorum constitit oris:
ergo eadem supplex venio et sanctum mihi numen
arma rogo, genetrix nato. te filia Nerei,
te potuit lacrimis Tithonia flectere coniunx.
385 aspice qui coeant populi, quae moenia clausis
ferrum acuant portis in me excidiumque meorum."
    Dixerat et niveis hinc atque hinc diva lacertis
cunctantem amplexu molli fovet. ille repente
accepit solitam flammam, notusque medullas
390 intravit calor et labefacta per ossa cucurrit,
non secus atque olim tonitru cum rupta corusco .

---

³⁹¹ non *PR*: haut (414) *M*

---

¹⁴ Thetis, the daughter of Nereus, asked Hephaestus (Vulcan)

Have the courage, my guest, to scorn riches; make yourself, too, worthy of deity, and come not disdainful of our poverty." He spoke, and beneath the roof of his lowly dwelling led towering Aeneas, and set him on a couch of strewn leaves and the skin of a Libyan bear. Night rushes down, and clasps the earth with dusky wings.

But Venus, her mother's heart dismayed by no idle fear, moved by the threats and fierce uprising of the Laurentes, addresses Vulcan, and in her golden nuptial chamber thus begins, breathing into her words divine allurement: "While the kings of Argos ravaged Troy's doomed towers in war, and her ramparts that were fated to fall by hostile flames, no aid for the sufferers did I ask, no weapons of your art and power; no, dearest husband, I did not wish to put you or your endeavors to work for nothing, heavy as was my debt to Priam's sons, and many the tears I shed for Aeneas' sore distress. Now, by Jove's commands, he has set foot in Rutulian territory; therefore, I, who never asked before, come as a suppliant, and ask arms of the deity I revere, a mother for her son. You the daughter of Nereus, you the spouse of Tithonus could sway with tears.[14] See what nations are mustering, what cities with closed gates whet the sword against me and the lives of my people!"

The goddess ceased, and as he falters throws her snowy arms round him and fondles him in soft embrace. At once he felt the usual flame; the familiar warmth passed into his marrow and ran through his melting frame: just as when at times, bursting amid the thunder's peal, a sparkling

to make armour for her son Achilles (*Iliad* 18.428 ff.). Aurora, wife of Tithonus, asked Vulcan to give armour to her son Memnon (cf. *Aen.* 1.489).

ignea rima micans percurrit lumine nimbos;
sensit laeta dolis et formae conscia coniunx.
tum pater aeterno fatur devinctus amore:
395 "quid causas petis ex alto? fiducia cessit
quo tibi, diva, mei? similis si cura fuisset,
tum quoque fas nobis Teucros armare fuisset;
nec pater omnipotens Troiam nec fata vetabant
stare decemque alios Priamum superesse per annos.
400 et nunc, si bellare paras atque haec tibi mens est,
quidquid in arte mea possum promittere curae,
quod fieri ferro liquidove potest electro,
quantum ignes animaeque valent, absiste precando
viribus indubitare tuis." ea verba locutus
405 optatos dedit amplexus placidumque petivit
coniugis infusus gremio per membra soporem.

Inde ubi prima quies medio iam noctis abactae
curriculo expulerat somnum, cum femina primum,
cui tolerare colo vitam tenuique Minerva
410 impositum, cinerem et sopitos suscitat ignis
noctem addens operi, famulasque ad lumina longo
exercet penso, castum ut servare cubile
coniugis et possit parvos educere natos:
haud secus ignipotens nec tempore segnior illo
415 mollibus e stratis opera ad fabrilia surgit.

Insula Sicanium iuxta latus Aeoliamque
erigitur Liparen fumantibus ardua saxis,
quam subter specus et Cyclopum exesa caminis
antra Aetnaea tonant, validique incudibus ictus
420 auditi referunt gemitus, striduntque cavernis

406 infusus *M*: infusum *PR*
420 gemitus *P*: gemitum *R*: gemitu *M*

streak of fire courses through the storm clouds with dazzling light. His consort knew it, rejoicing in her wiles and conscious of her beauty. Then spoke Father Vulcan, enchained by immortal love: "Why do you seek so far back for reasons? Where, goddess, has your faith in me fled to? Had your anxiety been the same then, in those days too it would have been right for me to arm the Trojans; neither the almighty Father nor Fate was unwilling that Troy stand or Priam live for ten years more. And now, if war is your purpose and this is your intent, whatever care I can promise in my craft, whatever can be achieved with iron or molten electrum, whatever fire and air may avail—cease to mistrust your powers by using entreaty!" Saying these words, he gave her the desired embrace and, melting in his wife's arms, sought quiet sleep in every limb.

Then, when repose had banished sleep, in the mid career of now waning night, at the time when a housewife, whose task it is to eke out life with her distaff and Minerva's humble toil, awakes the embers and slumbering fire, adding night to her day's work, and keeps her handmaids toiling by lamplight at the long task, so that she can keep her husband's bed chaste and rear her little sons: just so, and not more slothful at that hour, the Lord of Fire rises from his soft couch to the work of his smithy.

Hard by the Sicanian coast and Aeolian Lipare rises an island,[15] steep with smoking rocks. Beneath it thunders a cave, and the vaults of Aetna, scooped out by Cyclopean forges; strong strokes are heard echoing groans from the anvils, masses of Chalyb steel hiss in the caverns, and the

[15] Hiera, now Vulcano, one of the Aeolian isles.

stricturae Chalybum et fornacibus ignis anhelat,
Volcani domus et Volcania nomine tellus.
huc tunc ignipotens caelo descendit ab alto.
    Ferrum exercebant vasto Cyclopes in antro,
425 Brontesque Steropesque et nudus membra Pyracmon.
his informatum manibus iam parte polita
fulmen erat, toto genitor quae plurima caelo
deicit in terras, pars imperfecta manebat.
tris imbris torti radios, tris nubis aquosae
430 addiderant, rutili tris ignis et alitis Austri.
fulgores nunc terrificos sonitumque metumque
miscebant operi flammisque sequacibus iras.
parte alia Marti currumque rotasque volucris
instabant, quibus ille viros, quibus excitat urbes;
435 aegidaque horriferam, turbatae Palladis arma,
certatim squamis serpentum auroque polibant
conexosque anguis ipsamque in pectore divae
Gorgona desecto vertentem lumina collo.
"tollite cuncta" inquit "coeptosque auferte labores,
440 Aetnaei Cyclopes, et huc advertite mentem:
arma acri facienda viro. nunc viribus usus,
nunc manibus rapidis, omni nunc arte magistra.
praecipitate moras." nec plura effatus, at illi
ocius incubuere omnes pariterque laborem
445 sortiti. fluit aes rivis aurique metallum
vulnificusque chalybs vasta fornace liquescit.
ingentem clipeum informant, unum omnia contra
tela Latinorum, septenosque orbibus orbis
impediunt. alii ventosis follibus auras
450 accipiunt redduntque, alii stridentia tingunt

423 huc *P*: hoc *MR* (*archaic form of* huc, *say Servius, Priscian*)

fire pants in the furnace—it is the home of Vulcan and the land called Vulcania. To it the Lord of Fire then came down from high heaven.

In the vast cave the Cyclopes were forging iron— Brontes and Steropes and bare-limbed Pyracmon. They had a thunderbolt, which their hands had shaped, like the many that the Father hurls down from all over heaven upon earth, in part already polished, while part remained unfinished. Three shafts of twisted hail they had added to it, three of watery cloud, three of ruddy flame and the winged South Wind; now they were blending into the work terrifying flashes, noise, and fear, and wrath with pursuing flames. Elsewhere they were hurrying on for Mars a chariot and flying wheels, with which he stirs up men and cities; and eagerly with golden scales of serpents were burnishing the awful aegis, armour of wrathful Pallas, the interwoven snakes, and on the breast of the goddess the Gorgon herself, with neck severed and eyes revolving. "Away with all!" he cries. "Remove the tasks you have begun, Cyclopes of Aetna, and turn your thoughts to this! Arms for a brave warrior you must make. Now you have need of strength, now of swift hands, now of all your masterful skill. Throw off delay!" No more he said; but they with speed all bent to the toil, allotting the labour equally. Bronze and golden ore flow in streams, and wounding steel is molten in the vast furnace. A giant shield they shape, to confront alone all the weapons of the Latins, and weld it sevenfold, circle on circle. Some with panting bellows make the blasts come and go, others dip the hissing bronze in the lake, while the

---

450–454 *practically* = G.4.171–175

aera lacu; gemit impositis incudibus antrum;
illi inter sese multa vi bracchia tollunt
in numerum, versantque tenaci forcipe massam.
    Haec pater Aeoliis properat dum Lemnius oris,
455 Euandrum ex humili tecto lux suscitat alma
et matutini volucrum sub culmine cantus.
consurgit senior tunicaque inducitur artus
et Tyrrhena pedum circumdat vincula plantis.
tum lateri atque umeris Tegeaeum subligat ensem
460 demissa ab laeva pantherae terga retorquens.
nec non et gemini custodes limine ab alto
praecedunt gressumque canes comitantur erilem.
hospitis Aeneae sedem et secreta petebat
sermonum memor et promissi muneris heros.
465 nec minus Aeneas se matutinus agebat;
filius huic Pallas, illi comes ibat Achates.
congressi iungunt dextras mediisque residunt
aedibus et licito tandem sermone fruuntur.
    Rex prior haec . . .
470 "maxime Teucrorum ductor, quo sospite numquam
res equidem Troiae victas aut regna fatebor,
nobis ad belli auxilium pro nomine tanto
exiguae vires; hinc Tusco claudimur amni,
hinc Rutulus premit et murum circumsonat armis.
475 sed tibi ego ingentis populos opulentaque regnis
iungere castra paro, quam fors inopina salutem
ostentat: fatis huc te poscentibus adfers.

462 praecedunt *MR*: procedunt *P*

---

[16] The hide is brought round to the right side, so as not to be in the way of the sword hilt, which is on the left.

cavern groans under the anvils laid upon it. They with mighty force, now one, now another, raise their arms in measured cadence, and turn the metal with gripping tongs.

While on the Aeolian shores the lord of Lemnos speeds on this work, the kindly light and the morning songs of birds beneath the eaves roused Evander from his humble home. The old man rises, clothes his limbs in a tunic, and wraps his feet in Tyrrhenian sandals. Then to his side and shoulders he buckles his Tegean sword, twisting back the panther's hide that drooped from the left.[16] Moreover, two guardian dogs go ahead of him from the high threshold and attend their master's steps. To the secluded lodging of his guest, Aeneas, the hero made his way, mindful of his words and the service promised. Nor was Aeneas astir less early. With the one walked his son Pallas; with the other, Achates. As they meet, they clasp hands, sit down among the dwellings,[17] and at last enjoy free converse.

The king thus begins . . . "Mightiest captain of the Teucrians—for while you live, I will never admit that the power and realm of Troy have been vanquished—our strength to aid in war is weak to match such a name as ours.[18] On this side we are hemmed in by the Tuscan river; on that the Rutulian presses hard and thunders in arms about our wall. But I purpose to link mighty peoples with you and a camp rich in kingdoms[19]—the salvation that unforeseen chance reveals. It is at the call of Fate that you

[17] The conference takes place in the open air.

[18] It is Evander's name and fame that brought Aeneas hither.

[19] A reference to the twelve states of Etruria governed by their *Lucumones*.

haud procul hinc saxo incolitur fundata vetusto
urbis Agyllinae sedes, ubi Lydia quondam
480 gens, bello praeclara, iugis insedit Etruscis.
hanc multos florentem annos rex deinde superbo
imperio et saevis tenuit Mezentius armis.
quid memorem infandas caedes, quid facta tyranni
effera? di capiti ipsius generique reservent!
485 mortua quin etiam iungebat corpora vivis
componens manibusque manus atque oribus ora,
tormenti genus, et sanie taboque fluentis
complexu in misero longa sic morte necabat.
at fessi tandem cives infanda furentem
490 armati circumsistunt ipsumque domumque,
obtruncant socios, ignem ad fastigia iactant.
ille inter caedem Rutulorum elapsus in agros
confugere et Turni defendier hospitis armis.
ergo omnis furiis surrexit Etruria iustis,
495 regem ad supplicium praesenti Marte reposcunt.
his ego te, Aenea, ductorem milibus addam.
toto namque fremunt condensae litore puppes
signaque ferre iubent, retinet longaevus haruspex
fata canens: 'o Maeoniae delecta iuventus,
500 flos veterum virtusque virum, quos iustus in hostem
fert dolor et merita accendit Mezentius ira,
nulli fas Italo tantam subiungere gentem:
externos optate duces.' tum Etrusca resedit
hoc acies campo monitis exterrita divum.
505 ipse oratores ad me regnique coronam
cum sceptro misit mandatque insignia Tarchon,
succedam castris Tyrrhenaque regna capessam.

---

492 caedem *MR*: cedes *P*

come here. Not far from here, built of ancient stone, lies the site of the city of Agylla, where of old the war-famed Lydian race settled on the Etruscan heights. For many years it prospered, till King Mezentius ruled it with arrogant sway and cruel arms. Why recount the despot's heinous murders, his savage deeds? May the gods store up such treatment for his own head and for his breed! He would even link dead bodies with the living, fitting hand to hand and face to face (grim torture!), and, in the oozy slime and poison of that ghastly embrace, thus slay them by a lingering death. But at last his exhausted citizens take up arms and besiege the monstrous madman, himself and his palace, cut down his followers, and hurl fire on his roof. Amid the carnage, he flees for refuge to Rutulian soil and finds shelter among the weapons of Turnus his friend. So all Etruria has risen in righteous fury; threatening instant war they demand the king for punishment. Of these thousands, Aeneas, I will make you chief; for their ships throng all the shore clamouring, and they bid the standards advance, but the aged soothsayer restrains them with prophecy of fate: 'Chosen warriors of Maeonia, flower and chivalry of an ancient race, you whom just resentment launches against the foe, and Mezentius inflames with righteous wrath, it is not right that any man of Italy should control a race so proud: choose leaders from abroad!' At that the Etruscan lines settled down on yonder plain, awed by Heaven's warning; Tarchon himself has sent me envoys with the royal crown and sceptre, and offers the ensigns of power, bidding me join the camp and mount the Tuscan

sed mihi tarda gelu saeclisque effeta senectus
invidet imperium seraeque ad fortia vires.
510 natum exhortarer, ni mixtus matre Sabella
hinc partem patriae traheret. tu, cuius et annis
et generi fatum indulget, quem numina poscunt,
ingredere, o Teucrum atque Italum fortissime ductor.
hunc tibi praeterea, spes et solacia nostri,
515 Pallanta adiungam; sub te tolerare magistro
militiam et grave Martis opus, tua cernere facta
adsuescat, primis et te miretur ab annis.
Arcadas huic equites bis centum, robora pubis
lecta dabo, totidemque suo tibi munere Pallas."
520 Vix ea fatus erat, defixique ora tenebant
Aeneas Anchisiades et fidus Achates,
multaque dura suo tristi cum corde putabant,
ni signum caelo Cytherea dedisset aperto.
namque improviso vibratus ab aethere fulgor
525 cum sonitu venit et ruere omnia visa repente,
Tyrrhenusque tubae mugire per aethera clangor.
suspiciunt, iterum atque iterum fragor increpat ingens.
arma inter nubem caeli in regione serena
per sudum rutilare vident et pulsa tonare.
530 obstipuere animis alii, sed Troïus heros
agnovit sonitum et divae promissa parentis.
tum memorat: "ne vero, hospes, ne quaere profecto
quem casum portenta ferant: ego poscor Olympo.
hoc signum cecinit missuram diva creatrix,
535 si bellum ingrueret, Volcaniaque arma per auras
laturam auxilio . . .

519 munere *PR*: nomine (121) *M*

throne. But the frost of sluggish age, worn out with years, and strength too old for deeds of valour, begrudge me the command. My son I would urge to accept, were it not that, being of mixed blood, with a Sabine mother, he draws part of his nationality from her. You, to whose years and race Fate is kind, whom Heaven calls, take up your task, most valiant leader of Trojans and Italians both. Further, I will join with you Pallas here, our hope and comfort; under your guidance let him learn to endure warfare and the stern work of battle; let him behold your deeds, and revere you from his early years. To him I will give two hundred Arcadian cavalry, choice flower of our manhood, and as his own gift Pallas will give you as many more."

Scarce had he ended; and Aeneas son of Anchises and faithful Achates, holding their eyes downcast, would long have mused on many a trouble in their own sad hearts, had not Cythera's queen granted a sign from the cloudless sky. For unexpectedly, launched from heaven, comes a flash with thunder, and everything seemed suddenly to reel, while the Tyrrhenian trumpet blast pealed through the sky. They glance up; again and yet again crashed the mighty roar. In the serene expanse of the sky they see arms amid the clouds, gleaming red in the clear air and clashing in thunder. The rest stood aghast; but the Trojan hero knew the sound and the promise of his goddess mother. Then he cries: "Ask not, my friend, ask not, I pray, what fortune the portents bode; it is I who am summoned by Heaven. This sign the goddess who bore me foretold she would send if war was at hand, and to aid me would bring through the air

---

529 tonare *M, Servius Auctus*: sonare *PR*

heu quantae miseris caedes Laurentibus instant!
quas poenas mihi, Turne, dabis! quam multa sub undas
scuta virum galeasque et fortia corpora volves,
540 Thybri pater! poscant acies et foedera rumpant."
    Haec ubi dicta dedit, solio se tollit ab alto
et primum Herculeis sopitas ignibus aras
excitat, hesternumque larem parvosque penatis
laetus adit; mactat lectas de more bidentis
545 Euandrus pariter, pariter Troiana iuventus.
post hinc ad navis graditur sociosque revisit,
quorum de numero qui sese in bella sequantur
praestantis virtute legit; pars cetera prona
fertur aqua segnisque secundo defluit amni,
550 nuntia ventura Ascanio rerumque patrisque.
dantur equi Teucris Tyrrhena petentibus arva;
ducunt exsortem Aeneae, quem fulva leonis
pellis obit totum praefulgens unguibus aureis.
    Fama volat parvam subito vulgata per urbem
555 ocius ire equites Tyrrheni ad litora regis.
vota metu duplicant matres, propiusque periclo
it timor et maior Martis iam apparet imago.
tum pater Euandrus dextram complexus euntis
haeret inexpletus lacrimans ac talia fatur:
560 "o mihi praeteritos referat si Iuppiter annos,
qualis eram cum primam aciem Praeneste sub ipsa
stravi scutorumque incendi victor acervos
et regem hac Erulum dextra sub Tartara misi,

555 litora *MR*: limina *P*
559 inexpletus *M*: inpletus *R*: inexpletum *P* | lacrimans *PR*:
lacrimis *M*

arms wrought by Vulcan . . . Alas, what carnage awaits the hapless Laurentines! What a price, Turnus, will you pay me! How many shields and helmets and bodies of the brave will you, father Tiber, sweep beneath your waves! Let them call for battle and break their covenants!"

These words said, he rose from his lofty throne, and first quickens the slumbering altars with fire to Hercules, and gladly approaches the Lar of yesterday[20] and the lowly household gods. Evander alike and alike the warriors of Troy offer up ewes duly chosen. Next he goes to the ships and revisits his men, of whose number he chooses the foremost in valour to attend him to war; the rest glide down the stream and idly float with the favouring current, to bear news to Ascanius of his father and his fortunes. Horses are given to the Teucrians who seek the Tyrrhene fields; for Aeneas they lead forth a chosen steed, all caparisoned in a tawny lion's skin, glittering with claws of gold.

Suddenly, spreading through the little town, flies a rumour that horsemen are speeding to the shores of the Tyrrhene king. In alarm mothers redouble their vows; fear comes closer because of the danger, and the War God's image now looms larger. Then Evander, clasping the hand of his departing son, clings to him weeping insatiably and thus speaks: "If only Jupiter would bring me back the years that are sped, and make me what I was when under Praeneste's very walls I struck down the foremost ranks, burned the piled up shields in my triumph, and with this right hand sent down to Tartarus King Erulus, whom at his

[20] We are to assume that, on the day of his arrival, Aeneas had offered sacrifice to the Lar, or tutelary spirit, of the dwelling whose hospitality he enjoyed.

nascenti cui tris animas Feronia mater
565 (horrendum dictu) dederat, terna arma movenda—
ter leto sternendus erat; cui tunc tamen omnis
abstulit haec animas dextra et totidem exuit armis:
non ego nunc dulci amplexu divellerer usquam,
nate, tuo, neque finitimo Mezentius umquam
570 huic capiti insultans tot ferro saeva dedisset
funera, tam multis viduasset civibus urbem.
at vos, o superi, et divum tu maxime rector
Iuppiter, Arcadii, quaeso, miserescite regis
et patrias audite preces. si numina vestra
575 incolumem Pallanta mihi, si fata reservant,
si visurus eum vivo et venturus in unum,
vitam oro, patior quemvis durare laborem.
sin aliquem infandum casum, Fortuna, minaris,
nunc, nunc o liceat crudelem abrumpere vitam,
580 dum curae ambiguae, dum spes incerta futuri,
dum te, care puer, mea sera et sola voluptas,
complexu teneo, gravior neu nuntius auris
vulneret." haec genitor digressu dicta supremo
fundebat; famuli conlapsum in tecta ferebant.
585   Iamque adeo exierat portis equitatus apertis
Aeneas inter primos et fidus Achates,
inde alii Troiae proceres, ipse agmine Pallas
it medio, chlamyde et pictis conspectus in armis,
qualis ubi Oceani perfusus Lucifer unda,
590 quem Venus ante alios astrorum diligit ignis,
extulit os sacrum caelo tenebrasque resolvit.
stant pavidae in muris matres oculisque sequuntur

569 umquam *M*: usquam *PR*
579 nunc nunc o *MP²*: nunc nunc *P*: nunc o nunc (2.644) *R*

birth his mother Feronia had given (awful to tell!) three
lives with threefold armour to wear—three times he had
to be laid low in death; yet on that day this hand bereft him
of all his lives and as often stripped him of his armour—
then never should I now be torn, my son, from your sweet
embrace. Never on this his neighbour's head would
Mezentius have heaped scorn, dealt with the sword so
many cruel deaths, nor widowed the city of so many of her
sons! But you powers above, and you, Jupiter, mighty ruler
of the gods, pity, I pray, the Arcadian king, and hear a
father's prayer. If your will, if destiny keep my Pallas safe, if
I live still to see him, still to meet him, for life I pray; I have
patience to endure any toil. But if, Fortune, you threaten
some dread mischance, now, oh, now may I break the
thread of cruel life—while fears are doubtful, while hope
reads not the future, while you, beloved boy, my late and
lone delight, are held in my embrace; and may no heavier
tidings wound my ear!" These words the father poured
forth at their last parting; his servants bore him swooning
into the palace.

And now the horsemen had issued from the open gates,
Aeneas at their head with loyal Achates, then other princes
of Troy; Pallas himself rides at the column's centre, con-
spicuous in mantle and blazoned armour—just like the
Morning Star, whom Venus loves above all the starry fires,
when, bathed in Ocean's wave, he lifts up his sacred head
in heaven and melts the darkness. On the walls mothers
stand trembling, and follow with their eyes the dusty cloud

---

581 sera et sola *P*: sola et sera *MR*   582 complexu *MP*:
complexus *R*   583 dicta *PR*: maesta (3.482) *M*
588 it *Markland*: in *MPR*

pulveream nubem et fulgentis aere catervas.
olli per dumos, qua proxima meta viarum,
595 armati tendunt; it clamor, et agmine facto
quadripedante putrem sonitu quatit ungula campum.
    Est ingens gelidum lucus prope Caeritis amnem,
religione patrum late sacer; undique colles
inclusere cavi et nigra nemus abiete cingunt.
600 Silvano fama est veteres sacrasse Pelasgos,
arvorum pecorisque deo, lucumque diemque,
qui primi finis aliquando habuere Latinos.
haud procul hinc Tarcho et Tyrrheni tuta tenebant
castra locis, celsoque omnis de colle videri
605 iam poterat legio et latis tendebat in arvis.
huc pater Aeneas et bello lecta iuventus
succedunt, fessique et equos et corpora curant.
    At Venus aetherios inter dea candida nimbos
dona ferens aderat; natumque in valle reducta
610 ut procul egelido secretum flumine vidit,
talibus adfata est dictis seque obtulit ultro:
"en perfecta mei promissa coniugis arte
munera. ne mox aut Laurentis, nate, superbos
aut acrem dubites in proelia poscere Turnum."
615 dixit, et amplexus nati Cytherea petivit,
arma sub adversa posuit radiantia quercu.
ille deae donis et tanto laetus honore
expleri nequit atque oculos per singula volvit,
miraturque interque manus et bracchia versat
620 terribilem cristis galeam flammasque vomentem,
fatiferumque ensem, loricam ex aere rigentem,
sanguineam, ingentem, qualis cum caerula nubes

610 egelido *M*: et gelido *PR*

and the squadrons gleaming with bronze. Through the brushwood, where the journey's goal is nearest, the armed men move; a shout arises, they form in column, and with galloping tread the horse hoof shakes the crumbling plain.

Near Caere's cold stream there stands a vast grove, revered far and wide with ancestral awe; on all sides curving hills enclose it and girdle the woodland with dark fir trees. Rumour tells that the old Pelasgians who in time gone by first held the Latin borders dedicated both grove and festal day to Silvanus, god of fields and flock. Not far from there Tarchon and the Tyrrhenians camped in a sheltered spot, and now from a high hill all the host could be seen, their tents pitched in the wide fields. Hither come father Aeneas and the warriors chosen for battle, and refresh their steeds and wearied frames.

But Venus, lovely goddess, drew near, bearing her gifts amid the clouds of heaven; and when far off she saw her son apart in a secluded valley by the cool stream, she thus addressed him, suddenly presenting herself to view; "Behold the gifts perfected by my lord's promised skill, so that you do not shrink, my child, from soon challenging the haughty Laurentines or brave Turnus to battle." Cytherea spoke, and sought her son's embrace, and set up the radiant arms under an oak before him. Rejoicing in the divine gift and in this high honour, he cannot be sated as he moves his eyes from piece to piece, admiring and turning over in his hands and arms the helmet, terrifying with its plumes and spouting flames, the death-dealing sword, the stiff bronze corslet, blood-red and huge—just as when a dark

---

620 vomentem *MR*: minantem *P*

solis inardescit radiis longeque refulget;
tum levis ocreas electro auroque recocto,
625 hastamque et clipei non enarrabile textum.
    Illic res Italas Romanorumque triumphos
haud vatum ignarus venturique inscius aevi
fecerat ignipotens, illic genus omne futurae
stirpis ab Ascanio pugnataque in ordine bella.
630 fecerat et viridi fetam Mavortis in antro
procubuisse lupam, geminos huic ubera circum
ludere pendentis pueros et lambere matrem
impavidos, illam tereti cervice reflexa
mulcere alternos et corpora fingere lingua.
635 nec procul hinc Romam et raptas sine more Sabinas
consessu caveae, magnis Circensibus actis,
addiderat, subitoque novum consurgere bellum
Romulidis Tatioque seni Curibusque severis.
post idem inter se posito certamine reges
640 armati Iovis ante aram paterasque tenentes
stabant et caesa iungebant foedera porca,
654 Romuleoque recens horrebat regia culmo.
642 haud procul inde citae Mettum in diversa quadrigae
distulerant (at tu dictis, Albane, maneres!),
raptabatque viri mendacis viscera Tullus
645 per silvam, et sparsi rorabant sanguine vepres.
nec non Tarquinium eiectum Porsenna iubebat
accipere ingentique urbem obsidione premebat;
Aeneadae in ferrum pro libertate ruebant.
illum indignanti similem similemque minanti
650 aspiceres, pontem auderet quia vellere Cocles
et fluvium vinclis innaret Cloelia ruptis.

633 reflexa PR: reflexam M

blue cloud kindles with the sun's rays and gleams afar;
then the smooth greaves of electrum and refined gold, the
spear, and the shield's ineffable fabric.

There the story of Italy and the triumphs of Rome had
the Lord of Fire fashioned, not unversed in prophecy or
unknowing of the age to come; there, every generation of
the stock to spring from Ascanius, and the wars they fought
in their sequence. He had fashioned, too, the mother wolf
lying stretched out in the green cave of Mars; around her
teats the twin boys hung playing, and suckled their dam
without fear; with shapely neck bent back, she fondled
them by turns, and moulded their limbs with her tongue.
Not far from here he had set Rome and the Sabine maid-
ens, lawlessly carried off, when the great Circus games
were held, from the theatre's seated throng; then the sud-
den uprising of a fresh war between the sons of Romulus
and aged Tatius and his stern Cures. Next, the same kings,
their strife laid at rest, stood armed before Jove's altar, cup
in hand, and made covenant with each other over sacrifice
of swine, and the palace was rough, fresh with the thatch of
Romulus. Not far from there, four-horse chariots, driven
apart, had torn Mettus asunder (but you, Alban, should
have stood by your words!), and Tullus dragged the liar's
body through the woods, and the brambles dripped with
dew of blood. There, too, was Porsenna, bidding them ad-
mit the banished Tarquin, and oppressing the city with
mighty siege: the sons of Aeneas rushing on the sword
for freedom's sake. You could see him shown as angry, as
threatening, because Cocles dared to tear down the
bridge, and Cloelia broke her bonds and swam the river.

---

654 *after* 641 *Ribbeck*: *after* 653 *MPR*

In summo custos Tarpeiae Manlius arcis
stabat pro templo et Capitolia celsa tenebat.
655 atque hic auratis volitans argenteus anser
porticibus Gallos in limine adesse canebat;
Galli per dumos aderant arcemque tenebant
defensi tenebris et dono noctis opacae.
aurea caesaries ollis atque aurea vestis,
660 virgatis lucent sagulis, tum lactea colla
auro innectuntur, duo quisque Alpina coruscant
gaesa manu, scutis protecti corpora longis.
hic exsultantis Salios nudosque Lupercos
lanigerosque apices et lapsa ancilia caelo
665 extuderat, castae ducebant sacra per urbem
pilentis matres in mollibus. hinc procul addit
Tartareas etiam sedes, alta ostia Ditis,
et scelerum poenas, et te, Catilina, minaci
pendentem scopulo Furiarumque ora trementem,
670 secretosque pios, his dantem iura Catonem.
    Haec inter tumidi late maris ibat imago
aurea, sed fluctu spumabant caerula cano,
et circum argento clari delphines in orbem
aequora verrebant caudis aestumque secabant.
675 in medio classis aeratas, Actia bella,
cernere erat, totumque instructo Marte videres
fervere Leucaten auroque effulgere fluctus.
hinc Augustus agens Italos in proelia Caesar
cum patribus populoque, penatibus et magnis dis,

661 coruscant *MR*: coruscat *P*
672 spumabant χ: spumabat *MPR*

21 In 390 B.C., when the Gauls attacked the Capitol, they were

At the top of the shield Manlius, warder of the Tarpeian fort, stood before the temple and held the lofty Capitol. And here the silver goose,[21] fluttering through gilded colonnades, cried that the Gauls were on the threshold. The Gauls were close by in the thickets, laying hold of the fort, shielded by darkness, and the boon of shadowy night. Golden are their locks and golden their raiment; they glitter in striped cloaks, and their milk-white necks are entwined with gold; two Alpine pikes each brandishes in hand, and long shields guard their limbs. Here he had wrought the dancing Salii and naked Luperci, the crests bound with wool, and the shields that fell from heaven; and in cushioned carriages chaste matrons moved through the city in solemn progress.[22] At a distance from these he adds also the abodes of Hell, the high gates of Dis, the penalties of sin, and you, Catiline, hanging on a frowning cliff, and trembling at the sight of the Furies; and far apart, the good, with Cato giving them laws.

Among these scenes flowed wide the likeness of the swelling sea, all gold, but the blue water foamed with white billows, and round about dolphins, shining in silver, swept the seas with their tails in circles, and cleft the tide. In the centre could be seen bronze ships—the battle of Actium; you could see all Leucate aglow with War's array, and the waves ablaze with gold. On the one side Augustus Caesar stands on the lofty stern, leading Italians to strife, with Senate and People, the Penates of the state, and all the

driven back by Manlius, who had been roused from sleep by cackling geese.   [22] Roman matrons were allowed to ride at sacred processions in *pilenta*, because of their self-sacrifice after the capture of Veii, 395 B.C.

680 stans celsa in puppi, geminas cui tempora flammas
    laeta vomunt patriumque aperitur vertice sidus.
    parte alia ventis et dis Agrippa secundis
    arduus agmen agens, cui, belli insigne superbum,
    tempora navali fulgent rostrata corona.
685 hinc ope barbarica variisque Antonius armis,
    victor ab Aurorae populis et litore rubro,
    Aegyptum virisque Orientis et ultima secum
    Bactra vehit, sequiturque (nefas) Aegyptia coniunx.
    una omnes ruere ac totum spumare reductis
690 convulsum remis rostrisque tridentibus aequor.
    alta petunt; pelago credas innare revulsas
    Cycladas aut montis concurrere montibus altos,
    tanta mole viri turritis puppibus instant.
    stuppea flamma manu telisque volatile ferrum
695 spargitur, arva nova Neptunia caede rubescunt.
    regina in mediis patrio vocat agmina sistro,
    necdum etiam geminos a tergo respicit anguis.
    omnigenumque deum monstra et latrator Anubis
    contra Neptunum et Venerem contraque Minervam
700 tela tenent. saevit medio in certamine Mavors
    caelatus ferro, tristesque ex aethere Dirae,
    et scissa gaudens vadit Discordia palla,
    quam cum sanguineo sequitur Bellona flagello.
    Actius haec cernens arcum intendebat Apollo

> 680 stans *MP*: stat *R*
> 692 altos *MPR*: altis *known to Servius*
> 701 Dirae *MP*: divae *R*

---

23 See note on *Eclogues* 9.47.

mighty gods; his auspicious brows shoot forth a double flame, and on his head dawns his father's star.[23] Elsewhere, favored by winds and gods, high-towering Agrippa leads his column; his brows gleam with the beaks of the naval crown,[24] proud token won in war. On the other side comes Antony with barbaric might and motley arms, victorious over the nations of the dawn and the ruddy sea,[25] bringing in his train Egypt and the strength of the East and farthest Bactra; and there follows him (oh the shame of it!) his Egyptian wife. All rush on at once, and the whole sea foams, torn up by the sweeping oars and triple-pointed beaks. To the deep they race; you would think that the Cyclades, uprooted, were floating on the main, or that high mountains were clashing with mountains: in such huge ships the seamen attack the towered sterns. Flaming tow and shafts of winged steel are showered from their hands; Neptune's fields redden with strange slaughter. In the midst the queen calls upon her hosts with their native sistrum; not yet does she cast back a glance at the twin snakes behind.[26] Monstrous gods of every form and barking Anubis wield weapons against Neptune and Venus and against Minerva. In the middle of the fray storms Mavors, embossed in steel, with the grim Furies from on high; and in rent robe Discord strides exultant, while Bellona follows her with bloody scourge. Actian Apollo saw the sight, and

[24] The *corona navalis,* a crown adorned with ships' beaks, was a special distinction awarded to Agrippa.

[25] This is the *mare Erythraeum,* or Indian Ocean, not what we now call the Red Sea.

[26] The twin snakes are a symbol of death. Cf. *Aen.* 2.203, 7.450, 8.289.

705   desuper; omnis eo terrore Aegyptus et Indi,
    omnis Arabs, omnes vertebant terga Sabaei.
    ipsa videbatur ventis regina vocatis
    vela dare et laxos iam iamque immittere funis.
    illam inter caedes pallentem morte futura
710   fecerat ignipotens undis et Iapyge ferri,
    contra autem magno maerentem corpore Nilum
    pandentemque sinus et tota veste vocantem
    caeruleum in gremium latebrosaque flumina victos.
      At Caesar, triplici invectus Romana triumpho
715   moenia, dis Italis votum immortale sacrabat,
    maxima ter centum totam delubra per urbem.
    laetitia ludisque viae plausuque fremebant;
    omnibus in templis matrum chorus, omnibus arae;
    ante aras terram caesi stravere iuvenci.
720   ipse sedens niveo candentis limine Phoebi
    dona recognoscit populorum aptatque superbis
    postibus; incedunt victae longo ordine gentes,
    quam variae linguis, habitu tam vestis et armis.
    hic Nomadum genus et discinctos Mulciber Afros,
725   hic Lelegas Carasque sagittiferosque Gelonos
    finxerat; Euphrates ibat iam mollior undis,
    extremique hominum Morini, Rhenusque bicornis,
    indomitique Dahae, et pontem indignatus Araxes.

724,725 hic *MR*: hinc *P*

---

27 The Nile god "would be represented with a water-coloured robe, the bosom of which he would throw open" (Conington).

28 In August, 29 B.C., Augustus celebrated a triple triumph for victories in Dalmatia, at Actium, and at Alexandria.

from above was bending his bow; in terror at this all Egypt
and India, all Arabians, all Sabaeans, turned to flee. The
queen herself was seen to woo the winds, spread sail, andv
now, even now, fling loose the slackened sheets. Amid the
carnage, the Lord of Fire had fashioned her pale at the
coming of death, borne on by waves and the wind of Iapyx;
while over against her was the mourning Nile, of massive
body, opening wide his folds and with all his raiment wel-
coming the vanquished to his azure lap and sheltering
streams.[27]

But Caesar, entering the walls of Rome in triple tri-
umph,[28] was dedicating to Italy's gods his immortal votive
gift—three hundred mighty shrines throughout the city.
The streets were ringing with gladness and games and
shouting; in all the temples was a band of matrons, in all
were altars, and before the altars slain steers covered the
ground. He himself, seated at the snowy threshold of shin-
ing Phoebus, reviews the gifts of nations and hangs them
on the proud portals. The conquered peoples move in long
array, as diverse in fashion of dress and arms as in tongues.
Here Mulciber had portrayed the Nomad race and the un-
girt Africans, here the Leleges and Carians and quivered
Gelonians. Euphrates moved now with humbler waves,
and the Morini were there, furthest of mankind, and the
Rhine of double horn,[29] the untamed Dahae, and Araxes
chafing at his bridge.[30]

[29] Cf. 77 above, and see note 19 on *Georgics* 4.371. Here there
may be a reference to the two mouths, the Rhine and the Waal.

[30] A bridge over the Araxes, built by Alexander the Great, but
later swept away by a flood, was replaced by Augustus.

Talia per clipeum Volcani, dona parentis,
730 miratur rerumque ignarus imagine gaudet
attollens umero famamque et fata nepotum.

BOOK VIII

Such sights he admires on the shield of Vulcan, his mother's gift, and, though he knows not the events, he rejoices in their representation, raising up on his shoulder the fame and fortunes of his children's children.

LIBER IX

Atque ea diversa penitus dum parte geruntur,
Irim de caelo misit Saturnia Iuno
audacem ad Turnum. luco tum forte parentis
Pilumni Turnus sacrata valle sedebat.
5   ad quem sic roseo Thaumantias ore locuta est:
    "Turne, quod optanti divum promittere nemo
auderet, volvenda dies en attulit ultro.
Aeneas urbe et sociis et classe relicta
sceptra Palatini sedemque petît Euandri.
10 nec satis: extremas Corythi penetravit ad urbes
Lydorumque manum, collectos armat agrestis.
quid dubitas? nunc tempus equos, nunc poscere currus.
rumpe moras omnis et turbata arripe castra."
dixit, et in caelum paribus se sustulit alis
15 ingentemque fuga secuit sub nubibus arcum.
agnovit iuvenis duplicisque ad sidera palmas
sustulit ac tali fugientem est voce secutus:
"Iri, decus caeli, quis te mihi nubibus actam
detulit in terras? unde haec tam clara repente
20 tempestas? medium video discedere caelum
palantisque polo stellas. sequor omina tanta,

^{2} = 5.606 ^{11} manum *MR*: manus *P*
^{17} ac *P*: et *MR*

114

BOOK IX

And while in the far distance such deeds were done, Saturnian Juno sent Iris from heaven to gallant Turnus, who as it chanced was then seated in a hallowed vale, in the grove of his father Pilumnus. To him, with roseate lips, thus spoke the child of Thaumas:

"Turnus, what no god dared to promise to your prayers, see—the circling hour has brought unasked! Aeneas, leaving town, comrades and fleet, seeks the Palatine realm and Evander's dwelling. Nor does that suffice; he has won his way to Corythus' furthest cities,[1] and is mustering the Lydian country folk in armed bands. Why hesitate? Now, now is the hour to call for steed and chariot; break off delay, and seize the bewildered camp!" She spoke, and on poised wings rose into the sky, tracing in her flight a huge arch beneath the clouds. The youth knew her and, raising his two hands to heaven, with these words pursued her flight: "Iris, glory of the sky, who brought you down to me, wafted upon the clouds to earth? Whence this sudden brightness of the air? I see the heavens part asunder, and the stars that roam in the firmament.[2] I follow the mighty

[1] Corythus had founded Cortona, the principal Etruscan city.
[2] The mist veiling the heavens is rent asunder, revealing the stars beyond.

quisquis in arma vocas." et sic effatus ad undam
processit summoque hausit de gurgite lymphas
multa deos orans, oneravitque aethera votis.
25   Iamque omnis campis exercitus ibat apertis
dives equum, dives pictai vestis et auri;
Messapus primas acies, postrema coercent
28   Tyrrhidae iuvenes, medio dux agmine Turnus:
30   ceu septem surgens sedatis amnibus altus
per tacitum Ganges aut pingui flumine Nilus
FMPR cum refluit campis et iam se condidit alveo.
hic subitam nigro glomerari pulvere nubem
prospiciunt Teucri ac tenebras insurgere campis.
35   primus ab adversa conclamat mole Caicus:
"quis globus, o cives, caligine volvitur atra?
ferte citi ferrum, date tela, ascendite muros,
hostis adest, heia!" ingenti clamore per omnis
condunt se Teucri portas et moenia complent.
40   namque ita discedens praeceperat optimus armis
Aeneas: si qua interea fortuna fuisset,
neu struere auderent aciem neu credere campo;
castra modo et tutos servarent aggere muros.
ergo etsi conferre manum pudor iraque monstrat,
45   obiciunt portas tamen et praecepta facessunt,
armatique cavis exspectant turribus hostem.
     Turnus at ante volans tardum praecesserat agmen
viginti lectis equitum comitatus, et urbi
improvisus adest; maculis quem Thracius albis
50   portat equus cristaque tegit galea aurea rubra,

[26] pictai $M^2P^2\gamma$: pictae P: picta MR [29] = 7.784 χ] *om.*
MPR   [37] ascendite *MP*: et scandite *FR*
[47] at *Schenkl*: ut *FMPR*

omen, whoever you are who call me to arms!" And with
these words he went to the river, and took up water from
the brimming flood, calling many times on the gods and
burdening heaven with vows.

And now all the army was advancing on the open plain,
rich in horses, rich in embroidered robes and gold—
Messapus marshalling the van, the sons of Tyrrhus the
rear, and Turnus their captain in the centre of the line, like
Ganges, rising high in silence with his seven peaceful
streams, or Nile, when his rich flood ebbs from the fields
and at length he sinks into his channel. Here the Teucrians
descry a sudden cloud gathering in black dust, and dark-
ness rising on the plains. First from the rampart's front
Caïcus shouts, "What mass, my countrymen, rolls onward
in murky gloom? Quick, bring your swords! Give out weap-
ons, climb the walls! The enemy is upon us, ho!" With
mighty clamour the Teucrians seek shelter through all
the gates and man the ramparts. For so at his departure
Aeneas, best of warriors, had charged: were anything to
happen meanwhile, they should not dare to form their line
or entrust themselves to the field; let them only guard
camp and walls, secure behind their mound. Therefore,
though shame and wrath prompt them to conflict, yet they
bar the gates and do his bidding, awaiting the foe under
arms and inside the hollow towers.

But Turnus had hurried forward in advance of his tardy
column, with a following of twenty chosen horse, and
reaches the city sooner than expected: a Thracian steed,
spotted with white, bears him, and a golden helmet with

"ecquis erit mecum, iuvenes, qui primus in hostem—?
en," ait et iaculum attorquens emittit in auras,
principium pugnae, et campo sese arduus infert.
clamore excipiunt socii fremituque sequuntur
55 horrisono; Teucrum mirantur inertia corda,
non aequo dare se campo, non obvia ferre
arma viros, sed castra fovere. huc turbidus atque huc
lustrat equo muros aditumque per avia quaerit.
ac veluti pleno lupus insidiatus ovili
60 cum fremit ad caulas ventos perpessus et imbris
nocte super media; tuti sub matribus agni
balatum exercent, ille asper et improbus ira
saevit in absentis; collecta fatigat edendi
ex longo rabies et siccae sanguine fauces:
65 haud aliter Rutulo muros et castra tuenti
ignescunt irae, duris dolor ossibus ardet.
qua temptet ratione aditus, et quae via clausos
excutiat Teucros vallo atque effundat in aequum?
MPR classem, quae lateri castrorum adiuncta latebat,
70 aggeribus saeptam circum et fluvialibus undis,
invadit sociosque incendia poscit ovantis
atque manum pinu flagranti fervidus implet.
tum vero incumbunt (urget praesentia Turni),
atque omnis facibus pubes accingitur atris.
75 diripuere focos: piceum fert fumida lumen
taeda et commixtam Volcanus ad astra favillam.
    Quis deus, o Musae, tam saeva incendia Teucris
avertit? tantos ratibus quis depulit ignis?
dicite: prisca fides facto, sed fama perennis.

---

52 attorquens *FR*(?*P*): intorquens *M* (10.323)
54 clamore *FR*: clamorem *MP*

crimson crest guards his head. "Men, is there anyone who
with me will be first against the foe? See!" he cries, and
whirling a javelin sends it skyward to start the battle and
advances proudly over the plain. His comrades greet him
with a shout, and follow with dreadful din; they marvel at
the Teucrians' craven hearts, crying: "They cannot trust
themselves to a fair field, or face the foe in arms, but hug
the camp." Back and forth he rides wildly round the walls,
seeking entrance where way is none. And as when a wolf,
lying in wait at a crowded fold, growls beside the pens at
midnight, enduring winds and rains; safe beneath their
mothers the lambs keep bleating; fierce and reckless in his
wrath, he rages against the prey beyond his reach, tor-
mented by the long-gathering fury of famine, and by his
dry, bloodless jaws; just so, as he scans wall and camp, the
Rutulian's wrath is aflame; resentment is hot within his
iron bones. By what device can he attempt entrance? By
what path hurl the penned Teucrians from their rampart,
and pour them out over the plain? Close to the side of the
camp lay the fleet, fenced about with mounds and the flow-
ing river; he attacks it, calling to his exulting comrades for
fire, and in hot haste fills his hand with a blazing pine. Then
indeed they fall to, spurred on by Turnus' presence, and all
the band arm themselves with murky torches. They have
stripped the hearths; smoking brands fling a pitchy glare,
and the Fire God carries the sooty cloud to heaven.

What god, Muses, turned such fierce flames from the
Teucrians? Who drove such vast fires away from the ships?
Tell me; faith in the tale is old, but its fame is everlasting.

---

⁶⁶ duris *FMR*: durus *P*   ⁶⁷ quae *PR*: qua *FM*
⁶⁸ aequum *FMR*: aequor *P* (10.451)

80 tempore quo primum Phrygia formabat in Ida
Aeneas classem et pelagi petere alta parabat,
ipsa deum fertur genetrix Berecyntia magnum
vocibus his adfata Iovem: "da, nate, petenti,
quod tua cara parens domito te poscit Olympo.
85 pinea silva mihi multos dilecta per annos,
lucus in arce fuit summa, quo sacra ferebant,
nigranti picea trabibusque obscurus acernis.
has ego Dardanio iuveni, cum classis egeret,
laeta dedi; nunc sollicitam timor anxius angit.
90 solve metus atque hoc precibus sine posse parentem,
ne cursu quassatae ullo neu turbine venti
vincantur: prosit nostris in montibus ortas."
  Filius huic contra, torquet qui sidera mundi:
"o genetrix, quo fata vocas? aut quid petis istis?
95 mortaline manu factae immortale carinae
fas habeant? certusque incerta pericula lustret
Aeneas? cui tanta deo permissa potestas?
immo, ubi defunctae finem portusque tenebunt
Ausonios olim, quaecumque evaserit undis
100 Dardaniumque ducem Laurentia vexerit arva,
mortalem eripiam formam magnique iubebo
aequoris esse deas, qualis Nereïa Doto
et Galatea secant spumantem pectore pontum."
dixerat idque ratum Stygii per flumina fratris,
105 per pice torrentis atraque voragine ripas
adnuit, et totum nutu tremefecit Olympum.

91 ne *P*: neu *MR* (9.42)

In the days when on Phrygian Ida Aeneas was first fashioning his fleet and preparing to sail the deep seas, the very Mother of gods, it is said, the Berecyntian queen, spoke thus to mighty Jove: "Grant, son, to my prayer what your dear mother asks of you, now lord of Olympus.[3] A grove I had upon the mountain's crest, where men brought me offerings—a pine forest beloved for many years, dim with dusky firs and trunks of maple. These, when he lacked a fleet, I gave gladly to the Dardan youth; now anxious fear tortures my troubled breast. Relieve my terrors, and let a mother achieve this by her prayers: that they be overcome by neither stress of voyage nor blast of wind. Let their birth on our hills be a boon to them."

To her replied her son, who sways the starry world: "Mother, where are you summoning fate? What are you asking for these ships of yours? Should hulls framed by mortal hand have immortal rights? And should Aeneas in certainty traverse uncertain perils? To what god is such power allowed? Nay, when one day, their service done, they gain an Ausonian haven, from all the ships that have escaped the waves, and borne the Dardan chief to the fields of Laurentum, I will take away their mortal shape, and bid them be goddesses of the great sea, like Doto, Nereus' child, and Galatea, who cleave with their breasts the foaming deep." He had spoken, and by the waters of his Stygian brother, by the banks that seethe with pitch in the black swirling abyss, he nodded assent, and with the nod made all Olympus tremble.

[3] He therefore has power to grant her petition. Servius says that Cybele appeals to her son's gratitude, because when Cronos wished to devour him, she saved his life.

Ergo aderat promissa dies et tempora Parcae
debita complerant, cum Turni iniuria Matrem
admonuit ratibus sacris depellere taedas.
110 hic primum nova lux oculis offulsit et ingens
visus ab Aurora caelum transcurrere nimbus
Idaeique chori; tum vox horrenda per auras
excidit et Troum Rutulorumque agmina complet:
"ne trepidate meas, Teucri, defendere navis
115 neve armate manus; maria ante exurere Turno
quam sacras dabitur pinus. vos ite solutae,
ite deae pelagi; genetrix iubet." et sua quaeque
FMPR continuo puppes abrumpunt vincula ripis
delphinumque modo demersis aequora rostris
120 ima petunt. hinc virgineae (mirabile monstrum)
122 reddunt se totidem facies pontoque feruntur.
Obstipuere animis Rutuli, conterritus ipse
turbatis Messapus equis, cunctatur et amnis
125 rauca sonans revocatque pedem Tiberinus ab alto.
at non audaci Turno fiducia cessit;
ultro animos tollit dictis atque increpat ultro:
"Troianos haec monstra petunt, his Iuppiter ipse
auxilium solitum eripuit: non tela neque ignis
130 exspectant Rutulos. ergo maria invia Teucris,
nec spes ulla fugae: rerum pars altera adempta est,
terra autem in nostris manibus, tot milia gentes
arma ferunt Italae. nil me fatalia terrent,

110 offulsit *MR*: effulsit *P* (9.731)
121 = 10.223 χ] *om. MPR*
123 animis Rutuli *FR* (8.530): animi Rutulis *MP*

---

4 Cybele's attendants; cf. *Aen.* 3.111.

So the promised day was come, and the Destinies had fulfilled their appointed times, when Turnus' outrage warned the Mother to ward off the brands from her sacred ships. Then first there flashed upon the eyes a strange light, and from the Dawn a vast cloud was seen to speed across the sky, with Mount Ida's dancing bands[4] in its train; then through the air fell an awful voice, filling the Trojan and Rutulian ranks: "Trouble not, you Teucrians, to defend my ships, and take not weapons into your hands. Turnus shall have leave to burn up the seas sooner than my sacred pines. Go free, go, goddesses of ocean, the Mother bids it." And at once each ship rends her cable from the bank, and like dolphins they dip their beaks and dive to the water's depths; then as maiden forms—wondrous portent!—they resurface in like number and swim in the sea.

Amazed were the Rutulians at heart; Messapus himself was terror-stricken, his horses afraid; and the loud murmuring stream is stayed, as Tiberinus turns back his footsteps from the deep. But fearless Turnus did not lose heart; eagerly he raises their courage with his words, eagerly he chides them: "It is the Trojans that these portents are directed against; Jupiter himself has bereft them of their usual help; they do not await Rutulian sword and fire.[5] So the seas are pathless for the Teucrians, and they have no hope of flight. Half the world is lost to them, but the earth is in our hands: in such thousands are the nations of Italy under arms. I have no dread of all the fateful oracles of

[5] Their "usual help" (i.e. the ships, which the gods have taken away) is a gibe of Turnus, implying that the normal reaction of the Trojans is flight, thus forestalling the Rutuli, who would otherwise have destroyed them with fire and sword.

si qua Phryges prae se iactant, responsa deorum;
135   sat fatis Venerique datum, tetigere quod arva
fertilis Ausoniae Troes. sunt et mea contra
fata mihi, ferro sceleratam exscindere gentem
coniuge praerepta; nec solos tangit Atridas
iste dolor, solisque licet capere arma Mycenis.
140   'sed periisse semel satis est': peccare fuisset
ante satis, penitus modo non genus omne perosos
femineum, quibus haec medii fiducia valli
fossarumque morae, leti discrimina parva,
dant animos; at non viderunt moenia Troiae
145   Neptuni fabricata manu considere in ignis?
sed vos, o lecti, ferro quis scindere vallum
apparat et mecum invadit trepidantia castra?
non armis mihi Volcani, non mille carinis
est opus in Teucros. addant se protinus omnes
150   Etrusci socios. tenebras et inertia furta
Palladii caesis late custodibus arcis
ne timeant, nec equi caeca condemur in alvo:
luce palam certum est igni circumdare muros.
haud sibi cum Danais rem faxo et pube Pelasga
155   esse ferant, decimum quos distulit Hector in annum.
nunc adeo, melior quoniam pars acta diei,
quod superest, laeti bene gestis corpora rebus
procurate, viri, et pugnam sperate parari."
    Interea vigilum excubiis obsidere portas

135 datum *M* (2.291): datum est *FPR*   143 discrimina *PR*:
discrimine *FM* (3.685) | parva χ: parvo *FMP*²*R*: parvas *P*
   146 quis χ: qui *FMPR*   151 (= 2.166) *del. Bodoni: MPR*
   155 ferant *FP*: putent *MR*
   156 diei *FMP*: diei est *R*

heaven of which these Phrygians boast: to Fate and Venus all claims are paid, since the Trojans have touched our rich Ausonia's fields. I too have my own fate to meet theirs—to cut down with the sword a guilty race that has robbed me of my bride! Not only the sons of Atreus are touched by that pang, not only Mycenae has the right to take up arms. 'But to have perished once is enough!' Rather, to have sinned once would have been enough, provided that henceforth they utterly loathe well-nigh all womankind, these men to whom this trust in a sundering rampart, these delaying dykes—slight barriers against death—afford courage![6] But did they not see Troy's battlements, the work of Neptune's hand, sink in flames? But you, my chosen troops, who is ready to hew down the rampart with the sword and rush with me on their terrified camp? I do not need the arms of Vulcan nor a thousand ships, to meet the Trojans. Let all Etruria join them at once in alliance. Darkness and cowardly theft *of their Palladium, with slaughter of guards on the citadel,* they need not fear; nor shall we lurk in a horse's dark belly: in broad day, in the sight of all, I mean to gird their walls with fire. I will see to it that they know they do not have to deal with Danaans and Pelasgic youths, whom Hector kept at bay till the tenth year. Now, since the better part of the day is spent, for what remains, men, joyfully refresh yourselves after your good service, and be assured that we are preparing for war."

Meanwhile Messapus is charged to blockade the gates

[6] The argument is this: one would have expected them to be haters of women, rather than commit a second offence like that of abducting Helen, especially as they are cowards who refuse to face a fight.

160 cura datur Messapo et moenia cingere flammis.
bis septem Rutuli muros qui milite servent
delecti, ast illos centeni quemque sequuntur
purpurei cristis iuvenes auroque corusci.
discurrunt variantque vices, fusique per herbam
MPR indulgent vino et vertunt crateras aënos.
166 conlucent ignes, noctem custodia ducit
insomnem ludo . . .
    Haec super e vallo prospectant Troes et armis
alta tenent, nec non trepidi formidine portas
170 explorant pontisque et propugnacula iungunt,
tela gerunt. instat Mnestheus acerque Serestus,
quos pater Aeneas, si quando adversa vocarent,
rectores iuvenum et rerum dedit esse magistros.
omnis per muros legio sortita periclum
175 excubat exercetque vices, quod cuique tuendum est.
    Nisus erat portae custos, acerrimus armis,
Hyrtacides, comitem Aeneae quem miserat Ida
venatrix iaculo celerem levibusque sagittis,
et iuxta comes Euryalus, quo pulchrior alter
180 non fuit Aeneadum Troiana neque induit arma,
ora puer prima signans intonsa iuventa.
his amor unus erat pariterque in bella ruebant;
tum quoque communi portam statione tenebant.
Nisus ait: "dine hunc ardorem mentibus addunt,
185 Euryale, an sua cuique deus fit dira cupido?
aut pugnam aut aliquid iamdudum invadere magnum
mens agitat mihi, nec placida contenta quiete est.

171 instat *P*: instant *MR*

126

with posted sentries, and to encircle the battlements with fires. Twice seven Rutulians are chosen to guard the walls with soldiers; on each attend a hundred men, purple-plumed and sparkling with gold. Back and forth they rush, and take their turns on watch, or, stretched along the grass, drink their fill of wine and upturn bowls of bronze. The fires burn bright, and the guards spend the sleepless night in games . . .

On this scene the Trojans look forth from the rampart above, as in arms they hold the summit; in anxious haste they test the gates and build joining gangways[7] and bastions, bring up weapons. Mnestheus and valiant Serestus urge on the work, whom father Aeneas, should adversity ever require, appointed as leaders of the warriors and rulers of the state. Along the walls the whole host, sharing the peril, keeps watch, and serves in turns, each man at his allotted task.

Nisus was guardian of the gate, most valiant of warriors, son of Hyrtacus, whom Ida the huntress had sent in Aeneas' train, quick with javelin and light arrows. At his side was Euryalus—none fairer was among the Aeneadae, or wore Trojan armour—a boy who showed on his unshaven cheek the first bloom of youth. A common love was theirs; side by side they would charge into battle; now too they were mounting sentry together at the gate. Nisus says: "Do the gods, Euryalus, put this fire into hearts, or does his own wild longing become to each man a god? Long has my heart been astir to dare battle or some great deed, and it is not content with peaceful quiet. You see what faith in their

---

[7] The bridges or gangways connect towers standing outside the walls with the battlements.

cernis quae Rutulos habeat fiducia rerum:
lumina rara micant, somno vinoque soluti
190 procubuere, silent late loca. percipe porro
quid dubitem et quae nunc animo sententia surgat.
Aenean acciri omnes, populusque patresque,
exposcunt, mittique viros qui certa reportent.
si tibi quae posco promittunt (nam mihi facti
195 fama sat est), tumulo videor reperire sub illo
posse viam ad muros et moenia Pallantea."
obstipuit magno laudum percussus amore
Euryalus, simul his ardentem adfatur amicum:
"mene igitur socium summis adiungere rebus,
200 Nise, fugis? solum te in tanta pericula mittam?
non ita me genitor, bellis adsuetus Opheltes,
Argolicum terrorem inter Troiaeque labores
sublatum erudiit, nec tecum talia gessi
magnanimum Aenean et fata extrema secutus:
205 est hic, est animus lucis contemptor et istum
qui vita bene credat emi, quo tendis, honorem."
FMPR   Nisus ad haec: "equidem de te nil tale verebar,
nec fas; non ita me referat tibi magnus ovantem
Iuppiter aut quicumque oculis haec aspicit aequis.
210 sed si quis (quae multa vides discrimine tali)
si quis in adversum rapiat casusve deusve,
te superesse velim, tua vita dignior aetas.
sit qui me raptum pugna pretiove redemptum
mandet humo, aut solitas si qua Fortuna vetabit,
215 absenti ferat inferias decoretque sepulcro.
neu matri miserae tanti sim causa doloris,

214 aut solitas *J.E.Powell*: solita aut *FMPR* | qua *MacKay*: qua
id *FMPR*

fortunes possesses the Rutulians. Their gleaming lights are
far apart; relaxed with wine and slumber, they lie prone;
silence reigns far and wide. Learn then what I ponder, and
what purpose now rises in my mind. People and senate—
all demand that Aeneas be summoned, and men be sent to
bring him sure tidings. If they promise the boon I ask for
you—for to me the glory of the deed is enough—I think
that beneath that mound I can find a path to the walls and
fortress of Pallanteum." Euryalus was dazed, smitten with
mighty love of praise, and at once speaks thus to his ardent
friend: "Do you refuse then, Nisus, to let me join in this
great endeavour? Am I to send you alone into such great
perils? Not so did my father, the old warrior Opheltes,
train me as his child among Argive terrors and the travails
of Troy, nor at your side have I played my part so, following
high-souled Aeneas and his ultimate fate. Mine is a heart
that scorns the light, and believes that the glory that you
strive for is cheaply bought with life."

Nisus replied: "Indeed, of you I had no such fear, no—it
would be wrong; so may great Jupiter, or whoever looks on
this deed with favouring eyes, bring me back to you in tri-
umph! But if—as you see often in like hazards—if some
god or chance sweep me to disaster, I want you to survive;
your youth is worthier of life. Let there be someone to
commit me to earth, rescued from battle or ransomed at a
price, or, if some chance denies the usual rites, to render
them to me in my absence, and honour me with a tomb.[8]
And let me not, boy, be the cause of such grief to your poor

[8] I.e. a cenotaph.

quae te sola, puer, multis e matribus ausa
persequitur, magni nec moenia curat Acestae."
ille autem: "causas nequiquam nectis inanis
220 nec mea iam mutata loco sententia cedit.
acceleremus" ait, vigiles simul excitat. illi
succedunt servantque vices; statione relicta
ipse comes Niso graditur regemque requirunt.
　　Cetera per terras omnis animalia somno
225 laxabant curas et corda oblita laborum:
ductores Teucrum primi, delecta iuventus,
consilium summis regni de rebus habebant,
quid facerent quisve Aeneae iam nuntius esset.
stant longis adnixi hastis et scuta tenentes
230 castrorum et campi medio. tum Nisus et una
Euryalus confestim alacres admittier orant:
rem magnam pretiumque morae fore. primus Iulus
accepit trepidos ac Nisum dicere iussit.
tum sic Hyrtacides: "audite o mentibus aequis
MPR Aeneadae, neve haec nostris spectentur ab annis
236 quae ferimus. Rutuli somno vinoque sepulti
conticuere. locum insidiis conspeximus ipsi,
qui patet in bivio portae quae proxima ponto.
interrupti ignes aterque ad sidera fumus
240 erigitur. si fortuna permittitis uti,
242 mox hic cum spoliis ingenti caede peracta
243 adfore cernetis. nec nos via fallet euntis
241 quaesitum Aenean et moenia Pallantea.
244 vidimus obscuris primam sub vallibus urbem

---

236 sepulti *Servius Auctus*: soluti *MPR*　　　237 conticuere
MR: procubuere *P* (9.190)　　　241 *after* 243 χ, *known to Servius*:
after 240 *MPR*　　　243 fallet *M*: fallit *PR*

mother, who, alone of many mothers, dared to follow you to the end, and does not care for great Acestes' city.[9] But he replied: "Vainly you weave idle pleas, nor does my purpose now change or give way. Let us hurry!" he said, and at once rouses the guards. They come up, and take their turn; quitting his post, he walks by Nisus' side as they seek the prince.

All other creatures throughout all lands were soothing their cares in sleep, and their hearts were forgetful of sorrows, but the chief Teucrian captains, flower of their young men, held council on the people's affairs, what they should do, and who now should be messenger to Aeneas. They stand, leaning on their long spears and grasping their shields, between camp and plain.[10] Then Nisus and Euryalus together eagerly crave immediate audience; the matter, they say, is weighty and will repay the delay. Iülus was first to welcome the impatient pair, and bade Nisus speak. Then thus the son of Hyrtacus spoke: "Men of Aeneas, listen with kindly minds, and do not let our proposal be judged by our years. Buried in sleep and wine, the Rutulians lie silent; our own eyes have seen a place for an ambush that lies open in the forked way by the gate nearest the sea. The line of fires is broken and black smoke rises to the sky. If you permit us to use the chance, soon you will see us here again, laden with spoils after wreaking mighty slaughter. The road will not deceive us as we go to seek Aeneas and the walls of Pallanteum. Down the dim valleys in our frequent hunting we have seen the outskirts of the

[9] Cf. *Aen.* 5.715 and 5.750.

[10] I.e. in the middle of the open space which the Romans left in the centre of a camp.

131

245   venatu adsiduo et totum cognovimus amnem."
        Hic annis gravis atque animi maturus Aletes:
"di patrii, quorum semper sub numine Troia est,
non tamen omnino Teucros delere paratis,
cum talis animos iuvenum et tam certa tulistis
250   pectora." sic memorans umeros dextrasque tenebat
amborum et vultum lacrimis atque ora rigabat.
"quae vobis, quae digna, viri, pro laudibus istis
praemia posse rear solvi? pulcherrima primum
di moresque dabunt vestri: tum cetera reddet
255   actutum pius Aeneas atque integer aevi
Ascanius meriti tanti non immemor umquam."
"immo ego vos, cui sola salus genitore reducto,"
excipit Ascanius "per magnos, Nise, penatis
Assaracique larem et canae penetralia Vestae
260   obtestor, quaecumque mihi fortuna fidesque est,
in vestris pono gremiis. revocate parentem,
reddite conspectum; nihil illo triste recepto.
bina dabo argento perfecta atque aspera signis
pocula, devicta genitor quae cepit Arisba,
265   et tripodas geminos, auri duo magna talenta,
cratera antiquum quem dat Sidonia Dido.
si vero capere Italiam sceptrisque potiri
contigerit victori et praedae dicere sortem,
vidisti, quo Turnus equo, quibus ibat in armis
270   aureus; ipsum illum, clipeum cristasque rubentis
excipiam sorti, iam nunc tua praemia, Nise.
praeterea bis sex genitor lectissima matrum
corpora captivosque dabit suaque omnibus arma,
insuper his campi quod rex habet ipse Latinus.

274 quod *PR*: quos *M*

town and have come to know the whole river."

Then said Aletes, stricken in years and sage in council:
"Gods of our fathers, whose presence ever watches over
Troy, despite all you do not intend utterly to blot out the
Trojan race, since you have brought us such spirit in our
youths and such unwavering souls." So saying, he held
them both by shoulder and hand, while tears rained down
his cheeks and face. "What reward, men, shall I deem
worthy to be paid you for deeds so glorious? The first and
fairest the gods and your own hearts shall give; then the
rest the good Aeneas will straightway repay, and the youth-
ful Ascanius, never forgetful of service so noble." "No,"
breaks in Ascanius, "rather I, whose sole safety lies in my
father's return, adjure you both, Nisus, by the great gods of
the house, by the Lar of Assaracus, and by hoary Vesta's
shrine—all my fortune, all my hope, I lay upon your knees;
recall my father, give back the sight of him; if he is recov-
ered all grief vanishes. A pair of goblets I will give, wrought
in silver and rough with chasing, that he took when Arisba
was vanquished; and two tripods, two great talents of gold,
and an ancient bowl that Dido of Sidon gave. But if it is
our lot to take Italy, to wield a victor's sceptre and to assign
the spoil, you have seen the horse that Turnus rode and
the armour he wore, all gold—that same horse, the shield
and the crimson plumes I will set apart from the lot, your
reward, Nisus, even now. Moreover my father will give
twelve matrons of choicest beauty, and men captives, each
with his armour, and, beyond these, whatever land King

275 te vero, mea quem spatiis propioribus aetas
insequitur, venerande puer, iam pectore toto
accipio et comitem casus complector in omnis.
nulla meis sine te quaeretur gloria rebus:
seu pacem seu bella geram, tibi maxima rerum

280 verborumque fides." contra quem talia fatur
Euryalus: "me nulla dies tam fortibus ausis
dissimilem arguerit; tantum fortuna secunda
haud adversa cadat. sed te super omnia dona
unum oro: genetrix Priami de gente vetusta

285 est mihi, quam miseram tenuit non Ilia tellus
mecum excedentem, non moenia regis Acestae.
hanc ego nunc ignaram huius quodcumque pericli est
inque salutatam linquo (nox et tua testis
dextera), quod nequeam lacrimas perferre parentis.

290 at tu, oro, solare inopem et succurre relictae.
hanc sine me spem ferre tui, audentior ibo
in casus omnis." percussa mente dedere
Dardanidae lacrimas, ante omnis pulcher Iulus,
atque animum patriae strinxit pietatis imago.

295 tum sic effatur . . .
"sponde digna tuis ingentibus omnia coeptis.
namque erit ista mihi genetrix nomenque Creusae
solum defuerit, nec partum gratia talem
parva manet. casus factum quicumque sequentur,

300 per caput hoc iuro, per quod pater ante solebat:
quae tibi polliceor reduci rebusque secundis,
haec eadem matrique tuae generique manebunt."
sic ait inlacrimans; umero simul exuit ensem

²⁸³ haud *MPR*: aut *M²*, *Servius*   ²⁸⁷ est *M²*: *om. MPR*
²⁹² dedere *M*: dederunt *PR*

Latinus himself holds.[11] But you, revered youth, whom my age follows more closely, at once I take all to my heart, and embrace as my comrade in every chance. No glory shall be sought for my own lot without you; whether in peace or war, you will have my greatest trust in deed and word." To him spoke thus Euryalus in reply: "Never shall time prove me unfit for such bold deeds; only let Fortune prove kind, not cruel. But from you, above all your gifts, this one thing I ask. A mother I have, of Priam's ancient line, whom neither the Ilian land nor King Acestes' city could keep, unhappy woman, from leaving with me. I now leave her without knowledge of this peril, whatever it be, and without word of farewell, because—night and your right hand be witness—I could not bear a mother's tears. But, I pray, comfort her in her helplessness and relieve her desolation. Let me take with me this hope of you; I will meet all hazards more boldly." Touched to the heart, the Dardanians shed tears—fair Iülus more than all, and the picture of filial love touched his heart. Then he spoke thus . . .: "Assure yourself that all I do shall be worthy of your mighty enterprise; for she shall be a mother to me, lacking but the name Creüsa; no small honour awaits the bearing of such a son. Whatever chance attends your deed, I swear by this head, by which my father was wont to swear, what I promise to you on your prosperous return shall abide the same for your mother and your house." So he speaks weeping; and at the same time strips from his shoulder the gilded

[11] I.e. the land now held by the king, the royal domain, is to go to Nisus.

auratum, mira quem fecerat arte Lycaon
305   Cnosius atque habilem vagina aptarat eburna.
dat Niso Mnestheus pellem horrentisque leonis
exuvias, galeam fidus permutat Aletes.
protinus armati incedunt; quos omnis euntis
primorum manus ad portas, iuvenumque senumque,
310   prosequitur votis. nec non et pulcher Iulus,
ante annos animumque gerens curamque virilem,
multa patri mandata dabat portanda; sed aurae
omnia discerpunt et nubibus inrita donant.
    Egressi superant fossas noctisque per umbram
315   castra inimica petunt, multis tamen ante futuri
exitio. passim somno vinoque per herbam
corpora fusa vident, arrectos litore currus,
inter lora rotasque viros, simul arma iacere,
vina simul. prior Hyrtacides sic ore locutus:
320   "Euryale, audendum dextra: nunc ipsa vocat res.
hac iter est. tu, ne qua manus se attollere nobis
a tergo possit, custodi et consule longe;
haec ego vasta dabo et lato te limite ducam."
sic memorat vocemque premit, simul ense superbum
325   Rhamnetem adgreditur, qui forte tapetibus altis
exstructus toto proflabat pectore somnum,
rex idem et regi Turno gratissimus augur,
sed non augurio potuit depellere pestem.
tris iuxta famulos temere inter tela iacentis
330   armigerumque Remi premit aurigamque sub ipsis
nactus equis ferroque secat pendentia colla.
tum caput ipsi aufert domino truncumque relinquit
sanguine singultantem; atro tepefacta cruore
terra torique madent. nec non Lamyrumque Lamumque
335   et iuvenem Serranum, illa qui plurima nocte

sword, fashioned with wondrous art by Lycaon of Cnosus and fitted for use with ivory sheath. To Nisus Mnestheus gives a skin, spoil of a shaggy lion: faithful Aletes exchanges his helmet. At once they advance in arms and as they go all the company of princes, young and old, escorts them to the gate with vows. Likewise fair Iülus, with a man's mind and a spirit beyond his years, gave many a charge to carry to his father. But the breezes scatter all and give them fruitless to the clouds.

They leave and cross the trenches, and through the shadow of night seek that fatal camp—yet destined first to be the doom of many. Everywhere they see bodies stretched along the grass in drunken sleep, chariots atilt on the shore, men lying among wheels and harness, their arms and flagons all about. First the son of Hyrtacus thus began: "Euryalus, now for a daring hand; now the occasion itself calls us; here lies our way. Watch that no arm be raised against us from behind, and keep wide outlook. Here I will deal destruction, and by a broad path show you the way." So he speaks, then checks his voice, and at once drives his sword at haughty Rhamnes, who, it happened, pillowed on high coverlets, was breathing forth sleep from all his breast—a king himself, and King Turnus' best-beloved augur; but not by augury could he avert his doom. Three attendants he slew at his side, as they lay carelessly among their arms, and Remus' armour bearer, and the charioteer, catching him at the horses' feet. Their drooping necks he severs with the sword; then lops off the head of their lord himself, and leaves the trunk spurting blood; ground and couch reek with the warm black gore. Lamyrus, too, he slays, and Lamus, and youthful Serranus, of wondrous

luserat, insignis facie, multoque iacebat
membra deo victus—felix, si protinus illum
aequasset nocti ludum in lucemque tulisset:
impastus ceu plena leo per ovilia turbans
340 (suadet enim vesana fames) manditque trahitque
molle pecus mutumque metu, fremit ore cruento.
nec minor Euryali caedes; incensus et ipse
perfurit ac multam in medio sine nomine plebem,
Fadumque Herbesumque subit Rhoetumque Abarimque
345 ignaros; Rhoetum vigilantem et cuncta videntem,
sed magnum metuens se post cratera tegebat.
pectore in adverso totum cui comminus ensem
condidit adsurgenti et multa morte recepit.
purpuream vomit ille animam et cum sanguine mixta
350 vina refert moriens, hic furto fervidus instat.
iamque ad Messapi socios tendebat; ibi ignem
deficere extremum et religatos rite videbat
carpere gramen equos, breviter cum talia Nisus
MPRV (sensit enim nimia caede atque cupidine ferri)
355 "absistamus" ait, "nam lux inimica propinquat.
poenarum exhaustum satis est, via facta per hostis."
multa virum solido argento perfecta relinquunt
armaque craterasque simul pulchrosque tapetas.
Euryalus phaleras Rhamnetis et aurea bullis
360 cingula, Tiburti Remulo ditissimus olim
quae mittit dona, hospitio cum iungeret absens,
Caedicus; ille suo moriens dat habere nepoti;
post mortem bello Rutuli pugnaque potiti:
haec rapit atque umeris nequiquam fortibus aptat.
365 tum galeam Messapi habilem cristisque decoram

beauty, who had played long that night, and lay with limbs vanquished by the god's abundance;[12] happy he, had he played on, making that game one with the night, and pursuing it to the dawn! Just so, an unfed lion, rioting through full sheepfolds—for the madness of hunger constrains him—mangles and rends the feeble flock that is dumb with fear, and growls with blood-stained mouth. Nor less is the slaughter of Euryalus; he too, all aflame, rages, and falls on the vast unnamed multitude before him, Fadus and Herbesus, Rhoetus and Abaris, all unaware; but Rhoetus was awake and saw it all, yet in his fear crouched behind a mighty bowl. Right in his breast, as he rose, the foe in close encounter plunged his sword its full length, and drew it back steeped in death. Rhoetus belches forth his red life, and dying casts up wine mixed with blood; the other hotly pursues his stealthy work. And now he drew near Messapus' followers. There he saw the last fires flickering, and horses, duly tethered, cropping the grass; when Nisus briefly speaks thus—for he saw his comrade swept away by reckless lust of carnage: "Let us away; for the unfriendly dawn is near. Vengeance is sated to the full; a path is cut through the foe." Many a soldier's arms, wrought in solid silver, they leave behind—and bowls as well, and beautiful carpets. Euryalus takes the trappings of Rhamnes and his gold-studded sword belt, gifts that long ago wealthy Caedicus sent to Remulus of Tibur, when plighting friendship far away; he when dying gave them to his grandson for his own; after his death the Rutulians captured them in war and battle. These he tears away, and fits upon his valiant breast—all in vain. Then he dons Messapus' shapely

12 The god is Sleep.

induit. excedunt castris et tuta capessunt.
    Interea praemissi equites ex urbe Latina,
cetera dum legio campis instructa moratur,
ibant et Turno regi responsa ferebant,
370 ter centum, scutati omnes, Volcente magistro.
iamque propinquabant castris murosque subibant
cum procul hos laevo flectentis limite cernunt,
et galea Euryalum sublustri noctis in umbra
prodidit immemorem radiisque adversa refulsit.
375 haud temere est visum. conclamat ab agmine Volcens:
"state, viri. quae causa viae? quive estis in armis?
quove tenetis iter?" nihil illi tendere contra,
sed celerare fugam in silvas et fidere nocti.
obiciunt equites sese ad divortia nota
380 hinc atque hinc, omnemque abitum custode coronant.
silva fuit late dumis atque ilice nigra
horrida, quam densi complerant undique sentes;
rara per occultos lucebat semita callis.
Euryalum tenebrae ramorum onerosaque praeda
385 impediunt, fallitque timor regione viarum.
Nisus abit; iamque imprudens evaserat hostis
atque locos qui post Albae de nomine dicti
Albani (tum rex stabula alta Latinus habebat),
ut stetit et frustra absentem respexit amicum:
390 "Euryale infelix, qua te regione reliqui?
quave sequar?" rursus perplexum iter omne revolvens
fallacis silvae simul et vestigia retro
observata legit dumisque silentibus errat.

369 regi *MPRV* (*cf.* 9.327): regis *Servius Auctus*
371 muros *PV*: muro *MR* (7.161)
380 abitum *M*: aditum *RV*: aditu *P*

helmet with its graceful plumes. They leave the camp and make for safety.

Meanwhile horsemen, sent forward from the Latin city, while the rest of the force halts drawn up on the plain, came bringing a reply to King Turnus—three hundred, all bearing shields, with Volcens as leader. And now they were nearing the camp and coming under the walls, when at a distance they see the two turning away by a pathway to the left; and in the glimmering shadows of night his helmet betrayed the thoughtless Euryalus, as it flashed back the light. Not in vain was it seen. From his column shouts Volcens: "Halt, men! What is the reason for your journey? Who are you in arms? And where are you going?" They offer no response, but speed their flight to the wood and trust to night. On this side and that the horsemen bar the well-known crossways, and with sentinels surround every outlet. The forest spread wide with thickets and dark ilex; dense briers filled it on every side; here and there the path glimmered through the hidden glades. Euryalus is hampered by the shadowy branches and the burden of his spoil, and fear misleads him in the line of the paths. Nisus gets clear; and now, in his heedless course, he had escaped the foe to the place later called Alban from Alba's name (at that time King Latinus had there his stately stalls) when he halted and looked back in vain for his lost friend. "Unhappy Euryalus, where have I left you? Where shall I follow, again unthreading the whole tangled path of the treacherous wood?" At the same time he scans and retraces his footsteps, and wanders in the silent thickets. He

---

382 complerant *PRV*: complebant *M*

audit equos, audit strepitus et signa sequentum;
395   nec longum in medio tempus, cum clamor ad auris
pervenit ac videt Euryalum, quem iam manus omnis
fraude loci et noctis, subito turbante tumultu,
oppressum rapit et conantem plurima frustra.
quid faciat? qua vi iuvenem, quibus audeat armis
400   eripere? an sese medios moriturus in enses
inferat et pulchram properet per vulnera mortem?
ocius adducto torquet hastile lacerto
suspiciens altam Lunam et sic voce precatur:
"tu, dea, tu praesens nostro succurre labori,
405   astrorum decus et nemorum Latonia custos.
MPR si qua tuis umquam pro me pater Hyrtacus aris
dona tulit, si qua ipse meis venatibus auxi
suspendive tholo aut sacra ad fastigia fixi,
hunc sine me turbare globum et rege tela per auras."
410   dixerat et toto conixus corpore ferrum
conicit. hasta volans noctis diverberat umbras
et venit aversi in tergum Sulmonis ibique
frangitur, ac fisso transit praecordia ligno.
volvitur ille vomens calidum de pectore flumen
415   frigidus et longis singultibus ilia pulsat.
diversi circumspiciunt. hoc acrior idem
ecce aliud summa telum librabat ab aure.
dum trepidant, ît hasta Tago per tempus utrumque
stridens traiectoque haesit tepefacta cerebro.
420   saevit atrox Volcens nec teli conspicit usquam
auctorem nec quo se ardens immittere possit.

    400 enses *P*: hostis *MRV* (2.511; 9.554)   402 torquet *Wagner*: torquens *MPRV*   403 altam *MP*: altam ad *RV*
    412 aversi χ: adversi *MR*   418 it *MR*: iit *P*

hears the horses, hears the shouts and signals of pursuit.
And the interval was not long, when a cry reaches his ears,
and he sees Euryalus, whom, now betrayed by the ground
and night and bewildered by the sudden turmoil, the
whole band is dragging away overpowered and struggling
violently in vain. What can he do? With what force, what
arms dare he rescue the youth? Shall he cast himself on his
doom among the swords and win with wounds a swift and
glorious death? Quickly he draws back his arm with poised
spear and, looking up to the moon on high, thus prays:
"Goddess, be present and aid our endeavour, Latona's
daughter, glory of the stars and guardian of the groves; if
ever my father Hyrtacus brought any gifts for me to your
altars, if ever I have honoured you with any from my own
hunting, have hung offerings in your dome, or fastened
them on your holy roof,[13] grant me to confound that troop,
and guide my weapons through the air." He ended, and
with all his straining body flung the steel. The flying spear
whistles through the shadows of night, strikes the turned
back of Sulmo, then snaps, and with the broken wood
pierces the midriff. Spouting a warm torrent from his
breast he rolls over chill in death, and long gasps heave his
sides. Turning this way and that they gaze round. All the
fiercer now he balances another weapon close to his ear.
While they hesitate, the spear goes whizzing through both
of Tagus' temples, and lodged warm in the cloven brain.
Volcens storms with rage, but nowhere espies the sender
of the dart, nor where to vent his rage. "Yet you, mean-

---

[13] By *fastigia* is meant the gable roof of the exterior, over the
entrance; the *tholus* is the domed interior.

"tu tamen interea calido mihi sanguine poenas
persolves amborum" inquit; simul ense recluso
ibat in Euryalum. tum vero exterritus, amens,
425 conclamat Nisus nec se celare tenebris
amplius aut tantum potuit perferre dolorem:
"me, me, adsum qui feci, in me convertite ferrum,
o Rutuli! mea fraus omnis, nihil iste nec ausus
nec potuit; caelum hoc et conscia sidera testor;
430 tantum infelicem nimium dilexit amicum."
talia dicta dabat, sed viribus ensis adactus
transabiit costas et candida pectora rumpit.
volvitur Euryalus leto, pulchrosque per artus
it cruor inque umeros cervix conlapsa recumbit:
435 purpureus veluti cum flos succisus aratro
languescit moriens, lassove papavera collo
demisere caput pluvia cum forte gravantur.
at Nisus ruit in medios solumque per omnis
Volcentem petit, in solo Volcente moratur.
440 quem circum glomerati hostes hinc comminus atque hinc
proturbant. instat non setius ac rotat ensem
fulmineum, donec Rutuli clamantis in ore
condidit adverso et moriens animam abstulit hosti.
tum super exanimum sese proiecit amicum
445 confossus, placidaque ibi demum morte quievit.
      Fortunati ambo! si quid mea carmina possunt,
nulla dies umquam memori vos eximet aevo,
dum domus Aeneae Capitoli immobile saxum
accolet imperiumque pater Romanus habebit.
450 Victores praeda Rutuli spoliisque potiti

432 transabiit *R*: -adigit *M²P*: -adibit *M* (*conflation of variants*)

while, with your hot blood, will pay me vengeance for both," he cried and, as he spoke, rushed with drawn sword on Euryalus. Then indeed, frantic with terror, Nisus shouts aloud; no longer could he hide himself in darkness or endure such agony: "On me—on me—here am I who did the deed—on me turn your steel, Rutulians! Mine is all the guilt; he neither dared nor could have done it; heaven be witness of this and the all-seeing stars! He but loved his hapless friend too well." Thus was he pleading; but the sword, driven with force, passes through the ribs and rends the snowy breast. Euryalus rolls over in death; over his lovely limbs runs the blood, and his drooping neck sinks on his shoulder, as when a purple flower, severed by the plough, droops in death; or as poppies, with weary neck, bow the head, when weighted by a chance shower. But Nisus rushes among them, and among them all seeks only Volcens, to Volcens alone gives heed. Round him the foe cluster, and on every side try to hurl him back. Onward none the less he presses, whirling his lightning blade, till he plunged it full in the face of the shrieking Rutulian and, dying, bereft his foe of life. Then, pierced through and through, he flung himself on his lifeless friend, and there at length, in the peace of death, found rest.

Happy pair! If my poetry has any power, no day shall ever blot you from the memory of time, so long as the house of Aeneas dwells on the Capitol's unshaken rock, and the Father of Rome holds sovereign sway![14]

The victorious Rutulians, masters of plunder and

[14] By the *domus Aeneae* is meant not merely the Julian house, but the Roman people. The *pater Romanus* refers to the imperial line.

Volcentem exanimum flentes in castra ferebant.
nec minor in castris luctus Rhamnete reperto
exsangui et primis una tot caede peremptis,
Serranoque Numaque. ingens concursus ad ipsa
455 corpora seminecisque viros, tepidaque recentem
caede locum et pleno spumantis sanguine rivos.
agnoscunt spolia inter se galeamque nitentem
Messapi et multo phaleras sudore receptas.

Et iam prima novo spargebat lumine terras
460 Tithoni croceum linquens Aurora cubile.
iam sole infuso, iam rebus luce retectis
Turnus in arma viros armis circumdatus ipse
suscitat: aeratasque acies in proelia cogunt,
quisque suos, variisque acuunt rumoribus iras.
465 quin ipsa arrectis (visu miserabile) in hastis
praefigunt capita et multo clamore sequuntur
Euryali et Nisi . . .
Aeneadae duri murorum in parte sinistra
opposuere aciem (nam dextera cingitur amni),
470 ingentisque tenent fossas et turribus altis
stant maesti; simul ora virum praefixa movebant
nota nimis miseris atroque fluentia tabo.

Interea pavidam volitans pennata per urbem
nuntia Fama ruit matrisque adlabitur auris
475 Euryali. at subitus miserae calor ossa reliquit,
excussi manibus radii revolutaque pensa.
evolat infelix et femineo ululatu
scissa comam muros amens atque agmina cursu

---

455 tepida *Servius*: tepidam *M*: tepidum *PR*
456 pleno *MP*[2]: plenos *PR* | spumantis *MPR*: spumanti χ
459–60 = 4.584–5

spoils, wept as they bore lifeless Volcens to the camp. Nor in that camp was the wailing less when Rhamnes was found drained of life, and so many chieftains slain in a single massacre, here Serranus, and here Numa. A mighty throng rushes to the dead and dying men, to the ground fresh with warm slaughter and streams foaming with copious blood. As they talk together, they recognize the spoils, Messapus' shining helmet, and the trappings won back with much sweat.

And now early Dawn, leaving the saffron bed of Tithonus, was sprinkling her fresh rays upon the earth; now that the sun streamed in, now that day unveiled the world, Turnus, himself in armour clad, summons his men to arms; the leaders marshal the mailed lines to battle, each his own men, and whet their anger with divers tales. On uplifted spears (piteous sight!) they affix and follow with loud clamour the heads, the very heads, of Euryalus and Nisus. . . . On the rampart's left side—for the right is girded by the river—the hardy sons of Aeneas have set their opposing line, hold the broad trenches, and on the high towers stand sorrowing, moved by those uplifted heads that they know too well, now dripping with dark gore.

Meanwhile, winged Fame, flitting through the fearful town, speeds with the news and steals to the ears of Euryalus' mother. Then at once warmth left her hapless frame: the shuttle is dashed from her hands, and the thread unwound. Forth flies the unhappy lady and, with a woman's shrieks and torn tresses, in her madness makes

463 cogunt *Wagner*: cogit *MPR*
464 suos *PR*: suas *M*

prima petit, non illa virum, non illa pericli
480 telorumque memor, caelum dehinc questibus implet:
"hunc ego te, Euryale, aspicio? tune ille senectae
sera meae requies, potuisti linquere solam,
crudelis? nec te sub tanta pericula missum
adfari extremum miserae data copia matri?
485 heu, terra ignota canibus date praeda Latinis
alitibusque iaces! nec te tua funere mater
produxi pressive oculos aut vulnera lavi,
veste tegens tibi quam noctes festina diesque
urgebam, et tela curas solabar anilis.
490 quo sequar? aut quae nunc artus avulsaque membra
et funus lacerum tellus habet? hoc mihi de te,
nate, refers? hoc sum terraque marique secuta?
figite me, si qua est pietas, in me omnia tela
conicite, o Rutuli, me primam absumite ferro;
495 aut tu, magne pater divum, miserere, tuoque
invisum hoc detrude caput sub Tartara telo,
quando aliter nequeo crudelem abrumpere vitam."
hoc fletu concussi animi, maestusque per omnis
it gemitus, torpent infractae ad proelia vires.
500 illam incendentem luctus Idaeus et Actor
Ilionei monitu et multum lacrimantis Iuli
corripiunt interque manus sub tecta reponunt.
    At tuba terribilem sonitum procul aere canoro
increpuit, sequitur clamor caelumque remugit.
505 accelerant acta pariter testudine Volsci
et fossas implere parant ac vellere vallum;

485 date χ: data *MPR*
486 funere *Bembo*: funera *MPR*

for the walls and the foremost ranks—she is heedless of men, heedless of peril and of darts; then she fills the sky with her plaints: "Is this you, Euryalus, that I see? You who were the last solace of my age, could you bring yourself to leave me alone, cruel one? And when you were sent on so perilous an errand, did you not give your poor mother a chance to bid you a last farewell? Alas! You lie in a strange land, given as prey to the dogs and fowls of Latium! Nor did I, your mother, escort you to the grave, or close your eyes, or bathe your wounds, shrouding you with the robe which, in haste, night and day, I toiled at for your sake, beguiling with the loom the sorrows of age.[15] Where am I to follow? What land now holds your mangled limbs and dismembered body? Is this all, my son, you bring back to me of yourself? Is it this I have followed by land and sea? Pierce me, if you have any feeling, on me hurl all your weapons, Rutulians; destroy me first with your steel; or you, great Father of the gods, be pitiful, and with your bolt hurl down to hell this hateful life, since in no other way can I break life's cruel bonds!" At that wailing their spirits were shaken, and a groan of sorrow passed through all; their strength for battle is numbed and crushed; and as thus she kindles grief, Idaeus and Actor, bidden by Ilioneus and the sorely weeping Iülus, catch her up and carry her indoors in their arms.

But the trumpet with brazen song rang out afar its fearful call; a shout follows and the sky re-echoes. Forth the Volscians speed in even line, driving on their roof of shields, and prepare to fill the moat and pull down the pali-

[15] She had been making a rich robe as a gift for her son, but it could not even adorn his corpse.

quaerunt pars aditum et scalis ascendere muros,
qua rara est acies interlucetque corona

FMPR non tam spissa viris. telorum effundere contra
510 omne genus Teucri ac duris detrudere contis,
adsueti longo muros defendere bello.
saxa quoque infesto volvebant pondere, si qua
possent tectam aciem perrumpere, cum tamen omnis
ferre iuvat subter densa testudine casus.

515 nec iam sufficiunt. nam qua globus imminet ingens,
immanem Teucri molem volvuntque ruuntque,
quae stravit Rutulos late armorumque resolvit
tegmina. nec curant caeco contendere Marte
amplius audaces Rutuli, sed pellere vallo

520 missilibus certant . . .
parte alia horrendus visu quassabat Etruscam
pinum et fumiferos infert Mezentius ignis;
at Messapus equum domitor, Neptunia proles,
rescindit vallum et scalas in moenia poscit.

525 Vos, o Calliope, precor, aspirate canenti
quas ibi tum ferro strages, quae funera Turnus
ediderit, quem quisque virum demiserit Orco,
et mecum ingentis oras evolvite belli.
et meministis enim, divae, et memorare potestis.

530 Turris erat vasto suspectu et pontibus altis,
opportuna loco, summis quam viribus omnes
expugnare Itali summaque evertere opum vi
certabant, Troes contra defendere saxis
perque cavas densi tela intorquere fenestras.

535 princeps ardentem coniecit lampada Turnus

514 iuvat *F*[2]: iubet *P*: lubat *M*: libet *FM*[2]*R*
523 = 7.691, 12.128   529 = 7.645 (*R*)] *om. FMP*

sade. Some seek an entrance, and try to scale the walls with ladders, where the line is thin and light gleams through a less dense ring of men. In return, the Teucrians hurl missiles of every sort, and thrust the foe down with strong poles, trained by long warfare to defend their walls. Stones too they rolled of deadly weight, in the hope of breaking through the sheltered ranks: but beneath their compact shield, the enemy delight to brave all dangers. But now they fail; for where a massed throng threatens, the Teucrians roll up and hurl down a mighty mass, that laid low the Rutulians far and wide and broke their coverlet of armour. And the bold Rutulians care no longer to contend in blind warfare, but strive with darts to clear the ramparts. . . . Elsewhere, grim to behold, Mezentius was brandishing his Etruscan pine and hurls smoking brands; while Messapus, the seed of Neptune, tamer of horses, tears down the rampart and calls for ladders to mount the battlements.

Calliope, I pray, inspire me, you Muses, while I sing, what slaughter, what deaths Turnus dealt on that day, and whom each warrior sent down to doom; and unroll with me the mighty scroll of war. *For you, divine ones, remember and can recount.*

A tower loomed high above, with lofty gangways,[16] posted on vantage ground, which all the Italians strove with utmost strength to storm, and with utmost force of skill to overthrow; the Trojans in turn made defence with stones, and hurled showers of darts through the open loopholes. First Turnus flung a blazing torch and made fast its

---

[16] See note on 170 above.

MPR et flammam adfixit lateri, quae plurima vento
corripuit tabulas et postibus haesit adesis.
turbati trepidare intus frustraque malorum
velle fugam. dum se glomerant retroque residunt
540 in partem quae peste caret, tum pondere turris
procubuit subito et caelum tonat omne fragore.
semineces ad terram immani mole secuta
confixique suis telis et pectora duro
transfossi ligno veniunt. vix unus Helenor
545 et Lycus elapsi; quorum primaevus Helenor,
Maeonio regi quem serva Licymnia furtim
sustulerat vetitisque ad Troiam miserat armis,
ense levis nudo parmaque inglorius alba.
isque ubi se Turni media inter milia vidit,
550 hinc acies atque hinc acies astare Latinas,
ut fera, quae densa venantum saepta corona
contra tela furit seseque haud nescia morti
inicit et saltu supra venabula fertur—
haud aliter iuvenis medios moriturus in hostis
555 inruit et qua tela videt densissima tendit.
at pedibus longe melior Lycus inter et hostis
inter et arma fuga muros tenet, altaque certat
prendere tecta manu sociumque attingere dextras.
quem Turnus pariter cursu teloque secutus
560 increpat his victor: "nostrasne evadere, demens,
sperasti te posse manus?" simul arripit ipsum
pendentem et magna muri cum parte revellit:
qualis ubi aut leporem aut candenti corpore cycnum
sustulit alta petens pedibus Iovis armiger uncis,
565 quaesitum aut matri multis balatibus agnum

fire in the side; fanned by the wind, it seized the planks and lodged in the gateways it consumed. Within, troubled and terrified, men vainly seek escape from disaster. While they huddle close and retreat to the side free from ruin, under the sudden weight the tower fell, and all the sky thunders with the crash. Half dead they fall to the ground, the monstrous mass behind them, pierced by their own weapons, and their breasts impaled by cruel splinters. Only Helenor and Lycus barely escape—Helenor in the prime of youth, whom a Licymnian slave had borne secretly to the Maeonian king, and had sent to Troy in forbidden arms, lightly accoutred with naked sword and white shield, as yet unfamed.[17] When he saw himself in the midst of Turnus' thousands, with the Latin lines standing on this side and that, like a wild beast that, hedged about by the hunters' serried ring, rages against their shafts, flings itself knowingly on death, and with a bound springs upon the spears—just so the youth rushes to death among the foe and makes his way where he sees the weapons thickest. But Lycus, far swifter of foot, among foes, among weapons, gains the walls and strives to clutch the coping, and reach the hands of his comrades. Turnus, following him with both foot and spear, taunts thus in triumph: "Fool, did you hope to escape our hands?" At the same time he seizes him as he hangs, and tears him down with a mighty mass of wall: just as when the bearer of Jove's bolt, as he soars aloft, has swept up in his crooked talons a hare or snowy-bodied swan; or as when the wolf of Mars[18] has snatched from the

[17] He was too young to win distinction and therefore had no device on his shield.   [18] Because Romulus and Remus, the offspring of Mars, were suckled by a she-wolf.

Martius a stabulis rapuit lupus. undique clamor
tollitur: invadunt et fossas aggere complent,
ardentis taedas alii ad fastigia iactant.
Ilioneus saxo atque ingenti fragmine montis
570 Lucetium portae subeuntem ignisque ferentem,
Emathiona Liger, Corynaeum sternit Asilas,
hic iaculo bonus, hic longe fallente sagitta,
Ortygium Caeneus, victorem Caenea Turnus,
Turnus Ityn Cloniumque, Dioxippum Promolumque
575 et Sagarim et summis stantem pro turribus Idan,
Privernum Capys. hunc primo levis hasta Themillae
strinxerat, ille manum proiecto tegmine demens
ad vulnus tulit; ergo alis adlapsa sagitta
et laevo infixa est alte lateri, abditaque intus
580 spiramenta animae letali vulnere rupit.
stabat in egregiis Arcentis filius armis
pictus acu chlamydem et ferrugine clarus Hibera,
insignis facie, genitor quem miserat Arcens
eductum matris luco Symaethia circum
585 flumina, pinguis ubi et placabilis ara Palici:
stridentem fundam positis Mezentius hastis
ipse ter adducta circum caput egit habena
et media adversi liquefacto tempora plumbo
diffidit ac multa porrectum extendit harena.
590   Tum primum bello celerem intendisse sagittam
dicitur ante feras solitus terrere fugacis
Ascanius, fortemque manu fudisse Numanum,
cui Remulo cognomen erat, Turnique minorem
germanam nuper thalamo sociatus habebat.
595 is primam ante aciem digna atque indigna relatu

579 ‹alte› lateri *Housman*: lateri manus *MPR*

154

fold a lamb that its mother seeks with much bleating. On all sides a shout goes up; on they press, and with heaps of earth fill up the trenches; some toss blazing brands on to the roofs. Ilioneus lays Lucetius low with a rock, huge fragment of a mountain, as, carrying fire, he nears the gate. Liger slays Emathion, Asilas Corynaeus; the one skilled with the javelin, the other with the arrow deceiving from afar. Caeneus fells Ortygius; Turnus victorious Caeneus; Turnus Itys and Clonius, Dioxippus and Promolus, and Sagaris, and Idas, as he stood on the topmost towers; Capys slays Privernus. Themillas' spear had first grazed him lightly; in his madness he cast down his shield and carried his hand to the wound. So the arrow winged its way and lodged deep in his left side; burying itself inside, it tore the breathing ways of life with fatal wound. The son of Arcens stood in glorious arms, his mantle embroidered with the needle, and bright with Iberian blue—of noble form, whom his father Arcens had sent, a youth reared in his mother's grove by the streams of Symaethus, where Palicus' altar stands, gift-laden and gracious. But dropping his spears Mezentius with tight-drawn thong thrice whirled about his head the whistling sling, with moulded lead shot split in two the temples of his opposing foe, and stretched him at full length in the deep sand.

Then first, it is said, Ascanius aimed his swift shaft in war, till now used to scare wild beasts in flight, and with his hand laid low brave Numanus, Remulus by surname, who but lately had won as bride Turnus' younger sister. He strode ahead of the foremost line, shouting words meet

---

584 matris γ, *Macrobius* 5.19.15: Martis *MPR*

vociferans tumidusque novo praecordia regno
ibat et ingentem sese clamore ferebat:
"non pudet obsidione iterum valloque teneri,
bis capti Phryges, et morti praetendere muros?
600 en qui nostra sibi bello conubia poscunt!
quis deus Italiam, quae vos dementia adegit?
non hic Atridae nec fandi fictor Ulixes:
durum a stirpe genus natos ad flumina primum
deferimus saevoque gelu duramus et undis;
605 venatu invigilant pueri silvasque fatigant,
flectere ludus equos et spicula tendere cornu;
at patiens operum parvoque adsueta iuventus
aut rastris terram domat aut quatit oppida bello.
omne aevum ferro teritur, versaque iuvencum
610 terga fatigamus hasta, nec tarda senectus
debilitat viris animi mutatque vigorem:
canitiem galea premimus, semperque recentis
comportare iuvat praedas et vivere rapto.
vobis picta croco et fulgenti murice vestis,
615 desidiae cordi, iuvat indulgere choreis,
et tunicae manicas et habent redimicula mitrae.
o vere Phrygiae, neque enim Phryges, ite per alta
Dindyma, ubi adsuetis biforem dat tibia cantum.
tympana vos buxusque vocat Berecyntia Matris
620 Idaeae; sinite arma viris et cedite ferro."
　　Talia iactantem dictis ac dira canentem
non tulit Ascanius, nervoque obversus equino

---

19 The Oriental *mitra* was like a bonnet, fastened with rib-
bons, cf. *Aen.* 4.216. Tunics with sleeves were regarded as effemi-
nate by the Romans.

and unmeet to utter, his heart puffed up with new-won royalty, and loudly boasted his mighty prowess: "Are you not shamed, twice captured Phrygians, again to be cooped inside beleaguered ramparts, and to ward off death with walls? See: these are the men who go to war to claim our brides for themselves! What god, what madness, has driven you to Italy? Here are no sons of Atreus, no fable-forging Ulysses! A race of hardy stock, we first bring our newborn sons to the river, and harden them with the water's cruel cold; as boys they keep vigil for the chase, and tire the forests; their sport is to rein the steed and shoot arrows from the bow; but patient of toil, and inured to want, our youth tames earth with the hoe or shakes cities in battle. All our life is worn down with iron's use; with spear reversed we goad our bullocks' flanks, and sluggish age does not weaken our hearts' strength or change our vigour. On to white hairs we press the helmet, and we ever delight to drive in fresh booty and live on plunder. But you wear embroidered saffron and gleaming purple; sloth is your joy, your delight is to enjoy the dance; your tunics have sleeves and your turbans ribbons.[19] Phrygian women, in-deed!—for Phrygian men you are not—go over the heights of Dindymus, where to accustomed ears the pipe utters music from double mouths! The timbrels call you, and the Berecynthian boxwood of the mother of Ida:[20] leave arms to men, and quit the sword."

As he makes these boasts in words of ominous strain, Ascanius did not endure it but faced him and levelled his

[20] The pipe, timbrels, and boxwood flute were accompaniments of the worship of Cybele, which came from Phrygia. Cf. 3.111.

157

contendit telum diversaque bracchia ducens
constitit, ante Iovem supplex per vota precatus:
625 "Iuppiter omnipotens, audacibus adnue coeptis.
ipse tibi ad tua templa feram sollemnia dona,
et statuam ante aras aurata fronte iuvencum
candentem pariterque caput cum matre ferentem,
iam cornu petat et pedibus qui spargat harenam."
630 audiit et caeli genitor de parte serena
intonuit laevum, sonat una fatifer arcus.
effugit horrendum stridens adducta sagitta
perque caput Remuli venit et cava tempora ferro
traicit. "i, verbis virtutem inlude superbis!
635 bis capti Phryges haec Rutulis responsa remittunt":
hoc tantum Ascanius. Teucri clamore sequuntur
laetitiaque fremunt animosque ad sidera tollunt.
    Aetheria tum forte plaga crinitus Apollo
desuper Ausonias acies urbemque videbat
640 nube sedens, atque his victorem adfatur Iulum:
"macte nova virtute, puer, sic itur ad astra,
dis genite et geniture deos. iure omnia bella
gente sub Assaraci fato ventura resident,
nec te Troia capit." simul haec effatus ab alto
645 aethere se mittit, spirantis dimovet auras
Ascaniumque petit; formam tum vertitur oris
antiquum in Buten. hic Dardanio Anchisae
armiger ante fuit fidusque ad limina custos;

623 contendit *MR*: in- *P*
631 fatifer *MR*: letifer *P* (10.169)
632 effugit *M*: et fugit *PR* | adducta *MR*: adlapsa *P* (9.578)
634 traicit *M*: transigit *P*: transiit *P²*: transadigit *R*
646 formam *M*: forma *PR*

shaft from the horsehair string, and holding his arms wide apart paused, first invoking Jove with suppliant vows: "Jupiter almighty, give assent to my bold undertaking! My own hand shall bring you yearly gifts in your temple, and set before your altar a bullock with gilded brow, snowy white, carrying his head as high as his mother, that already can butt with his horn and can spurn the sand with his hoof." The Father heard, and from a clear space of sky thundered on the left; at that moment the fatal bow twanged. With awful whirr speeds forth the tight-drawn shaft, passes through the head of Remulus, and cleaves the hollow temples with its steel. "Go, mock valour with haughty words! This is the answer that the twice captured Phrygians send back to the Rutulians." Ascanius said no more. The Teucrians second him with cheers, they shout for joy, and raise their spirits to the skies.

Then it chanced that in the realm of sky long-haired Apollo, cloud-enthroned, was looking down on the Ausonian lines and town, and thus he addresses triumphant Iülus: "A blessing, boy, on your young valour! So man scales the stars, you son of gods and sire of gods to be![21] All the wars that fate may bring will justly cease under the house of Assaracus; nor can Troy contain you." So saying, he darts from high heaven, parts the breathing gales, and seeks Ascanius. Then he changes the fashion of his features to those of aged Butes, who in time gone by was armour bearer to Dardan Anchises, and trusty watcher at

[21] The "gods to be" are the future Caesars, descended from Aeneas and Ascanius, who are of "the house of Assaracus." There is a reference in 642f. to the closing of the temple of Janus by Augustus in 29 B.C.

    tum comitem Ascanio pater addidit. ibat Apollo
650 omnia longaevo similis vocemque coloremque
    et crinis albos et saeva sonoribus arma,
    atque his ardentem dictis adfatur Iulum:
    "sit satis, Aenide, telis impune Numanum
    oppetiisse tuis. primam hanc tibi magnus Apollo
655 concedit laudem et paribus non invidet armis;
    cetera parce, puer, bello." sic orsus Apollo
    mortalis medio aspectus sermone reliquit
    et procul in tenuem ex oculis evanuit auram.
    agnovere deum proceres divinaque tela
660 Dardanidae pharetramque fuga sensere sonantem.
    ergo avidum pugnae dictis ac numine Phoebi
    Ascanium prohibent, ipsi in certamina rursus
    succedunt animasque in aperta pericula mittunt.
    it clamor totis per propugnacula muris,
665 intendunt acris arcus amentaque torquent.
    sternitur omne solum telis, tum scuta cavaeque
    dant sonitum flictu galeae, pugna aspera surgit:
    quantus ab occasu veniens pluvialibus Haedis
    verberat imber humum, quam multa grandine nimbi
670 in vada praecipitant, cum Iuppiter horridus Austris
    torquet aquosam hiemem et caelo cava nubila rumpit.
      Pandarus et Bitias, Idaeo Alcanore creti,
    quos Iovis eduxit luco silvestris Iaera
    abietibus iuvenes patriis in montibus aequos,
675 portam, quae ducis imperio commissa, recludunt
    freti armis, ultroque invitant moenibus hostem.
    ipsi intus dextra ac laeva pro turribus astant

      658 = 4.278   661 ac *PR*: et *M*   667 flictu *P*: adflictu *MR*
      674 in *Bryant* (*cf. Homer, Iliad* 12.132): et *MPR*

his gate; thereafter the child's father made him henchman
to Ascanius. On strode Apollo, in all things like the old
man, in voice and hue, in white locks and savage-sounding
arms, and speaks these words to fiery Iülus: "Let it be
enough, son of Aeneas, that beneath your shafts Numanus
has fallen unavenged; this first taste of glory great Apollo
vouchsafes you, and does not grudge the weapons that
match his own; for the rest, child, refrain from war." Thus
Apollo began but, while yet speaking , left the sight of men
and far away from their eyes vanished into thin air. The
Dardan princes knew the god and his heavenly arms, and
heard his quiver rattle as he flew. Therefore, at the behest
and will of Phoebus, they check Ascanius, eager though he
is for the fray, they themselves go back into the fight and
fling their lives into open dangers. The shout runs from
tower to tower, all along the walls; they bend their eager
bows and whirl their thongs.[22] All the ground is strewn
with spears; shields and hollow helms ring as they clash;
the fight swells fierce: mighty as the storm that, coming
from the west, beneath the rainy Kids lashes the ground;
thick as the hail that storm clouds shower on the deep,
when Jupiter, grim with southern gales, whirls the watery
tempest, and bursts the hollow clouds in heaven.

Pandarus and Bitias, sprung from Alcanor of Ida, whom
the wood nymph Iaera bore in the grove of Jupiter—
youths tall as pines on their native hills—fling open the
gate entrusted to them by their captain's charge and, rely-
ing on their arms, freely invite the foe to enter the walls.
They themselves stand in the gateway, to right and left

[22] The thong, fastened to the middle of the shaft, gave impetus
to the throw.

armati ferro et cristis capita alta corusci:
quales aëriae liquentia flumina circum
680 sive Padi ripis Athesim seu propter amoenum
consurgunt geminae quercus intonsaque caelo
attollunt capita et sublimi vertice nutant.
inrumpunt aditus Rutuli ut videre patentis:
continuo Quercens et pulcher Aquiculus armis
685 et praeceps animi Tmarus et Mavortius Haemon
agminibus totis aut versi terga dedere
aut ipso portae posuere in limine vitam.
tum magis increscunt animis discordibus irae,
et iam collecti Troes glomerantur eodem
690 et conferre manum et procurrere longius audent.
    Ductori Turno diversa in parte furenti
turbantique viros perfertur nuntius, hostem
fervere caede nova et portas praebere patentis.
deserit inceptum atque immani concitus ira
695 Dardaniam ruit ad portam fratresque superbos.
et primum Antiphaten (is enim se primus agebat),
Thebana de matre nothum Sarpedonis alti,
coniecto sternit iaculo: volat Itala cornus
aëra per tenerum stomachoque infixa sub altum
700 pectus abit; reddit specus atri vulneris undam
spumantem, et fixo ferrum in pulmone tepescit.
tum Meropem atque Erymanta manu, tum sternit
    Aphidnum,
tum Bitian ardentem oculis animisque frementem,
non iaculo (neque enim iaculo vitam ille dedisset),
705 sed magnum stridens contorta phalarica venit
fulminis acta modo, quam nec duo taurea terga
nec duplici squama lorica fidelis et auro
sustinuit; conlapsa ruunt immania membra,

before the towers, sheathed in iron, with waving plumes upon their lofty heads: just as high in air beside flowing streams, whether on Padus' banks or by pleasant Athesis, twin oaks soar aloft, raising to heaven their unshorn heads and nodding their lofty crowns. The Rutulians rush in when they see the entrance clear. Straightway Quercens and Aquicolus, beautiful in arms, and Tmarus, reckless at heart, and Haemon, seed of Mars, with all their columns are routed and turn to flight, or in the very gateway lay down their life. At this, wrath waxes fiercer in their battling souls, and now the Trojans rally and swarm to the spot, and venture to close hand to hand and to sally farther out.

To Turnus the chief, as far away he storms and confounds his foe, comes news that the enemy, flushed with fresh slaughter, is flinging wide his gates. He quits the work in hand and, stirred with giant fury, rushes to the Dardan gate and the proud brothers. And first Antiphates (for he was first to advance), the bastard son of tall Sarpedon by a Theban mother, he slays with a javelin cast. Through the yielding air flies the Italian cornel shaft and, lodging in the gullet, runs deep into the breast; the wound's dark chasm gives back a foaming tide, and the steel grows warm in the pierced lung. Then Meropes and Erymas, then Aphidnus his hand lays low; then Bitias falls, fire in his eyes and rage in his heart, not under a javelin— for to a javelin he would not have given his life—but with a mighty hiss a whirled pike sped, driven like a thunderbolt. Not two bulls' hides nor the trusty corslet with double scales of gold could withstand it. The giant limbs totter and

dat tellus gemitum et clipeum super intonat ingens.
710 talis in Euboico Baiarum litore quondam
saxea pila cadit, magnis quam molibus ante
constructam ponto iaciunt, sic illa ruinam
prona trahit penitusque vadis inlisa recumbit;
miscent se maria et nigrae attolluntur harenae,
715 tum sonitu Prochyta alta tremit durumque cubile
Inarime Iovis imperiis imposta Typhoeo.
    Hic Mars armipotens animum virisque Latinis
addidit et stimulos acris sub pectore vertit,
immisitque Fugam Teucris atrumque Timorem.
720 undique conveniunt, quoniam data copia pugnae,
bellatorque animo deus incidit . . .
Pandarus, ut fuso germanum corpore cernit
et quo sit fortuna loco, qui casus agat res,
portam vi magna converso cardine torquet
725 obnixus latis umeris, multosque suorum
moenibus exclusos duro in certamine linquit;
ast alios secum includit recipitque ruentis,
demens, qui Rutulum in medio non agmine regem
viderit inrumpentem ultroque incluserit urbi,
730 immanem veluti pecora inter inertia tigrim.
continuo nova lux oculis effulsit et arma
horrendum sonuere, tremunt in vertice cristae
sanguineae clipeoque micantia fulmina mittit.
agnoscunt faciem invisam atque immania membra
735 turbati subito Aeneadae. tum Pandarus ingens
emicat et mortis fraternae fervidus ira

723 qui *M*: quis *PR*
724 magna *M*: multa *PR* (1.231)

fall; earth groans, and the huge shield thunders over him.
So on the Euboic shore of Baiae falls at times a rocky mass,
which, built up first of mighty blocks, men cast into the
sea:[23] so as it falls, it trails havoc, and crashing into the
waters finds rest in the depths; the seas are in turmoil and
the black sands mount upward; then at the sound lofty
Prochyta trembles, and Inarime's rugged bed, laid by
Jove's command above Typhoeus.

At this Mars, the mighty in war, lent fresh strength and
valour to the Latins, and in their hearts plied his keen
goads, and let slip Flight and dark Terror among the
Teucrians. From all sides gather the Latins, since scope for
fight is given, and the god of battle seizes on their souls.
Pandarus, when he sees his brother's fallen form, sees
how fortune stands, and what chance sways the day, with
mighty effort pushes with his broad shoulders and swings
the gate round on its hinge, leaving many a comrade shut
outside the walls in the cruel fray; but others he encloses
with himself, welcoming them as they rush in. Madman!
not to have seen the Rutulian prince bursting in among the
throng, and wantonly to have shut him up in the town, like
a monstrous tiger among helpless herds. Straightway a
new light flashed from Turnus' eyes and his armour rang
terribly; the blood-red plumes quiver on his crest, and
lightnings shoot gleaming from his shield. In sudden dis-
may the sons of Aeneas recognize that hateful form and
those giant limbs. Then huge Pandarus springs forward
and, blazing with wrath for his brother's death, cries: "This

[23] A reference to the building of massive piers running out
into the sea, whether as a breakwater or as the foundation of a pro-
jecting villa.

effatur: "non haec dotalis regia Amatae,
nec muris cohibet patriis media Ardea Turnum.
castra inimica vides, nulla hinc exire potestas."
740 olli subridens sedato pectore Turnus:
"incipe, si qua animo virtus, et consere dextram,
hic etiam inventum Priamo narrabis Achillem."
dixerat. ille rudem nodis et cortice crudo
intorquet summis adnixus viribus hastam;
745 excepere aurae, vulnus Saturnia Iuno
detorsit veniens, portaeque infigitur hasta.
"at non hoc telum, mea quod vi dextera versat,
effugies, neque enim is teli nec vulneris auctor":
sic ait, et sublatum alte consurgit in ensem
750 et mediam ferro gemina inter tempora frontem
dividit impubisque immani vulnere malas.
fit sonus, ingenti concussa est pondere tellus;
conlapsos artus atque arma cruenta cerebro
sternit humi moriens, atque illi partibus aequis
755 huc caput atque illuc umero ex utroque pependit.
    Diffugiunt versi trepida formidine Troes,
et si continuo victorem ea cura subisset,
rumpere claustra manu sociosque immittere portis,
ultimus ille dies bello gentique fuisset.
760 sed furor ardentem caedisque insana cupido
egit in adversos . . .
principio Phalerim et succiso poplite Gygen
excipit, hinc raptas fugientibus ingerit hastas
in tergus, Iuno viris animumque ministrat.
765 addit Halyn comitem et confixa Phegea parma,
ignaros deinde in muris Martemque cientis

[764] tergus *PR*: tergum *M*

is not Amata's bridal palace, nor is it midmost Ardea, hold-
ing Turnus within his native walls. This is a foeman's camp
that you see; there is no chance to escape from here." To
him said Turnus, smiling in untroubled mood: "Begin, if
your heart has any courage, and close with me: you will
tell Priam that here too an Achilles has been found." He
ended; the other, striving with all his might, hurls his spear,
rough with knots and unpeeled bark. The winds received
it; Saturnian Juno turned aside the coming blow, and the
spear lodges in the gate. "But you will not escape from this
weapon that my right arm brandishes; for not such is the
wielder of weapon and wound." So saying, he rises high
with his uplifted sword; the steel cleaves the brow in two
right between the temples, and with ghastly wound severs
the beardless cheeks. There is a crash, earth is shaken by
the vast weight; dying, he stretches on the ground his faint-
ing limbs and brain-bespattered armour, while in equal
halves his head dangles this way and that from either
shoulder.

The Trojans turn and scatter in hasty terror; and, if at
once the victor had taken thought to burst the bars by force
and let in his comrades at the gates, that day would have
been the last for the war and the nation. But rage and the
mad lust of slaughter drove him in fury on the enemy fac-
ing him . . . First he catches Phaleris, and Gyges, whom he
hamstrings; then, seizing their spears, he hurls them at the
backs of the flying crowd; Juno lends strength and cour-
age. Halys he sends to join them and Phegeus, his shield
transfixed; then, as, all unwitting, on the walls they rouse

Alcandrumque Haliumque Noëmonaque Prytanimque.
Lyncea tendentem contra sociosque vocantem
vibranti gladio conixus ab aggere dexter
770   occupat, huic uno deiectum comminus ictu
cum galea longe iacuit caput. inde ferarum
vastatorem Amycum, quo non felicior alter
unguere tela manu ferrumque armare veneno,
et Clytium Aeoliden et amicum Crethea Musis,
775   Crethea Musarum comitem, cui carmina semper
et citharae cordi numerosque intendere nervis,
semper equos atque arma virum pugnasque canebat.
    Tandem ductores audita caede suorum
conveniunt Teucri, Mnestheus acerque Serestus,
780   palantisque vident socios hostemque receptum.
et Mnestheus: "quo deinde fugam, quo tenditis?" inquit.
"quos alios muros, quaeve ultra moenia habetis?
unus homo et vestris, o cives, undique saeptus
aggeribus tantas strages impune per urbem
785   ediderit? iuvenum primos tot miserit Orco?
non infelicis patriae veterumque deorum
et magni Aeneae, segnes, miseretque pudetque?"
    Talibus accensi firmantur et agmine denso
consistunt. Turnus paulatim excedere pugnae
790   et fluvium petere ac partem quae cingitur unda.
acrius hoc Teucri clamore incumbere magno
et glomerare manum, ceu saevum turba leonem
cum telis premit infensis; at territus ille,
asper, acerba tuens, retro redit et neque terga

773 unguere P^2R: ungere M: tinguere P^1(?), *Bentley*
782 quaeve P: quae iam MR
789 pugnae PR (10.441): pugna M

the fray, Alcander and Halius, Noemon and Prytanis. As Lynceus moves to meet him and calls on his comrades he, from the rampart on the right, with sweep of flashing sword, smites him; severed by a single blow at close quarters, his head with its helmet lay far away. Next fell Amycus, scourge of beasts, whom none excelled in skill of hand in anointing the dart and arming the steel with venom; and Clytius, son of Aeolus, and Cretheus, delight of the Muses—Cretheus, the Muses' comrade, whose joy was ever in song and lyre and in stringing notes upon the chords; ever he sang of steeds and weapons, of men and battles.

At last, hearing of the slaughter of their men, the Teucrian captains, Mnestheus and gallant Serestus, come up, and see their comrades scattered and the foe within the gates. And Mnestheus: "Where then, where are you going? What other walls, what other battlements do you have elsewhere? My countrymen, shall one man, hemmed in on every side by your ramparts, deal such carnage throughout the city and go unpunished? Shall he send down to death so many of our noblest youths? Cowards, have you no pity, no shame, for your unhappy country, for your ancient gods, for great Aeneas?"

Kindled by such words, they take heart and halt in dense array. Step by step Turnus withdraws from the fight, making for the river and the place encircled by the stream. All the more fearlessly the Teucrians press on him with loud shouts and mass their ranks—as when a crowd with levelled spears beset a savage lion: but he, affrighted, yet fierce and glaring angrily, gives ground, and neither

795 ira dare aut virtus patitur, nec tendere contra
ille quidem hoc cupiens potis est per tela virosque.
haud aliter retro dubius vestigia Turnus
improperata refert et mens exaestuat ira.
quin etiam bis tum medios invaserat hostis,
800 bis confusa fuga per muros agmina vertit;
sed manus e castris propere coit omnis in unum
nec contra viris audet Saturnia Iuno
sufficere; aëriam caelo nam Iuppiter Irim
demisit germanae haud mollia iussa ferentem,
805 ni Turnus cedat Teucrorum moenibus altis.
ergo nec clipeo iuvenis subsistere tantum
nec dextra valet, iniectis sic undique telis
obruitur. strepit adsiduo cava tempora circum
tinnitu galea et saxis solida aera fatiscunt
810 discussaeque iubae, capiti nec sufficit umbo
ictibus; ingeminant hastis et Troes et ipse
fulmineus Mnestheus. tum toto corpore sudor
liquitur et piceum (nec respirare potestas)
flumen agit, fessos quatit aeger anhelitus artus.
815 tum demum praeceps saltu sese omnibus armis
in fluvium dedit. ille suo cum gurgite flavo
accepit venientem ac mollibus extulit undis
et laetum sociis abluta caede remisit.

wrath nor courage lets him turn his back, nor yet, desirous though he be, can he make his way through hunters and through spears. Just so Turnus in doubt retraces his unhurried steps, his heart seething with rage. Indeed, even then twice he attacked the foe, twice he drove them in flying rout along the walls: but the whole host hastily gathers in a body from the camp, and Saturnian Juno did not dare grant him strength to oppose them, for Jupiter sent Iris down through the sky from Heaven, charged with no gentle behests for his sister,[24] should Turnus not leave the Teucrians' lofty ramparts. Therefore, with neither shield nor sword arm can the soldier hold his own: with such a hail of missiles is he overwhelmed on all sides. Round his hollow temples the helmet echoes with ceaseless clash; the solid brass gapes beneath the rain of stones; the horsehair crest is torn from his head, and the shield's boss withstands not the blows: the Trojans and Mnestheus himself, of lightning force, launch a storm of spears. Then all over his body flows the sweat and runs in pitchy stream, and he has no breathing space; a sickly panting shakes his wearied limbs. Then at length, with headlong leap, he plunges in full armour into the river. Tiber with his yellow flood received him as he came, lifted him up on buoyant waters and, washing away the carnage, returned the joyous hero to his comrades.

[24] Juno, who is *et soror et coniunx* (*Aen.* 1.47).

LIBER X

MPRV Panditur interea domus omnipotentis Olympi
conciliumque vocat divum pater atque hominum rex
sideream in sedem, terras unde arduus omnis
castraque Dardanidum aspectat populosque Latinos.
5 considunt tectis bipatentibus, incipit ipse:
"caelicolae magni, quianam sententia vobis
versa retro tantumque animis certatis iniquis?
abnueram bello Italiam concurrere Teucris.
quae contra vetitum discordia? quis metus aut hos
10 aut hos arma sequi ferrumque lacessere suasit?
adveniet iustum pugnae (ne arcessite) tempus,
cum fera Karthago Romanis arcibus olim
exitium magnum atque Alpes immittet apertas:
tum certare odiis, tum res rapuisse licebit.
15 nunc sinite et placitum laeti componite foedus."
    Iuppiter haec paucis; at non Venus aurea contra
pauca refert . . .
"o pater, o hominum rerumque aeterna potestas
(namque aliud quid sit quod iam implorare queamus?),
20 cernis ut insultent Rutuli, Turnusque feratur

20–21 feratur . . . tumidusque (*PRV*) *om. M by homoeoteleuton*

172

BOOK X

Meanwhile the palace of omnipotent Olympus is thrown open, and the Sire of gods and King of men calls a council to his starry dwelling, from where, high-throned, he surveys all lands, the Dardan camp, and the Latin peoples. In the double-doored hall[1] they take their seats, and the king begins: "Mighty sons of Heaven, why is your decision reversed, and why do you quarrel with hearts so discordant? I forbade Italy to clash in war with Troy. What feud is this, in face of my command? What terror has bidden these or those to rush to arms and provoke the sword? There shall come—do not hasten it—a lawful time for battle, when fierce Carthage shall one day let loose upon the heights of Rome mighty destruction, and open upon her the Alps.[2] Then it will be lawful to vie in hate, then to ravage; now let be and cheerfully assent to the covenant I ordain."

Thus Jupiter in brief; but not briefly golden Venus makes reply . . . : "Father, eternal sovereignty of men and things—for what else can there be which we may now entreat?—do you see how insolent the Rutulians are, and

[1] The palace of Olympus has doors at the east and west ends. Through the former the sun comes out at dawn; through the latter it returns at night.

[2] A reference to Hannibal's invasion of Italy in 218 B.C.

per medios insignis equis tumidusque secundo
Marte ruat? non clausa tegunt iam moenia Teucros;
quin intra portas atque ipsis proelia miscent
aggeribus murorum, et inundant sanguine fossae.
25 Aeneas ignarus abest. numquamne levari
obsidione sines? muris iterum imminet hostis
MPR nascentis Troiae nec non exercitus alter,
atque iterum in Teucros Aetolis surgit ab Arpis
Tydides. equidem credo, mea vulnera restant
30 et tua progenies mortalia demoror arma.
si sine pace tua atque invito numine Troes
Italiam petiere, luant peccata neque illos
iuveris auxilio; sin tot responsa secuti
quae superi manesque dabant, cur nunc tua quisquam
35 vertere iussa potest aut cur nova condere fata?
quid repetam exustas Erycino in litore classis,
quid tempestatum regem ventosque furentis
Aeolia excitos aut actam nubibus Irim?
nunc etiam manis (haec intemptata manebat
40 sors rerum) movet et superis immissa repente
Allecto medias Italum bacchata per urbes.
nil super imperio moveor. speravimus ista,
dum fortuna fuit. vincant, quos vincere mavis.
si nulla est regio Teucris quam det tua coniunx
45 dura, per eversae, genitor, fumantia Troiae
excidia obtestor: liceat dimittere ab armis
incolumem Ascanium, liceat superesse nepotem.
Aeneas sane ignotis iactetur in undis

²⁴ murorum] moerorum ("*pro* murorum *antique*" *Servius*) *P*,
as at 144 and 11.382 *in the same phrase* | fossae *MR*: fossas *PV*
³⁵ iussa *MP*: iura *R*   ⁴⁸ sane *MP*: procul *R*

how Turnus is borne conspicuous through the crowd upon
his chariot, and rushes in swollen pride along the tide of
war? No longer do barred walls shelter the Teucrians;
rather, inside the gates and even on the rampart walls
they join battle, and the trenches are flooded with blood.
Aeneas, unknowing, is far away. Will you never suffer the
siege to be raised? Once more a foe, a second army, threat-
ens the walls of infant Troy; and once more against the Tro-
jans there rises from Aetolian Arpi a son of Tydeus. Truly, I
think, my wounds are yet to come, and I, your offspring,
delay a mortal spear.[3] If without your leave and despite
your deity the Trojans have sought Italy, let them expiate
their sin, and do not aid them with succour. But if they
have followed all the oracles given by gods above and gods
below, why is anyone now able to overthrow your bidding
or build the fates anew? Why should I recall the fleet
burned on the strand of Eryx?[4] Why the king of storms,
and his raging gales roused from Aeolia,[5] or Iris wafted
from the clouds? Now she even stirs the shades—this
quarter of the world was yet untried—and Allecto,
launched suddenly on the upper world, raves through the
midst of Italian towns. I care nothing for empire; that was
my hope while our Fortune stood; let those win whom you
would prefer to win. If there is no country for your relent-
less consort to bestow upon the Teucrians, by the smoking
ruins of desolate Troy I beseech you, Father, let me dis-
miss Ascanius unscathed from arms—let my grandson still
live! Aeneas, indeed, may well be tossed on unknown

[3] Diomedes, son of Tydeus, wounded Venus when she rescued
Aeneas. See Homer, *Iliad* 5.336.

[4] Cf. *Aen.* 5.604f.   [5] Cf. *Aen.* 1.50f.

et, quacumque viam dederit Fortuna, sequatur:
50 hunc tegere et dirae valeam subducere pugnae.
est Amathus, est celsa mihi Paphus atque Cythera
Idaliaeque domus: positis inglorius armis
MPRV exigat hic aevum. magna dicione iubeto
Karthago premat Ausoniam; nihil urbibus inde
55 obstabit Tyriis. quid pestem evadere belli
iuvit et Argolicos medium fugisse per ignis
totque maris vastaeque exhausta pericula terrae,
dum Latium Teucri recidivaque Pergama quaerunt?
non satius cineres patriae insedisse supremos
60 atque solum quo Troia fuit? Xanthum et Simoenta
redde, oro, miseris iterumque revolvere casus
da, pater, Iliacos Teucris." tum regia Iuno
acta furore gravi: "quid me alta silentia cogis
rumpere et obductum verbis vulgare dolorem?
65 Aenean hominum quisquam divumque subegit
bella sequi aut hostem regi se inferre Latino?
Italiam petiit fatis auctoribus (esto)
Cassandrae impulsus furiis: num linquere castra
hortati sumus aut vitam committere ventis?
70 num puero summam belli, num credere muros,
Tyrrhenamque fidem aut gentis agitare quietas?
quis deus in fraudem, quae dura potentia nostra
egit? ubi hic Iuno demissave nubibus Iris?
indignum est Italos Troiam circumdare flammis
75 nascentem et patria Turnum consistere terra,
cui Pilumnus avus, cui diva Venilia mater:
quid face Troianos atra vim ferre Latinis,
arva aliena iugo premere atque avertere praedas?

49 quacumque *P*: quamcumque *MR*

176

waters, and follow wherever Fortune points out a path: let me avail to shield this child and withdraw him from the dreadful fray. Amathus is mine, mine high Paphus and Cythera, and Idalia's shrine: here, laying arms aside, let him live out his inglorious days! Bid Carthage with mighty sway crush Ausonia; from Ausonia shall come no hindrance to Tyrian towns. What has it availed to escape the plague of war, to have fled through the midst of Argive fires, to have exhausted all the perils of sea and desolate lands, while his Teucrians seek Latium and a newborn Troy? Would it not be better to have settled on the last ashes of their country, and the soil where once was Troy? Restore, I pray, Xanthus and Simoïs to a hapless people, and let the Teucrians relive once more the woes of Ilium!" Then royal Juno, spurred by fierce frenzy: "Why do you force me to break my deep silence and publish to the world my hidden sorrow? Did any man or god constrain Aeneas to seek war and advance as a foe upon King Latinus? 'He sought Italy at the call of Fate.' So be it—driven on by Cassandra's raving! Did I urge him to quit the camp, or entrust his life to the winds? To commit the issue of war, the charge of battlements, to a boy? To tamper with Tyrrhene faith or stir up peaceful peoples? What god, what pitiless power of mine drove him to his harm? Where in this is Juno, or Iris sent down from the clouds? It is indeed shameful that Italians should gird your infant Troy with flames, and that Turnus set foot on his native soil—Turnus, whose grandsire is Pilumnus, whose mother divine Venilia! But what about the Trojans with smoking brands assailing the Latins, setting their yoke upon the fields of others, and driving

---

71 Tyrrhenamque *MP*: Tyrrhenamve *RV*

MPR   quid soceros legere et gremiis abducere pactas,
80   pacem orare manu, praefigere puppibus arma?
    tu potes Aenean manibus subducere Graium
    proque viro nebulam et ventos obtendere inanis,
    et potes in totidem classem convertere nymphas:
    nos aliquid Rutulos contra iuvisse nefandum est?
85   'Aeneas ignarus abest': ignarus et absit.
    est Paphus Idaliumque tibi, sunt alta Cythera:
    quid gravidam bellis urbem et corda aspera temptas?
    nosne tibi fluxas Phrygiae res vertere fundo
    conamur? nos? an miseros qui Troas Achivis
90   obiecit? quae causa fuit consurgere in arma
    Europamque Asiamque et foedera solvere furto?
    me duce Dardanius Spartam expugnavit adulter,
    aut ego tela dedi fovive Cupidine bella?
    tum decuit metuisse tuis: nunc sera querelis
95   haud iustis adsurgis et inrita iurgia iactas."
      Talibus orabat Iuno, cunctique fremebant
    caelicolae adsensu vario, ceu flamina prima
    cum deprensa fremunt silvis et caeca volutant
    murmura venturos nautis prodentia ventos.
100 tum pater omnipotens, rerum cui prima potestas,
    infit (eo dicente deum domus alta silescit
    et tremefacta solo tellus, silet arduus aether,
    tum Zephyri posuere, premit placida aequora pontus).
      "Accipite ergo animis atque haec mea figite dicta.

83 classem *PR*: classes *M*
96 Iuno *MR*: dictis (6.124) *P*
100 prima *MR*: summa *P*
104 = 3.250

off the spoil? What about their choosing whose daughters
they shall wed, and dragging from her lover's breast the
plighted bride?[6] Their proffering peace with the hand but
arraying their ships with armour? You have power to steal
Aeneas from Greek hands, and in place of a man to offer
them mist and empty air, and you have power to turn their
fleet into as many nymphs:[7] but that we in turn have given
some aid to the Rutuli, is that monstrous? 'Aeneas un-
knowing is far away'; unknowing and far away let him be!
'Paphus is yours, Idalium, and high Cythera': why meddle
with savage hearts, and a city teeming with war? Is it I that
try to overthrow from the foundation Phrygia's tottering
state? Is it I? Or is it he who flung the hapless Trojans in the
Achaeans' path? What cause was there that Europe and
Asia should rise up in arms and break the bonds of peace
by treachery? Was it I that led the Dardan adulterer to rav-
age Sparta? Was it I that gave him weapons or fostered war
with lust? It was then that you should have feared for your
own; now too late you rise with unjust complaints, and
bandy bickering words in vain."

So argued Juno, and all the celestial company mur-
mured diverse assent, just as when rising blasts, caught
in the forest, murmur, and roll their unseen moanings,
betraying to sailors the coming of the gale. Then the
Father Almighty, prime potentate of the world, begins; as
he speaks, the high house of the gods grows silent and
earth trembles from her base; silent is high heaven; then
the Zephyrs are hushed; Ocean stills his waters to rest.

"Take therefore to heart and fix there these words of

6 The reference is to Aeneas, suing for the hand of Lavinia.
7 Cf. *Aen.* 9.80f.

105 quandoquidem Ausonios coniungi foedere Teucris
    haud licitum, nec vestra capit discordia finem,
    quae cuique est fortuna hodie, quam quisque secat spem,
    Tros Rutulusne fuat, nullo discrimine habebo,
    seu fatis Italum castra obsidione tenentur
110 sive errore malo Troiae monitisque sinistris.
    nec Rutulos solvo. sua cuique exorsa laborem
    fortunamque ferent. rex Iuppiter omnibus idem.
    fata viam invenient." Stygii per flumina fratris,
    per pice torrentis atraque voragine ripas
115 adnuit et totum nutu tremefecit Olympum.
    hic finis fandi. solio tum Iuppiter aureo
    surgit, caelicolae medium quem ad limina ducunt.
        Interea Rutuli portis circum omnibus instant
    sternere caede viros et moenia cingere flammis.
120 at legio Aeneadum vallis obsessa tenetur
    nec spes ulla fugae. miseri stant turribus altis
    nequiquam et rara muros cinxere corona
    Asius Imbrasides Hicetaoniusque Thymoetes
    Assaracique duo et senior cum Castore Thymbris,
125 prima acies; hos germani Sarpedonis ambo
    et Clarus et Thaemon Lycia comitantur ab alta.
    fert ingens toto conixus corpore saxum,
    haud partem exiguam montis, Lyrnesius Acmon,
    nec Clytio genitore minor nec fratre Menestheo.
130 hi iaculis, illi certant defendere saxis
    molirique ignem nervoque aptare sagittas.
    ipse inter medios, Veneris iustissima cura,
    Dardanius caput, ecce, puer detectus honestum,
    qualis gemma micat fulvum quae dividit aurum,

114–5 = 9.105–6   126 alta *MR*: Ida (12.412) *P*

mine. Since it may not be that Ausonians and Teucrians join alliance, and your disunion admits no end, whatever the fortune of each today, whatever the hope each pursues, be he Trojan or be he Rutulian, no distinction shall I make, whether it be Italy's fortune that holds the camp in siege, or Troy's baneful error and misleading prophecies. Nor do I exempt the Rutulians. Each one's own course shall bring him his suffering or success. Jupiter is king over all alike; the fates shall find their way." By the waters of his Stygian brother, by the banks that seethe with pitch and black swirling waters, he nodded assent, and with the nod made all Olympus tremble. So ended the parley. Then from his golden throne Jupiter rises, and the celestial company gather round and escort him to the threshold.

Meanwhile, around every gate the Rutulians press on, to slaughter the foe with the sword, and to gird the ramparts with flame. But the army of the Aeneadae is held pent up inside the palisades, and there is no hope of escape. Forlorn and helpless they stand on the high towers, and girdle the walls with scanty ring. Asius, son of Imbrasus, and Thymoetes, son of Hicetaon, and the two Assaraci, and Castor, and old Thymbris are the foremost rank; at their side are Sarpedon's two brothers, Clarus and Thaemon, come from lofty Lycia. One, straining his whole frame, lifts up a giant rock, no scant fragment of a mountain—Acmon of Lyrnesus, huge as his father Clytius or his brother Mnestheus. Some with darts and some with stones, they strive to ward off the foe, and hurl fire and fit arrows to the string. In their midst, the Dardan boy himself, Venus' most rightful care, his comely head uncovered, glitters like a jewel inset in yellow gold to adorn neck or

135   aut collo decus aut capiti, vel quale per artem
      inclusum buxo aut Oricia terebintho
      lucet ebur; fusos cervix cui lactea crinis
      accipit et molli subnectens circulus auro.
      te quoque magnanimae viderunt, Ismare, gentes
140   vulnera derigere et calamos armare veneno,
      Maeonia generose domo, ubi pinguia culta
      exercentque viri Pactolusque inrigat auro.
      adfuit et Mnestheus, quem pulsi pristina Turni
      aggere murorum sublimem gloria tollit,
145   et Capys: hinc nomen Campanae ducitur urbi.
        Illi inter sese duri certamina belli
      contulerant: media Aeneas freta nocte secabat.
      namque ut ab Euandro castris ingressus Etruscis
      regem adit et regi memorat nomenque genusque
150   quidve petat quidve ipse ferat, Mezentius arma
      quae sibi conciliet, violentaque pectora Turni
      edocet, humanis quae sit fiducia rebus
      admonet immiscetque preces, haud fit mora, Tarchon
      iungit opes foedusque ferit; tum libera fati
155   classem conscendit iussis gens Lydia divum
      externo commissa duci. Aeneïa puppis
      prima tenet rostro Phrygios subiuncta leones,
      imminet Ida super, profugis gratissima Teucris.
      hic magnus sedet Aeneas secumque volutat
160   eventus belli varios, Pallasque sinistro
      adfixus lateri iam quaerit sidera, opacae
      noctis iter, iam quae passus terraque marique.

[138] subnectens *PR*: subnectit *M*
[144] murorum] meorum *P* (*see on* 24)

head, or as ivory gleams, skilfully inlaid in boxwood or Orician terebinth; his milk-white neck, and the circlet clasping it with pliant gold, receives his streaming locks. You too, Ismarus, your high-souled clansmen saw aiming wounds and arming shafts with venom, you noble scion of a Lydian house, where men till rich fields and Pactolus waters them with gold. There too was Mnestheus, whom yesterday's triumph of thrusting Turnus from the rampart walls exalts to the stars; and Capys, from whom comes the name of the Campanian city.

Thus they had clashed in stubborn warfare's conflict: and Aeneas at midnight was cleaving the seas. For when, leaving Evander and entering the Tuscan camp, he meets the king, and to the king announces his name and his race, the aid he seeks, and the aid he himself offers; informs him of the forces Mezentius is gathering to his side, and the violence of Turnus' spirit; then warns him, what faith may be put in things human, and with pleas mingles entreaties— without delay Tarchon joins forces and strikes a treaty; then, freed from Fate,[8] the Lydian people embark under heaven's ordinance, entrusting themselves to a foreign leader. Aeneas' ship takes the lead with Phrygian lions beneath her beak; above them towers Ida, sight most welcome to Trojan exiles.[9] There sits great Aeneas, pondering the changing issues of war; and Pallas, staying close to his left side, asks him now about the stars, their guide through the dark night, and now of his trials by land and sea.

---

[8] Cf. *Aen.* 8.503. Now that they have a foreign leader, fate will not oppose them.   [9] The ship's figurehead is a representation of Mount Ida (doubtless the mountain god), while below it are the lions of Cybele. (Cf. *Aen.* 9.80f.)

Pandite nunc Helicona, deae, cantusque movete,
quae manus interea Tuscis comitetur ab oris
165   Aenean armetque rates pelagoque vehatur.
     Massicus aerata princeps secat aequora Tigri,
sub quo mille manus iuvenum, qui moenia Clusi
quique urbem liquere Cosas, quîs tela sagittae
gorytique leves umeris et letifer arcus.
170   una torvus Abas: huic totum insignibus armis
agmen et aurato fulgebat Apolline puppis.
sescentos illi dederat Populonia mater
expertos belli iuvenes, ast Ilva trecentos
insula inexhaustis Chalybum generosa metallis.
175   tertius ille hominum divumque interpres Asilas,
cui pecudum fibrae, caeli cui sidera parent
et linguae volucrum et praesagi fulminis ignes,
mille rapit densos acie atque horrentibus hastis.
hos parere iubent Alpheae ab origine Pisae,
180   urbs Etrusca solo. sequitur pulcherrimus Astur,
Astur equo fidens et versicoloribus armis.
ter centum adiciunt (mens omnibus una sequendi)
MPRV   qui Caerete domo, qui sunt Minionis in arvis,
et Pyrgi veteres intempestaeque Graviscae.
185   Non ego te, Ligurum ductor fortissime bello,
transierim, Cunere, et paucis comitate Cupavo,
cuius olorinae surgunt de vertice pennae
(crimen, Amor, vestrum) formaeque insigne paternae.

---

179 Alpheae *PR*: Alphea *M*   186 Cunere *Timpanaro*: cun-
are *Servius Auctus*: cunerae *P*: cummare *R*: cinyrae *M*: cinere *V*

---

10 The Chalybes were famous workers of iron; cf. *Aen.* 8.420.
11 I.e. to you, Love, and your mother, Venus. Cycnus, father of

Now fling wide Helicon, goddesses, and start your song—what band comes then with Aeneas from the Tuscan shores, arming the ships and riding over the sea.

At their head Massicus cleaves the waters in the bronze-plated Tiger; under him is a band of a thousand youths, who have left the walls of Clusium and the city of Cosae; their weapons are arrows, light quivers on the shoulders, and deadly bows. With him is grim Abas, all his train in dazzling armour, his vessel gleaming with a gilded Apollo. To him Populonia had given six hundred of her sons, all skilled in war, and Ilva three hundred—an island rich in the Chalybes' inexhaustible mines.[10] Third comes Asilas, famous interpreter between gods and men, whom the victims' entrails obey, and the stars of heaven, the tongues of birds, and prophetic lightning fires. A thousand men he hurries to war in serried array and bristling with spears. These Pisa bids obey him—city of Alphean birth, but set in Tuscan soil. Then follows Astur, of wondrous beauty—Astur, relying on his mount and many-coloured weapons. Three hundred more—all of one mind to follow—come from the men who have their home in Caere and in the plains of Minio, in ancient Pyrgi, and fever-stricken Graviscae.

Nor would I pass you by, Cunerus, bravest in war of Ligurian captains, or you, Cupavo, with your scanty train, from whose crest rise the swan plumes—a reproach, Cupid, to you and yours[11]—the badge of his father's form.

Cupavo, loved Phaëthon, and was a witness of this youth's destruction by Jupiter. Being plunged into grief, he was transformed into a swan. The sisters of Phaëthon were at the same time changed into poplars.

namque ferunt luctu Cycnum Phaëthontis amati,
190 populeas inter frondes umbramque sororum
dum canit et maestum Musa solatur amorem,
canentem molli pluma duxisse senectam
linquentem terras et sidera voce sequentem.
filius aequalis comitatus classe catervas
195 ingentem remis Centaurum promovet: ille
instat aquae saxumque undis immane minatur
arduus, et longa sulcat maria alta carina.

    Ille etiam patriis agmen ciet Ocnus ab oris,
fatidicae Mantus et Tusci filius amnis,
200 qui muros matrisque dedit tibi, Mantua, nomen,
Mantua dives avis, sed non genus omnibus unum:
gens illi triplex, populi sub gente quaterni,
ipsa caput populis, Tusco de sanguine vires.
hinc quoque quingentos in se Mezentius armat,
205 quos patre Benaco velatus harundine glauca
Mincius infesta ducebat in aequora pinu.
it gravis Aulestes centenaque arbore fluctum
verberat adsurgens, spumant vada marmore verso.
MPR hunc vehit immanis Triton et caerula concha
210 exterrens freta, cui laterum tenus hispida nanti
frons hominem praefert, in pristim desinit alvus,
spumea semifero sub pectore murmurat unda.
tot lecti proceres ter denis navibus ibant
subsidio Troiae et campos salis aere secabant.
215   Iamque dies caelo concesserat almaque curru
noctivago Phoebe medium pulsabat Olympum:

---

[12] In the territory of Mantua there were three races, each
master of four cities. Once head of a confederacy of twelve Tuscan

For they tell that Cycnus, in grief for his loved Phaëthon, while he is singing and with music solacing his woeful love amid the shade of his sisters' leafy poplars, drew over his form the soft plumage of white old age, leaving earth and seeking the stars with his cry. His son, following on shipboard with a band of like age, drives with oars the mighty Centaur; over the water towers the monster, and threatens to hurl a mighty rock into the waves from above, while with long keel he furrows the deep seas.

Ocnus, too, summons a host from his native shores, son of prophetic Manto and the Tuscan river, who gave you, Mantua, ramparts and his mother's name—Mantua, rich in ancestry, yet not all of one stock: three races are there, and under each race four peoples:[12] herself the head of the peoples, her strength from Tuscan blood. Hence, too, Mezentius arms five hundred against himself,[13] whom Mincius, child of Benacus, crowned with gray sedge, leads over the seas in their hostile ships of pine. On comes Aulestes heavily, lashing the waves as he rises to the stroke of a hundred oars; the waters foam as the surface is torn up. He sails in the huge Triton, whose shell alarms the blue billows: its shaggy front, as it floats, shows a man down to the waist, its belly ends in a fish; beneath the monster's breast the wave gurgles in foam. So many the chosen chiefs who sailed in thrice ten ships to the help of Troy, and cut the salty plains with bronze beak.

And now day had passed from the sky and gracious Phoebe was trampling mid-heaven with her night-roving

cities (cf. Livy 5.33), Mantua in the time of Pliny the Elder was the only Tuscan city north of the Po.   [13] Because his tyranny has led them to take up arms against him.

Aeneas (neque enim membris dat cura quietem)
ipse sedens clavumque regit velisque ministrat.
atque illi medio in spatio chorus, ecce, suarum
220   occurrit comitum: nymphae, quas alma Cybebe
numen habere maris nymphasque e navibus esse
iusserat, innabant pariter fluctusque secabant,
quot prius aeratae steterant ad litora prorae.
agnoscunt longe regem lustrantque choreis;
225   quarum quae fandi doctissima Cymodocea
pone sequens dextra puppim tenet ipsaque dorso
eminet ac laeva tacitis subremigat undis.
tum sic ignarum adloquitur: "vigilasne, deum gens,
Aenea? vigila et velis immitte rudentis.
230   nos sumus, Idaeae sacro de vertice pinus,
nunc pelagi nymphae, classis tua. perfidus ut nos
praecipitis ferro Rutulus flammaque premebat,
rupimus invitae tua vincula teque per aequor
quaerimus. hanc genetrix faciem miserata refecit
MPRV   et dedit esse deas aevumque agitare sub undis.
236   at puer Ascanius muro fossisque tenetur
tela inter media atque horrentis Marte Latinos.
iam loca iussa tenet forti permixtus Etrusco
Arcas eques; medias illis opponere turmas,
240   ne castris iungant, certa est sententia Turno.
surge age et Aurora socios veniente vocari
primus in arma iube, et clipeum cape quem dedit ipse
invictum ignipotens atque oras ambiit auro.
crastina lux, mea si non inrita dicta putaris,
245   ingentis Rutulae spectabit caedis acervos."

237 horrentis *MR*: ardentis *P*: *V illegible*
238 tenet *PR*: tenent *MV*   245 spectabit *RV*: spectabis *MP*

steeds; Aeneas, for care allows no rest to his limbs, sat at his post, his own hand guiding the rudder and tending the sails. And lo! in mid course a band of his own company meets him, for the nymphs whom gracious Cybele had ordered to be deities of the sea, and turn from ships to nymphs, came swimming abreast and cleaving the billows, as many as the bronze prows that once lay moored to shore. They recognize their king from afar, and encircle him with their dancing. From among them, Cymodocea, most skilled in speech, following behind, grasps the stern with her right hand, and herself rises breast high above the wave, while with her left hand she oars her way upon the silent waters. Then thus she addresses the prince, all unaware: "Are you awake, Aeneas, scion of gods? Wake and fling loose the sheets of your sails. We—pines of Ida, from her sacred crest, now nymphs of the sea—are your fleet! When the treacherous Rutulian was driving us headlong with fire and sword, we reluctantly broke your moorings and are seeking you over the waves. This new shape the Great Mother gave us in pity, and granted us to be goddesses and spend our life beneath the waves. But your son Ascanius is hemmed in by wall and trench, in the midst of arms and of Latins bristling with war. Already the Arcadian cavalry, joined with brave Etruscans, hold the appointed place; to bar their way with interposing squadrons, lest they approach the camp, is Turnus' fixed resolve. Up, then, and with the coming dawn first give orders that your friends be called to arms, and take invincible the shield which the Lord of Fire himself gave you and rimmed with gold. Tomorrow's light, if you do not consider my words idle, shall look on mighty heaps of Rutulian carnage." She

dixerat et dextra discedens impulit altam
haud ignara modi puppim: fugit illa per undas
ocior et iaculo et ventos aequante sagitta.
inde aliae celerant cursus. stupet inscius ipse
250   Tros Anchisiades, animos tamen omine tollit.
tum breviter supera aspectans convexa precatur:
"alma parens Idaea deum, cui Dindyma cordi
turrigeraeque urbes biiugique ad frena leones,
tu mihi nunc pugnae princeps, tu rite propinques
255   augurium Phrygibusque adsis pede, diva, secundo."
tantum effatus, et interea revoluta ruebat
matura iam luce dies noctemque fugarat;
principio sociis edicit signa sequantur
atque animos aptent armis pugnaeque parent se.
260   Iamque in conspectu Teucros habet et sua castra
stans celsa in puppi, clipeum cum deinde sinistra
MPR   extulit ardentem. clamorem ad sidera tollunt
Dardanidae e muris, spes addita suscitat iras,
tela manu iaciunt, quales sub nubibus atris
265   Strymoniae dant signa grues atque aethera tranant
cum sonitu, fugiuntque Notos clamore secundo.
at Rutulo regi ducibusque ea mira videri
Ausoniis, donec versas ad litora puppis
respiciunt totumque adlabi classibus aequor.
270   ardet apex capiti, tristisque a vertice flamma
funditur et vastos umbo vomit aureus ignis:
non secus ac liquida si quando nocte cometae
sanguinei lugubre rubent, aut Sirius ardor

---

251 supera *R*: super *MPV*
256 ruebat *M²PR*: rubebat *P²*: *V illegible*
270 tristisque *Faernus*: cristisque *MPR* | a *M*: ac *PR*

ended, and as she departed with her right hand she drove the tall ship on, well knowing how; it speeds on over the wave, fleeter than javelin and wind-swift arrow. Then the rest quicken their speed. Marvelling, the Trojan son of Anchises is amazed, but cheers his soul with the omen. Then, looking at the vault above, he briefly prays: "Gracious lady of Ida, mother of the gods, to whom Dindymus is dear, and tower-crowned cities, and lions harnessed to your reins, be now my leader in the fight, duly prosper the omen, and attend your Phrygians, goddess, with favouring step!" So much he said; and meanwhile the returning day was rushing on with fulness of light, and had chased away the night. First he commands his comrades to follow his signals, ready their hearts for combat and fit themselves for the fray.

And now, as he stands on the high stern, he had the Trojans and his camp in view, when at once he lifted high in his left hand his blazing shield. The Dardans from the walls raise a shout to the sky; fresh hope kindles wrath; they hurl their weapons—just as below black clouds Strymonian cranes give signal, while clamorously they skim the air, and flee before the south winds with joyous cries.[14] But to the Rutulian king and the Ausonian captains these things seemed marvelous, till, looking back, they behold the shoreward-facing sterns, and the whole sea moving with the ships. On the hero's head the helmet peak blazes, and a dreadful flame streams from its top, and the shield's golden boss spouts floods of fire—just as when in the clear night comets glow blood-red and baneful; or as fiery Sirius,

[14] They are returning, at the end of winter, to their home on the Strymon.

ille sitim morbosque ferens mortalibus aegris
275 nascitur et laevo contristat lumine caelum.
   Haud tamen audaci Turno fiducia cessit
litora praecipere et venientis pellere terra.
ultro animos tollit dictis atque increpat ultro,
   "quod votis optastis adest, perfringere dextra.
280 in manibus Mars ipse, viri! nunc coniugis esto
quisque suae tectique memor, nunc magna referto
facta, patrum laudes. ultro occurramus ad undam
dum trepidi egressisque labant vestigia prima.
audentis Fortuna iuvat . . ."
285 haec ait, et secum versat quos ducere contra
vel quibus obsessos possit concredere muros.
   Interea Aeneas socios de puppibus altis
pontibus exponit. multi servare recursus
languentis pelagi et brevibus se credere saltu,
290 per remos alii. speculatus litora Tarchon,
qua vada non spirant nec fracta remurmurat unda,
sed mare inoffensum crescenti adlabitur aestu,
advertit subito proram sociosque precatur:
"nunc, o lecta manus, validis incumbite remis;
295 tollite, ferte rates, inimicam findite rostris
hanc terram, sulcumque sibi premat ipsa carina.
frangere nec tali puppim statione recuso
arrepta tellure semel." quae talia postquam
effatus Tarchon, socii consurgere tonsis
300 spumantisque rates arvis inferre Latinis,
donec rostra tenent siccum et sedere carinae
omnes innocuae. sed non puppis tua, Tarchon:

278 (= 9.127) R] *om. MP*   280 viri R: viris *MP*
281 referto *MR*: referte *P*

that bearer of drought and pestilence to feeble mortals,
rises and saddens the sky with baleful light.

But fearless Turnus did not lose his firm hope of seizing
the shore first, and driving the approaching foe from land.
*Nay, he raises their courage with his words—nay, he
chides them:* "What you have desired in your prayers is now
possible—to break through with the sword! The war god's
self is in your hands, men. Now let each be mindful of his
wife and home; now recall the great deeds, the glories of
our sires! Let us meet them at the water's edge, while they
are confused and their feet falter as first they land. Fortune
aids the daring . . ." So saying, he ponders with himself
whom to lead to the attack, and to whom he can entrust the
beleaguered walls.

Meanwhile Aeneas lands his crews from the tall ships
by gangways. Many watch for the ebb of the spent sea, and
boldly leap into the shallows; others use oars. Tarchon,
marking the shore where the shallows do not heave and
the broken billow does not roar, but the sea glides up un-
checked with spreading flow, suddenly turns his prow
thither and implores his men: "Now, chosen band, bend to
your stout oars! Raise, drive on your ships; cleave with your
beaks this hostile shore, and let the keel herself plough a
furrow. I do not shrink from shipwreck in such an anchor-
age, when once I win the land." When Tarchon has thus
spoken, his comrades rise to their oars, and drive their
foaming ships upon the Latin fields, till the beaks gain the
dry land and every hull comes to rest unscathed. But not

---

namque inflicta vadis, dorso dum pendet iniquo
anceps sustentata diu fluctusque fatigat,
305 solvitur atque viros mediis exponit in undis,
fragmina remorum quos et fluitantia transtra
impediunt retrahitque pedes simul unda relabens.
   Nec Turnum segnis retinet mora, sed rapit acer
totam aciem in Teucros et contra in litore sistit.
310 signa canunt. primus turmas invasit agrestis
Aeneas, omen pugnae, stravitque Latinos
occiso Therone, virum qui maximus ultro
Aenean petit. huic gladio perque aerea suta,
per tunicam squalentem auro latus haurit apertum.
315 inde Lichan ferit exsectum iam matre perempta
et tibi, Phoebe, sacrum: casus evadere ferri
quo licuit parvo? nec longe Cissea durum
immanemque Gyan sternentis agmina clava
deiecit leto; nihil illos Herculis arma
320 nec validae iuvere manus genitorque Melampus,
Alcidae comes usque gravis dum terra labores
praebuit. ecce Pharo, voces dum iactat inertis,
intorquens iaculum clamanti sistit in ore.
tu quoque, flaventem prima lanugine malas
325 dum sequeris Clytium infelix, nova gaudia, Cydon,
Dardania stratus dextra, securus amorum
qui iuvenum tibi semper erant, miserande iaceres,
ni fratrum stipata cohors foret obvia, Phorci
progenies, septem numero, septenaque tela
330 coniciunt; partim galea clipeoque resultant
inrita, deflexit partim stringentia corpus

---

307 pedes *MPR*: pedem *M*2   317 quo *P*2: quod *MP*: cui *R*
323 clamanti *R*: clamantis *MP*

your ship, Tarchon; for while, dashing against the shallows, she hangs upon an uneven ridge, long poised in doubtful balance, and wearies the waves, she breaks up and plunges her crew among the billows. Broken oars and floating thwarts entangle them, while the ebbing wave sucks back their feet.

Nor does dull delay hold Turnus back, but swiftly he sweeps his whole army at the Trojans, and plants it against them on the shore. The trumpets sound. First Aeneas dashed on the rustic ranks—fair omen for the fight—and laid low the Latins, slaying Theron, who in his might dared assail the hero Aeneas. Driven through the seams of bronze and through the tunic rough with gold, the sword drank from his pierced side. Next he strikes Lichas, who was cut from his dead mother's womb, and consecrated to you, Phoebus: but why was he suffered at birth to escape the peril of steel? Soon after, he cast down to death sturdy Cisseus and giant Gyas, as with clubs they laid low the ranks: the arms of Hercules did not help them, nor their stout hands and their father Melampus, Alcides' comrade all the time that earth yielded him grievous travails. Lo! as Pharus flings forth idle words, Aeneas launches his javelin and plants it in his bawling mouth. You too, hapless Cydon, while you follow your new delight, Clytius, whose cheeks are golden with early down—you would have fallen under the Dardan hand and lain, a piteous sight, forgetful of all your youthful loves, had not the serried band of your brothers met the foe—children of Phorcus, seven in number, and seven the darts they throw. Some from helmet and shield glance idly; some kindly Venus turned aside so that

alma Venus. fidum Aeneas adfatur Achaten:
"suggere tela mihi, non ullum dextera frustra
torserit in Rutulos, steterunt quae in corpore Graium
335   Iliacis campis." tum magnam corripit hastam
et iacit: illa volans clipei transverberat aera
Maeonis et thoraca simul cum pectore rumpit.
huic frater subit Alcanor fratremque ruentem
sustentat dextra: traiecto missa lacerto
340   protinus hasta fugit servatque cruenta tenorem,
dexteraque ex umero nervis moribunda pependit.
tum Numitor iaculo fratris de corpore rapto
Aenean petiit: sed non et figere contra
est licitum, magnique femur perstrinxit Achatae.
345   Hic Curibus, fidens primaevo corpore, Clausus
advenit et rigida Dryopem ferit eminus hasta
sub mentum graviter pressa, pariterque loquentis
vocem animamque rapit traiecto gutture; at ille
fronte ferit terram et crassum vomit ore cruorem.
350   tris quoque Threicios Boreae de gente suprema
et tris quos Idas pater et patria Ismara mittit,
per varios sternit casus. accurrit Halaesus
Auruncaeque manus, subit et Neptunia proles,
insignis Messapus equis. expellere tendunt
355   nunc hi, nunc illi: certatur limine in ipso
Ausoniae. magno discordes aethere venti
proelia ceu tollunt animis et viribus aequis;
non ipsi inter se, non nubila, non mare cedit;
anceps pugna diu, stant obnixa omnia contra:
360   haud aliter Troianae acies aciesque Latinae
concurrunt, haeret pede pes densusque viro vir.
     At parte ex alia, qua saxa rotantia late

they but grazed the body. Thus Aeneas speaks to loyal Achates: "Bring me plenty of weapons; my hand will hurl none at Rutulians in vain, of all that once on Ilium's plains were lodged in the bodies of Greeks." Then he seizes a great spear and hurls it; flying, it crashes through the brass of Maeon's shield, rending corslet and breast at once. His brother Alcanor comes to his aid, and with his right arm upholds his falling brother; piercing the arm, the spear flies right onward, keeping its bloody course, and the dying arm hung by the sinews from the shoulder. Then Numitor, tearing the lance from his brother's body, aimed at Aeneas, but he could not strike him in return, but grazed the thigh of great Achates.

Now comes up Clausus from Cures, trusting in his youthful frame, and from a distance smites Dryops under the chin with his stiff shaft driven with force, and piercing his throat robs him, as he speaks, of voice and life together; Dryops smites the ground with his forehead, and from his mouth vomits thick blood. Three Thracians, too, of the exalted race of Boreas, and three whom their father Idas and their native Ismarus sent forth, he lays low in divers ways. Halaesus runs to his side, and the Auruncan bands; the scion, too, of Neptune comes up, Messapus glorious with his steeds. Now these, now those, strain to thrust back the foe; on Ausonia's very threshold is the struggle. As in wide heaven warring winds rise to battle, matched in spirit and strength; they yield not to one another—not winds, not clouds, not sea; long is the battle doubtful; all things stand locked in struggle; just so clash the ranks of Troy and the ranks of Latium, foot against foot, and man pressed close against man.

But in another part, where a torrent had driven rolling

impulerat torrens arbustaque diruta ripis,
Arcadas insuetos acies inferre pedestris
365 ut vidit Pallas Latio dare terga sequaci,
aspera aquis natura loci dimittere quando
suasit equos, unum quod rebus restat egenis,
nunc prece, nunc dictis virtutem accendit amaris;
"quo fugitis, socii? per vos et fortia facta,
370 per ducis Euandri nomen devictaque bella
spemque meam, patriae quae nunc subit aemula laudi,
fidite ne pedibus. ferro rumpenda per hostis
est via. qua globus ille virum densissimus urget,
hac vos et Pallanta ducem patria alta reposcit.
375 numina nulla premunt, mortali urgemur ab hoste
mortales; totidem nobis animaeque manusque.
ecce maris magna claudit nos obice pontus,
deest iam terra fugae: pelagus Troiamne petamus?"
haec ait, et medius densos prorumpit in hostis.
380 Obvius huic primum fatis adductus iniquis
fit Lagus. hunc, magno vellit dum pondere saxum,
intorto figit telo, discrimina costis
per medium qua spina dabat, hastamque receptat
ossibus haerentem. quem non super occupat Hisbo,
385 ille quidem hoc sperans; nam Pallas ante ruentem,
dum furit, incautum crudeli morte sodalis
excipit atque ensem tumido in pulmone recondit.
hinc Sthenium petit et Rhoeti de gente vetusta
Anchemolum thalamos ausum incestare novercae.

363 impulerat *M*: intulerat *PR*
366 aquis *Madvig*: quis *MR*: quos *P*
378 petamus *PR*: petemus *M*
381 magno vellit *M*: vellit magno *PR*

boulders far and wide and bushes torn from the banks, when Pallas saw his Arcadians, unused to charge on foot, turn to flight before pursuing Latium—for the nature of the ground, roughened by waters, persuaded them for once to dismiss their horses—then, as the one hope in such straits, now with entreaties, now with bitter words, he fires their courage: "Friends, where are you running? By your brave deeds I pray you, by your King Evander's name, by the wars you have won, by my hopes now springing up to match my father's renown—trust not to flight. We must hew a way through the foe with the sword. Where the mass of men presses thickest, there your noble country calls you back, with Pallas at your head. No gods press upon us; by mortal foes are we mortals driven; we have as many lives, as many hands as they. See, the ocean hems us in with mighty barrier of sea; there is now no land for our flight; are we to make for the sea or Troy?" He speaks these words and dashes on into the midst of the serried foe.

First Lagus meets him, drawn there by unkind fate; him, while tearing at a stone of vast weight, he pierces with hurled javelin where the spine midway between the ribs made a parting, and plucks back the spear from its lodging in the bones. Nor does Hisbo surprise him by falling on him from above, hopeful though he is; for Pallas, as he rushes on, reckless and enraged over his comrade's cruel death, has welcome ready and buries his sword in his distended chest.[15] Next he assails Sthenius, and Anchemolus of Rhoetus' ancient line, who dared defile his step-

[15] I.e. swollen with rage.

390 vos etiam, gemini, Rutulis cecidistis in arvis,
Daucia, Laride Thymberque, simillima proles,
indiscreta suis gratusque parentibus error;
at nunc dura dedit vobis discrimina Pallas.
nam tibi, Thymbre, caput Euandrius abstulit ensis;
395 te decisa suum, Laride, dextera quaerit
semianimesque micant digiti ferrumque retractant.
Arcadas accensos monitu et praeclara tuentis
facta viri mixtus dolor et pudor armat in hostis.
    Tum Pallas biiugis fugientem Rhoetea praeter
400 traicit. hoc spatium tantumque morae fuit Ilo;
Ilo namque procul validam derexerat hastam,
quam medius Rhoeteus intercipit, optime Teuthra,
te fugiens fratremque Tyren, curruque volutus
caedit semianimis Rutulorum calcibus arva.
405 ac velut optato ventis aestate coortis
dispersa immittit silvis incendia pastor,
correptis subito mediis extenditur una
horrida per latos acies Volcania campos,
ille sedens victor flammas despectat ovantis:
410 non aliter socium virtus coit omnis in unum
teque iuvat, Palla. sed bellis acer Halaesus
tendit in adversos seque in sua colligit arma.
hic mactat Ladona Pheretaque Demodocumque,
Strymonio dextram fulgenti deripit ense
415 elatam in iugulum, saxo ferit ora Thoantis
ossaque dispersit cerebro permixta cruento.
fata canens silvis genitor celarat Halaesum;
ut senior leto canentia lumina solvit,
iniecere manum Parcae telisque sacrarunt

398 pudor *MP*: furor *R*

mother's bed. You twin brothers, too, fell on Rutulian plains, Larides and Thymber, sons of Daucus, most like in semblance, indistinguishable to kindred, and to their own parents a sweet perplexity. But now Pallas has made a grim difference between you. For your head, Thymber, Evander's sword swept off; while your severed hand, Larides, seeks its master, and the dying fingers twitch and clutch again at the sword. Fired by his chiding and beholding his glorious deeds, the Arcadians are armed by mingled wrath and shame to face the foe.

Then Pallas pierces Rhoeteus, as he flies past in his chariot. So much respite, so much delay Ilus gained; for at Ilus he had launched from afar his strong spear, and Rhoeteus intercepts it midway, fleeing from you, noble Teuthras, and from Tyres your brother. Rolling from the car in death, he spurns with his heels the Rutulian fields. And as in summer, when the winds he longed for have risen, some shepherd kindles fires here and there among the woods; suddenly the spaces between catch fire, and Vulcan's bristling battleline spreads unbroken over the broad fields; he, from his seat, gazes down victorious on the revelling flames: just so all your comrades' chivalry rallies to one point in aid of you, Pallas! But Halaesus, bold in war, advances to confront them, and gathers himself behind his shield. He slays Ladon, and Pheres, and Demodocus; with gleaming sword he lops off Strymonius' hand, raised against his throat; then smites Thoas in the face with a stone, and scattered the bones, mingled with blood and brains. His sire, prophetic of fate, had hidden Halaesus in the woods: when, with advance of age, he relaxed his glazing eyes in death, the Fates laid hand on Helaesus and devoted him to Evander's darts. Him Pallas

420 Euandri. quem sic Pallas petit ante precatus:
"da nunc, Thybri pater, ferro, quod missile libro,
fortunam atque viam duri per pectus Halaesi.
haec arma exuviasque viri tua quercus habebit."
audiit illa deus; dum texit Imaona Halaesus,
425 Arcadio infelix telo dat pectus inermum.
　　At non caede viri tanta perterrita Lausus,
pars ingens belli, sinit agmina: primus Abantem
oppositum interimit, pugnae nodumque moramque.
sternitur Arcadiae proles, sternuntur Etrusci
430 et vos, o Grais imperdita corpora, Teucri.
agmina concurrunt ducibusque et viribus aequis;
extremi addensent acies nec turba moveri
tela manusque sinit. hinc Pallas instat et urget,
hinc contra Lausus, nec multum discrepat aetas,
435 egregii forma, sed quîs Fortuna negarat
in patriam reditus. ipsos concurrere passus
haud tamen inter se magni regnator Olympi;
mox illos sua fata manent maiore sub hoste.
　　Interea soror alma monet succedere Lauso
440 Turnum, qui volucri curru medium secat agmen.
ut vidit socios: "tempus desistere pugnae;
solus ego in Pallanta feror, soli mihi Pallas
debetur; cuperem ipse parens spectator adesset."
haec ait, et socii cesserunt aequore iussi.
445 at Rutulum abscessu iuvenis tum iussa superba
miratus stupet in Turno corpusque per ingens

　　　432 addensent *P*: addensant *MR*
　　　441 pugnae *MP*: pugna *R*
　　　444 iussi *Aldine ed.*: iusso *MPR*

assails, first praying thus: "Grant now, father Tiber, to the steel I poise and hurl, a prosperous way through stout Halaesus' breast; your oak shall hold these weapons and the hero's spoils." The god heard the prayer; while Halaesus shielded Imaon, the luckless man offers his defenceless breast to the Arcadian lance.

But Lausus, a mighty portion of the war, does not allow his ranks to be dismayed by the hero's vast carnage: first he cuts down Abas, who faces him, the battle's knot[16] and barrier. Then falls the youth of Arcadia, the Etruscans fall, and you Trojans, whose bodies the Greeks did not destroy. The armies close, matched in captains as in might; the rearmost crowd upon the van, and the throng does not allow weapons or hands to move. Here Pallas presses and strains; there Lausus confronts him; the two were nearly matched in years, and peerless in beauty, but to them fortune had denied return to their homeland. But the king of great Olympus did not permit them to meet face to face; each has his own fate awaiting him soon beneath a greater foe.

Meanwhile his gracious sister warns Turnus to go to Lausus' aid, and with his swift chariot he cleaves the ranks between. As he saw his comrades, he cried: "It is time to stand aside from battle; I alone attack Pallas; to me alone Pallas is due; I wish that his father himself were here to see!" He said this, and his comrades withdrew from the field at his bidding. But when the Rutulians retired, then the youth, marvelling at the haughty command, stands amazed at Turnus, throws his eyes over that giant frame,

---

[16] The metaphor comes from the image of a knot in wood, difficult to cut through.

lumina volvit obitque truci procul omnia visu,
talibus et dictis it contra dicta tyranni:
"aut spoliis ego iam raptis laudabor opimis
450 aut leto insigni: sorti pater aequus utrique est.
tolle minas." fatus medium procedit in aequor;
frigidus Arcadibus coit in praecordia sanguis.
desiluit Turnus biiugis, pedes apparat ire
comminus; utque leo, specula cum vidit ab alta
455 stare procul campis meditantem in proelia taurum,
advolat, haud alia est Turni venientis imago.
hunc ubi contiguum missae fore credidit hastae,
ire prior Pallas, si qua fors adiuvet ausum
viribus imparibus, magnumque ita ad aethera fatur:
460 "per patris hospitium et mensas, quas advena adisti,
MR te precor, Alcide, coeptis ingentibus adsis.
cernat semineci sibi me rapere arma cruenta
victoremque ferant morientia lumina Turni."
audiit Alcides iuvenem magnumque sub imo
465 corde premit gemitum lacrimasque effundit inanis.
tum genitor natum dictis adfatur amicis:
"stat sua cuique dies, breve et inreparabile tempus
omnibus est vitae; sed famam extendere factis,
hoc virtutis opus. Troiae sub moenibus altis
470 tot gnati cecidere deum, quin occidit una
Sarpedon, mea progenies; etiam sua Turnum
fata vocant metasque dati pervenit ad aevi."
sic ait, atque oculos Rutulorum reicit arvis.
    At Pallas magnis emittit viribus hastam
475 vaginaque cava fulgentem deripit ensem.

<hr />

455 in *MR*: *om. P*
475 deripit γ*R*: diripit *M*

and with fierce glance scans all from afar, then with these words answers the monarch's words: "Soon I shall win praise either for kingly spoils or for a glorious death; my sire is equal to either fate: away with your threats!" So saying, he advances to the middle of the field: cold blood gathers at the hearts of the Arcadians. Down from his chariot leapt Turnus; he makes ready to close with the other on foot. And as, when from some lofty outlook a lion has seen a bull stand far off on the plain, meditating battle, on he rushes, no different seemed the coming of Turnus. But Pallas, when he thought his foe within range of a spearcast, moved forward first, in the hope that chance would aid the venture of his ill-matched strength, and thus to great heaven he cries: "By my father's welcome, and the table to which you came as a stranger, I beseech you, Alcides, aid my great enterprise. May Turnus see me strip the bloody arms from his dying limbs, and may his glazing eyes endure a conqueror!" Alcides heard the youth, and deep in his heart stifled a heavy groan, and shed useless tears. Then with kindly words the Father addresses his son:[17] "Each has his day appointed; short and irretrievable is the span of life for all: but to lengthen fame by deeds— that is valour's task. Under Troy's high walls fell those many sons of gods; indeed, with them fell my own child Sarpedon.[18] For Turnus too his own fate calls, and he has reached the goal of his allotted years." So he speaks, and turns his eyes away from the Rutulian fields.

But Pallas hurls his spear with all his strength and plucks his flashing sword from its hollow scabbard. On flies

---

[17] Hercules was son of Jupiter by Alcmena.
[18] Cf. Homer, *Iliad* 16.477f.

illa volans umeri surgunt qua tegmina summa
incidit, atque viam clipei molita per oras
tandem etiam magno strinxit de corpore Turni.
hic Turnus ferro praefixum robur acuto
480 in Pallanta diu librans iacit atque ita fatur:
"aspice num mage sit nostrum penetrabile telum."
dixerat; at clipeum, tot ferri terga, tot aeris,
quem pellis totiens obeat circumdata tauri,
vibranti cuspis medium transverberat ictu
485 loricaeque moras et pectus perforat ingens.
ille rapit calidum frustra de vulnere telum:
una eademque via sanguis animusque sequuntur.
corruit in vulnus (sonitum super arma dedere)
et terram hostilem moriens petit ore cruento.
490 quem Turnus super adsistens . . .
"Arcades, haec" inquit "memores mea dicta referte
Euandro: qualem meruit, Pallanta remitto.
quisquis honos tumuli, quidquid solamen humandi est,
largior. haud illi stabunt Aeneïa parvo
495 hospitia." et laevo pressit pede talia fatus
exanimem rapiens immania pondera baltei
impressumque nefas: una sub nocte iugali
caesa manus iuvenum foede thalamique cruenti,
quae Clonus Eurytides multo caelaverat auro;
500 quo nunc Turnus ovat spolio gaudetque potitus.
nescia mens hominum fati sortisque futurae
et servare modum rebus sublata secundis!
Turno tempus erit magno cum optaverit emptum

484 cuspis medium *M*: medium cuspis *γR*
486 vulnere *M*: corpore (744) *γ*: pectore *R*
490 *Mγ give as an unfinished line*: sic ore profatur *add. R*

the shaft and strikes where the top of the mail rises to guard the shoulder; then, forcing a way through the shield's rim, at last even grazed the mighty frame of Turnus. At this, Turnus, long poising his oaken shaft tipped with sharp steel, hurls it against Pallas, speaking thus: "See whether my weapon is not sharper!" He had spoken; and with quivering stroke the point tears through the centre of the shield, with all its plates of iron, all its plates of bronze, all the bull hide's overlaying folds; then pierces the corslet's barrier and the mighty breast. In vain he plucks the warm dart from the wound; by one and the same road follow blood and life. He falls prone upon the wound, his armour clashes over him, and, dying, he smites the hostile earth with blood-stained mouth. Then standing over him Turnus cries: "Arcadians, give heed, and bear these words of mine back to Evander: I send him back Pallas as he has deserved to receive him.[19] Whatever honour a tomb gives, whatever solace a burial, I freely grant; but his welcome of Aeneas shall cost him dear." So saying, with his left foot he trod upon the dead man, tearing away the belt's huge weight and the story of the crime engraved on it[20]—the youthful band foully slain on one nuptial night, and the chambers drenched with blood—which Clonus, son of Eurytus, had richly chased in gold. Now Turnus exults in the spoil, and glories in the winning. O mind of man, knowing not fate or coming doom or how to keep bounds when uplifted with favouring fortune! To Turnus shall come the hour when for

[19] I.e. dead. Evander has earned or merited this affliction, by reason of his treason to Italy.

[20] The story of the murder of the sons of Aegyptus by the daughters of Danaus.

intactum Pallanta, et cum spolia ista diemque
505 oderit. at socii multo gemitu lacrimisque
impositum scuto referunt Pallanta frequentes.
o dolor atque decus magnum rediture parenti,
haec te prima dies bello dedit, haec eadem aufert,
MPR cum tamen ingentis Rutulorum linquis acervos!
510   Nec iam fama mali tanti, sed certior auctor
advolat Aeneae tenui discrimine leti
esse suos, tempus versis succurrere Teucris.
proxima quaeque metit gladio latumque per agmen
ardens limitem agit ferro, te, Turne, superbum
515 caede nova quaerens. Pallas, Euandrus, in ipsis
omnia sunt oculis, mensae quas advena primas
tunc adiit, dextraeque datae. Sulmone creatos
quattuor hic iuvenes, totidem quos educat Ufens,
viventis rapit, inferias quos immolet umbris
520 captivoque rogi perfundat sanguine flammas.
inde Mago procul infensam contenderat hastam:
ille astu subit, at tremibunda supervolat hasta,
et genua amplectens effatur talia supplex:
"per patrios manis et spes surgentis Iuli
525 te precor, hanc animam serves gnatoque patrique.
est domus alta, iacent penitus defossa talenta
caelati argenti, sunt auri pondera facti
infectique mihi. non hic victoria Teucrum
vertitur aut anima una dabit discrimina tanta."
530 dixerat. Aeneas contra cui talia reddit:
"argenti atque auri memoras quae multa talenta
gnatis parce tuis. belli commercia Turnus
sustulit ista prior iam tum Pallante perempto.

515 Euandrus *Bentley*: Euander *MγR, Servius Auctus*

a great price he will long to have bought an unscathed Pallas, and when he will abhor those spoils and that day. But with many moans and tears his friends throng round Pallas and bear him back lying on his shield. O you who will go home as a great grief and yet great glory to your father, this day first gave you to war, this also takes you from it, the day when yet you leave behind vast piles of Rutulian dead!

And now no mere rumour of the bitter blow but a surer messenger flies to Aeneas—that his men are but a hair's breadth removed from death, that it is time to succour the routed Teucrians. With the sword he mows down all the nearest ranks, and fiercely drives a broad path through the host with the steel, seeking you, Turnus, still flushed with fresh slaughter. Pallas, Evander, everything is before his eyes—the board to which he came then, a stranger, and the right hands pledged. Then four youths, sons of Sulmo, and as many reared by Ufens, he takes alive, to offer as victims to the dead and to sprinkle the funeral flame with captive blood. Next at Magus from a distance he had aimed the hostile lance. Deftly he cowers—the lance flies quivering over him—and, clasping the hero's knees, he speaks thus in supplication: "By the spirit of your father, by your hope in growing Iülus, I entreat you, save my life for a son and for a father. I have a lofty house; buried deep inside lie talents of chased silver, and I have masses of gold, wrought and unwrought. Not on me does the victory of Troy turn, nor will one life make a difference so great." He spoke, and Aeneas thus replied: "Those many talents of silver and gold that you tell of, keep them for your sons. Such trafficking in war Turnus put away before now, even at the time when

521 contenderat *MP*: contorserat *R*

hoc patris Anchisae manes, hoc sentit Iulus."
535   sic fatus galeam laeva tenet atque reflexa
cervice orantis capulo tenus applicat ensem.
nec procul Haemonides, Phoebi Triviaeque sacerdos,
infula cui sacra redimibat tempora vitta,
totus conlucens veste atque insignibus albis.
540   quem congressus agit campo, lapsumque superstans
immolat ingentique umbra tegit, arma Serestus
lecta refert umeris tibi, rex Gradive, tropaeum.
    Instaurant acies Volcani stirpe creatus
Caeculus et veniens Marsorum montibus Umbro.
545   Dardanides contra furit: Anxuris ense sinistram
et totum clipei terrae deiecerat orbem
(dixerat ille aliquid magnum vimque adfore verbo
crediderat, caeloque animum fortasse ferebat
MPRV   canitiemque sibi et longos promiserat annos);
550   Tarquitus exsultans contra fulgentibus armis,
silvicolae Fauno Dryope quem nympha crearat,
obvius ardenti sese obtulit. ille reducta
loricam clipeique ingens onus impedit hasta,
tum caput orantis nequiquam et multa parantis
555   dicere deturbat terrae, truncumque tepentem
provolvens super haec inimico pectore fatur:
"istic nunc, metuende, iace. non te optima mater
condet humi patrioque onerabit membra sepulcro:
alitibus linquere feris, aut gurgite mersum
560   unda feret piscesque impasti vulnera lambent."
protinus Antaeum et Lucam, prima agmina Turni,

---

[536] orantis *MR*: oranti *P*   [539] albis (*P?*), *Probus*: armis
MP²R   [546] terrae *Jasper*: ferro *MPR*   [558] humi *MPR*:
humo *M²* | patrioque *M*: patriove PR (*V illegible*)

Pallas was slain. Thus judges my father Anchises' spirit, thus Iülus." So speaking, he grasps the helmet with his left hand and, bending back the suppliant's neck, drives the sword in up to the hilt. Close by was Haemon's son, priest of Phoebus and Trivia, his temples wreathed in the fillet's sacred band, all glittering in his white robe and armour. Him Aeneas meets and drives over the plain; then, bestriding the fallen man, slaughters him and wraps him in mighty darkness; his armour Serestus gathers and carries away on his shoulders, a trophy, King Gradivus, for you!

Caeculus, born of Vulcan's race, and Umbro, who comes from the Marsian hills, repair the ranks. The Dardan storms against them. His sword had felled Anxur's left arm to the ground with the whole circle of his shield— he had uttered some brave vaunt and thought his hand would match his word, and perhaps he was raising his spirit and had promised himself white-haired old age and length of years—when, in the pride of gleaming arms, Tarquitus, whom the Nymph Dryope had borne to silvan Faunus, crossed his fiery course. Drawing back his spear, he pins the corslet and the shield's huge burden together; then, as the youth vainly pleaded and tried to say many a word, he strikes his head to the ground and, as he spurns the trunk, still warm, speaks these words over him from his pitiless heart: "Lie there now, terrible man! No loving mother shall lay you in the earth, nor weigh down your limbs with an ancestral tomb. You will be left for the birds of prey; or, sunk beneath the flood, the wave will carry you along, and hungry fish will lick your wounds." Next he overtakes Antaeus and Lucas, foremost of Turnus' ranks, and brave Numa,

persequitur, fortemque Numam fulvumque Camertem,
magnanimo Volcente satum, ditissimus agri
qui fuit Ausonidum et tacitis regnavit Amyclis.
565 Aegaeon qualis, centum cui bracchia dicunt
centenasque manus, quinquaginta oribus ignem
pectoribusque arsisse, Iovis cum fulmina contra
tot paribus streperet clipeis, tot stringeret ensis:
sic toto Aeneas desaevit in aequore victor
570 ut semel intepuit mucro. quin ecce Niphaei
quadriiugis in equos adversaque pectora tendit.
atque illi longe gradientem et dira frementem
ut videre, metu versi retroque ruentes
effunduntque ducem rapiuntque ad litora currus.
MPR   Interea biiugis infert se Lucagus albis
576 in medios fraterque Liger; sed frater habenis
flectit equos, strictum rotat acer Lucagus ensem.
haud tulit Aeneas tanto fervore furentis;
inruit adversaque ingens apparuit hasta.
580 cui Liger . . .
"non Diomedis equos nec currum cernis Achilli
aut Phrygiae campos: nunc belli finis et aevi
his dabitur terris." vesano talia late
dicta volant Ligeri. sed non et Troïus heros
585 dicta parat contra, iaculum nam torquet in hostis.
Lucagus ut pronus pendens in verbera telo
admonuit biiugos, proiecto dum pede laevo
aptat se pugnae, subit oras hasta per imas
fulgentis clipei, tum laevum perforat inguen;
590 excussus curru moribundus volvitur arvis.
quem pius Aeneas dictis adfatur amaris:
"Lucage, nulla tuos currus fuga segnis equorum

and tawny Camers, son of noble Volcens, who was wealthiest in the land of the Ausonians, and reigned over silent Amyclae. Like Aegaeon, who, men say, had a hundred arms and a hundred hands, and flashed fire from fifty mouths and breasts, when against Jove's thunders he clanged with as many like shields, and bared as many swords;[21] so Aeneas over the whole plain gluts his victorious rage, when once his sword grew warm. Now see! he makes for Niphaeus' four-horse chariot and the chests that faced him; when they saw his long strides and deadly rage, in terror they turn and rush backward, flinging forth their master and dragging the chariot to the shore.

Meanwhile, with their two white steeds, Lucagus and Liger his brother dash into the fray; but the brother guides the horses with the reins, while Lucagus fiercely brandishes his drawn sword. Aeneas could not brook their furious onset, but rushed upon them, and towered gigantic with his opposing spear. To him Liger . . . : "It is not Diomedes' horses that you see, nor Achilles' car, nor the plains of Phrygia; now you will find an end of your warfare and your life in this land." Such words fly abroad from mad Liger's lips. But not in words does the Trojan hero shape a reply, for he hurls his javelin against the foe. Then, as Lucagus, leaning forward to the stroke, urged on his steeds with the sword, while with left foot advanced he prepares for the fray, the spear comes through the lowest rim of his gleaming shield, then pierces the left groin; tumbling from the chariot, he rolls dying on the ground while loyal Aeneas addresses him with bitter words: "Lucagus, it is not a cowardly flight by your horses that betrayed your chariot;

[21] I.e. fifty shields, all alike, and fifty swords.

prodidit aut vanae vertere ex hostibus umbrae:
ipse rotis saliens iuga deseris." haec ita fatus
595 arripuit biiugos; frater tendebat inertis
infelix palmas curru delapsus eodem:
"per te, per qui te talem genuere parentes,
vir Troiane, sine hanc animam et miserere precantis."
pluribus oranti Aeneas: "haud talia dudum
600 dicta dabas. morere et fratrem ne desere frater."
tum latebras animae pectus mucrone recludit.
talia per campos edebat funera ductor
Dardanius torrentis aquae vel turbinis atri
more furens. tandem erumpunt et castra relinquunt
605 Ascanius puer et nequiquam obsessa iuventus.
    Iunonem interea compellat Iuppiter ultro:
"o germana mihi atque eadem gratissima coniunx,
ut rebare, Venus (nec te sententia fallit)
Troianas sustentat opes, non vivida bello
610 dextra viris animusque ferox patiensque pericli."
cui Iuno summissa: "quid, o pulcherrime coniunx,
sollicitas aegram et tua tristia iussa timentem?
si mihi, quae quondam fuerat quamque esse decebat,
vis in amore foret, non hoc mihi namque negares,
615 omnipotens, quin et pugnae subducere Turnum
et Dauno possem incolumem servare parenti.
nunc pereat Teucrisque pio det sanguine poenas.
ille tamen nostra deducit origine nomen
Pilumnusque illi quartus pater, et tua larga
620 saepe manu multisque oneravit limina donis."
cui rex aetherii breviter sic fatur Olympi:
"si mora praesentis leti tempusque caduco

612 iussa *M*: dicta *PR*

and it is not the empty shadow from a foe that has turned them back; it is you yourself, leaping from the wheels, who forsakes your beasts." So saying, he seized the horses; as he slid down from the same chariot, his brother piteously outstretched his helpless hands: "By yourself, by the parents who gave life to such a son, hero of Troy, spare this life, and have pity on my prayer!" As he continued to plead, Aeneas said: "Not such were your words before. Die, and let not brother forsake brother!" Then with the sword he cleft open his breast, where life lies hidden. Such were the deaths the Dardan chieftain wrought over the plains, raging like a brook in torrent or a black tempest. At last the boy Ascanius and the warriors besieged in vain break out and leave the camp.

Meanwhile Jupiter of his own will addresses Juno: "O you who are both sister and dearest wife to me, it is Venus, as you supposed—your judgment is not wrong—who upholds the Trojan power, not their own right hands quick for war and their proud souls patient of peril." To him Juno speaks meekly: "Why, my fairest lord, do you vex my sick heart, that fears your stern commands? Had my love the force that once it had, and still should have, this boon surely you would not deny me—the power to withdraw Turnus from the fray, and preserve him in safety for his father Daunus. But now let him perish and with innocent blood make atonement to the Trojans! Yet from our lineage he derives his name, for Pilumnus was his sire four generations gone; and often he has heaped your threshold with many a gift from a lavish hand." To her the king of heavenly Olympus thus briefly spoke: "If your prayer is for a respite

oratur iuveni meque hoc ita ponere sentis,
tolle fuga Turnum atque instantibus eripe fatis:
625 hactenus indulsisse vacat. sin altior istis
sub precibus venia ulla latet totumque moveri
mutarive putas bellum, spes pascis inanis."
et Iuno adlacrimans: "quid si, quae voce gravaris,
mente dares atque haec Turno rata vita maneret?
630 nunc manet insontem gravis exitus, aut ego veri
vana feror. quod ut o potius formidine falsa
ludar, et in melius tua, qui potes, orsa reflectas!"
    Haec ubi dicta dedit, caelo se protinus alto
misit agens hiemem nimbo succincta per auras,
635 Iliacamque aciem et Laurentia castra petivit.
tum dea nube cava tenuem sine viribus umbram
in faciem Aeneae (visu mirabile monstrum)
Dardaniis ornat telis, clipeumque iubasque
divini adsimulat capitis, dat inania verba,
640 dat sine mente sonum gressusque effingit euntis,
morte obita qualis fama est volitare figuras
aut quae sopitos deludunt somnia sensus.
at primas laeta ante acies exsultat imago
inritatque virum telis et voce lacessit.
645 instat cui Turnus stridentemque eminus hastam
conicit; illa dato vertit vestigia tergo.
tum vero Aenean aversum ut cedere Turnus
credidit atque animo spem turbidus hausit inanem:
"quo fugis, Aenea? thalamos ne desere pactos;
650 hac dabitur dextra tellus quaesita per undas."
talia vociferans sequitur strictumque coruscat

from present death, and a reprieve for the doomed youth—if you understand that such is my will, take Turnus away in flight, and snatch him from impending fate. Thus far there is room for indulgence. But if thought of deeper favour lurks beneath your prayers, and you think that the war's whole course may be moved or altered, you are nursing an idle hope." And Juno weeping: "What if your heart were to grant what your tongue begrudges, and this life I crave were to remain assured to Turnus? Now a heavy doom awaits him for no guilt, or I wander empty of truth. O may I rather be mocked by my lying fears, and you, who can, bend your purposes to a better end!"

When she had spoken these words, she darted at once from high heaven through the air, driving her storm chariot and girdled in cloud, and sought the army of Ilium and the camp of Laurentum. Then the goddess from hollow mist fashions a thin, strengthless phantom in the likeness of Aeneas, a monstrous marvel to behold, decks it with Dardan weapons, and counterfeits the shield and plumes on his godlike head, gives it unreal words, gives a voice without thought, and mimics his gait as he moves; like shapes that flit, it is said, after death or like dreams that mock the slumbering senses. But the phantom stalks exultant in front of the foremost ranks, provokes the foe with weapons, and with cries defies him. Turnus rushes at it, and from afar hurls a hissing spear; the phantom wheels round in flight. Then indeed, when Turnus thought that Aeneas had turned and yielded, and drank this empty hope into his confused mind, he cried: "Where are you fleeing, Aeneas? Forsake not your plighted marriage; this hand of mine will give you the land you have sought over the seas." With such clamour he chases him and brandishes his

mucronem, nec ferre videt sua gaudia ventos.
    Forte ratis celsi coniuncta crepidine saxi
expositis stabat scalis et ponte parato,
655 qua rex Clusinis advectus Osinius oris.
huc sese trepida Aeneae fugientis imago
conicit in latebras, nec Turnus segnior instat
exsuperatque moras et pontis transilit altos.
vix proram attigerat, rumpit Saturnia funem
660 avulsamque rapit revoluta per aequora navem.
663 tum levis haud ultra latebras iam quaerit imago,
664 sed sublime volans nubi se immiscuit atrae.
661 illum autem Aeneas absentem in proelia poscit;
662 obvia multa virum demittit corpora morti,
665 cum Turnum medio interea fert aequore turbo.
respicit ignarus rerum ingratusque salutis
et duplicis cum voce manus ad sidera tendit:
"omnipotens genitor, tanton me crimine dignum
duxisti et talis voluisti expendere poenas?
670 quo feror? unde abii? quae me fuga quemve reducit?
Laurentisne iterum muros aut castra videbo?
quid manus illa virum, qui me meaque arma secuti?
quosne (nefas) omnis infanda in morte reliqui
et nunc palantis video, gemitumque cadentum
675 accipio? quid ago? aut quae iam satis ima dehiscat
terra mihi? vos o potius miserescite, venti;
in rupes, in saxa (volens vos Turnus adoro)
ferte ratem saevisque vadis immittite syrtis,
quo nec me Rutuli nec conscia fama sequatur."

663–4 *after* 660 χ, *Brunck: after* 662 *MPR*   661 illum *M*:
ille *PR* | Aeneas *M*: Aenean *PR*   668 tanton *MR*: tanto *P*
673 quosne *b, Asper cited by Servius:* quosque *MR:* quosve *M2P*

naked blade; he does not see that the winds are carrying his triumph away.

It chanced that, moored to the ledge of a lofty rock, with ladders let down and gangway ready, stood the ship in which king Osinius sailed from the coasts of Clusium. Hither the hurrying phantom of flying Aeneas flings itself into shelter; and with no less speed Turnus follows, surmounts all hindrances, and springs across the lofty bridge. Scarce had he touched the prow when Saturn's daughter snaps the cable and sweeps the ship, torn from its moorings, over the ebbing waters. Then the airy phantom seeks shelter no longer, but soaring aloft blends with a dark cloud. But meantime Aeneas is challenging his absent foe to battle, and sends down to death many bodies of warriors who cross his path, while the gale carries Turnus over mid ocean. Unknowing of the truth and unthankful for escape, he looks back and raises his voice and clasped hands to heaven: "Almighty Father, did you think me worthy of so much reproach, and is it your will that I pay such a penalty? Whither am I bound? Where have I come from? What flight withdraws me, and in what guise? Shall I look again on the camp or walls of Laurentium? What of that band of warriors who followed me and my standard? One and all— Oh, the shame!—I have left them in the jaws of a cruel death, and now I see them scattered and hear their groans as they fall. What shall I do? What earth could now gape deep enough for me? Rather, you winds take pity on me! On rock, on reef drive the ship—from my heart I, Turnus, implore you—and cast it on some sandbank's ruthless shoal, where neither Rutuli nor Rumour that knows my

680 haec memorans animo nunc huc, nunc fluctuat illuc,
an sese mucrone ob tantum dedecus amens
induat et crudum per costas exigat ensem,
fluctibus an iaciat mediis et litora nando
curva petat Teucrumque iterum se reddat in arma.
685 ter conatus utramque viam, ter maxima Iuno
continuit iuvenemque animi miserata repressit.
labitur alta secans fluctuque aestuque secundo
et patris antiquam Dauni defertur ad urbem.
   At Iovis interea monitis Mezentius ardens
690 succedit pugnae Teucrosque invadit ovantis.
concurrunt Tyrrhenae acies atque omnibus uni,
uni odiisque viro telisque frequentibus instant.
ille (velut rupes vastum quae prodit in aequor,
obvia ventorum furiis expostaque ponto,
695 vim cunctam atque minas perfert caelique marisque
ipsa immota manens) prolem Dolichaonis Hebrum
sternit humi, cum quo Latagum Palmumque fugacem,
sed Latagum saxo atque ingenti fragmine montis
occupat os faciemque adversam, poplite Palmum
700 succiso volvi segnem sinit, armaque Lauso
donat habere umeris et vertice figere cristas.
nec non Euanthen Phrygium Paridisque Mimanta
aequalem comitemque, una quem nocte Theano
in lucem genitore Amyco dedit et face praegnas
705 Cisseis regina Parin; Paris urbe paterna
occubat, ignarum Laurens habet ora Mimanta.
ac velut ille canum morsu de montibus altis

704 genitore *Bentley*: genitori *MPR*
705 Paris *Bentley*: creat *MPR*

shame may follow!" So saying, he wavers in spirit this way and that, whether because of disgrace so foul he should in madness throw himself on his sword and drive the cruel steel through his ribs, or plunge into the waves, and gain the winding shore by swimming, and once more cast himself against the Trojan arms. Thrice he tried each way; thrice mighty Juno stayed his hand and held him back in pity of heart. On he glides, cleaving the deep, with wave and tide to speed him, and is borne home to his father Daunus' ancient city.[22]

But meanwhile at Jove's behest fiery Mezentius takes up the battle and attacks the triumphant Teucrians. The Tyrrhene ranks rush together, and press on him alone with all their hatred, on him alone with all their ceaseless weapons. Like a cliff that juts into the vast deep, exposed to the raving winds and braving the main, that endures all the stress, all the menace of sky and sea, itself fixed unshaken—so he lays low on earth Hebrus, son of Dolichaon, and with him Latagus and Palmus, swift of foot; but Latagus he smites suddenly full in the mouth and face with a huge fragment of mountain rock, while Palmus he hamstrings, and leaves him slowly writhing; his armour he gives Lausus to wear upon his shoulders, and his plumes to fix upon his crest. Evanthes too, the Phrygian, and Mimas, comrade of Paris and his peer in age, whom Theano bore, his father being Amycus, on the very night that Cisseus' royal daughter, pregnant with a firebrand,[23] gave birth to Paris: Paris sleeps in the city of his fathers; Mimas, unknown, rests on the Laurentine shore. And just as a boar, driven by sharp-toothed hounds from mountain heights,

[22] Ardea in Latium.   [23] See 7.319f., with note.

actus aper, multos Vesulus quem pinifer annos
defendit multosque palus Laurentia silva
710 pascit harundinea, postquam inter retia ventum est,
substitit infremuitque ferox et inhorruit armos,
nec cuiquam irasci propiusve accedere virtus,
sed iaculis tutisque procul clamoribus instant;
717 ille autem impavidus partis cunctatur in omnis
718 dentibus infrendens et tergo decutit hastas:
714 haud aliter, iustae quibus est Mezentius irae,
non ulli est animus stricto concurrere ferro,
missilibus longe et vasto clamore lacessunt.
719   Venerat antiquis Corythi de finibus Acron,
720 Graius homo, infectos linquens profugus hymenaeos.
hunc ubi miscentem longe media agmina vidit,
purpureum pennis et pactae coniugis ostro,
impastus stabula alta leo ceu saepe peragrans
(suadet enim vesana fames), si forte fugacem
725 conspexit capream aut surgentem in cornua cervum,
gaudet hians immane comasque arrexit et haeret
visceribus super incumbens; lavit improba taeter
ora cruor . . .
sic ruit in densos alacer Mezentius hostis.
730 sternitur infelix Acron et calcibus atram
tundit humum exspirans infractaque tela cruentat.
MPRV atque idem fugientem haud est dignatus Oroden
sternere nec iacta caecum dare cuspide vulnus;
obvius adversoque occurrit seque viro vir
735 contulit, haud furto melior sed fortibus armis.

---

710 pascit *Bentley*: pastus *MPR*   712 propiusve *MR*:
propiusque *P*   717–8 *after* 713 (*omitted by homoeoteleuton* . . .
instant . . . hastas) *Scaliger*: *after* 716 *MPR*

one which pine-crowned Vesulus has sheltered for many years, or one which for many years the Laurentine marsh pastures on thick-growing reeds, when it reaches the nets, halts, snorts savagely, and raises its hackles, and no one is brave enough to rage or come near it, but all at safe distance assail it with darts and shouts, but undaunted it halts, turning in all directions with gnashing teeth, and shakes the javelins from its back—just so, of all those who had righteous hatred of Mezentius, none had heart to meet him with drawn sword; from a distance they provoke him with missiles and far-echoing shouts.

There had come from the ancient bounds of Corythus Acron, a Greek, an exile leaving a marriage incomplete. When Mezentius saw him far off, dealing havoc among the ranks, bright in crimson plumes and the bright purple of his plighted bride, just as often an unfed lion, ranging the deep coverts—for maddening hunger prompts him—if by chance he spies a timorous roe or stately antlered stag, exults with mouth terribly agape, bristles his mane, and clings crouching over the flesh, his cruel mouth bathed in foul gore . . . so Mezentius leaps eagerly upon the massed foemen. Down goes hapless Acron, hammers the black ground with his heels as he breathes his last, and dyes the broken spear with blood. And the same arm did not deign to lay Orodes low as he fled, nor to give an unseen wound with a spear cast; full face to face he ran to meet him and opposed him man against man, prevailing not by stealth but by strength of weapons. Then, planting his foot on the

---

[727] incumbens (5.858) *M*: accumbens *PR*, *Macrobius*

tum super abiectum posito pede nixus et hasta:
"pars belli haud temnenda, viri, iacet altus Orodes."
conclamant socii laetum paeana secuti;
ille autem exspirans: "non me, quicumque es, inulto,
740 victor, nec longum laetabere; te quoque fata
prospectant paria atque eadem mox arva tenebis."
ad quem subridens mixta Mezentius ira:
"nunc morere. ast de me divum pater atque hominum rex
viderit." hoc dicens eduxit corpore telum.
745 olli dura quies oculos et ferreus urget
somnus, in aeternam clauduntur lumina noctem.
    Caedicus Alcathoum obtruncat, Sacrator Hydaspen
Partheniumque Rapo et praedurum viribus Orsen,
Messapus Cloniumque Lycaoniumque Erichaeten,
750 illum infrenis equi lapsu tellure iacentem,
hunc peditem. pedes et Lycius processerat Agis,
quem tamen haud expers Valerus virtutis avitae
deicit; at Thronium Salius Saliumque Nealces,
insignis iaculo et longe fallente sagitta.
755   Iam gravis aequabat luctus et mutua Mavors
funera; caedebant pariter pariterque ruebant
victores victique, neque his fuga nota neque illis.
di Iovis in tectis iram miserantur inanem
MPR amborum et tantos mortalibus esse labores;
760 hinc Venus, hinc contra spectat Saturnia Iuno.
pallida Tisiphone media inter milia saevit.
    At vero ingentem quatiens Mezentius hastam
turbidus ingreditur campo. quam magnus Orion,
cum pedes incedit medii per maxima Nerei

742 ad quem *R*: atqu(a)e *MPV*   745–6 = 12.309–10
754 insignis *M*: insidiis *PRV*

fallen foe and straining at his spear, he cries, "See, men! Low lies great Orodes—no mean portion of the war!" His comrades join their shouts with his, taking up the joyous cry of triumph. But, breathing his last, Orodes says: "Not unavenged shall I be, my conqueror, whoever you are, nor will you long exult; for a like doom keeps watch for you too, and in these same fields you will soon lie." Mezentius answered him, smiling in his wrath: "Now die; but as for me let the father of gods and king of men look to it!" So saying, he drew the weapon from the hero's body; stern repose and iron slumber press upon his eyes, and their light closes into everlasting night.

Caedicus slaughters Alcathous, Sacrator Hydaspes, Rapo Parthenius, and Orses of wondrous strength; Messapus slays Clonius and Ericetes, Lycaon's son—the one as he lay on the ground, fallen from his unbridled steed, the other as he came on foot. On foot too Lycian Agis had advanced; but Valerus, lacking none of his ancestors' prowess, struck him down; Thronius was killed by Salius, and Salius by Nealces, famed for the javelin and the arrow that surprises from a distance.

Now the heavy hand of Mars was dealing out equal woe and mutual death. Alike they slew and alike they fell—victors and vanquished, and neither these nor those knew flight. The gods in Jove's halls pity the useless rage of both armies, and grieve that mortals should endure such toils. Here Venus looks on, there, facing her, Saturnian Juno; pale Tisiphone rages among the thousands of men.

But now Mezentius, brandishing his mighty spear, advances like a whirlwind on the plain. Great as Orion, when cleaving a path he stalks on foot through the vast pools of

765 stagna viam scindens, umero supereminet undas,
 aut summis referens annosam montibus ornum
 ingrediturque solo et caput inter nubila condit,
 talis se vastis infert Mezentius armis.
 hunc contra Aeneas speculatus in agmine longe
770 obvius ire parat. manet imperterritus ille
 hostem magnanimum opperiens, et mole sua stat;
 atque oculis spatium emensus quantum satis hastae:
 "dextra mihi deus et telum, quod missile libro,
 nunc adsint! voveo praedonis corpore raptis
775 indutum spoliis ipsum te, Lause, tropaeum
 Aeneae." dixit, stridentemque eminus hastam
 iecit. at illa volans clipeo est excussa proculque
 egregium Antoren latus inter et ilia figit,
 Herculis Antoren comitem, qui missus ab Argis
780 haeserat Euandro atque Itala consederat urbe.
 sternitur infelix alieno vulnere, caelumque
 aspicit et dulcis moriens reminiscitur Argos.
 tum pius Aeneas hastam iacit; illa per orbem
 aere cavum triplici, per linea terga tribusque
785 transiit intextum tauris opus, imaque sedit
 inguine, sed viris haud pertulit. ocius ensem
 Aeneas viso Tyrrheni sanguine laetus
 eripit a femine et trepidanti fervidus instat.
 ingemuit cari graviter genitoris amore,
790 ut vidit, Lausus, lacrimaeque per ora volutae—
 hic mortis durae casum tuaque optima facta,
 si qua fidem tanto est operi latura vetustas,
 non equidem nec te, iuvenis memorande, silebo—

769 hunc *M*: huc *P*: huic *R* | longe *R*: longo *MP*
791 optima *MP*: optime *R*

mid-ocean, towers with his shoulder above the waves, or, carrying off an aged ash from mountain heights, walks the ground with head hidden in the clouds: like him Mezentius strode in his giant armour. On the other side Aeneas, spying him far off in the battleline, moves to meet him. He stands his ground undaunted, awaiting his noble foe, and steadfast in his bulk; then, with eye measuring the distance that would suffice his spear, he says: "May this right hand, my deity, and the hurtling weapon I poise, now aid me! I vow you, Lausus, your very self, clad in spoils stripped from the robber's corpse, as my trophy over Aeneas."[24] He spoke, and threw from far his whistling spear; as it flew, it glanced from the shield, and pierces noble Antores nearby between side and flank—Antores, comrade of Hercules, who, sent from Argos, had joined Evander, and settled in an Italian town. He falls, unlucky man, by a wound meant for another, and gazes on the sky and, dying, dreams of his sweet Argos. Then loyal Aeneas casts a spear; through the hollow shield of threefold bronze, through the layers of linen and the inwoven work of triple bull hides, it sped, and lodged low in the groin; but it did not drive its force home. Quickly Aeneas, gladdened by the sight of the Tuscan's blood, snatches his sword from the thigh and presses eagerly on his confused foe. Deeply Lausus groaned for love of his dear father, when he saw the sight, and tears rolled down his face—and here the fate of cruel death and your most glorious deeds (if at all antiquity can win belief in such prowess) I will not leave unsung, nor you yourself,

---

[24] Instead of the usual trunk of wood, hung with the arms of the vanquished foe, the living Lausus, clothed in the armour of Aeneas, is to be his trophy.

ille pedem referens et inutilis inque ligatus
795 cedebat clipeoque inimicum hastile trahebat.
proripuit iuvenis seseque immiscuit armis,
iamque adsurgentis dextra plagamque ferentis
Aeneae subiit mucronem ipsumque morando
sustinuit; socii magno clamore sequuntur,
800 dum genitor nati parma protectus abiret,
telaque coniciunt perturbantque eminus hostem
missilibus. furit Aeneas tectusque tenet se.
ac velut effusa si quando grandine nimbi
praecipitant, omnis campis diffugit arator
805 omnis et agricola, et tuta latet arce viator
aut amnis ripis aut alti fornice saxi,
dum pluit in terris, ut possint sole reducto
exercere diem: sic obrutus undique telis
Aeneas nubem belli, dum detonet omnis,
810 sustinet et Lausum increpitat Lausoque minatur:
"quo moriture ruis maioraque viribus audes?
fallit te incautum pietas tua." nec minus ille
exsultat demens, saevae iamque altius irae
Dardanio surgunt ductori, extremaque Lauso
815 Parcae fila legunt. validum namque exigit ensem
per medium Aeneas iuvenem totumque recondit;
transiit et parmam mucro, levia arma minacis,
et tunicam molli mater quam neverat auro,
implevitque sinum sanguis; tum vita per auras
820 concessit maesta ad Manis corpusque reliquit.
    At vero ut vultum vidit morientis et ora,
ora modis Anchisiades pallentia miris,
ingemuit miserans graviter dextramque tetendit,

796 proripuit *M*: prorupit *PR*

228

young man, so worthy to be sung!—the father, disabled
and encumbered, was now giving ground with retreating
steps, trailing from his shield his foeman's lance. The youth
dashed forward and plunged into the fray; and just as
Aeneas' hand rose to deal a blow, he caught up the hero's
point and checked him by this delay. His comrades follow
with loud cries, until the father, guarded by his son's shield,
could withdraw; and showering their javelins beat back the
foe with missiles from a distance. Aeneas rages but keeps
himself under shelter. And as, when at times storm clouds
pour down in showers of hail, every ploughman, every hus-
bandman flees the fields, and the wayfarer cowers in a safe
stronghold, a river's bank or a vault of lofty rock, while the
rain falls upon the lands, so that, when the sun returns,
they may pursue the day's task: just so, overwhelmed by
javelins on all sides, Aeneas endures the war cloud until all
its thunder is spent, while he chides Lausus and threatens
Lausus: "Where are you rushing to death, with your daring
beyond your strength? Your love is betraying you into rash-
ness." But none the less the youth rages insanely; now
fierce wrath rises higher in the Dardan leader's heart, and
the Fates gather up Lausus' last threads; for Aeneas drives
the sword sheer through the youth's body, and buries it to
the hilt. The point pierced the targe—frail armour for one
so threatening—and the tunic his mother had woven him
of pliant gold; blood filled his breast, then through the air
the life fled sorrowing to the Shades, and left the body.

But when Anchises' son saw the look on that dying
face—that face so strangely pale—he groaned heavily in
pity, and stretched out his hand, as the likeness of his own

<hr/>

815 fila *MR*: lina *P*

et mentem patriae subiit pietatis imago.
825 "quid tibi nunc, miserande puer, pro laudibus istis,
quid pius Aeneas tanta dabit indole dignum?
arma, quibus laetatus, habe tua; teque parentum
manibus et cineri, si qua est ea cura, remitto.
hoc tamen infelix miseram solabere mortem:
830 Aeneae magni dextra cadis." increpat ultro
cunctantis socios et terra sublevat ipsum
sanguine turpantem comptos de more capillos.
    Interea genitor Tiberini ad fluminis undam
vulnera siccabat lymphis corpusque levabat
835 arboris acclinis trunco. procul aerea ramis
dependet galea et prato gravia arma quiescunt.
stant lecti circum iuvenes; ipse aeger anhelans
colla fovet fusus propexam in pectora barbam;
multa super Lauso rogitat, multumque remittit
840 qui revocent maestique ferant mandata parentis.
at Lausum socii exanimem super arma ferebant
flentes, ingentem atque ingenti vulnere victum.
agnovit longe gemitum praesaga mali mens.
canitiem multo deformat pulvere et ambas
845 ad caelum tendit palmas et corpore inhaeret.
"tantane me tenuit vivendi, nate, voluptas,
ut pro me hostili paterer succedere dextrae,
quem genui? tuane haec genitor per vulnera servor
morte tua vivens? heu, nunc misero mihi demum
850 exilium infelix, nunc alte vulnus adactum!
idem ego, nate, tuum maculavi crimine nomen,
pulsus ob invidiam solio sceptrisque paternis.

824 subiit *P*: subit *R*: strinxit (9.294) *M*
850 exilium *P, Servius*: exitium *MR*

love for his father entered his heart. "What now, unhappy boy, will loyal Aeneas give you in recognition of these glorious deeds of yours? What reward worthy of such a heart? Keep for your own the arms in which you delighted; and if you care at all for this, I return you to the spirits and ashes of your forebears. This at least, unhappy man, will console you for your sad death: you fall by the hand of great Aeneas." Further, he chides his laggard comrades and raises their chief from the ground, where he was befouling his ordered locks with blood.

Meanwhile by the wave of the Tiber river, the father staunched his wounds with water, and rested his reclining frame against the trunk of a tree. Nearby his bronze helmet hangs from the boughs, and his heavy weapons lie in peace on the meadow. Chosen men stand round; he himself, sick and panting, eases his neck, while over his chest streams his flowing beard. Many a time he asks for Lausus, and many a time he sends messengers to recall him, and convey the orders of his grieving father. But his weeping comrades were bearing Lausus lifeless on his armour—a mighty man and laid low by a mighty wound. The ill-boding heart knew their wail from far off. He defiles his hoary hair with dust, raises both hands to heaven, and clings to the body: "My son, did such joy of life possess me that in my stead I let you meet the foeman's sword—you whom I begot? Am I, your father, saved by these wounds of yours, alive through your death? Alas! now at last I know, wretch that I am, the bitterness of exile; now my wound is driven deep! I myself, my son, have stained your name with guilt—I, driven in loathing from the throne and sceptre of

debueram patriae poenas odiisque meorum:
omnis per mortis animam sontem ipse dedissem!
855 nunc vivo neque adhuc homines lucemque relinquo.
sed linquam." simul hoc dicens attollit in aegrum
se femur et, quamquam vis alto vulnere tardat,
haud deiectus equum duci iubet. hoc decus illi,
hoc solamen erat, bellis hoc victor abibat
860 omnibus. adloquitur maerentem et talibus infit:
"Rhaebe, diu, res si qua diu mortalibus ulla est,
viximus. aut hodie victor spolia illa cruenta
et caput Aeneae referes Lausique dolorum
ultor eris mecum, aut, aperit si nulla viam vis,
865 occumbes pariter; neque enim, fortissime, credo,
iussa aliena pati et dominos dignabere Teucros."
dixit, et exceptus tergo consueta locavit
membra manusque ambas iaculis oneravit acutis,
aere caput fulgens cristaque hirsutus equina.
870 sic cursum in medios rapidus dedit. aestuat ingens
uno in corde pudor mixtoque insania luctu.
873   Atque hic Aenean magna ter voce vocavit.
Aeneas agnovit enim laetusque precatur:
875 "sic pater ille deum faciat, sic altus Apollo!
incipias conferre manum . . ."
tantum effatus et infesta subit obvius hasta.
ille autem: "quid me erepto, saevissime, nato
terres? haec via sola fuit qua perdere posses:
880 nec mortem horremus nec divum parcimus ulli.
desine, nam venio moriturus et haec tibi porto
dona prius." dixit, telumque intorsit in hostem;

862 cruenta *P²*: cruenti *MPR*
872 = 12.668 (χ)] *om. MPR*

232

my fathers. Long have I owed my punishment to my country and my people's hate; by any form of death I would myself have yielded up my guilty life. Now I live on, and do not yet leave the light of day and mankind; but leave I will." And as he speaks he raises himself on his stricken thigh and, though his force flags from the deep wound, yet, undismayed, he bids his horse be brought. This was his pride, this his solace; on this he rode victorious from every battle. He addresses the grieving beast and accosts it thus: "Rhaebus, we have lived long, if anything lasts long for mortals. Today you will either carry away in victory those bloody spoils and the head of Aeneas, and with me avenge the sufferings of Lausus, or, if no force opens a way, you will die with me; for you, gallant steed, will not deign, I think, to endure a stranger's orders and a Trojan lord!" He spoke and, mounting the beast, settled his limbs as was his wont, and burdened each hand with sharp javelins, his head glittering with bronze and bristling with horsehair plume. Thus he swiftly dashed into the fray. In that single heart surges a vast tide of shame and madness mingled with grief.

And now thrice in loud tones he called Aeneas. Aeneas knew the call, and offers joyful prayer: "So may the great father of the gods grant it, so Apollo on high! Let you begin the combat! . . ." So much said, he moves forward to meet him with levelled spear. But he speaks: "Why seek to frighten me, fierce foe, now that my son is taken? This was the only way in which you could destroy me. We do not shrink from death, nor do we heed any of the gods. Cease; for I come to die, first bringing these gifts." He spoke, and

inde aliud super atque aliud figitque volatque
ingenti gyro, sed sustinet aureus umbo.
885 ter circum astantem laevos equitavit in orbis
tela manu iaciens, ter secum Troïus heros
immanem aerato circumfert tegmine silvam.
inde ubi tot traxisse moras, tot spicula taedet
vellere, et urgetur pugna congressus iniqua,
890 multa movens animo iam tandem erumpit et inter
bellatoris equi cava tempora conicit hastam.
tollit se arrectum quadripes et calcibus auras
verberat, effusumque equitem super ipse secutus
implicat eiectoque incumbit cernuus armo.
895 clamore incendunt caelum Troesque Latinique.
advolat Aeneas vaginaque eripit ensem
et super haec: "ubi nunc Mezentius acer et illa
effera vis animi?" contra Tyrrhenus, ut auras
suspiciens hausit caelum mentemque recepit:
900 "hostis amare, quid increpitas mortemque minaris?
nullum in caede nefas, nec sic ad proelia veni,
nec tecum meus haec pepigit mihi foedera Lausus.
unum hoc per si qua est victis venia hostibus oro:
corpus humo patiare tegi. scio acerba meorum
905 circumstare odia: hunc, oro, defende furorem
et me consortem nati concede sepulcro."
haec loquitur, iuguloque haud inscius accipit ensem
undantique animam diffundit in arma cruore.

---

883 figitque *R*: fugitque *MP*

hurled a javelin at his foe; then plants another and yet another, wheeling in wide circle; but the boss of gold withstands them. Thrice round his watchful foe he rode, turning to the left and launching darts from his hand; thrice the Trojan hero bears round with him the dreadful growth of spears upon his bronze shield. Then, weary of dragging out so many delays, of plucking out so many weapons, and hard pressed in the unequal fray, at last with much pondering at heart, he bursts out and hurls his lance full between the war horse's hollow temples. The steed rears up, lashes the air with its feet, then throws the rider and itself coming down from above, entangles him; then falls on him in headlong plunge, and with shoulder out of joint. Trojans and Latins set heaven aflame with their cries. Aeneas rushes up, tears his sword from the scabbard, and standing over him cries: "Where now is bold Mezentius, and that wild fierceness of soul?" In answer the Tuscan said, as with eyes raised to the air he drank in the heaven and regained his senses: "Bitter foe, why do you taunt me and threaten me with death? It is no sin to slay me; not on such terms did I come to battle, nor is such the pact my Lausus pledged between me and you. This alone I ask, by whatever grace a vanquished foe may claim: let my body to be laid in earth. I know that my people's fierce hatred besets me. Guard me, I pray, from their fury, and grant me fellowship with my son in the tomb." So he speaks, and, unfaltering, welcomes the sword to his throat, and pours forth his life over his armour in streams of blood.

LIBER XI

MPR Oceanum interea surgens Aurora reliquit:
Aeneas, quamquam et sociis dare tempus humandis
praecipitant curae turbataque funere mens est,
vota deum primo victor solvebat Eoo.[1]
5   ingentem quercum decisis undique ramis
constituit tumulo fulgentiaque induit arma,
Mezenti ducis exuvias, tibi magne tropaeum
bellipotens; aptat rorantis sanguine cristas
telaque trunca viri, et bis sex thoraca petitum
10 perfossumque locis, clipeumque ex aere sinistrae
subligat atque ensem collo suspendit eburnum.
tum socios (namque omnis eum stipata tegebat
turba ducum) sic incipiens hortatur ovantis:
     "Maxima res effecta, viri; timor omnis abesto,
15 quod superest; haec sunt spolia et de rege superbo
primitiae manibusque meis Mezentius hic est.
nunc iter ad regem nobis murosque Latinos.
arma parate animis, et spe praesumite bellum,
ne qua mora ignaros, ubi primum vellere signa
20 adnuerint superi pubemque educere castris,

     [1] = 4.129

_____

     [1] Aeneas has two duties to perform, to bury the dead and to

236

BOOK XI

Meanwhile dawn rose and left the ocean. Aeneas, though his sorrows urge him to give time to his comrades' burial, and death has confused his soul, yet, as the Day Star rose, began to pay the gods his vows of victory.[1] A mighty oak, its branches lopped all round, he plants on a mound, and arrays in the gleaming arms stripped from Mezentius the chief, a trophy to you, great Lord of War.[2] To it he fastens the crests dripping with blood, the warrior's broken spears, and the breastplate smitten and pierced twice six times; to the left hand he binds the bronze shield, and from the neck hangs the ivory sword. Then his triumphant comrades—for the whole band of chieftains thronged close about him—he thus begins to exhort:

"Mighty deeds have we wrought, my men; for the future, away with all fear! These are the spoils and firstfruits of a haughty king; and this is Mezentius, as fashioned by my hands. Now we must march to Latium's king and walls. Prepare your weapons with courage and with your hopes anticipate the war, so that when the gods above grant us to raise our standards and lead out the army from the camp

pay his vow. The latter he attends to first, according to Roman ritual; his inclination would have led him to bury his comrades first.

[2] In the trophy here described, the tree trunk represents the body of the vanquished foe.

impediat segnisve metu sententia tardet.
interea socios inhumataque corpora terrae
mandemus, qui solus honos Acheronte sub imo est.
ite," ait "egregias animas, quae sanguine nobis
25   hanc patriam peperere suo, decorate supremis
muneribus, maestamque Euandri primus ad urbem
mittatur Pallas, quem non virtutis egentem
abstulit atra dies et funere mersit acerbo."
    Sic ait inlacrimans, recipitque ad limina gressum
30   corpus ubi exanimi positum Pallantis Acoetes
servabat senior, qui Parrhasio Euandro
armiger ante fuit, sed non felicibus aeque
tum comes auspiciis caro datus ibat alumno.
circum omnis famulumque manus Troianaque turba
35   et maestum Iliades crinem de more solutae.
ut vero Aeneas foribus sese intulit altis
ingentem gemitum tunsis ad sidera tollunt
pectoribus, maestoque immugit regia luctu.
ipse caput nivei fultum Pallantis et ora
40   ut vidit levique patens in pectore vulnus
cuspidis Ausoniae, lacrimis ita fatur obortis:
"tene," inquit "miserande puer, cum laeta veniret,
invidit Fortuna mihi, ne regna videres
nostra neque ad sedes victor veherere paternas?
45   non haec Euandro de te promissa parenti
discedens dederam, cum me complexus euntem
mitteret in magnum imperium metuensque moneret
acris esse viros, cum dura proelia gente.
et nunc ille quidem spe multum captus inani

---

21 segnisve *MR*: segnisque *P*   23 imo est *M*: *om.* est *PR*
28 = 6.429   30 exanimi *P*: exanimis *R*: exanime *M*

no delay may impede us, taken unawares, or faltering purpose retard us through fear. Meanwhile let us commit to earth the unburied bodies of our comrades—their only honour in the depths of Acheron. Go," he continues, "grace with the last rites those noble souls who with their blood have won for us this our country; and first to Evander's mourning city let Pallas be sent, whom, though he did not lack courage, the black day swept away and plunged in bitter death."

So he speaks weeping, and retraces his steps to the threshold where Pallas' lifeless body was laid, watched by old Acoetes, who in former time was armour bearer to Parrhasian Evander, but now with less happy auspices went as appointed guardian to his beloved foster-child. Around stood all the attendant train and Trojan throng, with the Ilian women, their hair unbound for mourning according to custom. But when Aeneas entered the lofty portal, they smote their breasts and raised a mighty wail to the stars, and the royal dwelling rang with their sorrowful lamentation. He, when he saw the pillowed head and face of Pallas, snowy-white, and, on his smooth breast, the gaping wound from an Ausonian spear, speaks thus, amid welling tears: "Was it you, unhappy boy, that Fortune begrudged me in her happy hour, so that you would not look upon my realm, nor ride triumphant to your father's home? Not this was the parting promise about you that I gave your father Evander, when he embraced me as I went, and sent me forth to win great empire, but warned me in fear that valiant were the men and hardy the race we confronted. And now he, much beguiled by vain hope, is

50 fors et vota facit cumulatque altaria donis,
   nos iuvenem exanimum et nil iam caelestibus ullis
   debentem vano maesti comitamur honore.
   infelix, nati funus crudele videbis!
   hi nostri reditus, exspectatique triumphi?
55 haec mea magna fides? at non, Euandre, pudendis
   vulneribus pulsum aspicies, nec sospite dirum
   optabis nato funus pater. ei mihi quantum
   praesidium, Ausonia, et quantum tu perdis, Iule!"
      Haec ubi deflevit, tolli miserabile corpus
60 imperat, et toto lectos ex agmine mittit
   mille viros qui supremum comitentur honorem
   intersintque patris lacrimis, solacia luctus
   exigua ingentis, misero sed debita patri.
   haud segnes alii cratis et molle feretrum
65 arbuteis texunt virgis et vimine querno
   exstructosque toros obtentu frondis inumbrant.
   hic iuvenem agresti sublimem stramine ponunt:
   qualem virgineo demessum pollice florem
   seu mollis violae seu languentis hyacinthi,
70 cui neque fulgor adhuc nec dum sua forma recessit,
   non iam mater alit tellus virisque ministrat.
   tum geminas vestis auroque ostroque rigentis
   extulit Aeneas, quas illi laeta laborum
   ipsa suis quondam manibus Sidonia Dido
75 fecerat et tenui telas discreverat auro.
   harum unam iuveni supremum maestus honorem
   induit arsurasque comas obnubit amictu,
   multaque praeterea Laurentis praemia pugnae
   aggerat et longo praedam iubet ordine duci;

60 agmine *M*: ordine (7.152) *PR*   75 = 4.264

perhaps offering vows and heaping the altars high with gifts; we in sorrow attend with empty rites the lifeless son, who owes no more to any gods of heaven. Unhappy man, you will see the bitter funeral of your son! Is this our return, our awaited triumph? Is this my sure pledge? But your eyes, Evander, will not look on your son routed with shameful wounds nor will you, his father, pray for a death accursed because your son is alive. Ah me! how great a protection is lost to you, Ausonia, how great a one to you, Iülus!"

His lamentation ended, he bids them raise the piteous corpse, and sends a thousand men chosen from his whole army to attend the last rite and share the father's tears—scant solace for grief so vast, but owed to a father's sorrow. Others in haste plait the wicker frame of a soft bier with arbute shoots and oaken twigs, and shroud the high-piled couch with a leafy canopy. Here they lay the youth high on his rustic bed, like a flower culled by a girl's finger, tender violet or drooping hyacinth, whose sheen and native grace have not yet faded, but no more does its mother earth give it strength and nurture. Then Aeneas brought forth two robes, stiff with gold and purple, which Sidonian Dido, delighting in the toil, had once herself with her own hands wrought for him, interweaving the web with threads of gold. Of these he sadly drapes one round the youth as a last honour, and in its covering veils those locks that the fire will claim; and as well he heaps up many a prize from the Laurentine fray,[3] and bids that the spoils be borne in a long

[3] The Latin forces led by Turnus included the Laurentes, whose capital was Lavinium.

241

80 addit equos et tela quibus spoliaverat hostem.
   vinxerat et post terga manus, quos mitteret umbris
   inferias, caeso sparsurus sanguine flammas,
   indutosque iubet truncos hostilibus armis
   ipsos ferre duces inimicaque nomina figi.
85 ducitur infelix aevo confectus Acoetes,
   pectora nunc foedans pugnis, nunc unguibus ora,
   sternitur et toto proiectus corpore terrae;
   ducunt et Rutulo perfusos sanguine currus.
   post bellator equus positis insignibus Aethon
90 it lacrimans guttisque umectat grandibus ora.
   hastam alii galeamque ferunt, nam cetera Turnus
   victor habet. tum maesta phalanx Teucrique sequuntur
   Tyrrhenique omnes et versis Arcades armis.
   postquam omnis longe comitum praecesserat ordo,
95 substitit Aeneas gemituque haec addidit alto:
   "nos alias hinc ad lacrimas eadem horrida belli
   fata vocant: salve aeternum mihi, maxime Palla,
   aeternumque vale." nec plura effatus ad altos
   tendebat muros gressumque in castra ferebat.
100   Iamque oratores aderant ex urbe Latina
   velati ramis oleae veniamque rogantes:
   corpora, per campos ferro quae fusa iacebant,
   redderet ac tumulo sineret succedere terrae;
   nullum cum victis certamen et aethere cassis;
105 parceret hospitibus quondam socerisque vocatis.

82 flammas *MP*: flammam *R*
93 omnes *MP*: duces *R*
95 addidit *MP*: edidit *R*
101 rogantes *MP*: precantes *R*

train; then he adds the horses and armour of which he had
stripped the foe. He had bound behind their backs the
hands of those whom he meant to send as offerings to the
Shades, sprinkling the flames with the blood of the slain.
He bids the chiefs themselves bear tree trunks draped in
hostile weapons with the foemen's names affixed. Hapless
Acoetes, worn out with years, is led along, marring now his
breast with clenched fists, now his face with nails, and he
falls full-length on the ground. Chariots too they lead,
bespattered with Rutulian blood. Behind, the war-steed
Aethon, his trappings laid aside, goes weeping, and big
drops wet his face.[4] Others carry the spear and helmet:
for all else Turnus, as victor, holds. Then follows a mourn-
ful host—the Teucrians, and all the Tuscans and the
Arcadians with arms reversed. When all the retinue of his
comrades had advanced far ahead, Aeneas halted, and
with deep sigh spoke this word more: "The same grim
destiny of war summons me hence to other tears: hail for
evermore, noblest Pallas, and for evermore farewell!" And
without further words he turned to the lofty walls and bent
his steps towards the camp.

And now came envoys from the Latin city, shaded with
olive boughs and asking for truce; the bodies that lay
strewn by the sword all over the plain they prayed him to
return and allow to rest beneath a mound of earth. There
can be, they plead, no quarrel with vanquished men, bereft
of the light of heaven; let him spare men who were once
called hosts and fathers of their brides![5] To them good

[4] Cf. *Iliad* 17.426ff., where the horses of Achilles weep.

[5] Latinus had promised his daughter to Aeneas, and perhaps
similar alliances were arranged.

quos bonus Aeneas haud aspernanda precantis
prosequitur venia et verbis haec insuper addit:
"quaenam vos tanto fortuna indigna, Latini,
implicuit bello, qui nos fugiatis amicos?
110 pacem me exanimis et Martis sorte peremptis
oratis? equidem et vivis concedere vellem.
nec veni, nisi fata locum sedemque dedissent,
nec bellum cum gente gero; rex nostra reliquit
hospitia et Turni potius se credidit armis.
115 aequius huic Turnum fuerat se opponere morti.
si bellum finire manu, si pellere Teucros
apparat, his mecum decuit concurrere telis:
vixet cui vitam deus aut sua dextra dedisset.
nunc ite et miseris supponite civibus ignem."
120 dixerat Aeneas. illi obstipuere silentes
conversique oculos inter se atque ora tenebant.
    Tum senior semperque odiis et crimine Drances
infensus iuveni Turno sic ore vicissim
orsa refert: "o fama ingens, ingentior armis,
125 vir Troiane, quibus caelo te laudibus aequem?
iustitiaene prius mirer belline laborum?
nos vero haec patriam grati referemus ad urbem
et te, si qua viam dederit Fortuna, Latino
iungemus regi. quaerat sibi foedera Turnus.
130 quin et fatalis murorum attollere moles
saxaque subvectare umeris Troiana iuvabit."
dixerat haec unoque omnes eadem ore fremebant.
bis senos pepigere dies, et pace sequestra
per silvas Teucri mixtique impune Latini

118 sua *MR*: cui *P*
126 iustitiaene *P*: iustitiane *MR* | laborum *MP*: laborem *R*

Aeneas courteously grants the prayer he could not spurn, and adds these words besides: "What undeserved chance, Latins, has entangled you in so terrible a war, that you fly from us your friends? Do you ask me peace for the dead slain by the lot of battle? Gladly would I grant it to the living too. I would not have come, had not fate assigned me here a place and home, nor do I wage war with your people: it is your king who forsook our alliance and preferred to trust himself to Turnus' sword. It would have been juster for Turnus to face this death. If he seeks to end the war by force, if he seeks to drive out the Trojans, he should have fought against me with these weapons: the one of us would have lived to whom heaven or his own right hand had granted life. Now go, and kindle the fire beneath your hapless countrymen." Aeneas ceased; they stood dumb in silence, and kept their eyes and faces turned on one another.

Then aged Drances, who always pursued youthful Turnus with hate and calumny, thus speaks in reply: "Hero of Troy, great in glory, greater in arms, how may I extol you to the sky with my praises? Am I to marvel first at your justice or at your toils in war? We indeed will gratefully bear these words back to our native city and, if fortune grants a way, will unite you with Latinus our king. Let Turnus seek alliances for himself! It will rather be our delight to rear those massive walls which your destiny ordains, and to bear on our shoulders the stones of Troy." He had spoken, and all with one voice murmured assent. For twice six days they made truce, and, with peace interposing, Teucrians and Latins roamed unharmed over the forest heights

135 erravere iugis. ferro sonat alta bipenni
 fraxinus, evertunt actas ad sidera pinus,
 robora nec cuneis et olentem scindere cedrum
 nec plaustris cessant vectare gementibus ornos.
  Et iam Fama volans, tanti praenuntia luctus,
140 Euandrum Euandrique domos et moenia replet,
 quae modo victorem Latio Pallanta ferebat.
 Arcades ad portas ruere et de more vetusto
 funereas rapuere faces; lucet via longo
 ordine flammarum et late discriminat agros.
145 contra turba Phrygum veniens plangentia iungit
 agmina. quae postquam matres succedere tectis
 viderunt, maestam incendunt clamoribus urbem.
 at non Euandrum potis est vis ulla tenere,
 sed venit in medios. feretro Pallanta reposto
150 procubuit super atque haeret lacrimansque gemensque,
 et via vix tandem voci laxata dolore est:
 "non haec, o Palla, dederas promissa parenti,
 cautius ut saevo velles te credere Marti.
 haud ignarus eram quantum nova gloria in armis
155 et praedulce decus primo certamine posset.
 primitiae iuvenis miserae bellique propinqui
 dura rudimenta, et nulli exaudita deorum
 vota precesque meae! tuque, o sanctissima coniunx,
 felix morte tua neque in hunc servata dolorem!
160 contra ego vivendo vici mea fata, superstes
 restarem ut genitor. Troum socia arma secutum
 obruerent Rutuli telis! animam ipse dedissem
 atque haec pompa domum me, non Pallanta, referret!

149 Pallanta M²: Pallante MPR
151 voci PR: vocis P²: voces M

246

together. The lofty ash rings under the two-edged axe; they lay low star-towering pines, and ceaselessly their wedges cleave oak and fragrant cedar, and groaning wagons convey the mountain ash.

And now Rumour in her flight, heralding this piercing woe, fills Evander's ears, his palace and his city— Rumour that but now was proclaiming the triumph of Pallas to the dwellers in Latium. The Arcadians hurry to the gates, having after ancient custom snatched up torches for the funeral. The road gleams with a long procession of flames, which stretches like a broad boundary line across the fields. Meeting them, the Trojan column unites with theirs its company of mourners. When the women saw them approach their homes, their shrieks set the city ablaze with grief. But no restraint can hold Evander back: he rushes into their midst and, as soon as the bier is set down, flings himself on Pallas, clinging to him amid tears and groans, till scarce at last does choking grief allow a path for speech: "Not this, my Pallas, was the promise you gave your father, that you would with caution entrust yourself to the savage god of war. Well did I know the spell upon the young of glory in arms and how passing sweet is honour won in the maiden fight. Alas for the bitter first fruits of your youth and your harsh schooling in a war so close to home! Alas for my prayers and entreaties, to which no god gave ear! And you, Queen of blessed memory, happy were you in the death that saved you from this sorrow! I on the other hand by living on have outpassed my destiny, a father left to survive his son. Would that I had marched with the allied standards of Troy and had fallen beneath the enemy's fire! Would that I had given up my own life, and this cortege were bringing me, not Pallas, home! Yet I

nec vos arguerim, Teucri, nec foedera nec quas
165 iunximus hospitio dextras: sors ista senectae
debita erat nostrae. quod si immatura manebat
mors gnatum, caesis Volscorum milibus ante
ducentem in Latium Teucros cecidisse iuvabit.
quin ego non alio digner te funere, Palla,
170 quam pius Aeneas et quam magni Phryges et quam
Tyrrhenique duces, Tyrrhenum exercitus omnis.
magna tropaea ferunt quos dat tua dextera leto;
tu quoque nunc stares immanis truncus in armis,
esset par aetas et idem si robur ab annis,
175 Turne. sed infelix Teucros quid demoror armis?
vadite et haec memores regi mandata referte:
quod vitam moror invisam Pallante perempto,
dextera causa tua est, Turnum gnatoque patrique
quam debere vides. meritis vacat hic tibi solus
180 fortunaeque locus. non vitae gaudia quaero
(nec fas), sed gnato manis perferre sub imos."
    Aurora interea miseris mortalibus almam
extulerat lucem, referens opera atque labores:
iam pater Aeneas, iam curvo in litore Tarchon
185 constituere pyras. huc corpora quisque suorum
more tulere patrum, subiectisque ignibus atris
conditur in tenebras altum caligine caelum.
ter circum accensos cincti fulgentibus armis
decurrere rogos, ter maestum funeris ignem
190 lustravere in equis ululatusque ore dedere.
spargitur et tellus lacrimis, sparguntur et arma,
it caelo clamorque virum clangorque tubarum.

173 armis *MPR, not to be altered*: arvis *Bentley*

would not blame you, Trojans, nor our covenant, nor the hands we clasped in friendship: this fate was owed to my gray hairs. But if untimely death awaited my son, it will be my joy that, after slaying Volscian thousands, he fell leading the Trojans into Latium! Indeed, Pallas, I could think you worthy of no other death than loyal Aeneas does, than the mighty Phrygians, than the Tyrrhene captains, and all the Tyrrhenian host. Great are the trophies those men bring, to whom your hand deals death;[6] you, too, Turnus, would now be standing, a monstrous trunk arrayed in arms, had your age and strength of years been like his! But why do I, poor wretch, stay the Teucrians from conflict? Go, and forget not to bear this message to your king: if I drag on a life that is hateful now that Pallas is slain, the reason is your right hand, which you know owes Turnus to son and to father. That field alone is open for your merits and your fortune. I ask not for joy in life—that cannot be—but to bear the word to my son in the shades below."

Meanwhile Dawn had lifted up her kindly light for weary men, recalling them to task and toil. Now father Aeneas, now Tarchon, had set up pyres on the winding shore. Here, after the fashion of their fathers, they each brought the bodies of their kin, and as the murky fires are lit beneath, high heaven is veiled in the gloom of darkness. Thrice, girt in glittering armour, they ran their course round the blazing piles; thrice on horseback they circled the mournful funeral-fire and uttered the cries of wailing. Tears stream on earth, and stream on armour; cries of men and blare of trumpets mount to heaven. And now some

---

[6] The slain warriors themselves are said to bring the trophies Pallas can display.

hic alii spolia occisis derepta Latinis
coniciunt igni, galeas ensisque decoros
195 frenaque ferventisque rotas; pars munera nota,
ipsorum clipeos et non felicia tela.
multa boum circa mactantur corpora Morti,
saetigerosque sues raptasque ex omnibus agris
in flammam iugulant pecudes. tum litore toto
200 ardentis spectant socios semustaque servant
busta, neque avelli possunt, nox umida donec
invertit caelum stellis ardentibus aptum.

   Nec minus et miseri diversa in parte Latini
innumeras struxere pyras, et corpora partim
205 multa virum terrae infodiunt, avectaque partim
finitimos tollunt in agros urbique remittunt.
cetera confusaeque ingentem caedis acervum
nec numero nec honore cremant; tunc undique vasti
certatim crebris conlucent ignibus agri.
210 tertia lux gelidam caelo dimoverat umbram:
maerentes altum cinerem et confusa ruebant
ossa focis tepidoque onerabant aggere terrae.
iam vero in tectis, praedivitis urbe Latini,
praecipuus fragor et longi pars maxima luctus.
215 hic matres miseraeque nurus, hic cara sororum
pectora maerentum puerique parentibus orbi
dirum exsecrantur bellum Turnique hymenaeos;
ipsum armis ipsumque iubent decernere ferro,
qui regnum Italiae et primos sibi poscat honores.
220 ingravat haec saevus Drances solumque vocari
testatur, solum posci in certamina Turnum.

    [202] ardentibus *MP* (4.482, 6.797): fulgentibus *R* (*because of*
ardentis 200)

fling on the fire spoils stripped from slain Latins, helmets and handsome swords, bridles and scorching wheels; others, offerings familiar to the dead—their own shields and luckless weapons. Around, many cattle are sacrificed to Death; bristly swine and animals seized from all the country are slaughtered over the flames. Then, all along the shore, they watch their comrades burning, and keep guard above the charred pyres, and they cannot tear themselves away till dewy night rolls round the heaven, inset with gleaming stars.

No less, elsewhere, do the hapless Latins build pyres innumerable. Of their many dead, some they bury in the earth, some they lift up and carry to the neighbouring fields or send home to the city; the rest, a mighty mass of indistinguishable slaughter, they burn uncounted and unhonoured: then on all sides the broad fields compete with their clusters of fire. The third dawn had withdrawn chill darkness from the sky; mournfully they stirred from the pyres the bones mingled with thick ash, and heaped above them a warm mound of earth. But inside the walls, in the city of rich Latinus, is the chief uproar and most of the prolonged wailing. Here mothers and their sons' unhappy brides, here the loving hearts of sorrowing sisters, and boys bereft of their fathers, curse the dreadful war and Turnus' marriage: "He, he himself," they cry, "should decide the issue by arms and the sword, he who claims for himself the realm of Italy and foremost honours." Fierce Drances weights the scale, and bears witness that Turnus alone is called, alone is summoned to battle. At the same time,

---

[220] haec *MR*: et *P*

multa simul contra variis sententia dictis
pro Turno, et magnum reginae nomen obumbrat,
multa virum meritis sustentat fama tropaeis.
225   Hos inter motus, medio in flagrante tumultu,
ecce super maesti magna Diomedis ab urbe
legati responsa ferunt: nihil omnibus actum
tantorum impensis operum, nil dona neque aurum
nec magnas valuisse preces, alia arma Latinis
230 quaerenda, aut pacem Troiano ab rege petendum.
deficit ingenti luctu rex ipse Latinus:
fatalem Aenean manifesto numine ferri
admonet ira deum tumulique ante ora recentes.
ergo concilium magnum primosque suorum
235 imperio accitos alta intra limina cogit.
olli convenere fluuntque ad regia plenis
tecta viis. sedet in mediis et maximus aevo
et primus sceptris haud laeta fronte Latinus.
atque hic legatos Aetola ex urbe remissos
240 quae referant fari iubet, et responsa reposcit
ordine cuncta suo. tum facta silentia linguis,
et Venulus dicto parens ita farier infit:
    "Vidimus, o cives, Diomedem Argivaque castra,
atque iter emensi casus superavimus omnis,
245 contigimusque manum qua concidit Ilia tellus.
ille urbem Argyripam patriae cognomine gentis
victor Gargani condebat Iapygis agris.
postquam introgressi et coram data copia fandi,
munera praeferimus, nomen patriamque docemus,
250 qui bellum intulerint, quae causa attraxerit Arpos.

230 petendum *Servius*: petendam *MPR*
236 fluunt *PR*: ruunt *M*

opposed to them, many an opinion in varied phrase speaks for Turnus; the queen's great name is his shelter, and many a tale with well-won trophies supports the hero.

Amid this stir, at the fiery turmoil's height, lo! to crown everything, gloomy envoys bring the answer from Diomedes' great city: nothing has been gained at cost of so much toil; nothing have their gifts of gold or strong prayers achieved: Latium must seek other arms or sue for peace to the Trojan king. Beneath his weight of grief even king Latinus sinks. That Aeneas is called by fate, guided by heaven's clear will, is the warning given by angry gods and the fresh graves before his eyes. Therefore his high council, the foremost of his people, he summons by royal command and convenes within his lofty portals. They assembled, streaming to the king's palace through the crowded streets. In their midst, oldest in years and first in regal state, with little joy upon his brow, sits Latinus, and now bids the envoys, returned from the Aetolian city, tell what tidings they bring back, and demands full answers, each in turn. Then silence fell on all tongues and, obedient to his word, Venulus thus begins:

"Citizens, we have seen Diomedes and his Argive camp; we have achieved our journey, overcome all perils, and grasped the hand by which the land of Ilium fell. He was founding his city of Argyripa, named after his father's race, in the conquered fields of Iapygian Garganus. When we entered, and liberty was given to speak before him, we proffer our gifts, and declare our name and country, who are its invaders, and what cause has led us to Arpi. He

---

243 Diomedem χ: Diomeden *MPR*: Diomede χ

auditis ille haec placido sic reddidit ore:
　　'O fortunatae gentes, Saturnia regna,
antiqui Ausonii, quae vos fortuna quietos
sollicitat suadetque ignota lacessere bella?
255　quicumque Iliacos ferro violavimus agros
(mitto ea quae muris bellando exhausta sub altis,
quos Simois premat ille viros) infanda per orbem
supplicia et scelerum poenas expendimus omnes,
vel Priamo miseranda manus; scit triste Minervae
260　sidus et Euboicae cautes ultorque Caphereus.
militia ex illa diversum ad litus abacti
Atrides Protei Menelaus adusque columnas
exsulat, Aetnaeos vidit Cyclopas Ulixes.
266　ipse Mycenaeus magnorum ductor Achivum
coniugis infandae prima inter limina dextra
268　oppetiit, devictam Asiam subsedit adulter.
264　regna Neoptolemi referam versosque penatis
265　Idomenei? Libycone habitantis litore Locros?
269　invidisse deos, patriis ut redditus aris
270　coniugium optatum et pulchram Calydona viderem?
nunc etiam horribili visu portenta sequuntur
et socii amissi petierunt aethera pennis
fluminibusque vagantur aves (heu, dira meorum
supplicia!) et scopulos lacrimosis vocibus implent.
275　haec adeo ex illo mihi iam speranda fuerunt
tempore cum ferro caelestia corpora demens

255 violavimus *MP*: populavimus *R*
264–5 *after* 268 Ribbeck: *after* 263 *MPR*

---

[7] As the Greeks were returning from Troy, Pallas Minerva sent
a storm upon them, and Nauplius, king of Euboea, hung out false

heard and thus replied with unruffled mien:

"'O happy peoples of Saturn's realm, sons of old Ausonia, what chance vexes your calm and lures you to provoke unknown warfare? All we who with steel profaned the fields of Troy—I do not mention the sorrows we suffered in war beneath her high walls, the heroes drowned in the Simois—the wide world over, we have paid in nameless tortures all manner of penalties for our guilt, a band that even Priam might pity: witness Minerva's baleful star, the Euboic cliffs, and avenging Caphereus.[7] From that warfare driven to diverse shores, Menelaus, son of Atreus, is in exile so far away as the pillars of Proteus; and Ulysses has looked on the Cylopes of Aetna. Even the Mycenaean, the chief of the mighty Achaeans, scarce over the threshold, fell by his wicked wife's hand; after his conquest of Asia an adulterer lay in wait.[8] Need I tell of the realm of Neoptolemus and the home of Idomeneus overthrown, or of the Locrians who dwell on Libya's shore? To think that the gods begrudged me return to my country's altars, and sight of the wife I long for, and lovely Calydon! Even now portents of dreadful view pursue me; my lost comrades have winged their way to the sky or haunt the streams as birds—alas, the dire punishment of my people!—and fill the cliffs with their tearful cries.[9] This was the fate I had to expect from that moment when I insanely assailed celes-

lights, so that the fleet was wrecked on the promontory of Caphereus. [8] Aegisthus, Clytemnestra'a lover, aided her in the murder of her returning husband Agamemnon.

[9] Some of the companions of Diomedes were changed into sea birds, which haunted the Diomedean Islands off the Apulian promontory of Garganus.

appetii et Veneris violavi vulnere dextram.
ne vero, ne me ad talis impellite pugnas.
nec mihi cum Teucris ullum post eruta bellum
280 Pergama nec veterum memini laetorve malorum.
munera quae patriis ad me portatis ab oris
vertite ad Aenean. stetimus tela aspera contra
contulimusque manus: experto credite quantus
in clipeum adsurgat, quo turbine torqueat hastam.
285 si duo praeterea talis Idaea tulisset
terra viros, ultro Inachias venisset ad urbes
Dardanus, et versis lugeret Graecia fatis.
quidquid apud durae cessatum est moenia Troiae,
Hectoris Aeneaeque manu victoria Graium
290 haesit et in decimum vestigia rettulit annum.
ambo animis, ambo insignes praestantibus armis,
hic pietate prior. coeant in foedera dextrae,
qua datur; ast armis concurrant arma cavete.'
et responsa simul quae sint, rex optime, regis
295 audisti et quae sit magno sententia bello."

    Vix ea legati, variusque per ora cucurrit
Ausonidum turbata fremor, ceu saxa morantur
cum rapidos amnis, fit clauso gurgite murmur
vicinaeque fremunt ripae crepitantibus undis.
300 ut primum placati animi et trepida ora quierunt,
praefatus divos solio rex infit ab alto:

    "Ante equidem summa de re statuisse, Latini,
et vellem et fuerat melius, non tempore tali
cogere concilium, cum muros adsidet hostis.

---

[10] How Diomedes wounded Aphrodite is told in *Iliad* 5.318ff.

tial limbs with the sword, and profaned the hand of Venus with a wound.[10] Do not, do not urge me to such battles! I have no war with Teucer's race since Troy's towers fell, and I have no joyful memory of those ancient ills. The gifts that you bring me from your country, take them rather to Aeneas. We have faced his fierce weapons, and fought him hand to hand: trust one who has experienced it, how huge he looms above his shield, with what whirlwind he hurls his spear! Had Ida's land borne two others like him, the Trojans would even have stormed the towns of Inachus,[11] and Greece would be mourning, with fate reversed. In all the time we spent before the walls of stubborn Troy, it was by the hand of Hector and Aeneas that the Greeks' victory was delayed and driven back till the tenth year. Both were renowned for courage, both eminent in arms; Aeneas was first in loyalty. Join hand to hand in treaty, as best you may; but beware your swords clash not with his!' You have heard, noble King, what the King replies, and what he counsels on this mighty war."

Scarcely had the envoys spoken thus when a various murmur ran along the troubled lips of Ausonia's sons: just as, when rocks delay a rushing river, there rises a roar from the pent-up flood, and the neighbouring banks echo to the plashing waters. As soon as minds were calmed and restless tongues were hushed, the king, first calling on heaven, from his high throne begins:

"I wish that we had decided before now, Latins, about this supreme matter; it would have been better not to convene a council at such an hour, when the foe is seated at

[11] Inachus was the first king of Argos, and Argos indicates Greek cities in general.

305 bellum importunum, cives, cum gente deorum
    invictisque viris gerimus, quos nulla fatigant
    proelia nec victi possunt absistere ferro.
    spem si quam ascitis Aetolum habuistis in armis,
    ponite. spes sibi quisque; sed haec quam angusta videtis.
310 cetera qua rerum iaceant perculsa ruina,
    ante oculos interque manus sunt omnia vestras.
    nec quemquam incuso: potuit quae plurima virtus
    esse, fuit; toto certatum est corpore regni.
    nunc adeo quae sit dubiae sententia menti,
315 expediam et paucis (animos adhibete) docebo.
    est antiquus ager Tusco mihi proximus amni,
    longus in occasum, finis super usque Sicanos;
    Aurunci Rutulique serunt, et vomere duros
    exercent collis atque horum asperrima pascunt.
320 haec omnis regio et celsi plaga pinea montis
    cedat amicitiae Teucrorum, et foederis aequas
    dicamus leges sociosque in regna vocemus:
    considant, si tantus amor, et moenia condant.
    sin alios finis aliamque capessere gentem
325 est animus possuntque solo decedere nostro,
    bis denas Italo texamus robore navis;
    seu pluris complere valent, iacet omnis ad undam
    materies: ipsi numerumque modumque carinis
    praecipiant, nos aera, manus, navalia demus.
330 praeterea, qui dicta ferant et foedera firment
    centum oratores prima de gente Latinos
    ire placet pacisque manu praetendere ramos,
    munera portantis aurique eborisque talenta
    et sellam regni trabeamque insignia nostri.
335 consulite in medium et rebus succurrite fessis."

our walls. My countrymen, we are waging an ill-omened war with a race divine, with men unconquered; no battles weary them and even in defeat they cannot let go the sword. If you had any hope in alliance with Aetolian arms, resign it. Each is his own hope; but you see how slender this is. As for the rest of your fortunes, it is before your eyes, and all is in your grasp, in what wide ruin they lie smitten. I do not blame anyone; what valour's utmost could do is done; we have striven with our realm's whole strength. Now mark: the judgment of my wavering mind I will unfold and, if you pay heed, will instruct you in brief. There is an ancient domain of mine bordering the Tuscan river, stretching far westward, even beyond Sicanian bounds. Auruncans and Rutulians sow the seed, work the stubborn hills with the plough and graze their roughest slopes. Let all this tract, with a pine-clad belt of mountain height, pass to the Trojans in friendship; let us name just terms of treaty, and invite them to share our realm. Let them settle, if their desire is so strong, and build their city. But if they have a mind to lay hold of other territories and another nation, and can leave our soil, let us build twice ten ships of Italian oak; or, if they can man more, all the timber lies at the water's edge; let them prescribe the number and design of their vessels themselves; let us contribute bronze, labour, and docks. Further, to bring the news and seal the pact, I would have a hundred envoys go forth, Latins of noblest birth, holding boughs of peace in their hands, and carrying gifts—talent-weights of gold and ivory, and a throne and robe, signs of our royalty. Take counsel together and restore our weary fortunes!"

---

335 fessis *MR*: vestris *P*

Tum Drances idem infensus, quem gloria Turni
obliqua invidia stimulisque agitabat amaris,
largus opum et lingua melior, sed frigida bello
dextera, consiliis habitus non futtilis auctor,
340 seditione potens (genus huic materna superbum
nobilitas dabat, incertum de patre ferebat),
surgit et his onerat dictis atque aggerat iras:
"Rem nulli obscuram nostrae nec vocis egentem
consulis, o bone rex: cuncti se scire fatentur
345 quid fortuna ferat populi, sed dicere mussant.
det libertatem fandi flatusque remittat,
cuius ob auspicium infaustum moresque sinistros
(dicam equidem, licet arma mihi mortemque minetur)
lumina tot cecidisse ducum totamque videmus
350 consedisse urbem luctu, dum Troïa temptat
castra fugae fidens et caelum territat armis.
unum etiam donis istis, quae plurima mitti
Dardanidis dicique iubes, unum, optime regum,
adicias, nec te ullius violentia vincat
355 quin natam egregio genero dignisque hymenaeis
des pater, et pacem hanc aeterno foedere iungas.
quod si tantus habet mentes et pectora terror,
ipsum obtestemur veniamque oremus ab ipso:
cedat, ius proprium regi patriaeque remittat.
360 quid miseros totiens in aperta pericula civis
proicis, o Latio caput horum et causa malorum?
nulla salus bello, pacem te poscimus omnes,
Turne, simul pacis solum inviolabile pignus.

338 lingua *MR*: linguae *P*
356 iungas *MP*: firmes (330) *R*

Then Drances, hostile as before, whom the renown of Turnus goaded with the bitter stings of furtive envy, lavish of wealth and valiant of tongue, though his hand was cold in battle, in counsel deemed no mean adviser, in faction strong (his mother's high birth ennobled his lineage; from his father he drew obscure rank), rises and with these words loads and heaps high their wrath:

"A subject dark to no one and needing no voice of ours, gracious king, you consult us on. All admit that they know what course the public fortune prompts, but they shrink from speech. Let that man grant liberty of speech and abate his blustering pride, through whose ill-starred leadership and perverse ways (yes, I will speak, though he threaten me with arms and death) we see so many glorious leaders have fallen and the whole city is sunk in mourning, while he, confident in his ability to flee, assails the Trojan camp and frightens heaven with his weapons. Add one more to those many gifts you bid us send and promise to the sons of Dardanus—one more, most gracious king— and let no man's violence prevail to stop you from giving your daughter, as a father may, to a peerless son in a worthy marriage, and making this bond of peace in eternal covenant. But if such terror possesses our minds and hearts, let us entreat the prince himself and implore him, of his grace, to yield, and give up his own rights[12] to king and country. You who are the source and cause of these woes of Latium, why do you so often hurl your unhappy countrymen into open danger? There is no safety in war; for peace we ask you, Turnus, one and all, together with the one inviolable

[12] Called "his own rights" in irony. Latinus, of course, had the right to dispose of his daughter's hand.

primus ego, invisum quem tu tibi fingis (et esse
365 nil moror), en supplex venio. miserere tuorum,
pone animos et pulsus abi. sat funera fusi
vidimus ingentis et desolavimus agros.
aut, si fama movet, si tantum pectore robur
concipis et si adeo dotalis regia cordi est,
370 aude atque adversum fidens fer pectus in hostem.
scilicet ut Turno contingat regia coniunx,
nos animae viles, inhumata infletaque turba,
sternamur campis? etiam tu, si qua tibi vis,
si patrii quid Martis habes, illum aspice contra
375 qui vocat . . ."
    Talibus exarsit dictis violentia Turni.
dat gemitum rumpitque has imo pectore voces:
"larga quidem semper, Drance, tibi copia fandi
tum cum bella manus poscunt, patribusque vocatis
380 primus ades. sed non replenda est curia verbis,
quae tuto tibi magna volant, dum distinet hostem
agger murorum nec inundant sanguine fossae.
proinde tona eloquio (solitum tibi) meque timoris
argue tu, Drance, quando tot stragis acervos
385 Teucrorum tua dextra dedit, passimque tropaeis
insignis agros. possit quid vivida virtus
experiare licet, nec longe scilicet hostes
quaerendi nobis; circumstant undique muros.
imus in adversos—quid cessas? an tibi Mavors
390 ventosa in lingua pedibusque fugacibus istis
semper erit? . . .
pulsus ego? aut quisquam merito, foedissime, pulsum
arguet, Iliaco tumidum qui crescere Thybrim

---

382 murorum] moerorum *P* (*see on* 10.24)

pledge of peace. I first, I whom you imagine to be your
foe—but that I ignore—see, I come in suppliance! Pity
your own people; put away your pride; and, beaten as you
are, give way! Routed, we have seen enough of death and
have made wide lands desolate. Or, if glory moves you, if
you feel such strength in your heart, or if the dowry of a
palace is so dear to you, be bold, and fearlessly advance to
meet the foe. Oh yes, to be sure, so that Turnus can gain his
royal bride, let us, whose lives are worthless, be strewn
over the fields, a mob unburied and unwept. But you too, if
you have any strength, if you have any of the fighting spirit
of your fathers, look your challenger in the face! . . ."

At these words the fury of Turnus blazed out: he heaves
a groan, and from the depth of his heart breaks forth with
this cry: "Drances, you always have a full flow of speech at
the time when battle calls for hands; and when the sen-
ate is summoned, you are first to appear! But we need not
fill the council house with words—those big words that
fly from your lips when you are safe, while the rampart
walls keep off the foe, and the trenches are not yet swim-
ming with blood. Keep thundering on in eloquence (in
your usual way) and charge me with cowardice, Drances,
when your hand has produced such mounds of dead
Teucrians and marked out the fields everywhere with tro-
phies. You are free to test what lively courage can do; and,
as you see, we need not look far afield for enemies: they
surround the walls on every side. Are we going to advance
against the foe? Why do you hesitate? Will your spirit of
war always remain in your windy tongue and those run-
away feet of yours? . . . I beaten, you say? Rather, you foul
liar, will anyone rightly claim that I am beaten when he

sanguine et Euandri totam cum stirpe videbit
395   procubuisse domum atque exutos Arcadas armis?
haud ita me experti Bitias et Pandarus ingens
et quos mille die victor sub Tartara misi,
inclusus muris hostilique aggere saeptus.
nulla salus bello? capiti cane talia, demens,
400   Dardanio rebusque tuis. proinde omnia magno
ne cessa turbare metu atque extollere viris
gentis bis victae, contra premere arma Latini.
nunc et Myrmidonum proceres Phrygia arma tremescunt,
nunc et Tydides et Larisaeus Achilles,
405   amnis et Hadriacas retro fugit Aufidus undas.
vel cum se pavidum contra mea iurgia fingit,
artificis scelus, et formidine crimen acerbat.
numquam animam talem dextra hac (absiste moveri)
amittes: habitet tecum et sit pectore in isto.
410   Nunc ad te et tua magna, pater, consulta revertor.
si nullam nostris ultra spem ponis in armis,
si tam deserti sumus et semel agmine verso
funditus occidimus neque habet Fortuna regressum,
oremus pacem et dextras tendamus inertis.
415   quamquam o si solitae quicquam virtutis adesset!
ille mihi ante alios fortunatusque laborum
egregiusque animi, qui, ne quid tale videret,
procubuit moriens et humum semel ore momordit.
sin et opes nobis et adhuc intacta iuventus
420   auxilioque urbes Italae populique supersunt,
sin et Troianis cum multo gloria venit
sanguine (sunt illis sua funera, parque per omnis
tempestas), cur indecores in limine primo

404 *MPR*] = 2.197 (*del. Klouček*)   412 semel *MR*: simul *P*

sees the Tiber swollen with Trojan blood, and all Evander's house and line laid prostrate, and his Arcadians stripped of arms? Not such did Bitias and giant Pandarus find me, and the thousand men whom in one day my conquering arm sent down to hell, cooped though I was within their walls and girt by foemen's ramparts. There is no safety in war, you say. Chant such bodings, fool, for the Dardan's life and your own property! Go on, do not cease to disturb all with your great alarms, extol the might of a twice-conquered people, while you decry the arms of Latinus. Now the Myrmidon princes tremble before Phrygian arms, *now Tydeus' son and Achilles of Larissa,* and Aufidus' stream recoils from the Adriatic wave. Or what about when he pretends to fear my chiding—the knavish villain—and sharpens his charge against me with pretended terror! Never will you lose a life like yours—do not be anxious!—by this right hand: let it stay with you and abide in your craven breast!

Now, father, I return to you and this weighty debate of yours. If you put no further hope in our arms, if we are so forlorn and in one repulse of our forces have fallen on utter ruin, and Fortune cannot retrace her steps, let us pray for peace and stretch forth helpless hands! But if only we had any of our wonted valour! Blest beyond others in his toil and peerless in soul would I hold the man who, to avoid such a sight, has fallen in death and once for all has bitten the dust. But if we still have means and a manhood still unharmed, and the cities and nations of Italy still support us, if the Trojans too have won glory at the cost of much bloodshed (they too have their deaths, and the storm swept over all alike), why do we lose heart so shamefully at the

---

418 semel *M*²: semul *P*: simul *MR*

deficimus? cur ante tubam tremor occupat artus?
425 multa dies variique labor mutabilis aevi
rettulit in melius, multos alterna revisens
lusit et in solido rursus Fortuna locavit.
non erit auxilio nobis Aetolus et Arpi:
at Messapus erit felixque Tolumnius et quos
430 tot populi misere duces, nec parva sequetur
gloria delectos Latio et Laurentibus agris.
est et Volscorum egregia de gente Camilla
agmen agens equitum et florentis aere catervas.
quod si me solum Teucri in certamina poscunt
435 idque placet tantumque bonis communibus obsto,
non adeo has exosa manus Victoria fugit
ut tanta quicquam pro spe temptare recusem.
ibo animis contra, vel magnum praestet Achillem
factaque Volcani manibus paria induat arma
440 ille licet. vobis animam hanc soceroque Latino
Turnus ego, haud ulli veterum virtute secundus,
devovi. solum Aeneas vocat? et vocet oro;
nec Drances potius, sive est haec ira deorum,
morte luat, sive est virtus et gloria, tollat."
445   Illi haec inter se dubiis de rebus agebant
certantes: castra Aeneas aciemque movebat.
nuntius ingenti per regia tecta tumultu
ecce ruit magnisque urbem terroribus implet:
instructos acie Tiberino a flumine Teucros
450 Tyrrhenamque manum totis descendere campis.
extemplo turbati animi concussaque vulgi
pectora et arrectae stimulis haud mollibus irae.
arma manu trepidi poscunt, fremit arma iuventus,

432–3 *cf.* 7.803–4

very start? Why does trembling seize our limbs before the trumpet sounds? Many an ill has been repaired by time and the shifting toil of changing years; many a man Fortune, fitful visitant, has mocked, then once more set up upon firm ground. The Aetolian and his Arpi will be no help to us: but Messapus will be, and Tolumnius the fortunate, and all the leaders sent by many a nation; no scant fame will come to the flower of Latium and the Laurentine land. We have Camilla too, of the glorious Volscian race, leading her troop of horse and squadrons bright with bronze. But if I alone am called by the Teucrians to combat, and such is your will, and I am so great an obstruction of the common good, Victory has not fled from these hands of mine with such loathing that I refuse to dare anything for a hope so high. I will face him boldly, though he outmatch great Achilles and wear armour to match, wrought by Vulcan's hands. To you and my bride's father Latinus I, Turnus, second in valour to none of my fathers, dedicate my life. Aeneas alone challenges me, you say. I pray that he does challenge me, and that it is not Drances rather than I who appeases the gods by his death, if they are angry, or wins glory for his courage, if that is the prize here."

Thus, in mutual strife they were debating doubtful issues: Aeneas meanwhile moved from camp to field. Amid wild uproar, lo, a messenger rushes through the royal halls and fills the city with great alarms: in battle array, he cries, the Teucrians and the Tyrrhene force are sweeping down from the Tiber river over all the plain. At once the minds of the people are confounded, their hearts shaken, and their passions roused by ungentle spurs. Brandishing their fists they call for weapons; "Weapons!" the young men shout;

flent maesti mussantque patres. hic undique clamor
455 dissensu vario magnus se tollit in auras,
haud secus atque alto in luco cum forte catervae
consedere avium, piscosove amne Padusae
dant sonitum rauci per stagna loquacia cycni.
"immo," ait "o cives," arrepto tempore Turnus,
460 "cogite concilium et pacem laudate sedentes;
illi armis in regna ruunt." nec plura locutus
corripuit sese et tectis citus extulit altis.
"tu, Voluse, armari Volscorum edice maniplis,
duc" ait "et Rutulos. equitem Messapus in armis,
465 et cum fratre Coras latis diffundite campis.
pars aditus urbis firment turrisque capessant;
cetera, qua iusso, mecum manus inferat arma."
Ilicet in muros tota discurritur urbe.
concilium ipse pater et magna incepta Latinus
470 deserit ac tristi turbatus tempore differt,
multaque se incusat qui non acceperit ultro
Dardanium Aenean generumque asciverit urbi.
praefodiunt alii portas aut saxa sudesque
subvectant. bello dat signum rauca cruentum
475 bucina. tum muros varia cinxere corona
matronae puerique, vocat labor ultimus omnis.
nec non ad templum summasque ad Palladis arces
subvehitur magna matrum regina caterva
dona ferens, iuxtaque comes Lavinia virgo,
480 causa mali tanti, oculos deiecta decoros.
succedunt matres et templum ture vaporant

455 in *PR*: ad *M*
466 firment *MR*: firmet *P* | capessant *R*: capessat *MP*
480 mali tanti *P*: mali tantis *M*: malis tantis *R*

their unhappy fathers weep and moan. And now, from every side, there rises to heaven a loud din with varied discord just as when flocks of birds settle by chance in some tall grove, or when, by Padusa's fish-filled stream, hoarse-throated swans call among the clamorous pools. "Very well, then, my fellow citizens," cries Turnus, seizing the moment, "convene a council and sit there praising peace; our enemies are attacking our realm under arms." He said no more, but sprang up and sped swiftly forth from the high halls. "Volusus," he cries, "bid the Volscian squadrons arm, and lead out the Rutulians! You, Messapus, and you, Coras, with your brother deploy the cavalry under arms over the broad plains. Let some guard the city gates and man the towers; let the rest charge with me, where I shall command."

At once from all over the city there is a rush to the walls. Father Latinus himself, dismayed by the grimness of the hour, quits the council and postpones his high designs, often chiding himself that he did not give a ready welcome to Dardan Aeneas and did not, for the city's sake, adopt him as a son. Others dig trenches in front of the gates or shoulder stones and stakes. The hoarse clarion gives bloody signal for battle. Then a motley ring of matrons and boys girdles the walls; the final struggle summons them all. Moreover the queen, with a great throng of mothers, drives[13] up to the temple of Pallas and her towered heights, bearing gifts, and at her side the maiden Lavinia, the source of all that woe, her beautiful eyes lowered. As they go up, the matrons fill the temple with the smoke of

[13] As the Roman matrons drove in *pilenta* in their sacred processions (cf. *Aen.* 8.665).

et maestas alto fundunt de limine voces:
"armipotens, praeses belli, Tritonia virgo,
frange manu telum Phrygii praedonis, et ipsum
485 pronum sterne solo portisque effunde sub altis."
cingitur ipse furens certatim in proelia Turnus.
iamque adeo rutilum thoraca indutus aënis
horrebat squamis surasque incluserat auro,
tempora nudus adhuc, laterique accinxerat ensem,
490 fulgebatque alta decurrens aureus arce
exsultatque animis et spe iam praecipit hostem:
qualis ubi abruptis fugit praesepia vinclis
tandem liber equus, campoque potitus aperto
aut ille in pastus armentaque tendit equarum
495 aut adsuetus aquae perfundi flumine noto
emicat, arrectisque fremit cervicibus alte
luxurians luduntque iubae per colla, per armos.
    Obvia cui Volscorum acie comitante Camilla
occurrit portisque ab equo regina sub ipsis
500 desiluit, quam tota cohors imitata relictis
ad terram defluxit equis; tum talia fatur:
"Turne, sui merito si qua est fiducia forti,
audeo et Aeneadum promitto occurrere turmae
solaque Tyrrhenos equites ire obvia contra.
505 me sine prima manu temptare pericula belli,
tu pedes ad muros subsiste et moenia serva."
Turnus ad haec oculos horrenda in virgine fixus:
"o decus Italiae virgo, quas dicere grates
quasve referre parem? sed nunc, est omnia quando
510 iste animus supra, mecum partire laborem.
Aeneas, ut fama fidem missique reportant
exploratores, equitum levia improbus arma

incense and from the high threshold pour sad lamentations: "Mighty in arms, mistress in war, Tritonian maid, break with your hand the spear of the Phrygian pirate, hurl him prone to earth and stretch him prostrate beneath our high gates." As for Turnus, with emulous fury he girds himself for the fray. And now he had donned his flashing breastplate and bristled with bronze scales; his legs he had sheathed in gold, though his temples were yet bare, and he had buckled his sword to his side. He shone with gold as he ran down from the fortress height; he exults in courage, and in his hopes he is already seizing the foe—just as, when a horse, bursting his tether, has fled the stalls, free at last, and, lord of the open plain, either he makes for the pastures and herds of mares or, accustomed to bathe in a familiar river, he dashes away and, with head held high in wanton joy, neighs, while his mane plays over neck and shoulder.

Attended by the Volscian army, Camilla sped to meet him, and near the gates the queen leaped from her horse; at her example all her troop left their mounts and slid to the ground. Then thus she speaks: "Turnus, if the brave may justly put any trust in themselves, I dare and promise to face Aeneas' cavalry, and ride alone to meet the Tyrrhene horsemen. Let me try war's first perils with my hand while you stay on foot by the walls and guard the town." Turnus, with his eyes fixed upon the formidable maiden, replied: "Maiden, glory of Italy, what thanks can I try to utter or repay? But now, since your spirit soars above all, share the toil with me. Aeneas—so rumour tells, and scouts sent out confirm—has insolently sent forward his

---

483 praees *MPR*: praesens *M²P²*, *Macrobius*

praemisit, quaterent campos; ipse ardua montis
per deserta iugo superans adventat ad urbem.
515   furta paro belli convexo in tramite silvae,
ut bivias armato obsidam milite fauces.
tu Tyrrhenum equitem conlatis excipe signis;
tecum acer Messapus erit turmaeque Latinae
Tiburtique manus, ducis et tu concipe curam."
520   sic ait, et paribus Messapum in proelia dictis
hortatur sociosque duces et pergit in hostem.
    Est curvo anfractu valles, accommoda fraudi
armorumque dolis, quam densis frondibus atrum
urget utrimque latus, tenuis quo semita ducit
525   angustaeque ferunt fauces aditusque maligni.
hanc super in speculis summoque in vertice montis
planities ignota iacet tutique receptus,
seu dextra laevaque velis occurrere pugnae
sive instare iugis et grandia volvere saxa.
530   huc iuvenis nota fertur regione viarum
arripuitque locum et silvis insedit iniquis.
    Velocem interea superis in sedibus Opim,
unam ex virginibus sociis sacraque caterva,
compellabat et has tristis Latonia voces
535   ore dabat: "graditur bellum ad crudele Camilla,
o virgo, et nostris nequiquam cingitur armis,
cara mihi ante alias. neque enim novus iste Dianae
venit amor subitaque animum dulcedine movit.
pulsus ob invidiam regno virisque superbas
540   Priverno antiqua Metabus cum excederet urbe,
infantem fugiens media inter proelia belli

527 receptus *MP*: recessus *R, known to Servius*
534 tristis *MP*: tristi *R*

light cavalry to sweep the plains; he himself, climbing the ridge, marches by the mountain's lonely heights upon the town. I am laying snares of war in an over-arched pathway in the wood, to block the gorge's two entrances with armed troops. You, in battle array, must await the Tyrrhene cavalry; with you will be the valiant Messapus, the Latin squadrons, and Tiburtus' troop: you too must take the duty of a captain." So he speaks, and with similar words he heartens Messapus and the allied captains to battle, and moves against the foe.

There is a valley with sweeping curve, fit site for the stratagems and deceits of war, hemmed in on either side by a wall black with dense foliage. To it a narrow path leads, with straitened gorge and awkward approach. Above it, amid the watch towers of the mountain top, lies a hidden plain and a safe shelter, whether one plans to charge from right or left, or take stand upon the ridge and roll down enormous boulders. Hither the warrior hastens by a well-known road and, seizing his ground, lay in wait in the treacherous woods.

Meanwhile, in Heaven's halls Latona's daughter addressed swift Opis, one of her maiden sisterhood and sacred band, and opened her lips to these words of sorrow: "Camilla is marching to the cruel war, O maiden, and vainly girds on our arms, Camilla, whom I love as none besides. For no new love is this that has come upon Diana nor sudden the spell wherewith it has stirred her heart. When Metabus was driven from his realm by his subjects' hatred of his oppressive tyranny and was leaving Privernum's ancient city, as he fled amid the conflict of battle he took

sustulit exsilio comitem, matrisque vocavit
nomine Casmillae, mutata parte, Camillam.
ipse sinu prae se portans iuga longa petebat
545 solorum nemorum: tela undique saeva premebant
et circumfuso volitabant milite Volsci.
ecce fugae medio summis Amasenus abundans
spumabat ripis, tantus se nubibus imber
ruperat. ille innare parans infantis amore
550 tardatur caroque oneri timet. omnia secum
versanti subito vix haec sententia sedit:
telum immane manu valida quod forte gerebat
bellator, solidum nodis et robore cocto,
huic natam libro et silvestri subere clausam
555 implicat atque habilem mediae circumligat hastae;
quam dextra ingenti librans ita ad aethera fatur:
'alma, tibi hanc, nemorum cultrix, Latonia virgo,
ipse pater famulam voveo; tua prima per auras
tela tenens supplex hostem fugit. accipe, testor,
560 diva tuam, quae nunc dubiis committitur auris.'
dixit, et adducto contortum hastile lacerto
immittit: sonuere undae, rapidum super amnem
infelix fugit in iaculo stridente Camilla.
at Metabus magna propius iam urgente caterva
565 dat sese fluvio, atque hastam cum virgine victor
gramineo, donum Triviae, de caespite vellit.
non illum tectis ullae, non moenibus urbes
accepere (neque ipse manus feritate dedisset),
pastorum et solis exegit montibus aevum.
570 hic natam in dumis interque horrentia lustra

with him his infant child to share his exile, and from her mother Casmilla's name, slightly changed, called her Camilla. Carrying her before him on his breast, he made for a stretch of mountain ridges lonely and forest-clad. On every side hostile weapons pressed upon him, the Volscians hovering around him with their troops. While they were still in mid-flight, the Amasenus overflowed and foamed over the summit of its banks: so great a downpour had burst from the clouds. The exile, about to swim the flood, is checked by love of his child and fears for his precious burden. Quickly as he pondered all courses in his mind, he settled on this reluctant resolve: the giant spear, which the warrior chanced to be carrying in his stalwart hand, hard-knotted and of seasoned oak—to this he fastens his daughter, wrapped in bark of forest cork, and binds her closely round the centre of the shaft. Then, poising it in his mighty right hand, he cries thus to the heavens: "Gracious lady, dweller in the woods, virgin daughter of Latona, to your service I, her father, vow this child; yours is this first weapon that she clasps as a suppliant, speeding through the air in flight from her foe. Accept, goddess, for your own, I implore you, the child whom I now commit to the perils of the air!" He has spoken and, drawing back his arm, launches the spinning shaft: loud roared the waters, over the rushing river poor Camilla speeds her flight upon the strident steel. But Metabus, now that a great band pressed closer upon him, leaps into the stream, and in triumph plucks from the grassy turf his offering to Trivia, the spear and the maid. No cities received him to their homes or walls, nor in his wild mood would he himself have yielded to them: among shepherds and on the lonely mountains he passed his days. Here amid the woods and beasts' rugged

275

armentalis equae mammis et lacte ferino
nutribat teneris immulgens ubera labris.
utque pedum primis infans vestigia plantis
institerat, iaculo palmas armavit acuto
575 spiculaque ex umero parvae suspendit et arcum.
pro crinali auro, pro longae tegmine pallae
tigridis exuviae per dorsum a vertice pendent.
tela manu iam tum tenera puerilia torsit
et fundam tereti circum caput egit habena
580 Strymoniamque gruem aut album deiecit olorem.
multae illam frustra Tyrrhena per oppida matres
optavere nurum; sola contenta Diana
aeternum telorum et virginitatis amorem
intemerata colit. vellem haud correpta fuisset
585 militia tali conata lacessere Teucros:
cara mihi comitumque foret nunc una mearum.
verum age, quandoquidem fatis urgetur acerbis,
labere, nympha, polo finisque invise Latinos,
tristis ubi infausto committitur omine pugna.
590 haec cape et ultricem pharetra deprome sagittam:
hac, quicumque sacrum violarit vulnere corpus,
Tros Italusque, mihi pariter det sanguine poenas.
post ego nube cava miserandae corpus et arma
inspoliata feram tumulo patriaeque reponam."
595 dixit, at illa levis caeli delapsa per auras
insonuit nigro circumdata turbine corpus.

At manus interea muris Troiana propinquat,
Etruscique duces equitumque exercitus omnis
compositi numero in turmas. fremit aequore toto

592 Italusque *MPR*: Italusve *Servius*
595 delapsa *M*: demissa (10.73) *PR*

lairs he nursed his child on milk at the breast of a wild mare from the herd, squeezing the teats into her tender lips. And as soon as the baby had taken her earliest footsteps, he armed her hands with a pointed lance, and hung quiver and bow from the little child's shoulder. In place of gold to clasp her hair, in place of long trailing robe, there hung from her head and down her back a tiger's spoils. Even then with tender hand she hurled her childish spears, swung round her head the smooth-thonged sling, and struck down Strymonian crane or snowy swan. Many a mother in Tyrrhene towers longed in vain for her as daughter; content with Diana alone, she cherishes unsullied a lifelong love for her weapons and her maidenhood. I would that she had not been swept away in warfare such as this, nor tried to challenge the Teucrians: she would still be my darling and one of my companions. But come, since untimely doom weighs upon her, swoop down from heaven, nymph, and seek the Latin borders, where under evil omen they join in the dreadful fray. Take these,[14] and draw from the quiver an avenging shaft: with it may anyone, Trojan or Italian, who violates her sacred body with a wound pay me an equal penalty in his blood. Then in a hollow cloud I will bear the body and armour of the hapless maid unspoiled to the tomb, and bury them in her own land." She spoke; and Opis sped down with whirring sound through heaven's light air, her form shrouded in black whirlwind.

But meanwhile the Trojan band draws near the walls, with the Etruscan chiefs and all their mounted array, marshalled by number into squadrons. The warhorse prances

14 I.e. her bow and arrows.

600 insultans sonipes et pressis pugnat habenis
huc conversus et huc; tum late ferreus hastis
horret ager campique armis sublimibus ardent.
nec non Messapus contra celeresque Latini
et cum fratre Coras et virginis ala Camillae
605 adversi campo apparent, hastasque reductis
protendunt longe dextris et spicula vibrant,
adventusque virum fremitusque ardescit equorum.
iamque intra iactum teli progressus uterque
substiterat: subito erumpunt clamore furentisque
610 exhortantur equos, fundunt simul undique tela
crebra nivis ritu, caelumque obtexitur umbra.
continuo adversis Tyrrhenus et acer Aconteus
conixi incurrunt hastis primique ruinam
dant sonitu ingenti perfractaque quadripedantum
615 pectora pectoribus rumpunt; excussus Aconteus
fulminis in morem aut tormento ponderis acti
praecipitat longe et vitam dispergit in auras.
    Extemplo turbatae acies, versique Latini
reiciunt parmas et equos ad moenia vertunt;
620 Troes agunt, princeps turmas inducit Asilas.
iamque propinquabant portis rursusque Latini
clamorem tollunt et mollia colla reflectunt;
hi fugiunt penitusque datis referuntur habenis.
qualis ubi alterno procurrens gurgite pontus
625 nunc ruit ad terram scopulosque superiacit unda
spumeus extremamque sinu perfundit harenam,
nunc rapidus retro atque aestu revoluta resorbens
saxa fugit litusque vado labente relinquit:

601 conversus *MP*: obversus *R*
609 substiterat *P*: substituerant *R*: constiterant *M*

neighing all over the plain and, fighting the tight-drawn
rein, swerves this way and that: far and wide the field bris-
tles with the steel of spears, and the plains are ablaze with
raised weapons. On the other side, too, Messapus and the
fleet Latins, and Coras with his brother, and maid Camilla's
troop, come into view, confronting them on the plain; with
hands drawn far back they thrust the lance and brandish
the javelin; the marching of men and neighing of steeds
grows fierce. And now in its advance each army had halted
within a spear cast of the other; with a sudden shout they
dash forth, and spur on their furious steeds; together from
all sides they shower weapons as thick as snowflakes, and
the sky is veiled in darkness. At once Tyrrhenus and fierce
Aconteus charge each other full force with spears, and are
first to go down with a mighty crash, breaking and shatter-
ing their horses as they collide breast to breast. Flung
off like a thunderbolt or a stone shot from a catapult,
Aconteus is hurled headlong far away, and scatters his life
into the air.

At once the lines waver, and the routed Latins cast their
shields behind them, and turn their horses toward the
city walls. The Trojans give chase; Asilas in the van leads
the squadrons. And now they were approaching the gates
when again the Latins raise their shout, and wheel about
their horses' supple necks; the others flee, and retreat far
off with loosened rein: as when the ocean, advancing with
alternate flood, now rushes shoreward, dashes over the
cliffs in a wave of foam, and drenches the furthest sands
with its swelling curve; now flees in fast retreat and in its
wash sucks back rolling stones, leaving the sands dry as

---

612 adversis *P*: adversi *MR*

bis Tusci Rutulos egere ad moenia versos,
630 bis reiecti armis respectant terga tegentes.
tertia sed postquam congressi in proelia totas
implicuere inter se acies legitque virum vir,
tum vero et gemitus morientum et sanguine in alto
armaque corporaque et permixti caede virorum
635 semianimes volvuntur equi, pugna aspera surgit.
Orsilochus Remuli, quando ipsum horrebat adire,
hastam intorsit equo ferrumque sub aure reliquit;
quo sonipes ictu furit arduus altaque iactat
vulneris impatiens arrecto pectore crura,
640 volvitur ille excussus humi. Catillus Iollan
ingentemque animis, ingentem corpore et armis
deicit Herminium, nudo cui vertice fulva
caesaries nudique umeri nec vulnera terrent;
tantus in arma patet. latos huic hasta per armos
MR acta tremit duplicatque virum transfixa dolore.
646 funditur ater ubique cruor; dant funera ferro
certantes pulchramque petunt per vulnera mortem.
        At medias inter caedes exsultat Amazon
unum exserta latus pugnae, pharetrata Camilla,
650 et nunc lenta manu spargens hastilia denset,
nunc validam dextra rapit indefessa bipennem;
aureus ex umero sonat arcus et arma Dianae.
illa etiam, si quando in tergum pulsa recessit,
spicula converso fugientia derigit arcu.
655 at circum lectae comites, Larinaque virgo
Tullaque et aeratam quatiens Tarpeia securim,
Italides, quas ipsa decus sibi dia Camilla
delegit pacisque bonas bellique ministras:

the shallows retreat. Twice the Tuscans drove the routed
Rutulians to the city; twice, repulsed, they glance back-
wards, as they sling behind them their protecting shields.
But when, clashing in the third encounter, the lines stood
interlocked along their whole length, and man marked
man, then in truth there were groans of the dying, and
arms and bodies and horses, dying and mingled with
slaughtered riders, all weltering deep in blood: the fight
swells fiercely. Orsilochus hurled a lance at Remulus'
steed—for he feared to meet its lord—and left the steel
beneath its ear. At this blow the charger rears furious and,
unable to bear the wound, with chest raised flings his legs
on high; unseated, Remulus rolls on the ground. Catillus
strikes down Iollas, and Herminius, giant in courage, giant
in body and arms; on his bare head stream his tawny locks,
and bare are his shoulders; for him wounds have no ter-
rors; so vast a frame faces the steel. Through his broad
shoulders the driven spear comes quivering and, piercing
through, bends him double with pain. Everywhere the
dark blood streams; they deal carnage, clashing with the
sword, and seek a glorious death among the wounds.

But in the heart of the slaughter, like an Amazon, one
breast bared for the fray, and girt with a quiver, rages
Camilla; and now she showers tough javelins thick from
her hand, now she snatches a stout battle axe with unwea-
ried grasp; the golden bow, armour of Diana, clangs from
her shoulders. And even when, pressed from behind, she
withdraws, she turns her bow and aims arrows in her flight.
And round her are her chosen comrades, the maiden
Larina, and Tulla, and Tarpeia, wielding an axe of bronze,
daughters of Italy, whom godlike Camilla herself chose
to be her glory, good handmaids in both peace and war.

quales Threiciae cum flumina Thermodontis
660 pulsant et pictis bellantur Amazones armis,
seu circum Hippolyten seu cum se Martia curru
Penthesilea refert, magnoque ululante tumultu
feminea exsultant lunatis agmina peltis.
    Quem telo primum, quem postremum, aspera virgo,
665 deicis? aut quot humi morientia corpora fundis?
Eunaeum Clytio primum patre, cuius apertum
adversi longa transverberat abiete pectus.
sanguinis ille vomens rivos cadit atque cruentam
mandit humum moriensque suo se in vulnere versat.
670 tum Lirim Pagasumque super, quorum alter habenas
suffosso revolutus equo dum colligit, alter
dum subit ac dextram labenti tendit inermem,
praecipites pariterque ruunt. his addit Amastrum
Hippotaden, sequiturque incumbens eminus hasta
675 Tereaque Harpalycumque et Demophoonta Chrominque;
quotque emissa manu contorsit spicula virgo,
tot Phrygii cecidere viri. procul Ornytus armis
ignotis et equo venator Iapyge fertur,
cui pellis latos umeros erepta iuvenco
680 pugnatori operit, caput ingens oris hiatus
et malae texere lupi cum dentibus albis,
agrestisque manus armat sparus; ipse catervis
vertitur in mediis et toto vertice supra est.
hunc illa exceptum (neque enim labor agmine verso)
685 traicit et super haec inimico pectore fatur:
"silvis te, Tyrrhene, feras agitare putasti?
advenit qui vestra dies muliebribus armis
verba redarguerit. nomen tamen haud leve patrum

---

671 suffosso *M*: suffuso γ*R*

Such are the Amazons of Thrace, when they tramp over Thermodon's streams and war in blazoned armour, whether round Hippolyte, or when Penthesilea, child of Mars, returns in her chariot and, amid loud tumultuous cries, the army of women exult with crescent shields.

Fierce maiden, whom first, whom last do you strike down with your weapon? How many bodies do you lay low on the earth? First Euneus, son of Clytius, whose unguarded breast, as he faces her, she pierces through with her long pine-shaft. Coughing streams of blood, he falls, bites the gory dust and, dying, writhes upon his wound. Then she fells Liris, and Pagasus over him: while one, thrown from his stabbed horse, gathers up the reins and the other, coming up, stretches an unharmed hand to stay his fall, they fall headlong together. To these she adds Amastrus, son of Hippotas; and, bending to the task, she follows Tereus from far with her spear, and Harpalycus, and Demophoon, and Chromis; and as many weapons as she sent spinning from her hand, so many Phrygians fell. At a distance rides the hunter Ornytus in strange armour on an Iapygian steed: a hide stripped from a steer swathes the warrior's broad shoulders, his head is shielded by a wolf's huge gaping mouth and white-fanged jaws, and his hand is armed with a rustic pike; he himself moves in the midmost ranks, a full head above all. She caught—for it was easy amid the rout—and pierced him, then above him thus cries with pitiless heart: "Tuscan, did you think you were chasing beasts in the forests? The day is come that will refute your boasts with woman's weapons. But you will carry no small fame to your ancestral shades—that you fell

---

688 redarguerit *Priscian GLK* 2.503.12: redargueret *MγR*

manibus hoc referes, telo cecidisse Camillae."
690   Protinus Orsilochum et Buten, duo maxima Teucrum
MPR corpora, sed Buten aversum cuspide fixit
loricam galeamque inter, qua colla sedentis
lucent et laevo dependet parma lacerto;
Orsilochum fugiens magnumque agitata per orbem
695 eludit gyro interior sequiturque sequentem;
tum validam perque arma viro perque ossa securim
altior exsurgens oranti et multa precanti
congeminat; vulnus calido rigat ora cerebro.
incidit huic subitoque aspectu territus haesit
700 Appenninicolae bellator filius Auni,
haud Ligurum extremus, dum fallere fata sinebant.
isque ubi se nullo iam cursu evadere pugnae
posse neque instantem reginam avertere cernit,
consilio versare dolos ingressus et astu
705 incipit haec: "quid tam egregium, si femina forti
fidis equo? dimitte fugam et te comminus aequo
mecum crede solo pugnaeque accinge pedestri:
iam nosces ventosa ferat cui gloria fraudem."
dixit, at illa furens acrique accensa dolore
710 tradit equum comiti paribusque resistit in armis
ense pedes nudo puraque interrita parma.
at iuvenis vicisse dolo ratus avolat ipse
(haud mora), conversisque fugax aufertur habenis
quadripedemque citum ferrata calce fatigat.
715 "vane Ligus frustraque animis elate superbis,
nequiquam patrias temptasti lubricus artis,
nec fraus te incolumem fallaci perferet Auno."

---

[15] The Ligurians were notorious liars, and so long as he lived
he was conspicuous among them.

by the spear of Camilla!"

Next she slays Orsilochus and Butes, two Teucrians of mightiest frame. Butes she pierced with a spearpoint in the back, between corslet and helmet, where the rider's neck gleams, and the shield hangs from the left arm; as she flees from Orsilochus and is chased in a wide circle, she foils him, wheels into an inner ring and pursues the pursuer; then rising higher in the saddle, she drives her strong axe again and again through armour and through bone, while he implores and makes many prayers for mercy; the wound spatters his face with his warm brain. Now there fell in her way, and paused in terror at the sudden sight of her, the warrior son of Aunus, dweller upon the Apennine, not the least of the Ligurians while Fate allowed him to deceive.[15] When he sees that by no fleetness can he escape combat or divert the queen from her attack, he tries to concoct a stratagem with policy and craft and thus begins: "What great glory have you, woman, if you put your trust in your strong steed? Forget flight; dare to meet me hand to hand on equal ground, and gird yourself to fight on foot; soon you will know to whom windy vanity brings deception." He spoke, but she, furious and burning with the bitter smart, hands her horse over to a comrade and confronts him in equal arms, on foot and unafraid, with naked sword and shield unblazoned. But the youth, thinking that he had won by guile, himself darts away instantly and, turning his bridle, rushes off in flight, goading his charger to speed with iron spur. "Foolish Ligurian, vainly puffed up in pride of heart, in vain you have tried your slippery native tricks; cunning will not take you home unscathed to lying Aunus!"

haec fatur virgo, et pernicibus ignea plantis
transit equum cursu frenisque adversa prehensis
720 congreditur poenasque inimico ex sanguine sumit:
quam facile accipiter saxo sacer ales ab alto
consequitur pennis sublimem in nube columbam
comprensamque tenet pedibusque eviscerat uncis;
tum cruor et vulsae labuntur ab aethere plumae.
725   At non haec nullis hominum sator atque deorum
observans oculis summo sedet altus Olympo.
Tyrrhenum genitor Tarchonem in proelia saeva
suscitat et stimulis haud mollibus inicit iras.
ergo inter caedes cedentiaque agmina Tarchon
730 fertur equo variisque instigat vocibus alas
nomine quemque vocans, reficitque in proelia pulsos.
"quis metus, o numquam dolituri, o semper inertes
Tyrrheni, quae tanta animis ignavia venit?
femina palantis agit atque haec agmina vertit?
735 quo ferrum quidve haec gerimus tela inrita dextris?
at non in Venerem segnes nocturnaque bella,
MR aut ubi curva choros indixit tibia Bacchi.
exspectate dapes et plenae pocula mensae
(hic amor, hoc studium) dum sacra secundus haruspex
740 nuntiet ac lucos vocet hostia pinguis in altos!"
haec effatus equum in medios moriturus et ipse
concitat, et Venulo adversum se turbidus infert
dereptumque ab equo dextra complectitur hostem
et gremium ante suum multa vi concitus aufert.
745 tollitur in caelum clamor cunctique Latini

<hr>

728 inicit *R*: incitat *MP*: incutit *Heinsius*

So cries the maiden and with fleet foot, swift as lightning, she crosses the horse's path and, seizing the reins, meets him face to face and takes vengeance from his hated blood: as lightly as a falcon, bird of augury,[16] swooping from a lofty rock, overtakes a dove on the wing in a high cloud, then holds her in his clutch and with crooked claws tears out her heart, while blood and rent plumage flutter from the sky.

But with not unseeing eyes the father of gods and men sits throned on high Olympus, viewing the scene. He rouses Tyrrhenian Tarchon to the fierce battle, and fills him with wrath by no gentle spur. So, amid the slaughter and wavering columns, Tarchon rides, and goads his squadrons with diverse cries, calling each man by name, and rallying the routed to the fight. "You Tuscans, who will never be stung by shame, sluggards always, what fear, what utter cowardice has fallen on your hearts? Does a woman drive you in disorder and rout your ranks? For what reason do we bear swords, why these idle weapons, in our hands? But you are not laggard for love and nightly frays, or when the curved flute proclaims the Bacchic dance. Wait for the feasts and the cups on the loaded board (this is your passion, this your delight!) till the favouring seer announces the sacrifice, and the fat victim calls you to the deep groves!" So saying, he spurs his horse into the throng, ready himself also to die, and charges like a whirlwind full at Venulus; tearing the foe from his horse, he grips him with his right hand, clasps him to his breast, and, mightily spurring on his horse, carries him off. A shout rises to heaven, as all the Latins turned their eyes on the sight.

[16] As sacred to Apollo.

convertere oculos. volat igneus aequore Tarchon
arma virumque ferens; tum summa ipsius ab hasta
defringit ferrum et partis rimatur apertas,
qua vulnus letale ferat; contra ille repugnans
750 sustinet a iugulo dextram et vim viribus exit.
utque volans alte raptum cum fulva draconem
fert aquila implicuitque pedes atque unguibus haesit,
saucius at serpens sinuosa volumina versat
arrectisque horret squamis et sibilat ore
755 arduus insurgens, illa haud minus urget obunco
luctantem rostro, simul aethera verberat alis:
M   haud aliter praedam Tiburtum ex agmine Tarchon
portat ovans. ducis exemplum eventumque secuti
Maeonidae incurrunt. tum fatis debitus Arruns
760 velocem iaculo et multa prior arte Camillam
circuit, et quae sit fortuna facillima temptat.
qua se cumque furens medio tulit agmine virgo,
hac Arruns subit et tacitus vestigia lustrat;
qua victrix redit illa pedemque ex hoste reportat,
765 hac iuvenis furtim celeris detorquet habenas.
hos aditus iamque hos aditus omnemque pererrat
undique circuitum et certam quatit improbus hastam.
    Forte sacer Cybelo Chloreus olimque sacerdos
insignis longe Phrygiis fulgebat in armis
770 spumantemque agitabat equum, quem pellis aënis
in plumam squamis auro conserta tegebat.
ipse peregrina ferrugine clarus et ostro
spicula torquebat Lycio Gortynia cornu;

768 Cybelo *Ma, Servius*: Cybele γ: Cybelae *Macrobius*

Like lightning Tarchon flies over the plain, carrying away the arms and the man; then he breaks off the iron from the head of his foe's spear and searches for an unguarded place where he may deal a deadly wound; the other, struggling against him, keeps the hand from off his throat and baffles force with force. And as when a tawny eagle, soaring on high, carries a serpent she has caught, her feet entwined and her claws clinging tight, but the wounded snake writhes its sinuous coils, and rears its bristling scales, and hisses with its mouth, towering aloft; none the less with crooked beak she assails her struggling victim, while her wings beat the air: just so from the Tiburtian line Tarchon carries off his prey in triumph. Following their chief's example and success, Maeonia's sons attack. Then Arruns, his life owed to the fates, first circles round fleet Camilla with javelin and deep cunning and tries what chance may be easiest. Wherever the maiden rides among the ranks in her fury, there Arruns creeps up and silently tracks her footsteps; where she returns victorious and retires from the foe, there the youth stealthily turns his swift reins. He tries this approach and now that, and traverses the whole circuit round about, the unerring spear quivering in his relentless hand.

It chanced that Chloreus, sacred to Cybelus,[17] and once a priest, glittered resplendent from far off in his Phrygian armour, and spurred his foaming charger, whose covering was a skin plumed with bronze scales and clasped with gold. Himself ablaze in the deep hue of foreign purple, he launched Gortynian arrows from a Lycian bow: golden was

[17] Cybelus the mountain is here put for the deity worshipped upon it.

aureus ex umeris erat arcus et aurea vati
775 cassida; tum croceam chlamydemque sinusque crepantis
carbaseos fulvo in nodum collegerat auro
pictus acu tunicas et barbara tegmina crurum.
hunc virgo, sive ut templis praefigeret arma
Troïa, captivo sive ut se ferret in auro
780 venatrix, unum ex omni certamine pugnae
caeca sequebatur totumque incauta per agmen
femineo praedae et spoliorum ardebat amore,
MP telum ex insidiis cum tandem tempore capto
concitat et superos Arruns sic voce precatur:
785 "summe deum, sancti custos Soractis Apollo,
quem primi colimus, cui pineus ardor acervo
pascitur, et medium freti pietate per ignem
cultores multa premimus vestigia pruna,
da, pater, hoc nostris aboleri dedecus armis,
790 omnipotens. non exuvias pulsaeve tropaeum
virginis aut spolia ulla peto, mihi cetera laudem
facta ferent; haec dira meo dum vulnere pestis
MPR pulsa cadat, patrias remeabo inglorius urbes."
    Audiit et voti Phoebus succedere partem
795 mente dedit, partem volucris dispersit in auras:
sterneret ut subita turbatam morte Camillam
adnuit oranti; reducem ut patria alta videret
non dedit, inque Notos vocem vertere procellae.
ergo ut missa manu sonitum dedit hasta per auras,
800 convertere animos acris oculosque tulere
cuncti ad reginam Volsci. nihil ipsa nec aurae

799 ut *PR*: ubi *M*

290

that bow upon his shoulders, and golden was the seer's helmet; his saffron scarf and its rustling linen folds were gathered into a knot by yellow gold; his tunic and barbaric hose were embroidered with the needle. Whether hoping to fasten up Trojan arms in a temple or to flaunt herself in golden spoil, the maiden singled him out from all the battle fray and like a huntress was blindly pursuing him, recklessly raging through all the ranks with a woman's passion for booty and spoil, when at length, seizing the chance, Arruns from ambush rouses his lance, and thus prays aloud to Heaven: "Apollo, most high of gods, guardian of holy Soracte, whose chief worshippers are we, for whom the blaze of the pine wood heap is fed, while we, your votaries, pass through the fire in strength of faith and plant our steps on the deep embers[18]—grant that this disgrace be effaced by our arms, Father Almighty! I seek no plunder, no trophy of the maid's defeat, nor any spoils; other feats will bring me fame; if only this dread scourge fall stricken beneath my blow, I will return inglorious to the cities of my sires."

Phoebus heard, and in his heart vouchsafed that half the prayer should prosper; half he scattered to the flying breezes. He favoured the prayer that he might overthrow and strike down Camilla in sudden death; that his noble country should see his return he did not grant, and the blasts bore the prayer to the southern gates. Therefore, as the spear, sped from his hand, whistled through the air, all the Volscians turned their eager eyes and minds to the

[18] In the ancient rites on Mount Soracte, the worshippers walked three times through a pine fire, carrying offerings to the god. Cf. Pliny, *Nat. Hist.* 7.2.19.

nec sonitus memor aut venientis ab aethere teli,
hasta sub exsertam donec perlata papillam
haesit virgineumque alte bibit acta cruorem.
805 concurrunt trepidae comites dominamque ruentem
suscipiunt. fugit ante omnis exterritus Arruns
laetitia mixtoque metu, nec iam amplius hastae
credere nec telis occurrere virginis audet.
ac velut ille, prius quam tela inimica sequantur,
810 continuo in montis sese avius abdidit altos
occiso pastore lupus magnove iuvenco,
conscius audacis facti, caudamque remulcens
subiecit pavitantem utero silvasque petivit:
haud secus ex oculis se turbidus abstulit Arruns
815 contentusque fuga mediis se immiscuit armis.
illa manu moriens telum trahit, ossa sed inter
ferreus ad costas alto stat vulnere mucro.
labitur exsanguis, labuntur frigida leto
lumina, purpureus quondam color ora reliquit.
820 tum sic exspirans Accam ex aequalibus unam
adloquitur, fida ante alias quae sola Camillae
quicum partiri curas, atque haec ita fatur:
"hactenus, Acca soror, potui: nunc vulnus acerbum
conficit, et tenebris nigrescunt omnia circum.
825 effuge et haec Turno mandata novissima perfer:
succedat pugnae Troianosque arceat urbe.
iamque vale." simul his dictis linquebat habenas
ad terram non sponte fluens. tum frigida toto
paulatim exsolvit se corpore, lentaque colla
830 et captum leto posuit caput, arma relinquens,

826 urbe *MP*: urbi *R*
830 relinquens *M²P²*: reliquens *P*: relinquit *M*: reliquit *R*

queen. She herself noticed neither air nor sound nor weapon coming from the sky till the spear, borne home, found lodging beneath the bare breast and, driven deep, drank her maiden blood. In alarm, her comrades hurry around her, and catch their falling queen. More alarmed than the rest, Arruns flees in mingled joy and fear, and no more dares to trust his lance, or to meet the maiden's weapons. And just as the wolf, when he has slain a shepherd or a great steer, before hostile darts can pursue him, at once plunges by pathless ways among the high mountains, conscious of a reckless deed, and lowering his tail holds it quivering beneath his belly, and seeks the woods: just so does Arruns, in confusion, steal away from sight and, satisfied to escape, plunge into the armed throng. She tugs at the weapon with dying hand but in the deep wound the iron point stands fast between the bones, close to the ribs. Bloodless she sinks; her eyes sink, chill with death; the once radiant hue has left her face. Then, as her breath fails, she thus accosts Acca, one of her age-mates, true to Camilla beyond all the others, sole sharer of her cares, and thus she speaks: "So far, sister Acca, has my strength availed; now the bitter wound overpowers me, and all around grows dim and dark. Hurry away, and bring to Turnus my latest orders: to take my place in the battle, and ward off the Trojans from the town. And now farewell!" With these words she dropped the reins, slipping helplessly to earth. Then, growing chill, she slowly freed herself from all the body's bonds, drooped her nerveless neck and the head which Death had seized, letting fall her weapons,

vitaque cum gemitu fugit indignata sub umbras.
tum vero immensus surgens ferit aurea clamor
sidera: deiecta crudescit pugna Camilla;
incurrunt densi simul omnis copia Teucrum
835   Tyrrhenique duces Euandrique Arcades alae.
     At Triviae custos iamdudum in montibus Opis
alta sedet summis spectatque interrita pugnas.
utque procul medio iuvenum in clamore furentum
prospexit tristi multatam morte Camillam,
840   ingemuitque deditque has imo pectore voces:
"heu nimium, virgo, nimium crudele luisti
supplicium Teucros conata lacessere bello!
nec tibi desertae in dumis coluisse Dianam
profuit aut nostras umero gessisse pharetras.
845   non tamen indecorem tua te regina reliquit
extrema iam in morte, neque hoc sine nomine letum
per gentis erit aut famam patieris inultae.
nam quicumque tuum violavit vulnere corpus
morte luet merita." fuit ingens monte sub alto
850   regis Dercenni terreno ex aggere bustum
antiqui Laurentis opacaque ilice tectum;
hic dea se primum rapido pulcherrima nisu
sistit et Arruntem tumulo speculatur ab alto.
ut vidit fulgentem armis ac vana tumentem,
855   "cur" inquit "diversus abis? huc derige gressum,
huc periture veni, capias ut digna Camillae
praemia. tune etiam telis moriere Dianae?"
FMPR   dixit, et aurata volucrem Threissa sagittam
depromsit pharetra cornuque infensa tetendit

---

[831] = 12.952   [839] multatam χ: mulcatam MPR
[844] pharetras PR: sagittas M

and with a moan her life fled resentfully to the Shades below. Then indeed a boundless uproar rose, striking the golden stars: Camilla fallen, the fight waxes fiercer; on they rush in crowds together, all the Teucrian host, the Tyrrhene chiefs, and Evander's Arcadian squadrons.

But Opis, Trivia's sentinel, has long been seated high on the mountain top, and, undismayed, watches the combat. And when far off, amid the din of raging warriors, she saw that Camilla had paid the penalty of death, she sighed and from her heart's depth uttered these words: "Alas! too cruel, too cruel, maiden, the forfeit you have paid for trying to defy the Teucrians in battle! It has availed you nothing that, alone in the woodlands, you worshipped Diana and wore our quiver on your shoulder. But your queen has not left you unhonoured even in death's last hour; nor will your doom be without renown among the nations, nor will you bear the reproach of one unavenged; for whoever profaned your limbs with this wound will pay the debt of death." Under the mountain height stood a mound of earth, the mighty tomb of Dercennus, Laurentine king of old, screened by shadowy ilex; here first the beautiful goddess, with swift spring, plants her feet, and from the high barrow espies Arruns. When she saw him blazing in his armour and swelling with pride, she cried, "Why do you stray so far? Turn your steps this way, come this way to your death and for Camilla receive the reward you deserve! Shall you too die by Diana's darts?" So spoke the Thracian nymph, and from gilded quiver plucked a winged shaft, stretched the bow with full intent, and drew it far, till the

---

[845] reliquit *MR*: relinquet *P*   [854] fulgentem armis *PR*:
laetantem animis *M*   [856] Camillae *MP*: Camilla *R*

860 et duxit longe, donec curvata coirent
inter se capita et manibus iam tangeret aequis,
laeva aciem ferri, dextra nervoque papillam.
extemplo teli stridorem aurasque sonantis
audiit una Arruns haesitque in corpore ferrum.
865 illum exspirantem socii atque extrema gementem
obliti ignoto camporum in pulvere linquunt;
Opis ad aetherium pennis aufertur Olympum.
    Prima fugit domina amissa levis ala Camillae,
turbati fugiunt Rutuli, fugit acer Atinas,
870 disiectique duces desolatique manipli
tuta petunt et equis aversi ad moenia tendunt.
nec quisquam instantis Teucros letumque ferentis
sustentare valet telis aut sistere contra,
sed laxos referunt umeris languentibus arcus,
875 quadripedumque putrem cursu quatit ungula campum.
volvitur ad muros caligine turbidus atra
pulvis, et e speculis percussae pectora matres
femineum clamorem ad caeli sidera tollunt.
qui cursu portas primi inrupere patentis,
880 hos inimica super mixto premit agmine turba,
nec miseram effugiunt mortem, sed limine in ipso,
moenibus in patriis atque inter tuta domorum
confixi exspirant animas. pars claudere portas,
nec sociis aperire viam nec moenibus audent
885 accipere orantis, oriturque miserrima caedes
defendentum armis aditus inque arma ruentum.
exclusi ante oculos lacrimantumque ora parentum
pars in praecipitis fossas urgente ruina
volvitur, immissis pars caeca et concita frenis

882 inter *FP*: intra *MR*

curving ends met together and, with levelled hands, she could touch the steel's point with her left, her breast with her right and with the bow string. Straightway, at the self-same moment, Arruns heard the whistling dart and whirring air, and the steel was lodged in his breast. As he gasps and groans his last breaths, his forgetful comrades leave him on the unknown dust of the plain; Opis wings her way to heavenly Olympus.

Their mistress lost, Camilla's light squadron flees first; in rout the Rutulians flee, valiant Atinas flees; scattered captains, and troops left leaderless, make for shelter and, wheeling their horses, gallop to the walls. Nor can any check with their weapons the onset of the death-dealing Trojans, nor stand against it, but cast their unstrung bows on fainting shoulders, and in their galloping course the horsehoof shakes the crumbling plain. On to the walls rolls a cloud of dust, black and murky, and from the watch-towers mothers, beating their breasts, raise to the stars of heaven their womanish cries. Upon those who first broke at full speed through the open gates there presses hard a throng of foes, mingling with their ranks, nor do they escape a piteous death, but on the very threshold, their native walls about them, and within the shelter of their homes, they are pierced through, and gasp away their lives. Some close the gates, and dare not open a way to their friends, nor receive them inside the walls, implore as they may; and slaughter most pitiful ensues, both of those guarding the entry sword in hand, and of those rushing upon the sword. Shut out before the eyes and gaze of weeping parents, some, driven by the rout, roll headlong into the trenches; some, charging blindly with loosened

890   arietat in portas et duros obice postis.
ipsae de muris summo certamine matres
(monstrat amor verus patriae), ut videre Camillam,
tela manu trepidae iaciunt ac robore duro
stipitibus ferrum sudibusque imitantur obustis
895   praecipites, primaeque mori pro moenibus ardent.
MPR   Interea Turnum in silvis saevissimus implet
nuntius et iuveni ingentem fert Acca tumultum:
deletas Volscorum acies, cecidisse Camillam,
ingruere infensos hostis et Marte secundo
900   omnia corripuisse, metum iam ad moenia ferri.
ille furens (et saeva Iovis sic numina poscunt)
deserit obsessos collis, nemora aspera linquit.
vix e conspectu exierat campumque tenebat,
cum pater Aeneas saltus ingressus apertos
905   exsuperatque iugum silvaque evadit opaca.
sic ambo ad muros rapidi totoque feruntur
agmine nec longis inter se passibus absunt;
ac simul Aeneas fumantis pulvere campos
prospexit longe Laurentiaque agmina vidit,
910   et saevum Aenean agnovit Turnus in armis
adventumque pedum flatusque audivit equorum.
continuoque ineant pugnas et proelia temptent,
ni roseus fessos iam gurgite Phoebus Hibero
tingat equos noctemque die labente reducat.
915   considunt castris ante urbem et moenia vallant.

rein, batter at the gates and stoutly barred doors. The very mothers from the walls, in keenest rivalry (true love of country points the way), when they marked Camilla, fling weapons with trembling hands, and hastily do the work of steel with stout oaken poles and seared stakes, and burn to be the first to die defending their walls.

Meanwhile in the forests the woeful tidings fill Turnus' ears, and Acca brings the warrior her tale of mighty turmoil: the Volscian ranks destroyed, Camilla fallen, the foe fiercely advancing and sweeping the field in triumphant warfare, the panic now passing to the town. He, raging— and Jove's stern will so demands—quits the hills' ambush, and leaves the rough woodland. Scarce had he passed from view and reached the plain when father Aeneas, entering the unguarded pass, scales the ridge, and issues from the shady wood. So both march toward the walls, swiftly and in full force, and not far distant from each other: and at the same moment Aeneas descried far off the plain smoking with dust and saw the Laurentine hosts, and Turnus was aware of fell Aeneas in arms, and heard the march of feet and the snorting of steeds. And they would enter the fray at once and try the issue of battle, but ruddy Phoebus already bathes his weary team in the Iberian flood and, as day ebbs, brings back the night. Before the city they encamp and strengthen the ramparts.

LIBER XII

MPR Turnus ut infractos adverso Marte Latinos
defecisse videt, sua nunc promissa reposci,
se signari oculis, ultro implacabilis ardet
attollitque animos. Poenorum qualis in arvis
5 saucius ille gravi venantum vulnere pectus
tum demum movet arma leo, gaudetque comantis
excutiens cervice toros fixumque latronis
impavidus frangit telum et fremit ore cruento:
haud secus accenso gliscit violentia Turno.
10 tum sic adfatur regem atque ita turbidus infit:
"nulla mora in Turno; nihil est quod dicta retractent
ignavi Aeneadae, nec quae pepigere recusent:
congredior. fer sacra, pater, et concipe foedus.
aut hac Dardanium dextra sub Tartara mittam
15 desertorem Asiae (sedeant spectentque Latini),
et solus ferro crimen commune refellam,
aut habeat victos, cedat Lavinia coniunx."
    Olli sedato respondit corde Latinus:
"o praestans animi iuvenis, quantum ipse feroci
20 virtute exsuperas, tanto me impensius aequum est
consulere atque omnis metuentem expendere casus.
sunt tibi regna patris Dauni, sunt oppida capta

BOOK XII

When Turnus sees the Latins crushed and faint of heart through war's reverse, his own pledge now claimed, and himself the mark of every eye, forthwith he blazes with wrath unappeasable and raises his courage. As in Punic fields a lion, when wounded in the chest by huntsmen with a grievous stroke, only then wakes to war, joyously tosses from his neck his shaggy main, and undaunted breaks the robber's implanted dart, roaring with blood-stained mouth: even so in Turnus' kindling soul the fury swells. Then thus he accosts the king, and with these wild words begins: "No delay lies with Turnus! There is no reason for the coward sons of Aeneas to recall their words or to renounce their pact! I go to meet him. Bring on the holy rites, father, and frame the covenant. Either with this arm I will hurl to Tartarus the Dardan, the Asian runaway—let the Latins sit and see it—and with my sword alone refute the nation's shame,[1] or let him be lord of the vanquished, let Lavinia come to him as bride!"

To him Latinus with unruffled soul replied: "O youth of matchless spirit, the more you excel in proud valour, the more carefully it is right that I ponder and in fear weigh every chance. You have your father Daunus' realms, you

[1] All are under the slur of cowardice.

multa manu, nec non aurumque animusque Latino est;
sunt aliae innuptae Latio et Laurentibus arvis
25 nec genus indecores. sine me haec haud mollia fatu
sublatis aperire dolis, *simul hoc animo hauri:*
me natam nulli veterum sociare procorum
fas erat, idque omnes divique hominesque canebant.
victus amore tui, cognato sanguine victus
30 coniugis et maestae lacrimis, vincla omnia rupi;
promissam eripui genero, arma impia sumpsi.
ex illo qui me casus, quae, Turne, sequantur
bella, vides, quantos primus patiare labores.
bis magna victi pugna vix urbe tuemur
35 spes Italas; recalent nostro Tiberina fluenta
sanguine adhuc campique ingentes ossibus albent.
quo referor totiens? quae mentem insania mutat?
si Turno exstincto socios sum ascire paratus,
cur non incolumi potius certamina tollo?
40 quid consanguinei Rutuli, quid cetera dicet
Italia, ad mortem si te (fors dicta refutet!)
prodiderim, natam et conubia nostra petentem?
respice res bello varias, miserere parentis
longaevi, quem nunc maestum patria Ardea longe
45 dividit." haudquaquam dictis violentia Turni
flectitur; exsuperat magis aegrescitque medendo.
MR ut primum fari potuit, sic institit ore:
"quam pro me curam geris, hanc precor, optime, pro me

---

24 arvis *M*: agris (11.431) *PR*
26b (*MPR*)] *del. Peerlkamp*
35 Tiberina *Charisius*: Thybrina *MPR*
46 aegrescitque medendo *PR*: ardescitque tuendo (1.713) *M*
47 institit *R*: incipit (692) *Mγ*

have the many towns your hand has taken; Latinus, too, has gold and good will. Other unwed maids there are in Latium and Laurentum's fields, and of no ignoble birth. Suffer me to utter this hard saying, stripped of all disguise, *and drink it into your soul:* for me to ally my child to any of her old-time wooers was forbidden, and this all gods and men foretold.[2] Overborne by love of you, overborne by kindred blood[3] and the tears of my sorrowing queen, I broke all fetters, snatched the betrothed from her promised husband, and drew the unholy sword. From that day, Turnus, you see what perils, what wars pursue me, what heavy burdens you bear above all. Twice vanquished in terrible battle,[4] we can scarcely guard within our walls the hopes of Italy; Tiber's streams are still warm with our blood, the boundless plains still white with our bones. Why do I drift back so often?[5] What madness turns my purpose? If, with Turnus dead, I am ready to link them to me as allies, why not rather end the strife while he still lives? What will your Rutulian kinsmen say, what the rest of Italy, if—Fortune refute the word!—I should betray you to death, while you woo our daughter in marriage? Consider war's changes and chances; pity your aged father, whom now his native Ardea keeps far away from us in sorrow!" Not at all do his words bend the fury of Turnus; still higher it mounts, more inflamed with the healing. As soon as he could speak he thus began: "The care you have on my be-

---

[2] Cf. 7.95 above.   [3] Amata, wife of Latinus, was sister to Venilia, mother of Turnus.   [4] Perhaps a deliberate echo of the words in which the disaster of Lake Trasimene was announced to the crowd in the Forum: *pugna magna victi sumus* (Livy 22.7).

[5] I.e. from what must be his inevitable decision.

deponas letumque sinas pro laude pacisci.
50 et nos tela, pater, ferrumque haud debile dextra
spargimus, et nostro sequitur de vulnere sanguis.
longe illi dea mater erit, quae nube fugacem
feminea tegat et vanis sese occulat umbris."
    At regina nova pugnae conterrita sorte
55 flebat et ardentem generum moritura tenebat:
"Turne, per has ego te lacrimas, per si quis Amatae
tangit honos animum: spes tu nunc una, senectae
tu requies miserae, decus imperiumque Latini
te penes, in te omnis domus inclinata recumbit.
60 unum oro: desiste manum committere Teucris.
qui te cumque manent isto certamine casus
et me, Turne, manent; simul haec invisa relinquam
lumina nec generum Aenean captiva videbo."
accepit vocem lacrimis Lavinia matris
65 flagrantis perfusa genas, cui plurimus ignem
subiecit rubor et calefacta per ora cucurrit.
Indum sanguineo veluti violaverit ostro
si quis ebur, aut mixta rubent ubi lilia multa
alba rosa, talis virgo dabat ore colores.
70 illum turbat amor figitque in virgine vultus;
ardet in arma magis paucisque adfatur Amatam:
"ne, quaeso, ne me lacrimis neve omine tanto
prosequere in duri certamina Martis euntem,
o mater; neque enim Turno mora libera mortis.
75 nuntius haec, Idmon, Phrygio mea dicta tyranno
haud placitura refer. cum primum crastina caelo
puniceis invecta rotis Aurora rubebit,

---

6 In the *Iliad* (at 5.311ff.) Aeneas is rescued by Aphrodite, who

half, most gracious lord, on my behalf, I pray, resign, and
suffer me to barter death for fame. I too, father, can scatter
darts and no weakling steel from this right hand, and from
my strokes too flows blood. His goddess-mother will not be
at his side to shelter the runaway, woman-like, with a cloud
and hide herself in empty shadows."[6]

But the queen, dismayed by the new terms of conflict,
wept and, ready to die, clung to her fiery son: "Turnus, by
these my tears, by any reverence for Amata that yet may
touch your heart—you are now my only hope, the comfort
of my sad old age; in your hands are the honour and sover-
eignty of Latinus, on you rests all our sinking house—one
boon I beg: forbear to join combat with the Trojans. What-
ever perils await you in that combat await me also, Turnus;
with you I will quit this hateful light, and I will not in cap-
tivity see Aeneas as my son." Lavinia heard her mother's
words, her burning cheeks steeped in tears, while a deep
blush kindled its fire, and mantled her glowing face. As
when someone stains Indian ivory with crimson dye, or
white lilies blush when mingled with many a rose—such
hues her maiden features showed. Love throws Turnus
into turmoil, and he fastens his gaze upon the maid; then,
fired yet more for the fray, he briefly addresses Amata: "I
beseech you, mother, do not send me off with tears or such
ill omen as I go forth to stern war's conflicts; for Turnus is
not free to delay his death. Idmon, be my herald and bear
my message to the Phrygian king—a message he will not
welcome: as soon as tomorrow's Dawn, riding in crimson

spreads before him a fold of her garment. Elsewhere, however,
Apollo and Poseidon rescue him in a cloud (*Iliad* 5.344; 20.321 ff.;
cf. 3.380).

non Teucros agat in Rutulos, Teucrum arma quiescant
et Rutuli; nostro dirimamus sanguine bellum,
80 illo quaeratur coniunx Lavinia campo."
    Haec ubi dicta dedit rapidusque in tecta recessit,
poscit equos gaudetque tuens ante ora frementis,
Pilumno quos ipsa decus dedit Orithyia,
qui candore nives anteirent, cursibus auras.
85 circumstant properi aurigae manibusque lacessunt
pectora plausa cavis et colla comantia pectunt.
ipse dehinc auro squalentem alboque orichalco
circumdat loricam umeris, simul aptat habendo
ensemque clipeumque et rubrae cornua cristae,
90 ensem quem Dauno ignipotens deus ipse parenti
fecerat et Stygia candentem tinxerat unda.
exim quae mediis ingenti adnixa columnae
MPR aedibus astabat, validam vi corripit hastam,
Actoris Aurunci spolium, quassatque trementem
95 vociferans: "nunc, o numquam frustrata vocatus
hasta meos, nunc tempus adest: te maximus Actor,
te Turni nunc dextra gerit; da sternere corpus
loricamque manu valida lacerare revulsam
semiviri Phrygis et foedare in pulvere crinis
100 vibratos calido ferro murraque madentis."
his agitur furiis, totoque ardentis ab ore
scintillae absistunt, oculis micat acribus ignis,
mugitus veluti cum prima in proelia taurus
terrificos ciet atque irasci in cornua temptat
105 arboris obnixus trunco, ventosque lacessit
ictibus aut sparsa ad pugnam proludit harena.

---

92 columnae *MR*: columna γ   104 atque (*G*.3.232) *M*: aut
PR (<106?)   105–106 = *G*.3.233–234

chariot, reddens in the sky, let him not lead Teucrians against Rutulians—let Teucrian arms and Rutulians have rest—with our own blood let us settle the war; on that field let Lavinia be wooed and won!"

When he has spoken these words and hurried back into the palace, he calls for his steeds, and exults to see them neighing before his face—the steeds that Orithyia herself gave as a glory to Pilumnus, because they excelled the snows in whiteness and the gales in speed. The eager charioteers stand round, patting with hollow palms their sounding chests, and combing their flowing manes. Next he binds upon his shoulders a corslet stiff with gold and pale mountain bronze; at the same time he fits on sword and shield and the horns of his ruddy crest;[7] the sword the divine Lord of Fire had himself wrought for his father Daunus and dipped, all glowing, in the waters of Styx. Then, as it stood leaning on a giant column in the middle of the hall, he seizes with strong hand his mighty spear, spoil of Auruncan Actor, and shakes it quivering, while he cries aloud: "Now, spear that never failed my call, now the hour is come! Mighty Actor once bore you; now the hand of Turnus wields you. Grant me to lay low the body of the Phrygian eunuch, with strong hand to tear and rend away his corslet, and to defile in dust his locks, crisped with heated iron and drenched in myrrh!" Such is the frenzy driving him: from all his face shoot fiery sparks; his eager eyes flash flame—even as a bull, before the battle begins, raises a fearful bellowing, and, as he tries to throw wrath into his horns, charges a tree's trunk; he lashes the winds with his blows, and paws the sand in prelude for the fray.

[7] The crest rested upon two projecting sockets made of horn.

Nec minus interea maternis saevus in armis
Aeneas acuit Martem et se suscitat ira,
oblato gaudens componi foedere bellum.
110 tum socios maestique metum solatur Iuli
fata docens, regique iubet responsa Latino
certa referre viros et pacis dicere leges.
Postera vix summos spargebat lumine montis
orta dies, cum primum alto se gurgite tollunt
115 Solis equi lucemque elatis naribus efflant:
campum ad certamen magnae sub moenibus urbis
dimensi Rutulique viri Teucrique parabant
in medioque focos et dis communibus aras
gramineas. alii fontemque ignemque ferebant
120 velati limo et verbena tempora vincti.
procedit legio Ausonidum, pilataque plenis
agmina se fundunt portis. hinc Troïus omnis
Tyrrhenusque ruit variis exercitus armis,
haud secus instructi ferro quam si aspera Martis
125 pugna vocet. nec non mediis in milibus ipsi
ductores auro volitant ostroque superbi,
et genus Assaraci Mnestheus et fortis Asilas
et Messapus equum domitor, Neptunia proles;
utque dato signo spatia in sua quisque recessit,
130 defigunt tellure hastas et scuta reclinant.
tum studio effusae matres et vulgus inermum
invalidique senes turris ac tecta domorum
obsedere, alii portis sublimibus astant.

117 dimensi *PR*: demensi *M*
120 limo *Caper and Hyginus (Servius)*: lino *MPR*
126 superbi *M*: decori (5.133) *PR*
128 = 7.691; 9.523

No less, meantime, Aeneas, fierce in the arms his mother gave,[8] whets his valour and rouses his heart with wrath, rejoicing that the war is being settled by the compact offered. Then he comforts his comrades, and sad Iülus' fear, expounding the fates, and bids them bear firm answer to King Latinus and declare the terms of peace.

The next dawn was just beginning to sprinkle the mountain tops with light, at the time when the Sun's steeds first rise from the deep flood, and breathe light from raised nostrils: Rutulians and Teucrians had measured the field for the combat under the great city's walls, and in the middle were preparing hearths and grassy altars to their common deities. Others were bringing fountain water and fire, draped in aprons[9] and their brows bound with vervain. The Ausonian host comes forth, and the troops, close-ranked, pour from the crowded gates. On this side streams forth all the Trojan and Tyrrhene host in diverse accoutrements, armed in steel as if the harsh battle strife called them. No less, amid their thousands, do the captains dart to and fro, brilliant in gold and purple, Mnestheus of the line of Assaracus, and brave Asilas, and Messapus, tamer of horses, seed of Neptune. As soon as, on the given signal, each has retired to his own ground, they plant their spears in the earth, and rest their shields against them. Then, eagerly streaming forth, mothers and the unarmed throng, and feeble old men, have beset towers and housetops; others stand upon the lofty gates.

[8] Made by Vulcan at the request of Venus; cf. *Aen.* 8.608ff.

[9] The *limus* was an apron worn by priests, so called because it had a transverse stripe of purple.

At Iuno ex summo (qui nunc Albanus habetur;
135   tum neque nomen erat neque honos aut gloria monti)
prospiciens tumulo campum aspectabat et ambas
Laurentum Troumque acies urbemque Latini.
extemplo Turni sic est adfata sororem
diva deam, stagnis quae fluminibusque sonoris
140   praesidet (hunc illi rex aetheris altus honorem
Iuppiter erepta pro virginitate sacravit):
"nympha, decus fluviorum, animo gratissima nostro,
scis ut te cunctis unam, quaecumque Latinae
magnanimi Iovis ingratum ascendere cubile,
145   praetulerim caelique libens in parte locarim:
disce tuum, ne me incuses, Iuturna, dolorem.
qua visa est Fortuna pati Parcaeque sinebant
cedere res Latio, Turnum et tua moenia texi;
nunc iuvenem imparibus video concurrere fatis,
150   Parcarumque dies et vis inimica propinquat.
non pugnam aspicere hanc oculis, non foedera possum.
tu pro germano si quid praesentius audes,
perge; decet. forsan miseros meliora sequentur."
Vix ea, cum lacrimas oculis Iuturna profudit
155   terque quaterque manu pectus percussit honestum.
"non lacrimis hoc tempus" ait Saturnia Iuno:
"accelera et fratrem, si quis modus, eripe morti;
aut tu bella cie conceptumque excute foedus.
auctor ego audendi." sic exhortata reliquit
160   incertam et tristi turbatam vulnere mentis.
Interea reges ingenti mole Latinus
quadriiugo vehitur curru (cui tempora circum

---

142 gratissima *M*: carissima *PR*
154 profudit *M²P*: profundit *M*: profugit *R*

But Juno, from the hill now called Alban—at that time the mount had neither name nor fame nor honour—looking forth, gazed upon the plain, upon the double lines of Laurentum and Troy, and upon the city of Latinus. Straightway, goddess to goddess, she spoke thus to Turnus' sister, mistress of the ponds and sounding rivers: this honour Jupiter, heaven's high lord, assigned to her in return for theft of maidenhood: "Nymph, glory of rivers, most dear to my heart, you know how, above all Latin maids that have mounted to great-hearted Jove's thankless bed, I have preferred you alone, and have gladly given you a place in heaven: learn, Juturna, the grief that will be yours, lest you blame me. Where Fortune seemed to permit, and the Fates suffered Latium's state to prosper, I shielded Turnus and your city. Now I see the prince confront unequal destiny; the day of doom, and the enemy's stroke, draws nigh. Upon this battle, this treaty, my eyes cannot look: you, if you dare to do anything of more present help for your brother, go on; it befits you. Perhaps happier days will come to those who are now unhappy."

Scarcely had she said this when Juturna's eyes streamed with tears, and thrice, even four times her hand smote her comely breast. "This is no time for tears," cries Saturnian Juno; "hasten, and if there is any way, snatch your brother from death; or rouse battle, and strike from their hands the treaty they have framed. I it is who bid you dare." Having counselled thus, she left her doubtful and distracted by the cruel wound to her heart.

Meanwhile the kings ride forth, Latinus drawn in four-horse chariot of immense size, twelve golden rays circling

aurati bis sex radii fulgentia cingunt,
Solis avi specimen), bigis it Turnus in albis,
165 bina manu lato crispans hastilia ferro.
hinc pater Aeneas, Romanae stirpis origo,
sidereo flagrans clipeo et caelestibus armis
et iuxta Ascanius, magnae spes altera Romae,
procedunt castris, puraque in veste sacerdos
170 saetigeri fetum suis intonsamque bidentem
attulit admovitque pecus flagrantibus aris.
illi ad surgentem conversi lumina solem
dant fruges manibus salsas et tempora ferro
summa notant pecudum, paterisque altaria libant.
175 tum pius Aeneas stricto sic ense precatur:
    "Esto nunc Sol testis et haec mihi terra vocanti,
quam propter tantos potui perferre labores,
et pater omnipotens et tu Saturnia coniunx
(iam melior, iam, diva, precor), tuque inclute Mavors,
180 cuncta tuo qui bella, pater, sub numine torques;
fontisque fluviosque voco, quaeque aetheris alti
religio et quae caeruleo sunt numina ponto:
cesserit Ausonio si fors victoria Turno,
convenit Euandri victos discedere ad urbem,
185 cedet Iulus agris, nec post arma ulla rebelles
Aeneadae referent ferrove haec regna lacessent.
sin nostrum adnuerit nobis victoria Martem
(ut potius reor et potius di numine firment),
non ego nec Teucris Italos parere iubebo
190 nec mihi regna peto: paribus se legibus ambae

165 = 1.313
176 vocanti *PR*: precanti *M*
178 coniunx *PR*: Iuno (156) *M*

his gleaming brows, emblem of his ancestor the Sun;[10] Turnus drives behind a snow-white pair, his hand brandishing two spears with broad heads of steel. On this side father Aeneas, source of the Roman stock, ablaze with starry shield and celestial arms, and beside him Ascanius, second hope of mighty Rome, issue from the camp; while a priest in spotless raiment has brought the young of a bristly boar and an unshorn sheep of two years old, and set the beasts beside the blazing altars. The heroes, turning their eyes to the rising sun, sprinkle salted meal from their hands, mark the foreheads of the victims with the knife,[11] and from goblets pour libations on the altars. Then loyal Aeneas, drawing his sword, thus makes prayer:

"Let the Sun now be witness to my call, and this land, for whose sake I have been able to endure such travails, and the Father Almighty, and you, Saturnia, his consort— kinder now at last, I pray, goddess: and you, famed Mavors, you, father, who wield all warfare under your sway; and on Founts and Floods I call, on all the majesty of high heaven and the powers that belong to the blue seas: if by chance victory falls to Turnus the Ausonian, it is agreed that the vanquished withdraw to Evander's city. Iülus shall quit the land; and never in after time shall the sons of Aeneas return for renewed war, or attack this realm with the sword. But if Victory grant that the battle be ours—as I think more likely, and may the gods so confirm it with their power!—I will not bid the Italians be subject to Teucrians, nor do I seek the realm for mine; under equal terms let

[10] Latinus was descended from the Sun through Circe, mother of Faunus.

[11] I.e. by cutting off a lock of hair to be burnt.

invictae gentes aeterna in foedera mittant.
sacra deosque dabo; socer arma Latinus habeto,
imperium sollemne socer; mihi moenia Teucri
constituent urbique dabit Lavinia nomen."
195   Sic prior Aeneas, sequitur sic deinde Latinus
suspiciens caelum, tenditque ad sidera dextram:
"haec eadem, Aenea, terram, mare, sidera, iuro
Latonaeque genus duplex Ianumque bifrontem,
vimque deum infernam et duri sacraria Ditis;
200 audiat haec genitor qui foedera fulmine sancit.
tango aras, medios ignis et numina testor:
nulla dies pacem hanc Italis nec foedera rumpet,
quo res cumque cadent; nec me vis ulla volentem
avertet, non, si tellurem effundat in undas
205 diluvio miscens caelumque in Tartara solvat,
ut sceptrum hoc" (dextra sceptrum nam forte gerebat)
"numquam fronde levi fundet virgulta nec umbras,
cum semel in silvis imo de stirpe recisum
matre caret posuitque comas et bracchia ferro,
210 olim arbos, nunc artificis manus aere decoro
inclusit patribusque dedit gestare Latinis."
talibus inter se firmabant foedera dictis
conspectu in medio procerum. tum rite sacratas
in flammam iugulant pecudes et viscera vivis
215 eripiunt, cumulantque oneratis lancibus aras.
    At vero Rutulis impar ea pugna videri
iamdudum et vario misceri pectora motu,

202 rumpet *MR*: rumpit *P*: rumpat *P*2
213 conspectu *PR*: prospectu *M*

both nations, unconquered, enter upon an everlasting compact. I will give gods and their rites; Latinus, my father-in-law, is to keep the sword; my father-in-law is to keep his wonted command. The Teucrians shall raise walls for me, and Lavinia give the city her name."

Thus first Aeneas speaks, and after him Latinus thus follows, lifting eyes to heaven, and stretching his right hand to the stars: "By these same Powers I swear, Aeneas, by earth, sea, stars, Latona's twofold offspring, and two-faced Janus, and the might of gods below, and the shrines of cruel Dis: may the great Sire hear my words, who sanctions treaties with his thunderbolt! I touch the altars, I adjure these fires and gods that stand between us: no time shall break this peace and truce for Italy, however things befall; nor shall any force turn aside my will, not though, commingling all in deluge, it plunge land into water, and dissolve Heaven into Hell: just as this sceptre"[12] (for by chance in his hand he held his sceptre) "shall never sprout with light foliage into branch or shade, now that, once hewn in the forest from the lowest stem, it is bereft of its mother, and beneath the steel has shed its leaves and twigs; once a tree, now the craftsman's hand has cased it in fine bronze and given it to the elders of Latium to bear." With such words they sealed the treaty between them, in full view of the leaders; then over the flame they slay the duly hallowed beasts, and tear out the live entrails, and pile the altars with laden dishes.

But to the Rutulians the battle had long seemed unequal, and their hearts, swayed to and fro, had long been in

[12] Cf. the oath of Achilles in Homer, *Iliad* 1.234ff.

315

tum magis ut propius cernunt *non viribus aequis*.
adiuvat incessu tacito progressus et aram
220 suppliciter venerans demisso lumine Turnus
tabentesque genae et iuvenali in corpore pallor.
quem simul ac Iuturna soror crebrescere vidit
sermonem et vulgi variare labantia corda,
in medias acies formam adsimulata Camerti,
225 cui genus a proavis ingens clarumque paternae
nomen erat virtutis, et ipse acerrimus armis,
in medias dat sese acies haud nescia rerum
rumoresque serit varios ac talia fatur:
"non pudet, o Rutuli, pro cunctis talibus unam
230 obiectare animam? numerone an viribus aequi
non sumus? en, omnes et Troes et Arcades hi sunt,
fatalesque manus, infensa Etruria Turno:
vix hostem, alterni si congrediamur, habemus.
ille quidem ad superos, quorum se devovet aris,
235 succedet fama vivusque per ora feretur;
nos patria amissa dominis parere superbis
cogemur, qui nunc lenti consedimus arvis."
    Talibus incensa est iuvenum sententia dictis
iam magis atque magis, serpitque per agmina murmur:
240 ipsi Laurentes mutati ipsique Latini.
qui sibi iam requiem pugnae rebusque salutem
sperabant, nunc arma volunt foedusque precantur
infectum et Turni sortem miserantur iniquam.
his aliud maius Iuturna adiungit et alto

---

218 non viribus aequis (*MPR*) *del. Brunck as interpolated from*
5.809 *to fill a half-line*   221 tabentes χ: pubentes *MPR*
    232 fatalesque *MR*: fatalisque *P*
    237 arvis *PR*: armis *M*

turmoil; all the more now, when they beheld the combatants at closer view *in ill-matched strength*. Turnus swells the unrest by advancing with noiseless tread and as a suppliant venerating the altar with downcast eye—swells it by his wasted cheeks and by the pallor of his youthful frame. As soon as Juturna his sister saw these whispers spread, and the hearts of the throng wavering in doubt, into the midmost ranks, in feigned semblance of Camers—noble his ancestral house, glorious the renown of his father's worth, and he himself most valiant in arms—into the midmost ranks she comes, knowing well her task, scatters diverse rumours, and speaks these words: "Are you not ashamed, Rutulians, to set one man's life at hazard for so many men? Are we not their match in numbers and in might? See, all of them are here, both Trojans and Arcadians, and the fate-led troops of Etruria, hostile to Turnus: even if only every other man of us joins battle, there is scarcely an enemy for each of us. Turnus will mount on fame to the gods, on whose altars he has dedicated his life, and shall endure on the lips of men:[13] but we, our country lost, will submit perforce to haughty masters—we, who today sit listless in the fields!"

With such words the warriors' resolve is kindled yet more and more, and a murmur creeps from rank to rank. Even the Laurentines, even the Latins are changed; and they who but lately hoped for rest from the fray, and safety for their fortunes, now long for arms, pray that the covenant be undone, and pity Turnus' unjust fate. To these Juturna adds another and mightier impulse, and in high

[13] Cf. *Georgics* 3.9.

245 dat signum caelo, quo non praesentius ullum
turbavit mentes Italas monstroque fefellit.
namque volans rubra fulvus Iovis ales in aethra
litoreas agitabat avis turbamque sonantem
agminis aligeri, subito cum lapsus ad undas
250 cycnum excellentem pedibus rapit improbus uncis.
arrexere animos Itali, cunctaeque volucres
convertunt clamore fugam (mirabile visu),
aetheraque obscurant pennis hostemque per auras
facta nube premunt, donec vi victus et ipso
255 pondere defecit praedamque ex unguibus ales
proiecit fluvio, penitusque in nubila fugit.
    Tum vero augurium Rutuli clamore salutant
expediuntque manus, primusque Tolumnius augur
"hoc erat, hoc votis" inquit "quod saepe petivi.
260 accipio agnoscoque deos; me, me duce ferrum
corripite, o miseri, quos improbus advena bello
territat invalidas ut avis, et litora vestra
vi populat. petet ille fugam penitusque profundo
vela dabit. vos unanimi densete catervas
265 et regem vobis pugna defendite raptum."
    Dixit, et adversos telum contorsit in hostis
procurrens; sonitum dat stridula cornus et auras
certa secat. simul hoc, simul ingens clamor et omnes
turbati cunei calefactaque corda tumultu.
270 hasta volans, ut forte novem pulcherrima fratrum
corpora constiterant contra, quos fida crearat
una tot Arcadio coniunx Tyrrhena Gylippo,

264 densete *R*: densate *MP*

heaven shows a sign, than which none was more potent to confound Italian minds and cheat them with its miracle. Flying through the ruddy sky, Jove's golden bird was chasing the fowls of the shore and the clamorous rout of their winged troop, when, swooping suddenly to the water, he shamelessly snatches up in his crooked talons the leader swan. The Italians become alert and, wondrous to behold, all the birds clamorously wheel their flight and, darkening the sky with wings, in serried cloud drive their foe through the air till, overborne by the onset and the sheer weight, the bird gave way, dropped the booty from his talons into the stream, and sped deep into the clouds.

Then in truth the Rutulians hail the omen with a cheer and spread out their hands.[14] And first of all Tolumnius the augur cries: "This it was, this, that my prayers have often sought! I accept it, I acknowledge the gods. With me, me, at your head, snatch up the sword, hapless people, whom, like frail birds, a shameless alien affrights with war, and violently ravages your coasts. He too will take to flight, and spread sail far across the deep. With one accord close up your ranks, and in battle defend the king who has been snatched from you!"

He spoke, and, darting forward, hurled his spear full against the foe; the whistling cornel shaft sings, and splits the air, unerring. At this deed, at once rises a mighty shout, the crowds are all confusion, and their hearts hot with turmoil. The spear flew on where, as it chanced, nine brothers of fine stature stood in its path—all of them his one faithful Tuscan wife had borne to Arcadian Gylippus. One of these

[14] To indicate their wish to fight, according to Servius, this being a *consensio militaris*.

horum unum ad medium, teritur qua sutilis alvo
balteus et laterum iuncturas fibula mordet,
275 egregium forma iuvenem et fulgentibus armis,
transadigit costas fulvaque effundit harena.
at fratres, animosa phalanx accensaque luctu,
pars gladios stringunt manibus, pars missile ferrum
corripiunt caecique ruunt. quos agmina contra
280 procurrunt Laurentum, hinc densi rursus inundant
Troes Agyllinique et pictis Arcades armis:
sic omnis amor unus habet decernere ferro.
diripuere aras, it toto turbida caelo
tempestas telorum ac ferreus ingruit imber,
285 craterasque focosque ferunt. fugit ipse Latinus
pulsatos referens infecto foedere divos.
infrenant alii currus aut corpora saltu
subiciunt in equos et strictis ensibus adsunt.
    Messapus regem regisque insigne gerentem
290 Tyrrhenum Aulesten, avidus confundere foedus,
adverso proterret equo; ruit ille recedens
et miser oppositis a tergo involvitur aris
in caput inque umeros. at fervidus advolat hasta
Messapus teloque orantem multa trabali
295 desuper altus equo graviter ferit atque ita fatur:
"hoc habet, haec melior magnis data victima divis."
concurrunt Itali spoliantque calentia membra.
obvius ambustum torrem Corynaeus ab ara
corripit et venienti Ebyso plagamque ferenti
300 occupat os flammis: olli ingens barba reluxit

275 = (*and probably the source of*) 6.861

near the waist, where the stitched belt chafes the belly, and the buckle bites the linked sides[15]—a youth of comely form and gleaming armour—it pierces clean through the ribs and stretches on the yellow sand. But his brothers—a gallant band, and fired by grief—some draw their swords, some seize their spears, and rush blindly on. Against them charge the Laurentine columns; from the other side again Trojans and Agyllines pour thickly in and Arcadians with blazoned arms. Thus all are ruled by one passion—to let the sword decide. They have stripped the altars; through the whole sky flies a thickening storm of javelins and the iron rain falls fast; bowls and hearth fires are carried off. Latinus himself takes flight, carrying away his defeated gods, the covenant now void; the others rein their chariots or leap on to their horses and with drawn swords stand ready.

Messapus, eager to destroy the truce, with charging steed scares off Tuscan Aulestes, a king[16] and wearing a king's device. As he backs away, he trips and falls, poor wretch, on his head and shoulders on to the altars behind him. Messapus flashes forth like fire, spear in hand, and, high on his horse, strikes heavily down upon him with massive spear, though sorely he pleads; then he speaks thus: "He's had it,[17] this nobler victim given to the mighty gods!" The Italians crowd around and despoil his body before it is cold. Standing in their path, Corynaeus snatches up a charred brand from the altar and, as Ebysus comes up and aims a blow, dashes flames in his face: his mighty beard

---

[15] I.e. the ends of the belt.   [16] He was an Etruscan *Lucumo* or *Lars*.   [17] I.e. he has had his death blow: an expression used by spectators when a gladiator was fatally hit.

nidoremque ambusta dedit. super ipse secutus
caesariem laeva turbati corripit hostis
impressoque genu nitens terrae applicat ipsum;
sic rigido latus ense ferit. Podalirius Alsum
305 pastorem primaque acie per tela ruentem
ense sequens nudo superimminet; ille securi
adversi frontem mediam mentumque reducta
disicit et sparso late rigat arma cruore.
olli dura quies oculos et ferreus urget
310 somnus, in aeternam conduntur lumina noctem.
  At pius Aeneas dextram tendebat inermem
nudato capite atque suos clamore vocabat:
"quo ruitis? quaeve ista repens discordia surgit?
o cohibete iras! ictum iam foedus et omnes
315 compositae leges. mihi ius concurrere soli;
me sinite atque auferte metus. ego foedera faxo
firma manu; Turnum debent haec iam mihi sacra."
has inter voces, media inter talia verba
ecce viro stridens alis adlapsa sagitta est,
320 incertum qua pulsa manu, quo turbine adacta,
quis tantam Rutulis laudem, casusne deusne,
attulerit; pressa est insignis gloria facti,
nec sese Aeneae iactavit vulnere quisquam.
  Turnus ut Aenean cedentem ex agmine vidit
325 turbatosque duces, subita spe fervidus ardet;
poscit equos atque arma simul, saltuque superbus
emicat in currum et manibus molitur habenas.
multa virum volitans dat fortia corpora leto.
seminecis volvit multos: aut agmina curru

309–310 = 10.745–746
310 conduntur *P*: clauduntur (10.746) *MR*

322

blazed up, and sent forth a smell of burning. Then himself pursuing the stroke, he clutches in his left hand the locks of his bewildered foe, and with a thrust of his bended knee brings his body to the earth, and there strikes his side with unyielding sword. Podalirius, pursuing with naked steel, towers over the shepherd Alsus as in foremost line he rushes through the darts; but Alsus, swinging back his axe, cuts through the middle of his enemy's brow and chin, and drenches his armour with widely spattered gore. Stern repose and iron slumber press upon his eyes, and their sight is curtained in everlasting night.

But good Aeneas, with head bared, was stretching forth his unarmed hand, and calling loudly to his men: "Where are you going? What is this sudden outburst of strife? Curb your rage! The truce has already been struck and all its terms fixed; I alone have the right to do battle. Let me act; banish your fears; this hand will prove the treaty true; these rites make Turnus already mine!" Amid these cries, amid such words, against him a whizzing arrow winged its way, launched by what hand, sped whirling by whom, none knows, nor who—chance or god—brought the Rutulians such honour: the fame of that high deed is hidden, and no one boasted of the wounding of Aeneas.

As soon as Turnus saw Aeneas withdrawing from the ranks, and his captains in confusion, he burns with the fire of sudden hope, calls for horses and arms, with a bound leaps proudly into his chariot, and firmly grasps the reins. In his swift course many a brave man's body he gives to death; many men he tumbles half-slain, or crushes whole ranks under his chariot, or, seizing spear after spear, show-

330 proterit aut raptas fugientibus ingerit hastas.
qualis apud gelidi cum flumina concitus Hebri
sanguineus Mavors clipeo increpat atque furentis
bella movens immittit equos, illi aequore aperto
ante Notos Zephyrumque volant, gemit ultima pulsu
335 Thraca pedum circumque atrae Formidinis ora
Iraeque Insidiaeque, dei comitatus, aguntur:
talis equos alacer media inter proelia Turnus
fumantis sudore quatit, miserabile caesis
hostibus insultans; spargit rapida ungula rores
340 sanguineos mixtaque cruor calcatur harena.
iamque neci Sthenelumque dedit Thamyrumque
        Pholumque,
hunc congressus et hunc, illum eminus; eminus ambo
Imbrasidas, Glaucum atque Laden, quos Imbrasus ipse
nutrierat Lycia paribusque ornaverat armis
345 vel conferre manum vel equo praevertere ventos.
        Parte alia media Eumedes in proelia fertur,
antiqui proles bello praeclara Dolonis,
nomine avum referens, animo manibusque parentem,
qui quondam, castra ut Danaum speculator adiret,
350 ausus Pelidae pretium sibi poscere currus;
illum Tydides alio pro talibus ausis
adfecit pretio nec equis aspirat Achilli.
hunc procul ut campo Turnus prospexit aperto,
ante levi iaculo longum per inane secutus
355 sistit equos biiugis et curru desilit atque

330 aut *MP*: et *R*
332 increpat *P*: intonat (9.709) *MR*

ers them upon men trying to escape. Just as when by the streams of icy Hebrus blood-stained Mavors, stirred to fury, thunders with his shield and, rousing war, gives rein to his frenzied steeds; over the open plain they outstrip the South Wind and the West; furthest Thrace moans with the beat of their hoofs, and around him speed the forms of black Terror and Anger and Ambush, attendants on the god: with the same eagerness Turnus goads his sweat-smoking horses amid the fray, trampling on the foes, piteously slain; the galloping hoof splashes bloody dews, and spurns the gore and mingled sand. And now he has given Sthenelus to death, and Thamyrus, and Pholus, these in close encounter, the first from a distance; from a distance the sons of Imbrasus, Glaucus and Lades, whom Imbrasus himself had nurtured in Lycia and equipped with matched arms, either to fight hand to hand or on horseback to outstrip the winds.

Elsewhere Eumedes rides into the middle of the fray, war-famed offspring of old Dolon, in name renewing his grandfather, in heart and hand his father, who of old, for going as a spy to the Danaan camp, dared to ask as his reward the chariot of Peleus' son; but the son of Tydeus paid him a different reward for his daring and he does not aspire to Achilles' horses.[18] When Turnus saw him far off on the open plain, first following him with light javelin through the long space between them, he halts his twin-yoked horses and leaps from his chariot, descends on the

---

[18] The story of Dolon, who for the promised reward of Achilles' chariot and horses undertook to explore by night the Greek camp, but was put to death by Diomedes, the son of Tydeus, is told in Homer, *Iliad* 10.314ff.

semianimi lapsoque supervenit, et pede collo
impresso dextrae mucronem extorquet et alto
fulgentem tingit iugulo atque haec insuper addit:
"en agros et, quam bello, Troiane, petisti,
360 Hesperiam metire iacens: haec praemia, qui me
ferro ausi temptare, ferunt, sic moenia condunt."
huic comitem Asbyten coniecta cuspide mittit
Chloreaque Sybarimque Daretaque Thersilochumque
et sternacis equi lapsum cervice Thymoeten.
365 ac velut Edoni Boreae cum spiritus alto
insonat Aegaeo sequiturque ad litora fluctus,
qua venti incubuere, fugam dant nubila caelo:
sic Turno, quacumque viam secat, agmina cedunt
conversaeque ruunt acies; fert impetus ipsum
370 et cristam adverso curru quatit aura volantem.
non tulit instantem Phegeus animisque frementem
obiecit sese ad currum et spumantia frenis
ora citatorum dextra detorsit equorum.
dum trahitur pendetque iugis, hunc lata retectum
375 lancea consequitur rumpitque infixa bilicem
loricam et summum degustat vulnere corpus.
ille tamen clipeo obiecto conversus in hostem
ibat et auxilium ducto mucrone petebat,
cum rota praecipitem et procursu concitus axis
380 impulit effunditque solo, Turnusque secutus
imam inter galeam summi thoracis et oras
abstulit ense caput truncumque reliquit harenae.
     Atque ea dum campis victor dat funera Turnus,
interea Aenean Mnestheus et fidus Achates
385 Ascaniusque comes castris statuere cruentum
alternos longa nitentem cuspide gressus.

326

fallen, dying man and, planting his foot on his neck, wrests the sword from his hand, dyes the glittering blade deep in his throat, and adds these words besides: "See, Trojan, the fields and that Hesperia that you sought in war: lie there and measure them out! This is the reward of those who dare to tempt me with the sword; so do they establish their walls!" Then with cast of spear he sends Asbytes to keep him company, and Chloreus and Sybaris, Dares and Thersilochus, and Thymoetes, flung from the neck of his restive horse. And as when the blast of the Edonian North Wind roars on the deep Aegean and drives the billows shoreward; where the winds swoop, the clouds scud through the sky: so, wherever Turnus cleaves a path, the ranks give way and lines turn and run; his own speed bears him on, and the breeze, as his chariot meets it, tosses his flying plume. Phegeus could not meet his attack and fiery rage; he flung himself in front of the chariot and with his right hand wrenched aside the jaws of the furious horses, foaming on the bits. While he is dragged along clinging to the yoke, the broad spearhead reaches his unguarded side, rends the two-plated corslet where it has lodged, and with its wound just grazes the surface of the flesh. Yet he, with his shield before him, turned and was making for his foe, seeking aid from his drawn sword, when the wheel and axle, whirling onward, struck him headlong and flung him to the ground, and Turnus, following, with sweep of blade between the helmet's lowest rim and the breastplate's upper edge, struck off his head, and left the body on the sand.

And while Turnus victoriously deals this havoc over the plains, meantime Mnestheus and loyal Achates, and Ascanius by their side, set Aeneas down in the camp, bleeding and supporting every other step with his long

saevit et infracta luctatur harundine telum
eripere auxilioque viam, quae proxima, poscit:
ense secent lato vulnus telique latebram
390 rescindant penitus, seseque in bella remittant.
iamque aderat Phoebo ante alios dilectus Iapyx
Iasides, acri quondam cui captus amore
ipse suas artis, sua munera, laetus Apollo
augurium citharamque dabat celerisque sagittas.
395 ille, ut depositi proferret fata parentis,
scire potestates herbarum usumque medendi
maluit et mutas agitare inglorius artis.
stabat acerba fremens ingentem nixus in hastam
Aeneas magno iuvenum et maerentis Iuli
400 concursu, lacrimis immobilis. ille retorto
Paeonium in morem senior succinctus amictu
multa manu medica Phoebique potentibus herbis
nequiquam trepidat, nequiquam spicula dextra
sollicitat prensatque tenaci forcipe ferrum.
405 nulla viam Fortuna regit, nihil auctor Apollo
subvenit, et saevus campis magis ac magis horror
crebrescit propiusque malum est. iam pulvere caelum
stare vident: subeunt equites et spicula castris
densa cadunt mediis. it tristis ad aethera clamor
410 bellantum iuvenum et duro sub Marte cadentum.
    Hic Venus indigno nati concussa dolore
dictamnum genetrix Cretaea carpit ab Ida,

389 latebram *PR*: latebras *M*   394 dabat *PR*: dedit *M*
408 subeunt *P*: subeuntque *R*: *om. M*

---

19 Unlike music and prophecy, wherein the voice is used. But

spear. Raging, he struggles to pluck out the head of the broken shaft, and calls for the nearest means of relief, bidding them with broad sword cut the wound, tear open to the bottom the weapon's lair, and send him back to battle. And now Iapyx drew near, Iasus' son, dearest beyond others to Phoebus, to whom once Apollo himself, smitten with love's sting, gladly offered his own arts, his own powers— his augury, his lyre, and his swift arrows. He, to defer the fate of a father sick unto death, chose rather to know the virtues of herbs and the practice of healing, and to ply, inglorious, the silent arts.[19] Bitterly chafing, Aeneas stood propped on his mighty spear, amid a great concourse of warriors along with sorrowing Iülus, himself unmoved by their tears. The aged healer, with robe rolled back, and girt in Paeonian fashion, with healing hand and Phoebus' potent herbs works hard—in vain; in vain with his hand he pulls at the arrow, and with gripping tongs tugs at the steel. No Fortune guides his path, no help does Apollo's counsel give; and more and more the fierce alarm swells over the plains, and disaster draws closer. Now they see the sky supported on columns of dust; on come the horsemen, and shafts fall thick in the middle of the camp. The dismal cry rises to heaven, of men that fight and men that fall beneath the stern War God's hand.

At this Venus, shaken by her son's cruel pain, with a mother's care plucks from Cretan Ida dittany[20] clothed

the idea of obscurity is also included, for the profession of medicine does not lead to great fame.

[20] The dittany (*dictamnus*) takes its name from Mt. Dicte in Crete, where, according to Aristotle, Cicero, and others, wild goats found a cure for their wounds in the eating of the herb.

puberibus caulem foliis et flore comantem
purpureo; non illa feris incognita capris
415   gramina, cum tergo volucres haesere sagittae.
hoc Venus obscuro faciem circumdata nimbo
detulit, hoc fusum labris splendentibus amnem
inficit occulte medicans, spargitque salubris
ambrosiae sucos et odoriferam panaceam.
420   fovit ea vulnus lympha longaevus Iapyx
ignorans, subitoque omnis de corpore fugit
quippe dolor, omnis stetit imo vulnere sanguis.
iamque secuta manum, nullo cogente, sagitta
excidit, atque novae rediere in pristina vires.
425   "arma citi properate viro! quid statis?" Iapyx
conclamat primusque animos accendit in hostem.
"non haec humanis opibus, non arte magistra
proveniunt, neque te, Aenea, mea dextera servat:
maior agit deus atque opera ad maiora remittit."
430   ille avidus pugnae suras incluserat auro
hinc atque hinc oditque moras hastamque coruscat.
postquam habilis lateri clipeus loricaque tergo est,
Ascanium fusis circum complectitur armis
summaque per galeam delibans oscula fatur:
435   "disce, puer, virtutem ex me verumque laborem,
fortunam ex aliis. nunc te mea dextera bello
defensum dabit et magna inter praemia ducet.
tu facito, mox cum matura adoleverit aetas,
sis memor et te animo repetentem exempla tuorum
440   et pater Aeneas et avunculus excitet Hector."
     Haec ubi dicta dedit, portis sese extulit ingens,
telum immane manu quatiens; simul agmine denso

[440] = 3.343

with downy leaves and purple flower; that herb is not un-
known to wild goats, when winged arrows have lodged in
their flank. This Venus carried down, her face veiled in dim
mist; this she steeps with secret healing in river water
poured into a bright-brimming ewer, and sprinkles ambro-
sia's healing juices and fragrant panacea.[21] With this water
aged Iapyx bathed the wound, unwitting; and suddenly, in
truth, all pain fled from the body, all blood was staunched
deep in the wound. And now, following his hand, with no
force applied, the arrow fell out, and new strength re-
turned, as it was before. "Quick! Bring him arms! Why
stand there?" cries Iapyx loudly, and is the first to fire their
spirit against the foe. "Not by mortal aid does this cure
come, not by the art that guides me, nor is it my hand that
saves you, Aeneas; a mightier one—a god—is at work, and
sends you back to mightier deeds." Eager for the fray,
Aeneas had sheathed his legs in gold on this side and that
and, scorning delay, is brandishing his spear. As soon as the
shield is fitted to his side and the corslet to his back, he
clasps Ascanius in armed embrace and, lightly kissing his
lips through the helmet, says: "Learn valour from me, my
son, and true toil; fortune from others. Today my hand will
shield you in war and lead you to great rewards: see to it,
when later your years have grown to ripeness, that you re-
member, and, as you recall the example set by your kins-
men, that your father Aeneas and your uncle Hector stir
your soul!"

When he had spoken these words, he rushed out
through the gates in all his might, brandishing a massive

[21] Ambrosia, food of immortals, and panacea, the "cure for
all," are two mythical plants.

Antheusque Mnestheusque ruunt, omnisque relictis
turba fluit castris. tum caeco pulvere campus
445 miscetur pulsuque pedum tremit excita tellus.
vidit ab adverso venientis aggere Turnus,
videre Ausonii, gelidusque per ima cucurrit
ossa tremor; prima ante omnis Iuturna Latinos
audiit agnovitque sonum et tremefacta refugit.
450 ille volat campoque atrum rapit agmen aperto.
qualis ubi ad terras abrupto sidere nimbus
it mare per medium (miseris, heu, praescia longe
horrescunt corda agricolis: dabit ille ruinas
arboribus stragemque satis, ruet omnia late),
455 ante volant sonitumque ferunt ad litora venti:
MPRV talis in adversos ductor Rhoeteïus hostis
agmen agit, densi cuneis se quisque coactis
adglomerant. ferit ense gravem Thymbraeus Osirim,
Arcetium Mnestheus, Epulonem obtruncat Achates
460 Ufentemque Gyas; cadit ipse Tolumnius augur,
primus in adversos telum qui torserat hostis.
tollitur in caelum clamor, versique vicissim
pulverulenta fuga Rutuli dant terga per agros.
ipse neque aversos dignatur sternere morti
465 nec pede congressos nec equo nec tela ferentis
insequitur: solum densa in caligine Turnum
vestigat lustrans, solum in certamina poscit.
    Hoc concussa metu mentem Iuturna virago
aurigam Turni media inter lora Metiscum
470 excutit et longe lapsum temone reliquit;

444 fluit *MR*: ruit *P* (*cf.* 11.236)
465 nec equo *Servius Auctus*: aequo *MPRV*
470 reliquit *MPR*: relinquit *V*

332

spear in his hand: with him rush Antheus and Mnestheus
in serried column, and all the throng streams out of the
forsaken camp. Then the plain is a turmoil of blinding dust,
and the startled earth trembles under the tramp of feet.
From the facing rampart Turnus saw them coming; the
Ausonians saw, and a cold shudder ran through the marrow
of their bones; first before all the Latins Juturna heard and
knew the sound, and in terror fled away. Aeneas swoops
ahead and races his dark column over the open plain. As
when a tempest bursts, and a storm cloud moves towards
land over the deep sea, the hearts of hapless husbandmen,
alas! know it from afar and shudder—it will bring downfall
to trees and havoc to crops, it will overthrow everything far
and wide—before it the winds fly, and carry their voices
shoreward: just so the Rhoetean[22] chief brings up his band
full against the foe; densely they gather, one and all, to his
side in close-packed columns. Thymbraeus smites mighty
Osiris with the sword, Mnestheus slays Arcetius, Achates
Epulo, Gyas Ufens; even the augur Tolumnius falls, who
had been the first to hurl his spear full against the foe. A
shout rises to heaven, and in turn the routed Rutulians
turn their backs in clouds of dust, in flight across the fields.
Aeneas himself does not deign to lay low the fugitives in
death nor does he attack those who meet him on foot or
on horse or wield their weapons: Turnus alone he tracks
through the thick gloom with searching glance, Turnus
alone he summons to battle.

Stricken in heart with fear at this, Juturna the warrior
maid strikes Metiscus, Turnus' charioteer, out from among
the reins, and leaves him far off, fallen from the pole;

[22] I.e. Trojan.

ipsa subit manibusque undantis flectit habenas
cuncta gerens, vocemque et corpus et arma Metisci.
nigra velut magnas domini cum divitis aedes
pervolat et pennis alta atria lustrat hirundo
475 pabula parva legens nidisque loquacibus escas,
et nunc porticibus vacuis, nunc umida circum
stagna sonat: similis medios Iuturna per hostis
fertur equis rapidoque volans obit omnia curru,
iamque hic germanum iamque hic ostentat ovantem
480 nec conferre manum patitur, volat avia longe.
haud minus Aeneas tortos legit obvius orbis,
vestigatque virum et disiecta per agmina magna
voce vocat. quotiens oculos coniecit in hostem
alipedumque fugam cursu temptavit equorum,
485 aversos totiens currus Iuturna retorsit.
heu, quid agat? vario nequiquam fluctuat aestu,
diversaeque vocant animum in contraria curae.
huic Messapus, uti laeva duo forte gerebat
lenta, levis cursu, praefixa hastilia ferro,
490 horum unum certo contorquens derigit ictu.
substitit Aeneas et se collegit in arma
poplite subsidens; apicem tamen incita summum
hasta tulit summasque excussit vertice cristas.
tum vero adsurgunt irae, insidiisque subactus,
495 diversos ubi sensit equos currumque referri,
multa Iovem et laesi testatus foederis aras
iam tandem invadit medios et Marte secundo
terribilis saevam nullo discrimine caedem
suscitat, irarumque omnis effundit habenas.
500 Quis mihi nunc tot acerba deus, quis carmine caedes

---

495 sensit *PRV*: sentit *M*   496 testatus *MV*: testatur *PR*

she herself takes his place, and guides with her hands the flowing thongs, assuming all that belonged to Meniscus— his voice, form, weapons. As when a black swallow flits through a rich lord's great mansion and wings her way through lofty halls, gleaning for her chirping nestlings tiny crumbs and scraps of food, and twitters now in the empty courts, now about the watery pools: just so Juturna is borne by the steeds through the midst of the enemy, and winging her way in swift chariot scours all the field. And now here, and now there, she gives glimpses of her triumphant brother, but does not allow him to close in fight, but flits far away. None the less Aeneas threads the winding maze to meet him, and tracks his steps, and among the scattered ranks loudly calls him. As often as he cast eyes on his foe and strove by running to match the flight of the fleet-footed horses, so often did Juturna turn and wheel her car. Alas, what is he to do? Vainly he tosses on a shifting tide, and conflicting cares call his mind this way and that. Against him Messapus, who chanced to be carrying in his left hand two tough spears tipped with steel, lightly advancing, levels one and whirls it with unerring stroke. Aeneas halted, and gathered himself behind his shield, sinking upon his knee; but the swift spear took off the top of his helmet and dashed the topmost plumes from his head. Then indeed his wrath swells and driven on by this treachery, when he saw that the horses and chariot of his foe were far away, making many appeals to Jove and the altars of the broken treaty, at last he plunges into the fray and, with the War God supporting him, terribly awakes grim indiscriminate carnage, giving full rein to his anger.

What god can now unfold for me so many horrors, who

diversas obitumque ducum, quos aequore toto
inque vicem nunc Turnus agit, nunc Troïus heros,
expediat? tanton placuit concurrere motu,
Iuppiter, aeterna gentis in pace futuras?
505   Aeneas Rutulum Sucronem (ea prima ruentis
pugna loco statuit Teucros) haud multa morantem
excipit in latus et, qua fata celerrima, crudum
transadigit costas et cratis pectoris ensem.
MPR   Turnus equo deiectum Amycum fratremque Dioren,
510   congressus pedes, hunc venientem cuspide longa,
hunc mucrone ferit, curruque abscisa duorum
suspendit capita et rorantia sanguine portat.
ille Talon Tanaimque neci fortemque Cethegum,
tris uno congressu, et maestum mittit Oniten,
515   nomen Echionium matrisque genus Peridiae;
hic fratres Lycia missos et Apollinis agris
et iuvenem exosum nequiquam bella Menoeten,
Arcada, piscosae cui circum flumina Lernae
ars fuerat pauperque domus nec nota potentum
520   munera, conductaque pater tellure serebat.
ac velut immissi diversis partibus ignes
arentem in silvam et virgulta sonantia lauro,
aut ubi decursu rapido de montibus altis
dant sonitum spumosi amnes et in aequora currunt
525   quisque suum populatus iter: non segnius ambo
Aeneas Turnusque ruunt per proelia; nunc, nunc
fluctuat ira intus, rumpuntur nescia vinci

503 *MPR*: *om. V*
511 abscisa *PV*: abscissa *MR*
520 munera *PR*: limina *M*

in song can tell such diverse deaths, and the fall of captains, whom now Turnus, now the Trojan hero, drives in turn all over the plain? Was it your will, Jupiter, that in so vast a shock nations should clash that thereafter would dwell in everlasting peace? Aeneas, meeting Rutulian Sucro—this was the combat that first brought the Trojan attack to a halt—quickly smites him on the flank and drives the cruel steel where death comes speediest, through the ribs that fence the chest. Turnus unhorses Amycus and his brother Diores and, assailing them on foot, strikes the one with a long spear as he advances, the other with his sword; then, hanging from his car the severed heads of the two, he bears them off dripping with blood. Aeneas sends to death Talos and Tanaïs and brave Cethegus, three in one onslaught, and sad Onites, of Echionian name,[23] whose mother was Peridia; Turnus kills the brothers sent from Lycia and Apollo's fields,[24] and Menoetes of Arcadia, who in youth loathed warfare in vain: near fish-haunted Lerna's streams had been his craft and humble home, he did not know the patronage of the great, and his father sowed on hired soil. And like fires launched from opposite sides into a dry forest and thickets of crackling laurel, or as when in swift descent from mountain heights foaming rivers roar and race seaward, each leaving its own path waste: with no less fury the two, Aeneas and Turnus, sweep through the battle; now, now wrath surges within them; their unconquerable hearts are bursting, knowing not to yield; now

[23] I.e. of Theban name or stock. Echion was the mythical founder of Thebes.

[24] The brothers are not named but may be those mentioned in *Aen.* 10.126. Lycia was a favourite haunt of Apollo.

pectora, nunc totis in vulnera viribus itur.
    Murranum hic, atavos et avorum antiqua sonantem
530 nomina per regesque actum genus omne Latinos,
praecipitem scopulo atque ingentis turbine saxi
excutit effunditque solo; hunc lora et iuga subter
provolvere rotae, crebro super ungula pulsu
incita nec domini memorum proculcat equorum.
535 ille ruenti Hyllo animisque immane frementi
occurrit telumque aurata ad tempora torquet:
olli per galeam fixo stetit hasta cerebro.
dextera nec tua te, Graium fortissime Cretheu,
eripuit Turno, nec di texere Cupencum
540 Aenea veniente sui: dedit obvia ferro
pectora, nec misero clipei mora profuit aerei.
te quoque Laurentes viderunt, Aeole, campi
oppetere et late terram consternere tergo.
occidis, Argivae quem non potuere phalanges
545 sternere nec Priami regnorum eversor Achilles;
hic tibi mortis erant metae, domus alta sub Ida,
Lyrnesi domus alta, solo Laurente sepulcrum.
totae adeo conversae acies omnesque Latini,
omnes Dardanidae, Mnestheus acerque Serestus
550 et Messapus equum domitor et fortis Asilas
Tuscorumque phalanx Euandrique Arcades alae,
pro se quisque viri summa nituntur opum vi;
nec mora nec requies, vasto certamine tendunt.
    Hic mentem Aeneae genetrix pulcherrima misit
555 iret ut ad muros urbique adverteret agmen

---

541 aerei *Aldine ed.* (1501): aeris *MPR*

---

[25] According to Servius, *Cupencus* in the Sabine language

they rush into deadly combat with all their strength.

As Murranus boasts of his grandfathers and the ancient names of his ancestors and all his family traced through Latin kings, Aeneas dashes him down headlong with a stone and mighty whirling rock and tumbles him on the ground; under reins and yoke the wheels rolled him along, and over him, trampling him down with many a beat, rush the hoofs of the horses who remember not their master. Turnus meets Hyllus as he rushes on with boundless fury at heart, and whirls a dart at his gold-bound brow: piercing the helmet, the spear stood fast in his brain. And your right hand, Cretheus, bravest of the Greeks, did not save you from Turnus, nor did his gods shield Cupencus when Aeneas came:[25] he put his breast in the weapon's path, and the bronze shield's delay availed him not, poor wretch. You too, Aeolus, the Laurentine plains saw fall, and spread your frame widely over the earth: you fall whom the Argive battalions could not lay low, nor Achilles, destroyer of Priam's realms. Here was the end of your life's course; beneath Ida was your lofty home—your lofty home at Lyrnesus—in Laurentine soil your sepulchre. The whole lines turned to the fray—all the Latins and all the Trojans: Mnestheus and valiant Serestus; Messapus, tamer of horses, and brave Asilas; the Tuscan battalion and Evander's Arcadian squadrons—each doing his all, the men strain with utmost force of strength; there is no rest nor respite as they struggle in measureless conflict.

Now his lovely mother inspired Aeneas to advance on the walls, fling his column on the town, and confound the

means a priest, corresponding to *Flamen* and *Pontifex* in Latin. Hence *di sui*.

ocius et subita turbaret clade Latinos.
ille ut vestigans diversa per agmina Turnum
huc atque huc acies circumtulit, aspicit urbem
immunem tanti belli atque impune quietam.
560 continuo pugnae accendit maioris imago:
Mnesthea Sergestumque vocat fortemque Serestum
ductores, tumulumque capit quo cetera Teucrum
concurrit legio, nec scuta aut spicula densi
deponunt. celso medius stans aggere fatur:
565 "ne qua meis esto dictis mora, Iuppiter hac stat,
neu quis ob inceptum subitum mihi segnior ito.
urbem hodie, causam belli, regna ipsa Latini,
ni frenum accipere et victi parere fatentur,
eruam et aequa solo fumantia culmina ponam.
570 scilicet exspectem libeat dum proelia Turno
nostra pati rursusque velit concurrere victus?
hoc caput, o cives, haec belli summa nefandi.
ferte faces propere foedusque reposcite flammis."
dixerat, atque animis pariter certantibus omnes
575 dant cuneum densaque ad muros mole feruntur;
scalae improviso subitusque apparuit ignis.
discurrunt alii ad portas primosque trucidant,
ferrum alii torquent et obumbrant aethera telis.
ipse inter primos dextram sub moenia tendit
580 Aeneas, magnaque incusat voce Latinum
testaturque deos iterum se ad proelia cogi,
bis iam Italos hostis, haec altera foedera rumpi.
exoritur trepidos inter discordia civis:
urbem alii reserare iubent et pandere portas
585 Dardanidis ipsumque trahunt in moenia regem;

561 = 4.288   582 haec *MPR*: haec iam *M*²

340

Latins with sudden disaster. While he tracked Turnus here and there through the troops and swept his glance this way and that, he sees the city free from that fierce warfare, peaceful and unharmed. At once a vision of greater battle fires his heart; he calls Mnestheus and Sergestus and brave Serestus, and plants himself on a mound, where the rest of the Teucrian host throng thickly around without laying down shield or spear. Standing among them on the mounded height he cries: "Let nothing delay my command; Jupiter is on our side; and let no one, I pray, be slower to advance because the venture is so sudden. That city, the cause of war, the very seat of Latinus' realm, unless they consent to receive our yoke and to submit as vanquished, this very day I will overthrow, and lay its smoking roofs level with the ground. Am I to wait, do you suppose, till Turnus sees fit to do battle with me, and chooses to meet me a second time, beaten though he is? This, fellow citizens, is the head, this the sum, of the accursed war. Bring brands with speed, and with fire reclaim the treaty." He ceased, and with hearts equally emulous all form a wedge and advance in serried mass to the walls. In a moment ladders and sudden flames are seen. Some rush to the several gates and cut down the foremost guards; others hurl their steel and darken the sky with javelins. Himself in the van at the foot of the wall, Aeneas raises his hand, loudly reproaches Latinus, and calls the gods to witness that he is being forced into battle again, that the Italians have now twice become his foes, and that this treaty is the second broken. Strife rises among the anxious citizens: some bid unbar the town and throw wide the gates to the Dardans, and drag the king himself to the ramparts; others

arma ferunt alii et pergunt defendere muros,
inclusas ut cum latebroso in pumice pastor
vestigavit apes fumoque implevit amaro;
illae intus trepidae rerum per cerea castra
590 discurrunt magnisque acuunt stridoribus iras;
volvitur ater odor tectis, tum murmure caeco
intus saxa sonant, vacuas it fumus ad auras.
    Accidit haec fessis etiam fortuna Latinis,
quae totam luctu concussit funditus urbem.
595 regina ut tectis venientem prospicit hostem,
incessi muros, ignis ad tecta volare,
nusquam acies contra Rutulas, nulla agmina Turni,
infelix pugnae iuvenem in certamine credit
exstinctum et subito mentem turbata dolore
600 se causam clamat crimenque caputque malorum,
multaque per maestum demens effata furorem
purpureos moritura manu discindit amictus
et nodum informis leti trabe nectit ab alta.
quam cladem miserae postquam accepere Latinae,
605 filia prima manu flavos Lavinia crinis
et roseas laniata genas, tum cetera circum
turba furit, resonant late plangoribus aedes.
hinc totam infelix vulgatur fama per urbem:
demittunt mentes, it scissa veste Latinus
610 coniugis attonitus fatis urbisque ruina,
canitiem immundo perfusam pulvere turpans.
multaque se incusat, qui non acceperit ante
Dardanium Aenean generumque asciverit ultro.
    Interea extremo bellator in aequore Turnus

587 ut cum *PR*: veluti *M*
596 incessi *M²P, Servius*: incedi *M*: incensi *R*

bring arms, and hasten to defend the walls. As when some
shepherd has tracked bees to their lair in a rocky covert
and filled it with stinging smoke; inside, anxious for their
safety, they scurry to and fro through the wax fortress, and
with loud buzzing whet their rage; the black stench rolls
through their dwelling, the rocks within murmur with
blind hum, and smoke billows out into the empty air.

This further fate befell the weary Latins, and shook the
whole city to its base with grief: when from her palace the
queen sees the foe approaching, the walls assailed, flames
mounting to the roofs, but nowhere Rutulian ranks or any
troops of Turnus to meet them, the unhappy woman thinks
that Turnus has been slain in combat and, her mind dis-
traught by sudden anguish, cries out that she is the guilty
source and spring of sorrows, and uttering many a wild
word in the frenzy of grief, resolved to die she rends her
purple robes, and from a lofty beam fastens the noose of
a hideous death. As soon as the unhappy Latin women
learned this disaster, first her daughter Lavinia, her hand
tearing her golden tresses and rosy cheeks, falls into a
frenzy, then all the throng around her; the wide halls ring
with lamentations. From here the woeful rumour spreads
throughout the town. Hearts sink; Latinus goes with rent
raiment, dazed at his wife's doom and his city's downfall,
defiling his hoary hair with showers of unclean dust, *oft
chiding himself that he did not give a ready welcome to
Dardan Aeneas and adopt him as his son.*

Meanwhile Turnus, battling on the plain's far edge, is

---

605 flavos *MPR*: floros *Probus, according to Servius*
612–3 χ (= 11.471–472): *om. MPR*

615 palantis sequitur paucos iam segnior atque
iam minus atque minus successu laetus equorum.
attulit huc illi caecis terroribus aura
commixtum clamorem, arrectasque impulit auris
confusae sonus urbis et inlaetabile murmur.
620 "ei mihi! quid tanto turbantur moenia luctu?
quisve ruit tantus diversa clamor ab urbe?"
sic ait, adductisque amens subsistit habenis.
atque huic, in faciem soror ut conversa Metisci
aurigae currumque et equos et lora regebat,
625 talibus occurrit dictis: "hac, Turne, sequamur
Troiugenas, qua prima viam victoria pandit;
sunt alii qui tecta manu defendere possint.
ingruit Aeneas Italis et proelia miscet,
et nos saeva manu mittamus funera Teucris.
630 nec numero inferior pugnae neque honore recedes."
Turnus ad haec . . . :
"o soror, et dudum agnovi, cum prima per artem
foedera turbasti teque haec in bella dedisti,
et nunc nequiquam fallis dea. sed quis Olympo
635 demissam tantos voluit te ferre labores?
an fratris miseri letum ut crudele videres?
nam quid ago? aut quae iam spondet Fortuna salutem?
vidi oculos ante ipse meos me voce vocantem
Murranum, quo non superat mihi carior alter,
640 oppetere ingentem atque ingenti vulnere victum.
occidit infelix ne nostrum dedecus Ufens
aspiceret; Teucri potiuntur corpore et armis.
exscindine domos (id rebus defuit unum)
perpetiar, dextra nec Drancis dicta refellam?

617 huc χ: hunc *MPR*   624 regebat *MR*: gerebat *P*

pursuing the few stragglers, slacker now and less and less exultant in the triumph of his horses. To him the breeze bore a cry blended with terrors unknown, and the sound and joyless murmur of the town in turmoil fell on his straining ears. "Ah me! What is this great sorrow that shakes the walls? What is this cry that speeds from the distant town?" So he speaks, and in frenzy draws in the reins and halts. At this his sister, changed to the form of his charioteer Metiscus, as she guided chariot and horses and reins, meets him with these words: "This way, Turnus, let us chase the sons of Troy, where victory first opens a path; there are others whose hands can guard their homes. Aeneas is attacking the Italians with turmoil of battle; let our hand too deal fierce havoc among his Teucrians! Neither in number of slain nor in glory in battle will you come off the worse." To this Turnus . . .: "Sister, long ago I recognized you, when first you craftily upset the truce and flung yourself into this war; and now too you hide your deity in vain. But who willed that you be sent down from Olympus to bear such toils? Was it so that you would see your hapless brother's cruel death? For what can I do? What chance can now assure me of safety? Before my very eyes, as he called loudly upon me, I saw Murranus fall—no other dearer than he is left to me—a mighty soul and laid low by a mighty wound. Luckless Ufens fell so that he would not view our shame: the Teucrians hold his corpse and armour. Shall I endure the razing of their homes—the one thing lacking to my lot—and not refute Drances' taunts with my

---

635 tantos . . . ferre *MP*: tantosque . . . perferre *R*
641 ne nostrum *MR*: nostrum ne *P*

645 terga dabo et Turnum fugientem haec terra videbit?
usque adeone mori miserum est? vos o mihi, Manes,
este boni, quoniam superis aversa voluntas.
sancta atque istius ad vos anima inscia culpae
descendam magnorum haud umquam indignus avorum."
650   Vix ea fatus erat: medios volat ecce per hostis
MP vectus equo spumante Saces, adversa sagitta
saucius ora, ruitque implorans nomine Turnum:
"Turne, in te suprema salus, miserere tuorum.
fulminat Aeneas armis summasque minatur
655 deiecturum arces Italum excidioque daturum,
iamque faces ad tecta volant. in te ora Latini,
in te oculos referunt; mussat rex ipse Latinus
quos generos vocet aut quae sese ad foedera flectat.
praeterea regina, tui fidissima, dextra
660 occidit ipsa sua lucemque exterrita fugit.
soli pro portis Messapus et acer Atinas
sustentant acies. circum hos utrimque phalanges
stant densae strictisque seges mucronibus horret
ferrea; tu currum deserto in gramine versas."
665 obstipuit varia confusus imagine rerum
Turnus et obtutu tacito stetit; aestuat ingens
MPV uno in corde pudor mixtoque insania luctu
et furiis agitatus amor et conscia virtus.
ut primum discussae umbrae et lux reddita menti,
670 ardentis oculorum orbis ad moenia torsit
turbidus eque rotis magnam respexit ad urbem.
    Ecce autem flammis inter tabulata volutus
ad caelum undabat vertex turrimque tenebat,

647 aversa *PR*: adversa *M*   648 atque istius *before* ad vos
Housman: *before* inscia *MPR*   662 acies *M*: aciem *P*

sword? Shall I turn my back? Shall this land see Turnus in flight? Is dead so terrible? Be kind to me, Shades, since the gods above have turned their faces from me. I will descend to you a soul stainless and innocent of that reproach, never unworthy of my mighty forebears!"

Scarce had he spoken, when borne on a foaming steed through the foemen's midst speeds Saces, wounded full in face by an arrow and, rushing on, calls for aid by name on Turnus: "Turnus, in you lies our last hope; pity your people! Aeneas thunders in arms, and threatens to overthrow Italy's highest towers and give them to destruction: even now brands are flying to the roofs. To you the Latins turn their looks, to you their eyes; King Latinus himself mutters, in doubt whom to call his sons, or towards what alliance to incline. Moreover the queen, who trusted wholly in you, has fallen by her own hand and fled in terror from the light. Alone before the gates Messapus and valiant Atinas sustain our lines. Around them on either side stand serried squadrons, and a harvest of steel bristles with drawn swords, while you wheel your chariot over the deserted sward." Aghast and bewildered by the changing picture of disaster, Turnus stood mutely gazing; within that single heart surges mighty shame, and madness mingled with grief, and love stung by fury, and the consciousness of worth. As soon as the shadows scattered and light dawned afresh on his mind, he turned his blazing eyes wrathfully upon the walls and from his chariot looked back upon the spacious city.

But now from storey to storey a rolling spire of flame was eddying heavenward, and fastening upon a tower—a

---

666b–667 = 10.870b-871

turrim compactis trabibus quam eduxerat ipse
675 subdideratque rotas pontisque instraverat altos.
"iam iam fata, soror, superant, absiste morari;
quo deus et quo dura vocat Fortuna sequamur.
stat conferre manum Aeneae, stat, quidquid acerbi est,
morte pati, neque me indecorem, germana, videbis
680 amplius. hunc, oro, sine me furere ante furorem."
dixit, et e curru saltum dedit ocius arvis
perque hostis, per tela ruit maestamque sororem
deserit ac rapido cursu media agmina rumpit.
ac veluti montis saxum de vertice praeceps
685 cum ruit avulsum vento, seu turbidus imber
proluit aut annis solvit sublapsa vetustas;
MPRV   fertur in abruptum magno mons improbus actu
exsultatque solo, silvas armenta virosque
involvens secum: disiecta per agmina Turnus
690 sic urbis ruit ad muros, ubi plurima fuso
sanguine terra madet striduntque hastilibus aurae,
significatque manu et magno simul incipit ore:
"parcite iam, Rutuli, et vos tela inhibete, Latini.
quaecumque est fortuna, mea est; me verius unum
695 pro vobis foedus luere et decernere ferro."
discessere omnes medii spatiumque dedere.
    At pater Aeneas audito nomine Turni
deserit et muros et summas deserit arces
praecipitatque moras omnis, opera omnia rumpit
700 laetitia exsultans horrendumque intonat armis:
quantus Athos aut quantus Eryx aut ipse coruscis

677 quo dura *MV*: qua dura *P*

tower that he himself had reared of jointed beams and set on wheels and slung with lofty gangways.[26] "Now, my sister, now Fate triumphs: cease to hinder; where God and cruel Fortune call, let us follow! I am resolved to meet Aeneas, resolved to bear in death all its bitterness; no longer, sister, will you behold me shamed. Let me first, I beg, give vent to this madness." He spoke and leapt quickly from his chariot to the ground and, rushing through foes and through spears, leaves his sorrowing sister, and bursts in rapid course through their columns. And as when a rock from mountaintop rushes headlong, torn away by the blast—whether the whirling storm has washed it free, or time stealing on with lapse of years has loosened it, down the steep with mighty rush sweeps the reckless mass and bounds over the earth, rolling with it trees, herds, and men: so among the scattered ranks Turnus rushes to the city walls, where the ground is deepest drenched with spilled blood and the air is shrill with spears; then he beckons with his hand and thus begins aloud: "Forbear now, Rutulians, and you Latins, stay your darts. Whatever fortune is here is mine; it is better that I alone for your sake atone for the covenant, and decide the outcome with the sword." All those between them dispersed and gave him room.

But father Aeneas, hearing Turnus' name, forsakes the walls, forsakes the lofty fortress, flings aside all delay, breaks off all tasks and, exultant with joy, clashes his weapons terribly; vast as Athos, vast as Eryx or vast as Father

[26] Cf. the account at 9.530ff. These defensive towers were provided with wheels, and with gangways which could be lowered to the walls.

cum fremit ilicibus quantus gaudetque nivali
vertice se attollens pater Appenninus ad auras.
iam vero et Rutuli certatim et Troes et omnes
705 convertere oculos Itali, quique alta tenebant
moenia quique imos pulsabant ariete muros,
armaque deposuere umeris. stupet ipse Latinus
ingentis, genitos diversis partibus orbis,
inter se coiisse viros et cernere ferro.
710 atque illi, ut vacuo patuerunt aequore campi,
procursu rapido coniectis eminus hastis
invadunt Martem clipeis atque aere sonoro.
dat gemitum tellus; tum crebros ensibus ictus
congeminant, fors et virtus miscentur in unum.
715 ac velut ingenti Sila summove Taburno
cum duo conversis inimica in proelia tauri
frontibus incurrunt, pavidi cessere magistri,
stat pecus omne metu mutum, mussantque iuvencae
MPR quis nemori imperitet, quem tota armenta sequantur;
720 illi inter sese multa vi vulnera miscent
cornuaque obnixi infigunt et sanguine largo
colla armosque lavant, gemitu nemus omne remugit:
non aliter Tros Aeneas et Daunius heros
concurrunt clipeis, ingens fragor aethera complet.
725 Iuppiter ipse duas aequato examine lances
sustinet et fata imponit diversa duorum,
quem damnet labor et quo vergat pondere letum.
    Emicat hic impune putans et corpore toto
alte sublatum consurgit Turnus in ensem
730 et ferit; exclamant Troes trepidique Latini,

709 et cernere *P, Seneca* (*Ep*.58.3): et decernere *MRV*
714 miscentur *MPR*: miscetur *V*

Apennine himself, when he roars with his shimmering oaks, and joyously raises his snowy head to heaven. Now indeed, all eagerly turned their eyes—Rutulians, and Trojans, and Italians, both those who held the lofty ramparts, and those whose ram battered the walls below—and took off the armour from their shoulders. Latinus himself is amazed that these mighty men, born in different parts of the world, have met together and are deciding the outcome with the sword. And as soon as the fields were clear on the open plain, the two dash swiftly forward, first hurling their spears from far, and rush into battle with shields and clanging bronze. Earth groans; then with the sword they redouble blow on blow, chance and valour blending in one. And as in mighty Sila or on Taburnus' height, when two bulls charge, brow to brow, in mortal battle, in terror the keepers fall back, the whole herd stands mute with dread, and the heifers dumbly wait to see who will be lord of the forest, whom all the herds will follow; with mighty force they deal mutual wounds, gore with butting horns, and bathe neck and shoulders in streaming blood; all the woodland re-echoes with their bellowing: just so Trojan Aeneas and the Daunian hero clash shield on shield; the mighty crash fills the sky. Jupiter himself holds up two scales in even balance, and lays in them the diverse destinies of both—whom the strife dooms, and with whose weight death sinks down.[27]

Turnus springs forward, thinking it safe, he rises full height on his uplifted sword, and strikes. The Trojans and expectant Latins cry aloud; both armies are on tiptoe with

[27] For this weighing of the fates, see Homer, *Iliad* 22.209ff. The sinking scale means death.

arrectaeque amborum acies. at perfidus ensis
frangitur in medioque ardentem deserit ictu,
ni fuga subsidio subeat. fugit ocior Euro
ut capulum ignotum dextramque aspexit inermem.
735 fama est praecipitem, cum prima in proelia iunctos
conscendebat equos, patrio mucrone relicto,
dum trepidat, ferrum aurigae rapuisse Metisci;
idque diu, dum terga dabant palantia Teucri,
suffecit; postquam arma dei ad Volcania ventum est,
740 mortalis mucro glacies ceu futtilis ictu
dissiluit, fulva resplendent fragmina harena.
ergo amens diversa fuga petit aequora Turnus
et nunc huc, inde huc incertos implicat orbis;
undique enim densa Teucri inclusere corona
745 atque hinc vasta palus, hinc ardua moenia cingunt.
    Nec minus Aeneas, quamquam tardata sagitta
interdum genua impediunt cursumque recusant,
insequitur trepidique pedem pede fervidus urget:
inclusum veluti si quando flumine nactus
750 cervum aut puniceae saeptum formidine pennae
venator cursu canis et latratibus instat;
ille autem insidiis et ripa territus alta
mille fugit refugitque vias, at vividus Umber
haeret hians, iam iamque tenet similisque tenenti
755 increpuit malis morsuque elusus inani est;
tum vero exoritur clamor ripaeque lacusque
responsant circa et caelum tonat omne tumultu.
ille simul fugiens Rutulos simul increpat omnis
MP nomine quemque vocans notumque efflagitat ensem.

    732 ictu *P*: ictum *MR*   735 prima (103) *M*: primum *PR*
    741 resplendent fragmina *MP*: resplendet fragmen *R*

excitement. But the treacherous sword snaps, and in mid
stroke fails its ardent lord, did not flight come to his aid.
Swifter than the East Wind he flies, as soon as he sees an
unknown hilt in his defenceless hand. They say that in
his headlong haste, when first mounting behind his yoked
horses for battle, he left his father's blade behind and in his
haste snatched up the sword of Metiscus his charioteer;
and for long that served, while the straggling Teucrians
turned their backs; but when it met the god-wrought
armour of Vulcan, the mortal blade, like brittle ice, flew
asunder at the stroke; the fragments glitter on the yellow
sand. So Turnus madly flees this way and that over the
plain, and now in one direction and now in another he
entwines wavering circles; for on all sides the Teucrians
enclosed him in a crowded ring, and on one side a waste
fen, on another steep ramparts hem him in.

No less Aeneas, though at times his knees, slowed by
the arrow wound, impede him and deny their speed, pur-
sues and hotly presses, foot to foot, upon his panting foe; as
when a hunter hound has caught a stag, pent in by a stream
or hedged about by the terror of crimson feathers, and,
running and barking, presses him close; the stag, in terror
of the snares and the high bank, flees to and fro in a thou-
sand ways, but the keen Umbrian stays close with jaws
agape; he almost seizes him, and snaps his jaws as if he had
seized him, and baffled, bites on empty air. Then indeed a
din breaks out; the banks and pools around make answer,
and all heaven thunders with the tumult. Even as he flees,
even then Turnus upbraids all the Rutulians, calling each
by name, and clamouring for the sword he knows. Aeneas

---

744 densa Teucri *PR*: Teucri densa *M*

760 Aeneas mortem contra praesensque minatur
exitium, si quisquam adeat, terretque trementis
excisurum urbem minitans et saucius instat.
quinque orbis explent cursu totidemque retexunt
huc illuc; neque enim levia aut ludicra petuntur
765 praemia, sed Turni de vita et sanguine certant.
    Forte sacer Fauno foliis oleaster amaris
hic steterat, nautis olim venerabile lignum,
servati ex undis ubi figere dona solebant
Laurenti divo et votas suspendere vestis;
770 sed stirpem Teucri nullo discrimine sacrum
sustulerant, puro ut possent concurrere campo.
hic hasta Aeneae stabat, huc impetus illam
detulerat fixam et lenta radice tenebat.
incubuit voluitque manu convellere ferrum
775 Dardanides, teloque sequi quem prendere cursu
non poterat. tum vero amens formidine Turnus
"Faune, precor, miserere" inquit "tuque optima ferrum
Terra tene, colui vestros si semper honores,
quos contra Aeneadae bello fecere profanos."
780 dixit, opemque dei non cassa in vota vocavit.
namque diu luctans lentoque in stirpe moratus
viribus haud ullis valuit discludere morsus
roboris Aeneas. dum nititur acer et instat,
rursus in aurigae faciem mutata Metisci
785 procurrit fratrique ensem dea Daunia reddit.
quod Venus audaci nymphae indignata licere
accessit telumque alta ab radice revellit.
olli sublimes armis animisque refecti,
hic gladio fidens, hic acer et arduus hasta,

784 mutata *M*: conversa (623) *P*

354

in turn threatens death and instant doom, if anyone comes
near, and terrifies his trembling foes with threats to raze
the town; though wounded he presses on. Five circles they
cover, and unweave as many, running this way and that; for
no slight or sportive prize they seek, but strive for Turnus'
life and blood.

By chance a bitter-leaved wild olive, sacred to Faunus,
had stood here, a tree revered of old by mariners, on
which, when saved from the waves, they were wont to fas-
ten their gifts to the god of Laurentum and hang up their
votive garments; but the Teucrians, making no exception,
had removed the sacred stem, so that they could fight on
open ground. Here stood the spear of Aeneas; its force had
carried it here and was holding it fast in the tough root. The
Dardan stooped, meaning to pluck away the steel perforce
and follow with his javelin the man he could not catch by
speed of foot. Then indeed Turnus, frantic with terror,
cried: "Faunus, have pity, I pray, and you, most gracious
Earth, hold fast the steel, if ever I have honoured your
rites, which the sons of Aeneas, to the contrary, have
defiled by war." He spoke, and not in vain did he invoke the
aid of heaven. For though long he wrestled and lingered
over the stubborn stem, by no strength could Aeneas un-
lock the oaken bite. While fiercely he tugs and strains, the
Daunian goddess,[28] changing once again into the form of
charioteer Metiscus, runs forward and restores the sword
to her brother. But Venus, enraged that such license was
granted the bold nymph, drew near and plucked the
weapon from the deep root. At full height, in arms and
heart renewed, one trusting to his sword, the other fiercely

[28] Juturna.

790 adsistunt contra certamine Martis anheli.
    Iunonem interea rex omnipotentis Olympi
adloquitur fulva pugnas de nube tuentem:
"quae iam finis erit, coniunx? quid denique restat?
indigetem Aenean scis ipsa et scire fateris
795 deberi caelo fatisque ad sidera tolli.
quid struis? aut qua spe gelidis in nubibus haeres?
mortalin decuit violari vulnere divum?
aut ensem (quid enim sine te Iuturna valeret?)
ereptum reddi Turno et vim crescere victis?
800 desine iam tandem precibusque inflectere nostris,
ne te tantus edit tacitam dolor et mihi curae
saepe tuo dulci tristes ex ore recursent.
ventum ad supremum est. terris agitare vel undis
Troianos potuisti, infandum accendere bellum,
805 deformare domum et luctu miscere hymenaeos:
ulterius temptare veto." sic Iuppiter orsus;
sic dea summisso contra Saturnia vultu:
    "Ista quidem quia nota mihi tua, magne, voluntas,
Iuppiter, et Turnum et terras invita reliqui;
810 nec tu me aëria solam nunc sede videres
digna indigna pati, sed flammis cincta sub ipsa
starem acie traheremque inimica in proelia Teucros.
Iuturnam misero (fateor) succurrere fratri
suasi et pro vita maiora audere probavi,
815 non ut tela tamen, non ut contenderet arcum;
adiuro Stygii caput implacabile fontis,
una superstitio superis quae reddita divis.
et nunc cedo equidem pugnasque exosa relinquo.

---

⁷⁹⁰ certamine χ: certamina *MP*   ⁸⁰¹ edit *P, Diomedes,
Servius*: edat *M*   ⁸⁰⁹ reliqui *MP*: relinquo (818) *P²*

towering with his spear, breathless both, they stand face to face in the War God's strife.

Meanwhile the king of almighty Olympus addresses Juno, as from a golden cloud she gazes on the fray: "What now shall be the end, wife? What remains at the last? You yourself know, and admit that you know, that Aeneas, as Hero of the land, is claimed by heaven, and that the Fates exalt him to the stars. What are you planning? In what hope are you lingering in the chill clouds? Was it well that a god should be profaned by a mortal's wound? Or that the lost sword—for without you what could Juturna do?—be restored to Turnus, and the vanquished gain fresh force? Cease now, I pray, and yield to my entreaties so that your great grief may not consume you in silence, nor your bitter cares often return to me from your sweet lips. The end is reached. To chase the Trojans over land or wave, to kindle monstrous war, to mar a happy home and blend bridals with woe—this power you have had; I forbid you to try any further!" So Jupiter spoke: so, with downcast look, the goddess, child of Saturn, replied:

"It was indeed because I knew, great Jove, that this was your pleasure, that I reluctantly left Turnus and the earth; otherwise you would not see me now, alone on my airy throne, enduring fair and foul, but girt in flame I would be standing right in the battle line and dragging the Teucrians into deadly combat. As for Juturna, I counselled her, I own, to help her hapless brother, and for his life's sake sanctioned still greater deeds of daring, but not to level the arrow, not to bend the bow: I swear by the inexorable fountainhead of Styx, sole name of dread ordained for the gods above. And now I yield, yes, I yield, and quit the strife in

illud te, nulla fati quod lege tenetur,
820 pro Latio obtestor, pro maiestate tuorum:
cum iam conubiis pacem felicibus (esto)
component, cum iam leges et foedera iungent,
ne vetus indigenas nomen mutare Latinos
neu Troas fieri iubeas Teucrosque vocari
825 aut vocem mutare viros aut vertere vestem.
sit Latium, sint Albani per saecula reges,
sit Romana potens Itala virtute propago:
occidit, occideritque sinas cum nomine Troia."
    Olli subridens hominum rerumque repertor:
830 "es germana Iovis Saturnique altera proles,
MPR irarum tantos volvis sub pectore fluctus.
verum age et inceptum frustra summitte furorem:
do quod vis, et me victusque volensque remitto.
sermonem Ausonii patrium moresque tenebunt,
835 utque est nomen erit; commixti corpore tantum
subsident Teucri. morem ritusque sacrorum
adiciam faciamque omnis uno ore Latinos.
hinc genus Ausonio mixtum quod sanguine surget,
supra homines, supra ire deos pietate videbis,
840 nec gens ulla tuos aeque celebrabit honores."
adnuit his Iuno et mentem laetata retorsit;
interea excedit caelo nubemque relinquit.
    His actis aliud genitor secum ipse volutat
Iuturnamque parat fratris dimittere ab armis.
845 dicuntur geminae pestes cognomine Dirae,
quas et Tartaream Nox intempesta Megaeram
uno eodemque tulit partu, paribusque revinxit

825 vestem *M*: vestes *P*
835 tantum *MP*: tanto *R*

loathing. This boon, banned by no law of fate, I beg of you for Latium's sake, for your own kin's greatness:[29] when anon with happy bridal rites—so be it!—they plight peace, when anon they join in laws and treaties, do not command the native Latins to change their ancient name, nor to become Trojans and be called Teucrians, nor to change their language and alter their attire: let Latium be, let Alban kings endure through ages, let be a Roman stock, strong in Italian valour: Troy is fallen, and fallen let her be, together with her name!"

Smiling on her, the creator of men and things replied: "You are Jove's true sister, and Saturn's other child: such waves of wrath surge deep within your breast! But come, allay the anger that was stirred in vain. I grant your wish and relent, willingly won over. Ausonia's sons shall keep their fathers' speech and ways, and as it is now, so shall their name be: the Teucrians shall but sink down, merged in the mass. I will give them their sacred laws and rites and make them all Latins of one tongue. From them shall arise a race, blended with Ausonian blood, which you will see overpass men, overpass gods in loyalty, and no nation will celebrate your worship with equal zeal." Juno assented to this and joyfully changed her purpose; then she leaves heaven, and quits the cloud.

This done, the Father revolves another purpose in his heart, and prepares to withdraw Juturna from her brother's side. Men tell of twin fiends, named the Dread Ones, whom untimely Night bore in one and the same birth with hellish Megaera, wreathing them alike with snaky coils and

---

[29] Saturn, father of Jupiter, had once reigned in Latium, and from him Latinus was descended. Cf. *Aen.* 7.45–49.

serpentum spiris ventosasque addidit alas.
hae Iovis ad solium saevique in limine regis
850 apparent acuuntque metum mortalibus aegris,
si quando letum horrificum morbosque deum rex
molitur, meritas aut bello territat urbes.
harum unam celerem demisit ab aethere summo
Iuppiter inque omen Iuturnae occurrere iussit:
855 illa volat celerique ad terram turbine fertur.
non secus ac nervo per nubem impulsa sagitta,
armatam saevi Parthus quam felle veneni,
Parthus sive Cydon, telum immedicabile, torsit,
stridens et celeris incognita transilit umbras:
860 talis se sata Nocte tulit terrasque petivit.
postquam acies videt Iliacas atque agmina Turni,
alitis in parvae subitam collecta figuram,
quae quondam in bustis aut culminibus desertis
nocte sedens serum canit importuna per umbras—
865 hanc versa in faciem Turni se pestis ob ora
fertque refertque sonans clipeumque everberat alis.
illi membra novus solvit formidine torpor,
arrectaeque horrore comae et vox faucibus haesit.
    At procul ut Dirae stridorem agnovit et alas,
870 infelix crinis scindit Iuturna solutos
unguibus ora soror foedans et pectora pugnis:
"quid nunc te tua, Turne, potest germana iuvare?
aut quid iam durae superat mihi? qua tibi lucem
arte morer? talin possum me opponere monstro?
875 iam iam linquo acies. ne me terrete timentem,
obscenae volucres: alarum verbera nosco
letalemque sonum, nec fallunt iussa superba

865 ob ora *R*: ad ora *P*: inob (in *M*²) ora *M*

360

clothing them with wings of wind. These attend by the throne of Jove and on the threshold of that grim monarch, and whet the fears of feeble mortals, whenever heaven's king wreaks diseases and awful death, or terrifies guilty towns with war. Jove sent one of them swiftly down from high heaven, and bade her meet Juturna as a sign. She wings her way, and darts to earth in swift whirlwind. Like an arrow, shot from the bow string through a cloud, an arrow armed with the gall of fell poison, which a Parthian—a Parthian or a Cydonian—has launched, a shaft beyond all cure; whizzing, it leaps unseen through the swift shadows: so sped the child of Night and sought the earth. As soon as she sees the Ilian ranks and Turnus' troops, suddenly shrinking to the shape of that small bird which often, perched at night on tombs or deserted roofs, sings her late, ill-omened song among the shadows, so changed in form the fiend flits screaming to and fro before the face of Turnus, and beats his shield with her wings. A strange numbness slackened his limbs with dread; his hair stood up in terror and the voice cleaved to his throat.

But when his unhappy sister Juturna recognized the Dread One's whirring wings from afar, she tears her loosened hair, disfiguring her face with her nails, and her breasts with her fists: "What help, Turnus, can your sister give you now? What still awaits me, who have endured so much? With what contrivance can I prolong your life? Can I stand against this terrible portent? Now at last I quit the field. Do not terrify my fluttering soul, ill-boding birds! I know your beating wings, and their dreadful sound, and I do not mistake the haughty mandates of high-hearted

---

⁸⁶⁸ = 4.280   ⁸⁷¹ = 4.673

magnanimi Iovis. haec pro virginitate reponit?
quo vitam dedit aeternam? cur mortis adempta est
880 condicio? possem tantos finire dolores
nunc certe, et misero fratri comes ire per umbras!
immortalis ego? aut quicquam mihi dulce meorum
te sine, frater, erit? o quae satis ima dehiscat
terra mihi, Manisque deam demittat ad imos?"
885 tantum effata caput glauco contexit amictu
multa gemens et se fluvio dea condidit alto.
      Aeneas instat contra telumque coruscat
ingens arboreum, et saevo sic pectore fatur:
"quae nunc deinde mora est? aut quid iam, Turne,
      retractas?
890 non cursu, saevis certandum est comminus armis.
verte omnis tete in facies et contrahe quidquid
sive animis sive arte vales; opta ardua pennis
astra sequi clausumve cava te condere terra."
ille caput quassans: "non me tua fervida terrent
895 dicta, ferox; di me terrent et Iuppiter hostis."
nec plura effatus saxum circumspicit ingens,
saxum antiquum ingens, campo quod forte iacebat,
limes agro positus litem ut discerneret arvis.
vix illud lecti bis sex cervice subirent,
900 qualia nunc hominum producit corpora tellus;
ille manu raptum trepida torquebat in hostem
altior insurgens et cursu concitus heros.
sed neque currentem se nec cognoscit euntem
tollentemve manu saxumve immane moventem;
905 genua labant, gelidus concrevit frigore sanguis.
tum lapis ipse viri vacuum per inane volutus

883 quae *MR*: quam *P*   893 clausumve *P*: clausumque *MR*

Jove. Is this his repayment for my virginity? Why did he give me life eternal? Why am I deprived of the possibility of death? Then I could end this anguish, and pass through the shadows at my poor brother's side! I immortal! Will anything of mine be sweet to me without you, my brother? What ground can gape deep enough for me, and send me down, goddess as I am, to the deepest shades?" So saying, she veiled her head in a mantle of grey, and with many a moan the goddess plunged into the depths of the river.

Aeneas presses on against the foe, brandishing his great tree-like spear, and thus he cries in wrathful spirit: "What more delay is there now? Why, Turnus, do you still draw back? Not in a race, but hand to hand with savage weapons, must we contend. Change yourself into all shapes, muster all your powers of courage or skill; wing your flight, if you will, to the stars aloft, or hide within earth's hollow prison!" The other, shaking his head: "Your fiery words, proud one, do not daunt me; it is the gods who daunt me, and the enmity of Jove." Saying no more, he glances round and sees a huge stone, an ancient stone and huge which by chance lay upon the plain, set for a landmark to keep dispute from the fields. Twice six chosen men could scarce lift it on their shoulders, men of such frames as earth now produces: but the hero, with hurried grasp, seized and hurled it at his foe, rising to his height and at swiftest speed. But he does not recognize himself as he runs, nor as he moves, as he raises the mighty stone in his hand or throws it; his knees buckle, his blood is frozen cold. The very stone, whirled by the hero through the empty air, did not traverse the whole dis-

---

899 illud *PR*: illum *M*
904 tollentemve *PR*: tollentemque *M* | manu *P*: manus *MR*

nec spatium evasit totum neque pertulit ictum.
ac velut in somnis, oculos ubi languida pressit
nocte quies, nequiquam avidos extendere cursus
910 velle videmur et in mediis conatibus aegri
succidimus; non lingua valet, non corpore notae
sufficiunt vires nec vox aut verba sequuntur:
sic Turno, quacumque viam virtute petivit,
successum dea dira negat. tum pectore sensus
915 vertuntur varii; Rutulos aspectat et urbem
cunctaturque metu letumque instare tremescit,
nec quo se eripiat, nec qua vi tendat in hostem,
nec currus usquam videt aurigamve sororem.
    Cunctanti telum Aeneas fatale coruscat,
920 sortitus fortunam oculis, et corpore toto
eminus intorquet. murali concita numquam
tormento sic saxa fremunt nec fulmine tanti
dissultant crepitus. volat atri turbinis instar
exitium dirum hasta ferens orasque recludit
925 loricae et clipei extremos septemplicis orbis;
per medium stridens transit femur. incidit ictus
ingens ad terram duplicato poplite Turnus.
consurgunt gemitu Rutuli totusque remugit
mons circum et vocem late nemora alta remittunt.
930 ille humilis supplex oculos dextramque precantem
protendens "equidem merui nec deprecor" inquit;
"utere sorte tua. miseri te si qua parentis
tangere cura potest, oro (fuit et tibi talis
Anchises genitor) Dauni miserere senectae
935 et me, seu corpus spoliatum lumine mavis,
redde meis. vicisti et victum tendere palmas

916 letum *P*: telum MR

tance, nor drive home its blow. And as in dreams, when
languorous sleep has weighed down our eyes at night, we
seem to strive in vain to press on our eager course, and
in mid effort collapse helpless: our tongue lacks power,
our wonted strength fails our limbs, and neither voice nor
words will come: so to Turnus, however bravely he sought
to win his way, the dread goddess denies fulfilment. Then
shifting fancies whirl through his mind; he gazes on his
Rutulians and the town, he falters in fear, and trembles at
the death that looms; he sees nowhere to escape, nowhere
to attack his foe; he cannot see his chariot anywhere, or his
sister, the charioteer.

As he wavers, Aeneas brandishes the fateful spear, see-
ing a favorable chance, then hurls it from afar with all his
strength. Never do stones shot from a siege engine roar so
loud, never do such great crashes burst from a thunder-
bolt. Like a black whirlwind the spear flies on, bearing fell
destruction, and pierces the corslet's rim and the sevenfold
shield's outermost circle: whizzing it passes right through
the thigh. Under the blow, with his knee bent down to
earth beneath him, huge Turnus sank. The Rutulians start
up with a groan; all the hills re-echo round about, and far
and near the wooded slopes send back the sound. In sup-
plication he lowered his eyes and stretched out his right
hand: "I have earned it," he cried, "and I ask no mercy; use
your chance. If any thought of a parent's grief can touch
you, I beg you—you too had such a father in Anchises—
pity Daunus' old age, and give me—or, if you prefer, my
lifeless body—back to my kin. You are the victor; and the

Ausonii videre; tua est Lavinia coniunx,
ulterius ne tende odiis." stetit acer in armis
MP Aeneas volvens oculos dextramque repressit;
940 et iam iamque magis cunctantem flectere sermo
coeperat, infelix umero cum apparuit alto
balteus et notis fulserunt cingula bullis
Pallantis pueri, victum quem vulnere Turnus
straverat atque umeris inimicum insigne gerebat.
945 ille, oculis postquam saevi monumenta doloris
exuviasque hausit, furiis accensus et ira
terribilis: "tune hinc spoliis indute meorum
eripiare mihi? Pallas te hoc vulnere, Pallas
immolat et poenam scelerato ex sanguine sumit."
950 hoc dicens ferrum adverso sub pectore condit
fervidus; ast illi solvuntur frigore membra
vitaque cum gemitu fugit indignata sub umbras.

[952] = 11.831

Ausonians have seen me stretch forth my hands as the vanquished: Lavinia is your wife; do not press your hatred further." Fierce in his armour, Aeneas stood still shifting his eyes, and restrained his hand; and now, as he paused, these words began to sway him more and more, when high on the shoulder the luckless baldric met his gaze, and the belt flashed with its well-known studs—the belt of young Pallas, whom Turnus had wounded and stretched vanquished on the earth, and now he wore on his shoulders his foeman's fatal emblem. Aeneas, as soon as his eyes drank in the trophy, that memorial of cruel grief, ablaze with fury and terrible in his wrath: "Clad in the spoils of one of mine, are you to be snatched from my hands? Pallas it is, Pallas who sacrifices you with this stroke, and takes retribution from your guilty blood!" So saying, in burning rage he buries his sword full in Turnus' breast. His limbs grew slack and chill and with a moan his life fled resentfully to the Shades below.

APPENDIX VERGILIANA

Note. For *Aetna* and *Elegiae in Maecenatem* see the Loeb Classical Library edition of Minor Latin Poets, vol. I; for *De Est et Non* and *De Inst. Viri Boni* see Ausonius, vol. I; for *De Rosis Nascentibus* see Ausonius, vol. II.

INTRODUCTION

The creative artist is only incidentally a human being; he wins fame and immortality not by his human condition, which is terminated by his death, but by what he was inspired to create, which lives on. We know nothing about Homer the man and tantalizingly little about Shakespeare; the world acknowledges their genius without being able to explain it from their circumstances or to deduce from their productions the record of their private lives. A like situation confronts us in the case of Virgil, incomparably the greatest of Roman poets. Moreover, he was, judging by reports about him, shy almost to paranoia. Entrée to him can only be made through his literary creations: these are clearly authenticated by the capital manuscripts and the ancient line by line commentaries; and at the end of the *Georgics* the poet identifies himself as the author of the *Eclogues,* which he composed "in youth's boldness." But while *Eclogues, Georgics,* and *Aeneid* constitute, almost by definition, the authentic oeuvre of the poet, it is impossible to believe that his first steps in verse-making were the consummate pastorals, hardly conceived, let alone executed, before he was some thirty years old. What we can assert is that Virgil himself neither published nor acknowledged any earlier work, and that there is no evidence that Augustus or Varius or Horace or Propertius, for example, knew of any.

Nevertheless, this did not satisfy some early enthusiasts, who attributed to Virgil sundry items of heterogeneous verse which had come to their attention from sources we know not what or how. At first these sensational attributions led to an eager and uncritical acceptance of them as genuine: Lucan, Statius, and Martial all refer to *Culex* as Virgil's; and Quintilian, without giving a reference other than our author's name, quotes *Catalepton* 2. But in his *Life of Virgil* Donatus, i.e. Suetonius, gives a longer list of titles, lacking only the *Moretum* and three Ausonian poems to form the definitive list of the *Appendix Vergiliana,* as these questionable Virgilian items were labelled by Scaliger in 1572 and now appear in the 1968 Oxford Classical Text.

As was asserted at the outset, it is the greatness of *Eclogues, Georgics,* and *Aeneid* that determines the author Virgil and not the other way round. This consideration enables us to see that the principal question to be asked of the *Appendix* is not so much "Did Virgil compose these poems?" as "Do these poems or any of them reflect or presage the greatness of *Eclogues, Georgics,* and *Aeneid*?" The answer is an uncompromising no. For one thing, they are so disparate in subject matter and style as scarcely to be the products of a single author; and, for another, there is no hint of the genius which aspires to immortality: we meet with many an echo of Virgil, but nothing that is stamped as Virgilian.

Of the three longest poems in the collection Housman has this to say: "The authors of the Culex and Ciris and

Aetna were mediocre poets and worse; and the gods and men and booksellers whom they affronted by existing allotted them for transcription to worse than mediocre scribes. The Ciris was indited by a twaddler, and the Culex and Aetna by stutterers: but what they stuttered and twaddled was Latin, not double-Dutch; and great part of it is now double-Dutch, and Latin no more. The deep corruption of the mss is certified not merely by the jargon which they offer us, but by other and external proofs. For 150 verses of the Aetna we have the fragmentum Gyraldinum, and it reveals, for instance, that the mss on which we depend for the bulk of the poem have altered v. 227 *ingenium sacrare caputque* attollere *caelo* into *sacra per ingentem capitique* attollere *caelum*. For 100 verses of the Ciris we have the codex Bruxellensis, and it tells us that the other mss have substituted *secum heu* for *eheu* at 469 and *uexauit et aegros* for *uexarier undis* at 481. In the Culex the ms on which we chiefly rely can here and there be tested by other authorities, and they prove that it has corrupted *Zanclaea* to *metuenda* at 332[1] and *cui cessit Lydi timefacta* to *legitime cessit cui facta* at 366. Just as it is hard to tell, in Statius or Valerius Flaccus, whether this or that absurd expression is due to miscopying or to the divine afflatus of the bard, so in the Culex and Ciris and Aetna it is for ever to be borne in mind that they are the work of poetasters. Many a time it is impossible to say for certain where the badness of the author ends and the badness of the

---

[1] Actually Housman is guilty of a misjudgement here: *metuenda* is the true reading, and *Zanclaea* the interpolation; but his view of the depth of corruption indicated by some manuscript variants remains valid.

scribe begins" (*Classical Review* 16 [1902] 339 = *Collected Papers* 2.563).

It will be convenient to give here a catalogue of this ramshackle collection, with the numerals and lowercase letters assigned to them by Courtney (133) and approved by Reeve (1976, 238, n.24).

1 *Dirae* (Curses) and *Lydia*
2 *Culex* (The Gnat)
3 *Aetna*
4 *Copa* (The Hostess)
5 *Elegiae in Maecenatem* (Elegies on Maecenas)
6 *Ciris*
7 *Catalepton* (Slight Poems)
8 *Priapea*
9 *Moretum* (The Salad)
a *De Est et Non* (Yes and No)
b *De Institutione Viri Boni* (The Good Man)
c *De Rosis Nascentibus* (Budding Roses)

To this collection of pseudo-Vergiliana may be added two epigrams from the *Life* attributed to Donatus: 17 (on a schoolmaster Ballista, Virgil's "first" composition) and 36 (*Mantua me genuit,* his "last"), the former improbable, the latter impossible.

Dirae and *Lydia*

The verses entitled PUBLII VIRGILII MARONIS DIRAE appear in the manuscripts as a single poem and were only in 1792 recognized (by Friedrich Jacobs) as the compositions of two different authors, with different themes.

Dirae presupposes the same background as the first and ninth eclogues and contains a series of "Curses" by one who has been dispossessed of his lands; *Lydia* is a lament at being parted from his sweetheart by one who has also suffered eviction.

Yet another versifier has interpolated in *Dirae* some lines of farewell to Lydia in an attempt (exposed by Eduard Fraenkel) to give a unity to the two poems.

Culex

Although among the poems of the *Appendix* the external evidence for Virgilian authorship is strongest in the case of *Culex*, there can be little doubt that it is a fake: chronology forbids the claim of the composer's intimacy with Octavius in their student days, at a time when he was apparently able to echo passages from the *Eclogues, Georgics,* and *Aeneid.* Fraenkel quotes a particularly telling example: the phrase *hinc atque hinc* does not occur before the *Aeneid* (1.162, 500; 4.447; 8.387; 9.380, 440, 550; and 12.431) and rarely after it; but the author of *Culex* twice (16, 221) adopted this peculiarity of the *Aeneid* as he did many others.

Fraenkel is probably right in seeing behind *Culex* a Greek poem, the story of which was as follows. Overcome by the heat of the noonday sun, a shepherd falls asleep in the shade of a tree; however, a deadly serpent is creeping towards him and would undoubtedly have killed him, had not a kindly gnat warned him of his danger by stinging him in the eye; up jumps the shepherd in rage and at once crushes the insect; now fully awake he catches sight of the serpent, which he batters to death with a bough torn from a tree in desperation. As he sleeps that night he is haunted by the spirit of the gnat, which reproaches him for his ingratitude.

Nevertheless, most of *Culex* is taken up with a tour of the underworld, an absurdly grotesque pageant of heroes and heroines which has nothing to do with gnat or shepherd. Possibly the Hellenistic poem postulated took much from Homer's *Necyia* (*Odyssey* 11), but such fancies as *hic Fabii Deciique, hic est et Horatia virtus* can only have originated with the sixth book of the *Aeneid,* i.e. are post-Virgilian.

Aetna

Aetna, a didactic poem of 645 hexameters, attributed to Virgil (though Donatus adds that the attribution is disputed), must have been composed before A.D. 79 since Vesuvius' eruption in that year is not mentioned. The author, who writes as a scientist, but is no Lucretius, may have been influenced by Seneca's *Natural Questions.* Loeb Classical Library text and translation (by J. Wight Duff and Arnold M. Duff) are to be found in *Minor Latin Poets,* vol.I, pp. 349–419; index nominum, vol.II, pp. 831–838.

Copa

Amid the motley pinchbeck of the *Appendix Vergiliana, Copa* stands out as a pure pearl: it reflects the language of Virgil and the meter of Propertius, but its spirit is far removed from that of the classical world and foreshadows the carefree jollity of the Wandering Scholars of the Middle Ages. One would guess it to have been composed in the Neronian period, but as literature it is dateless.

The title of the poem refers to the hostess who runs a roadside inn for the benefit of weary travellers; she sings and dances to entertain them, and the poem as a whole represents her pitch to attract their custom. It has been asserted that the establishment is no more than a brothel, and its fare the shoddiest. However, the poet is not portraying reality, but the make-believe world of his dreams.

Elegiae in Maecenatem

Not even the most credulous of Virgil's aficionados can claim his authorship for these poems since they were composed shortly after 8 B.C. in commemoration of the death of Augustus' great political and literary adviser, when Virgil had already been dead eleven years. Even so, like other poems in the collection, they provide evidence for the literary scene of that time. Loeb Classical Library text and translation (by J. Wight Duff and Arnold M. Duff) are to be found in *Minor Latin Poets,* vol.I, pp. 113–139; index nominum, vol.II, pp. 831–838.

Ciris

Like *Culex,* this poem is an epyllion (though the term is not an ancient one), "a little epic" in hexameters. It was a short-lived genre, usually dealing with a mythological romance and named after the heroine. Cinna's *Smyrna,* unfortunately no longer extant, was much admired by Catullus, who in his poem 64 (possibly titled *Ariadne*) provides the best example of the type.

Many stories are told about Scylla, the central character of *Ciris:* in this poem she is not the companion of the Homeric Charybdis, but the daughter of Nisus, king of Megara. Though hotly attacked by the Cretan overlord Minos, he is divinely protected by a purple lock of hair in the middle of his head so long as this itself is unharmed. However, Scylla is madly in love with Minos, and thinking thereby to win his love, she stealthily cuts off Nisus' lock and so encompasses his death. So far from accepting her suit, Minos drowns her in disgust. But Heaven intervenes and changes her into a bird "impossible of identification, a poetical, half-imaginary bird" (D'Arcy Thompson, *Greek Birds,* p. 144) and Nisus into a sea eagle, which pursues her unceasingly.

Dedication to Messalla (d. A.D. 8) and numerous quotations from Virgil preclude the latter's authorship of *Ciris,* while various echoes of Catullus 64 rule out a late date such as is proposed by Lyne, for detailed knowledge of the text of Catullus had been lost by the end of the Neronian age. Moreover, in spite of Catullus' enthusiasm, and Cinna's praised performance, the genre did not catch on. Propertius, in his *Tarpeia* (4.4), successfully transfers to elegy the theme of the girl who betrays her country for love, but this tended to block any further development of the epyllion, and it was left to Ovid to create a wider scope by exploiting the theme of transformation, brilliantly accomplished by him in the *Metamorphoses.*

Catalepton

Catalepton (κατὰ λεπτόν, slight poems), an ill-assorted collection of pieces on different subjects and in varying meters, hardly by a single author, is still thought by some scholars to contain original work by Virgil. That they mostly date from Virgil's own lifetime there is no reason to doubt, and it is probably this consideration which has fueled belief in their authenticity. But there is so much in them that is obscure or tasteless or just plain trivial as to cast the gravest suspicion on the collection as a whole. The tenth poem is, admittedly, a clever piece of parody, which, however, like the second, is more likely to have been composed by some member of Catullus' circle than by Virgil, who shows little penchant for caricature or invective.

Priapea

The god Priapus, carved out of wood to represent a phallus and set up in gardens and orchards, was the inspiration for a collection of some eighty poems containing dire warnings against trespassers. Known as *Priapea,* it is nowadays generally imputed to an author of imperial date; but many contributed to the theme and enlarged it. Catullus 17 is the most famous example of the Priapean meter, but the classical poets contain many references to the god and his function.

Donatus' *Life* lists *Priapea* (unspecified) among the poet's early work, and from mss associated with the *Appendix Vergiliana* three (84–86 Bücheler) are commonly printed with or as part of the *Catalepton:* these purport to be spoken by the god himself and are typical examples of the genre. Another (83 B) is of an unusual kind, dealing, like Ovid's *Amores* 3.7 and poems of Petronius and Maximian, with the author's impotence; while in the Graz manuscript it is attributed to Virgil, it is also found, equally incongruously, in the *Appendix Tibulliana* (full commentary in Tränkle's edition).

There is no likelihood that any of these poems were composed by Virgil.

Moretum

This charming idyll of 122 lines is first attested in the ninth-century Murbach catalogue. The influence of Ovid's *Metamorphoses* (the Baucis and Philemon episode) rules out a Virgilian date. As Kenney suggests (ed. p. xxii), the

Moretum survived on its own merits until "in the wholesale transference of Latin literature from roll to codex, it was swept into the Virgilian net," very much as the poems of Lygdamus and Sulpicia were preserved by association with Tibullus. The poem describes in detail the preparation of his lunch by a ploughman with the aid of his African serving maid.

De Est et Non [Ausonius, ed. R. P. H. Green, XIV *Ecl.* 21. Loeb Classical Library text and translation (by H. G. Evelyn White) are to be found in Ausonius, vol.I, pp. 170–73];

De Institutione Viri Boni [Ausonius, ed. R. P. H. Green, XIV *Ecl.* 20. Loeb Classical Library text and translation (by H. P. Evelyn White) are to be found in Ausonius, vol.I, pp. 168–71];

De Rosis Nascentibus [Ausonius, ed. R. P. H. Green, Appendix A 3, *De R.N.*, pp. 669–671. Loeb Classical Library text and translation (by H. G. Evelyn White) are to be found in Ausonius, vol.II, pp. 276–81].

These three pieces are now acknowledged to be poems of Ausonius, whose oeuvre, like that of all creators who are both prolific and multifarious, poses difficulties for those compiling a complete canon; it is easy for minor pieces which are not obviously connected with larger portions of the author's work nor marked with his name to become detached. As with so much else in the *Appendix Vergiliana,* such anonymous fragments could conveniently be assigned to Virgil, whose poems were intimately known to Ausonius.

Text

Deep uncertainty surrounds the origins and transmission of the *Appendix Vergiliana*. It is essentially a heterogeneous collection; we know neither the circumstances in which it was put together nor the agent who was responsible. The items are identified by being mostly mentioned by Donatus and Servius, but the only clue to the textual tradition is an entry in a 9th-century Murbach catalogue which describes a manuscript containing the items 1–9 and a, b, c detailed above. Unfortunately this manuscript does not survive, and "since only two manuscripts contain as many as three works in the same order as the Murbacensis and only two late manuscripts contain in any order more than five, it is by no means clear that the Murbacensis or indeed any single manuscript gave rise to the extant tradition" (Reeve, 1983, 43).

In these circumstances my textual notes do not aspire to furnish more than first aid, and for the sake of clarity and simplicity the siglum Ω is employed to denote what seems to be the textual tradition of each item and thus will often refer to different mss; that such readings are archetypal and indeed those of the Murbacensis is conceivable though far from certain.

G items 67849: Graz fragment 1814: 9th cent.
L items 214abc9: the lost *Iuvenalis Ludi Libellus*, the source of
  W Trevirensis 1086: 9–10th cent.
  E Paris 8093: 10th cent.
  A Paris 7927: 10–11th cent.
  T Paris 8069: 11th cent.

S   items 2149cab3: Stabulensis, now Paris 17177: 10th cent.

F   items (a) 95; (b) 214⟨ab⟩c: Fiechtianus, now Mellicensis cim.2: 10th cent.

C   items 23: Cambridge Kk v 34: 10th cent.

M   items 95184: the source of
> m   Munich 305: 11–12th cent.
> n   Munich 18059: 11th cent.

B   items 6785: Brussels 10675–6: 12th cent.

V   items 28: Vat.2759: 13th cent.

Γ   item 2: Corsinianus 43 F 5: 14th cent.

Z   items 35678: the source of
> H   Helmstadiensis 332: 15th cent.
> A   Arundelianus 133: 15th cent.
> R   Rehdigeranus 125: 15th cent.

ρ, ς   item 6: other late mss

BIBLIOGRAPHY

Reference

Karl Büchner: "Vergilius," Paulys *Real-Encyclopaedie* VIIIA (1955–58) 1021–1486, also published separately Stuttgart 1961.

Francesco della Corte (ed.): *Enciclopedia virgiliana*, 6 vols, Rome 1984–91.

Editions

Otto Ribbeck: *P. Vergili Maronis Opera*, vol. 4: *Appendix Vergiliana* [2, 6, 4, 9, 7, 1], Leipzig 1895.

Appendix Vergiliana [2, 6, 9, 1, 4, 8 i–iii, 7, *a*, *b*, 5], ed. R. Ellis, Oxford Classical Texts, Oxford 1907, reissued with *Vitae Vergilianae Antiquae* (ed. Colin Hardie) 1954.

Joseph J. Mooney: *The Minor Poems of Vergil* [2, 1, 9, 4, 8 i–iii, 7] *metrically translated into English* (with notes; a translation of Foca's *Life*; and a Latin text of the poems), Birmingham 1916.

Poetae Latini Minores, ed. Fr. Vollmer, vol. I *Appendix Vergiliana* [2, 1, 4, 9, 6, 8 i–iii, 7, 5, 3], with supplement by Willy Morel; Bibliotheca Teubneriana, Leipzig 1927.

Appendix Vergiliana [2, 6, 1, 4, 9, 8 i–iii, 7, 5, *a*, *b*, *c*], ed. Remo Giomini, with introduction on the mss and editions, bibliography; full apparatus and translation (Italian) (*Biblioteca di Studi Superiori*), Florence 1953.

Appendix Vergiliana [1, 2, 3, 4, 5, 6, 8 i–iii, 7, 8 iv, 9, *b*, *a*, *c*], ed. W. V. Clausen, F. R. D. Goodyear, E. J. Kenney, J. A. Richmond, Oxford Classical Texts, Oxford 1966.

Individual Items

Dirae (1)

Eduard Fraenkel: "The Dirae" (text and commentary), *Journal of Roman Studies* 56 (1966) 142–155.

F. R. D. Goodyear: "The *Dirae*" (text and commentary: an attack on Fraenkel's views as published above), *Proceedings of the Cambridge Philological Society* 17 (1971) 30–43 (= *Papers on Latin Literature*, Duckworth, London 1992, pp. 9–22).

Culex (2)

Fr. Leo: *Culex* (introduction, text, apparatus, commentary; with text and apparatus of *Copa*), Weidmann, Berlin 1891.

A. E. Housman: "Remarks on the *Culex*," *Classical Review* 16 (1902) 339–346 (= *Collected Papers* 2.563–576).

A. E. Housman: "The Apparatus Criticus of the *Culex*," *Transactions of the Cambridge Philological Society* 6 (1908) 3–22 (= *Collected Papers* 2.773–786).

Eduard Fraenkel: "The Culex," *Journal of Roman Studies* 42 (1952) 1–9 (= *Kleine Beiträge* 2.181–197).

Copa (4)

Ulrich von Wilamowitz-Moellendorff: *Hellenistische Dichtung*, Weidmann, Berlin 1924, vol. 2, chap. 9, pp. 311–315 (repr. 1962).

F. R. D. Goodyear: "The *Copa*: A Text and Commentary," *Bulletin of the Institute of Classical Studies* 24 (1977) 117–131 (= *Papers on Latin Literature*, Duckworth, London 1992, pp. 27–45).

Ciris (6)

R. O. A. M. Lyne: *Ciris* (introduction, text, apparatus, commentary), Cambridge Classical Texts and Commentaries, Cambridge, 1978.

A. E. Housman: "Remarks on the *Ciris*," *Classical Review* 17 (1903) 303–311 (= *Collected Papers* 2.583–596).

Catalepton (7)

Theodor Birt: *Jugendverse und Heimatpoesie Vergils: Erklärung des Catalepton* (introduction, text, apparatus, commentary), Leipzig and Berlin, Teubner 1910.

P. Vergili Maronis . . . Catalepton, ed. R. E. H. Westendorp Boerma, Assen 1949 (pars prior, 1–8), 1963 (pars altera 9–15): bibliography, text, apparatus criticus, English (Loeb) translation; commentary (Latin).

Johannes and Maria Götte: *Vergil, Bucolica, Georgica, Catalepton*, also Karl Bayer, ed., *Vergil-viten* (Artemis edition, with German hexameter translation and extensive scholarly apparatus and bibliography of work by 333 authors), Munich, Heimeran 1981 (updated from 1959 edition).

Moretum (9)

E. J. Kenney: *The Ploughman's Lunch: Moretum* (bibliography, introduction, text, apparatus, translation, commentary), Bristol Classical Press 1984.

BIBLIOGRAPHY

Manuscript Tradition

E. Courtney: "The Textual Transmission of the *Appendix Vergiliana*," *Bulletin of the Institute of Classical Studies* 15 (1968) 133–141.

M. D. Reeve: "The Textual Tradition of *Aetna, Ciris*, and *Catalepton*," *Maia* 27 (1975) 231–247.

M. D. Reeve: "The Textual Tradition of the *Appendix Vergiliana*," *Maia* 28 (1976) 233–254.

Biographical Studies

Franz Skutsch: *Aus Vergils Frühzeit* (vol. 1); *Gallus und Vergil* (vol. 2), Leipzig and Berlin, Teubner 1901, 1906.

Norman Wentworth DeWitt: *Virgil's Biographia Litteraria*, Victoria College Press, Toronto (Oxford University Press) 1923.

Tenney Frank: *Vergil, A Biography*, Russell and Russell, New York 1965 (orig. ed. 1922).

DIRAE

Battare, cycneas repetamus carmine voces:
divisas iterum sedes et rura canamus,
rura quibus diras indiximus, impia vota.
ante lupos rapient haedi, vituli ante leones,
5   delphini fugient pisces, aquilae ante columbas,
et conversa retro rerum discordia gliscet—
multa prius fient quam non mea libera avena
montibus et silvis dicat tua facta, Lycurge.

"Impia Trinacriae sterilescant gaudia vobis
10 nec fecunda, senis nostri felicia rura,
semina parturiant segetes, non pascua colles,
non arbusta novas fruges, non pampinus uvas,
ipsae non silvae frondes, non flumina montes."

Rursus et hoc iterum repetamus, Battare, carmen:

15 "Effetas Cereris sulcis condatis avenas,
pallida flavescant aestu sitientia prata,
immatura cadant ramis pendentia mala,
desint et silvis frondes et fontibus umor,

mss: Ω = M (mn); SF; L (WBEAT)   meter: hexameter
8 dicat ç: dicam Ω

DIRAE

O Battarus, let my verse intone again the notes of the swan: again let us sing of our divided homes and lands, lands whereon we have pronounced our curses, unholy prayers. Sooner shall kids prey upon wolves, sooner calves upon lions; sooner shall dolphins flee before fishes, sooner eagles before doves, and worldwide chaos, again returning, shall burst forth—yea, many things shall come to pass before my shepherd's reed shall be silenced from telling your deeds, Lycurgus, to the woods and mountains.

"Unholy and unblest, may Trinacria's joys become barren for you and your fellows, and may the fruitful seeds in our old master's rich lands give birth to no corn crops, the hills to no pastures, the trees to no fresh fruits, the vines to no grapes, the very woods to no leafage, the mountains to no streams!"

Again and yet again, O Battarus, let us repeat this song:

"Outworn be the oats of Ceres that ye bury in the furrows; pale and wan may the meadows become, parched with the heat; unripened may the drooping apples fall from the boughs! Let leaves fail the woods, let water fail the

nec desit nostris devotum carmen avenis.
20 haec Veneris vario florentia serta decore,
purpureo campos quae pingunt verna colore
(hinc aurae dulces, hinc suavis spiritus agri),
mutent pestiferos aestus et taetra venena;
dulcia non oculis, non auribus ulla ferantur."

25 Sic precor, et nostris superent haec carmina votis:

"Lusibus et multum nostris cantata libellis,
optima silvarum, formosis densa virectis,
tondebis virides umbras, nec laeta comantis
iactabis mollis ramos inflantibus auris
30 (nec mihi saepe meum resonabit, Battare, carmen),
militis impia cum succidet dextera ferro
formosaeque cadent umbrae, formosior illis
ipsa cades, veteris domini felicia ligna—
nequiquam: nostris potius devota libellis
35 ignibus aetheriis flagrabis. Iuppiter (ipse
Iuppiter hanc aluit), cinis haec tibi fiat oportet.
Thraecis tum Boreae spirent immania vires,
Eurus agat mixtam fulva caligine nubem,
Africus immineat nimbis minitantibus imbrem.
40 cum tu, cyaneo resplendens aethere, silva,
. . . .
[non iterum dices, crebro quae 'Lydia' dixti]
vicinae flammae rapiant ex ordine vitis,
pascantur segetes, diffusis ignibus aura

21 pingunt verna *Naeke*: pingit avena Ω
26 lusibus *Sillig*: ludimus Ω
28 tondebis *Gronovius*: -emus Ω

streams, but let not the song that curses fail my reeds! May these flowery garlands of Venus, with their varied beauties, which in springtime paint the fields with brilliant hues (depart, ye breezes sweet; depart, ye fragrant odours of the field!)—may they change to blasting heats and loathsome poisons; may nothing sweet to eyes or ears be wafted!"

Thus I pray, and in my prayers may these strains prevail:

"You, best of woods, oft sung in my playful songs and verses, beautiful in your thick foliage, you will shear your green shade; nor will you toss your soft boughs' joyous foliage to the breezes blowing through them; nor, O Battarus, shall it oft resound for me with my song. When with his axe the soldier's impious hand shall fell it, and the lovely shadows fall, you, more lovely than they, shall fall, the old owner's happy timber. Yet all for naught! Rather, cursed by my verses, you will burn with heaven's fires. O Jupiter (it was Jupiter himself who nurtured this wood), this you must turn into ashes! Then let the strength of the Thracian North emit his mighty blasts; let the East drive a cloud with tawny darkness mixed; let the South-West menace with storm clouds threatening rain. When, O wood, ablaze in the dark-blue sky, ⟨you are utterly consumed by fire⟩, [you will not again say 'Lydia,' as you said so oft] let nearby flames tear the vines out of their regular order, let them feed on the crops, let the breeze, scattering sparks,

---

40 tu *Vollmer*: tua Ω

post 40 *lac. Fraenkel*

41 *del. Fraenkel* (dices ς: dicens Ω | quae *Schmidt*: tua Ω)

43 aura ς: auras Ω

transvolet, arboribus coniungat et ardor aristas.
45 pertica qua nostros metata est impia agellos,
qua nostri fines olim, cinis omnia fiat."

Sic precor, et nostris superent haec carmina votis:

"Undae, quae vestris pulsatis litora lymphis,
litora, quae dulcis auras diffunditis agris,
50 accipite has voces: migret Neptunus in arva
fluctibus et spissa campos perfundat harena;
qua Volcanus agros pastus Iovis ignibus arsit,
barbara dicatur Libycae soror, altera Syrtis."

Tristius hoc, memini, revocasti, Battare, carmen:

55 "Nigro multa mari dicunt portenta natare,
monstra repentinis terrentia saepe figuris,
cum subito emersere furenti corpora ponto;
haec agat infesto Neptunus caeca tridenti,
atrum convertens aestum maris undique ventis
60 et fuscum cinerem canis exhauriat undis.
dicantur mea rura ferum mare (nauta, caveto),
rura, quibus diras indiximus, impia vota."

Si minus haec, Neptune, tuas infundimus auris,
Battare, fluminibus tu nostros trade dolores:
65 nam tibi sunt fontes, tibi semper flumina amica.
nil est quod perdam ulterius: merito omnia Ditis.

---

52 arsit *Ribbeck*: arcet Ω
54 revocasti *H*: -asset Ω

fly across, and let the fire unite the corn ears with the trees. Where the wicked rod measured our fields, where once were our boundaries, let all be reduced to ash."

Thus I pray, and in my prayers may these strains prevail:

"O waves, that with your waters beat the shores; O shores that scatter sweet breezes o'er the fields, give ear to my prayers. Let Neptune with his waves invade the plains and cover the fields with thick sand! Where Vulcan, feeding on the lands, has burnt with the fires of Jupiter, let it be called a foreign sister of the Libyan sand, a second Syrtis."

This sadder strain, O Battarus, I remember you recalled:

"Many fearful things, they say, swim in the dark sea, monsters that often terrify with unexpected shapes, when suddenly their bodies have emerged from the raging deep. May Neptune drive these hidden beasts with threatening trident, on all sides upturning with the winds the black sea-surge and swallowing in his hoary waves the swarthy ashes![1] Let my lands be called a savage sea (sailor, beware), my lands on which I have invoked curses, wicked prayers."

If we do not pour this, Neptune, into your ears, do you, O Battarus, consign our sorrows to the streams; for to you the springs, to you the streams are ever friendly. No further ruin can I effect;[2] to Dis all belongs of right.

---

[1] I.e. left by the fire described above.
[2] I.e. by my curses.

"Flectite currentis lymphas, vaga flumina, retro;
flectite et adversis rursum diffundite campis:
incurrant amnes passim rimantibus undis
70 nec nostros servire sinant erronibus agros."

Dulcius hoc, memini, revocasti, Battare, carmen:

"Emanent subito sicca tellure paludes,
et metat hic iuncos, spicas ubi legimus olim;
incolat arguti grylli cava garrula rana."

75 Tristius hoc rursum dicat mea fistula carmen:

"Praecipitent altis fumantes montibus imbres,
et late teneant diffuso gurgite campos,
qui dominis infesta minantes stagna relinquant.
cum delapsa meos agros pervenerit unda,
80 piscetur nostris in finibus advena arator,
advena, civili qui semper crimine crevit."

O male devoti, raptorum crimina, agelli,
tuque inimica tui semper Discordia civis,
exsul ego indemnatus egens mea rura reliqui,
85 miles ut accipiat funesti praemia belli?
hinc ego de tumulo mea rura novissima visam,
hinc ibo in silvas: obstabunt iam mihi colles,
obstabunt montes, campos audire licebit:

[74] incolat *Maehly*: occulet Ω
[75] dicat ς: dicit Ω
[82] raptorum *Scaliger*: pratorum Ω

"Turn back your running waters, ye roving streams; turn back, and pour them again over the opposing fields: let brooks from all sides rush in with deep-cleaving waters, and let them not suffer our lands to be enslaved to vagabonds!"

This sweeter strain, O Battarus, I remember you recalled:

"Let marshes from parched ground suddenly spring forth, and, where once we gathered corn ears, let this man reap rushes; let the croaking frog dwell in the chirping cricket's hollow lairs!"

This sadder strain let my pipe give forth in turn:

"From high mountains let rains rush streaming down, and with outspread flood widely occupy the plains; then, menacing evil to their lords, let them leave stagnant pools! When the waters, rushing down, reach my fields, then let the foreign ploughman fish within my bounds—a foreigner, who has always gained wealth from civil strife."

Accursed fields that stand as an indictment of those who seized you, and you, O Discord, ever the foe of your fellow citizens, have I, a needy exile, though not condemned to that, left my lands that a soldier may receive the rewards of deadly war? From this mound will I look my last upon my lands; from this will I pass to the woods; soon will the hills, soon will the mountains obstruct my view, but the plains will be able to hear me.

["Dulcia rura, valete, et Lydia dulcior illis,
90   et casti fontes et, felix nomen, agelli."]

Tardius, a, miserae descendite monte capellae
(mollia non iterum carpetis pabula nota)
tuque resiste pater: en prima novissima nobis,
intueor campos: longum manet esse sine illis.

95   ["Rura valete iterum, tuque, optima Lydia, salve.
sive eris et si non, mecum morieris utrumque."]

Extremum carmen revocemus, Battare, avena:

"Dulcia amara prius fient et mollia dura,
candida nigra oculi cernent et dextera laeva,
100 migrabunt casus aliena in corpora rerum,
quam tua de nostris emigret cura medullis.
quamvis ignis eris, quamvis aqua, semper amabo."
[gaudia semper enim tua me meminisse licebit]

    89,90 *del. Fraenkel*
    93 en ç: et Ω
    95,96; 103 *del. Fraenkel*

["Sweet lands, farewell! And Lydia, sweeter still, farewell, and ye, pure fountains, and ye fields of happy name!"]

Ah! Poor she goats, come more slowly down the mountain: never again will ye browse on the soft familiar pastures; and do you, father of the flock, remain behind! Lo, upon the plains, my first and last possession, I gaze: to be bereft of them for ever remains my lot.

["Once more ye fields, farewell, and you, best Lydia, farewell; whether you live or not, in either case you will die with me."]

Our last strain, Battarus, let us recall on the reed!

"Sooner shall sweet become bitter, and soft hard; eyes shall see white as black, and right as left; atoms of things shall pass into bodies of other kinds before love of you shall pass from my heart. Though you become fire, though water, I shall always love you." [always I shall be allowed to recall your joys]

LYDIA

Invideo vobis, agri formosaque prata,
hoc formosa magis, mea quod formosa puella
in vobis tacite nostrum suspirat amorem;
vos nunc illa videt, vobis mea Lydia ludit,
5   vos nunc alloquitur, vos nunc arridet ocellis,
et mea submissa meditatur carmina voce,
cantat et interea, mihi quae cantabat in aurem.
    Invideo vobis, agri, discetis amare.
o fortunati nimium multumque beati,
10 in quibus illa pedis nivei vestigia ponet
aut roseis viridem digitis decerpserit uvam
(dulci namque tumet nondum vitecula Baccho)
aut inter varios, Veneris stipendia, flores
membra reclinarit teneramque illiserit herbam
15 et secreta meos furtim narrabit amores.
gaudebunt silvae, gaudebunt mollia prata
et gelidi fontes, aviumque silentia fient,
tardabunt rivi labentes (sistite, lymphae),
dum mea iucundas exponat cura querelas.
20   Invideo vobis, agri: mea gaudia habetis,
et vobis nunc est mihi quae fuit ante voluptas.
at male tabescunt morientia membra dolore,

mss: Ω = M (mn); SF; L (WBEAT)   meter: hexameter

LYDIA

I envy you, ye fields and lovely meadows, for this more lovely that in you my lovely girl sighs silently for my love. It is you she now sees, in you my Lydia plays, it is you she now addresses, on you she now turns her smiling eyes, hums my songs with voice subdued, and meanwhile sings those strains she used to sing into my ear.

I envy you, ye fields; you will learn to love. O too, too happy fields, yea, often blest, in which she will print the steps of her snowy feet, or with rosy fingers will pluck the green grape (for the little vine swells not yet with nectarous juice), or amid the coloured flowers, tribute to Venus, she will lay down her limbs and crush the tender grass, and all alone will stealthily recount the tale of my love. The woods will rejoice, the soft meadows and cool springs will rejoice, and the birds will keep silent. The gliding brooks will pause (halt, ye waters!) while my heart sets forth its fond complaints.

I envy you, ye fields; you possess what gives me joy, and now you have her, who before was my delight. But my dying limbs are wasting with grief, and warmth fails me,

---

3 in vobis *Heinsius*: est vobis Ω

18 sistite ς: currite Ω

21 mihi *Heinsius*: mea Ω

et calor infuso decedit frigore mortis,
quod mea non mecum domina est: non ulla puella
25   doctior in terris fuit aut formosior, ac, si
fabula non vana est, tauro Iove digna vel auro
(Iuppiter, avertas aurem) mea sola puella est.
    Felix taure, pater magni gregis et decus, a te
vaccula non umquam secreta cubilia captans
30   frustra te patitur silvis mugire dolorem.
et pater haedorum felix semperque beate,
sive petis montes praeruptos, saxa pererrans,
sive tibi silvis nova pabula fastidire
sive libet campis: tecum tua laeta capella est.
35   et mas quicumque est, illi sua femina iuncta
interpellatos numquam ploravit amores.
cur non et nobis facilis, natura, fuisti?
cur ego crudelem patior tam saepe dolorem?
    Sidera per viduum radiant cum pallida mundum
40   inque vicem Phoebi currens abit aureus orbis,
Luna, tuus tecum est: cur non est et mea mecum?
Luna, dolor nosti quid sit: miserere dolentis.
Phoebe, recens in te laurus celebravit amorem,
et quae pompa deûm (nisi vilis fama locuta est
45   somnia: vos scitis) secum sua gaudia gestat
aut inspersa videt mundo; quae dicere longum est.

35 quicumque ς: quo- Ω
37 fuisti *Salmasius*: fuisset Ω
39 viduum *Goold*: viridem Ω | radiant *Heinsius*: redeunt Ω
40 Phoebi *Heinsius*: Phoebo Ω | abit *Escuche*: atque Ω
43 recens *Naeke*: gerens Ω
44 vilis *Baehrens*: silvis Ω
45 somnia *Heinsius*: omnia Ω | scitis *Ribbeck*: estis Ω

steeped in the chill of death, because my sweetheart is not with me. No girl on earth was cleverer or lovelier; and if the story is not false, then my girl alone is as worthy of Jupiter as bull or bullion[1] (Jupiter, hearken not!).

O happy bull, father and pride of the mighty herd, never does the heifer, seeking stalls apart, suffer you to low your unhappiness vainly to the woods. And you, father of kids, happy and ever blest, whether, roaming over rocks, you seek steep mountains or, whether in woods or on plains, it is your pleasure to scorn fresh forage: with you is your happy mate. And whoever is a male, with him is joined his mate, and never has he lamented an interrupted love. Why, Nature, have you not been so kind to us as well? Why so often do I suffer bitter grief?

When the pale stars shine over a bereft[2] sky and the golden orb that runs in place of Phoebus is not there, then, O Moon, you are with your lover:[3] why is not also mine with me? O Moon, you know what grief is: pity one who grieves. Phoebus, the newfound laurel that you wear proclaims your love,[4] and so does that procession of gods (unless base rumour has spoken false—but ye know it to be true) which carries their fancies with them[5] or sees them scattered over the universe: to tell of these would prove a tedious task. Moreover, when the golden ages unrolled

---

[1] This is Mooney's attempt to reproduce the wordplay of *tauro . . . auro*; Jupiter seduced Europa after taking the form of a bull, and Danaë by turning himself into a shower of gold.

[2] Explained by the next line, i.e. bereft of the Moon.

[3] Endymion, whom in the interlunar period the Moon was fancied to visit on Mount Latmos.　　[4] For Daphne.

[5] As Pan his pipes (Syrinx).

aurea quin etiam cum saecula volvebantur,
condicio similis fuerat mortalibus illis.
haec quoque praetereo: notum Minoidos astrum
50 quaeque virum virgo, sicut captiva, secuta est.
laedere, caelicolae, potuit vos nostra quid aetas,
condicio nobis vitae quo durior esset?

    Ausus egon primus castos violare pudores,
sacratamque meae vittam temptare puellae
55 immatura mea cogor nece solvere fata?
istius atque utinam facti mea culpa magistra
prima foret! letum vita mihi dulcius esset.
non mea, non ullo moreretur tempore fama,
dulcia cum Veneris furatus gaudia primus
60 dicerer, atque ex me dulcis foret orta voluptas.
nunc mihi non tantum tribuerunt invida fata
auctor ut occulti noster foret error amoris.

    Iuppiter ante, sui semper mendacia factus,
cum Iunone, prius coniunx quam dictus uterque est,
65 gaudia libavit dulcem furatus amorem.
et moechum tenera gavisa est laedere in herba
purpureos flores, quos insuper accumbebat,
Cypria, formoso supponens bracchia collo;
tum, credo, fuerat Mavors distentus in armis,
70 nam certe Volcanus opus faciebat, et illi
tristi turpabat malam ac fuligine barbam.
non Aurora novos etiam ploravit amores

59 primus *ed. Bas.*: -um Ω
61 nunc *Schrader*: nam Ω | invida fata *Heinsius*: impia vota Ω
66 moechum *Baehrens*: mecum Ω
68 Cypria . . . bracchia *Putsch*: grandia . . . gaudia Ω
71 malam ac *Vollmer*: malas Ω

400

their course and mortals of that time enjoyed similar conditions—this also I pass over. To all is known the star of Minos' daughter,[6] and the maiden who, as a captive, followed her master. In what, ye heaven-dwellers, could our age have injured you, that therefore the way of life should be harder for us?

Was I the first who dared to violate the chaste purity and sully the sacred ribbon of his girl, that by my death I am forced to pay the penalty of an untimely fate? And O that my fault were the first prompter of that deed! Then would death be sweeter to me than life. Then would my fame not perish at any time, since it would be said that I first had stolen Love's sweet joys and from me had sprung that sweet delight. As it is, envious fate has not granted to me a boon so great, that our lapse should have given rise to clandestine love.

Once Jupiter, who could at all times counterfeit false forms of himself, and Juno too, before either was called a spouse, tasted the stolen delights of sweet love. The Cyprian also rejoiced that on the tender grass her lover[7] crushed the brilliant flowers on which she lay, as she threw her arms about his handsome neck; at that time, I imagine, Mars had been detained in warfare, for Vulcan was surely busied with work, which was defiling with unsightly soot the cheek and beard of that unhappy god. Has not Aurora, too, wept for a new love[8] and, blushing, veiled her eyes in

[6] Ariadne, raised to the stars by Dionysus (her master) as Corona Borealis, the crown he had given her at her wedding.

[7] Adonis.

[8] Her old love was Tithonus; her new one, Orion, who was killed by Diana's arrows.

atque rubens oculos roseo celavit amictu?
talia caelicolae. numquid minus aurea proles?
75 ergo quod deus atque heros, cur non minor aetas?
    Infelix ego, non illo qui tempore natus,
quo facilis natura fuit. sors o mea laeva
nascendi miserumque genus, cui sera libido est.
tantam Fata meae cordis fecere rapinam,
80 ut maneam quod vix oculis cognoscere possis.

74 proles *Vonck*: promo Ω
78 cui (quoi) *Naeke*: quo Ω
79 tantam Fata *Heinsius*: tantum vita Ω

her roseate mantle? Such things the heaven-dwellers have done: and the golden age, did it do less? Therefore what gods and heroes have done, why not a later age?

Unhappy I, who was not born in those days when Nature was kind! O my luckless lot in birth, and O the wretched race for whom desire is all too late! Such havoc have the Fates made of my heart that what remains of me your eyes would scarcely recognize.

CULEX

Lusimus, Octavi, gracili modulante Thalia
atque ut araneoli tenuem formavimus orsum;
lusimus: haec propter culicis sint carmina docta,
omnis ut historiae per ludum consonet ordo
5   notitiaeque ducum voces, licet invidus adsit.
quisquis erit culpare iocos Musamque paratus,
pondere vel culicis levior famaque feratur.
posterius graviore sono tibi Musa loquetur
nostra, dabunt cum securos mihi tempora fructus,
10 ut tibi digna tuo poliantur carmina sensu.
     Latonae magnique Iovis decus, aurea proles,
Phoebus erit nostri princeps et carminis auctor
et recinente lyra fautor, sive educat illum
Arna Chimaeraeo Xanthi perfusa liquore
15 seu decus Asteriae seu qua Parnasia rupes
hinc atque hinc patula praepandit cornua fronte,
Castaliaeque sonans liquido pede labitur unda.

mss: Ω = Γ; V; S; F; C; L [= WBEAT]   meter: hexameter
³ docta Ω: dicta V   ⁴ ut ç: et Ω
⁷ feratur *Scaliger*: feretur Ω   ¹⁴ Arna *Haupt:* alma Ω

---

[1] The later Augustus, who is still a *puer* (vv. 26, 37) when thus addressed. The young Octavius assumed the toga in his fifteenth year, in 48 B.C.: the poem, therefore, which purports to have been

CULEX

We have trifled, Octavius,[1] while a slender Muse marked the measure, and lo! like tiny spiders, have fashioned our thin-spun task. We have trifled: let our Gnat's song be a learned one, that for all its sportive mood the whole plot of the story and the speeches of the heroes be consistent with tradition, whatever carping critic be present. Let the man ready to blame our playful Muse be deemed lighter than even our Gnat in weight and name. In time to come our Muse will speak to you in graver tones, when the seasons yield me their fruits in peace, that you may find her verses polished and worthy of your taste.

The pride of Latona and mighty Jove, their golden child, even Phoebus, shall be the fount and source of my song, and he with resounding harp shall inspire, whether Arna nurture him—Arna, bathed with Xanthus' stream from Mount Chimaera—or the glory of Asteria,[2] or that land where Parnassus' ridge, with broad brow, spreads his horns this way and that, and Castalia's singing waves glide in their watery course.[3] Wherefore, come, ye sister

written before that date, must be a fake, containing, as it does, so many echoes of the mature Virgil.   [2] Delos.

[3] Far below the real summit of Parnassus, the rocky cliffs that tower above Delphi present two peaks, between which, in a deep chasm, flows the Castalian stream.

405

quare, Pierii laticis decus, ite, sorores
Naides, et celebrate deum ludente chorea.
20 et tu, sancta Pales, ad quam ventura recurrunt
agrestum bona fetura—sit cura tenentis
aërios nemorum cultus silvasque virentis:
te cultrice vagus saltus feror inter et antra.
   Et tu, cui meritis oritur fiducia tantis,
25 Octavi venerande, meis adlabere coeptis,
sancte puer: tibi namque canit non pagina bellum
triste Iovis ponitque acies quibus horruit olim
Phlegra, Giganteo sparsa est quae sanguine tellus,
nec Centaureos Lapithas compellit in enses;
30 urit Ericthonias Oriens non ignibus arces,
non perfossus Athos nec magno vincula ponto
iacta meo quaerent iam sera volumine famam,
non Hellespontus pedibus pulsatus equorum,
Graecia cum timuit venientis undique Persas:
35 mollia sed tenui decurrens carmina versu
viribus apta suis Phoebo duce ludere gaudet.
hoc tibi, sancte puer; memorabilis et tibi certet
gloria perpetuum lucens, mansura per aevum,
et tibi sede pia maneat locus, et tibi sospes
40 debita felices remoretur vita per annos,
grata bonis lucens. sed nos ad coepta feramur.
   Igneus aetherias iam sol penetrarat in arces
candidaque aurato quatiebat lumina curru,

24 tantis *Aldine*: chartis Ω
27 acies . . . olim *Bücheler*: canit . . . bellum (*from* 26) Ω
40 remoretur Γ, *Baehrens*: memoretur *VFCL*

Naiads,[4] glory of the Pierian spring, and throng about the god in sportive dance. You, too, holy Pales, to whom, as they appear, the blessings of rustics return with increase, be yours the care of him who keeps the lofty forest-homes and woodlands green; while you tend them, I freely roam among the glades and dells.

You, too, revered Octavius, who inspire confidence by your great merits, smile, holy youth, upon my undertaking! My page sings for you not Jove's deadly war[5] nor arrays the battle lines wherewith Phlegra once bristled, the land that was sprinkled with the Giants' blood, nor drives the Lapiths upon the Centaurs' swords; nor does the East consume the Erichthonian towers[6] with flames: it is not the channel cut through Athos nor the casting of fetters upon the mighty sea, not the Hellespont trampled by horses' hooves when Greece feared the Persians as they streamed from every side that at this late hour shall through my book seek fame: but it is her joy that her gentle songs run with slender foot and sport under Phoebus' guidance as befits her strength. This she sings for you, holy youth; may ennobling fame also strive for you, shining for all time and lasting throughout the ages; and may you be guaranteed a place in the abode of the blessed, and as your due be there extended a life of safety through happy years, shining for the joy of the good! But let me embark upon my theme.

The fiery sun had now penetrated into the heights of the upper sky,[7] and from gilded car was scattering his bril-

---

[4] The Muses.   [5] The battle between Jupiter and the Giants, fought in Phlegra.   [6] Athens, of which Erichthonius was an early king, burned by the Persians.   [7] I.e. from the lower world. The time is early morning, not midday.

crinibus et roseis tenebras Aurora fugarat:
45 propulit e stabulis ad pabula laeta capellas
pastor et excelsi montis iuga summa petivit,
rorida qua patulos velabant gramina colles.
iam silvis dumisque vagae, iam vallibus abdunt
corpora, iamque omni celeres e parte vagantes
50 tondebant tenero viridantia gramina morsu.
scrupea desertis errabant ad cava ripis,
pendula proiectis carpuntur et arbuta ramis,
densaque virgultis avide labrusca petuntur.
haec suspensa rapit carpente cacumina morsu
55 vel salicis lentae vel quae nova nascitur alnus,
haec teneras fruticum sentes rimatur, at illa
imminet in rivi, praestantis imaginis, umbram.
   O bona pastoris (si quis non pauperis usum
mente prius docta fastidiat et probet illis
60 somnia luxuriae spretis), incognita curis,
quae lacerant avidas inimico pectore mentes!
si non Assyrio fuerint bis lota colore
Attalicis opibus data vellera, si nitor auri
sub laqueare domus animum non angit avarum
65 picturaeque decus, lapidum nec fulgor in ulla
cognitus utilitate manet, nec pocula gratum
Alconis referent Boethique toreuma, nec Indi
conchea baca maris pretio est, at pectore puro
saepe super tenero prosternit gramine corpus,
70 florida cum tellus, gemmantis picta per herbas,
vere notat dulci distincta coloribus arva;

---

[47] rorida *Haupt*: lurida Ω

---

[8] Cf. *Georgics* 2.458ff.

liant rays, and Dawn with roseate locks had routed darkness, when a shepherd drove forth his goats to the happy pastures, and sought a mountain's highest ridges, where dewy grasses clothed the widespread slopes. As they roam, they hide themselves now in the woods and thickets, now in the valleys, and now, wandering swiftly to and fro, they cropped the rich grasses with nibbling bite. Leaving the banks, they strayed toward rocky hollows, the overhanging arbutes are shorn of their outstretched branches, and the wild vines' thick shoots are eagerly assailed. One, poised aloft, snatches with eager bite the tips, it may be of the pliant willow, or of fresh growing alder; this gropes amid the thickets' tender briars, while that hangs over the water of the stream, its wondrous mirror.

O the blessings of the shepherd[8]—if one would not, with mind already schooled, disdain the poor man's ways, and in scorn of them give approval to dreams of wealth— blessings those cares know not, that rend greedy hearts within warring breasts! If fleeces, twice dipped in Assyrian dye, have not been purchased with wealth of Attalus, if gleam of gold beneath the fretted ceiling of a house, and brilliancy of painting, move not a greedy soul, if flashing gems be never deemed to have aught of worth, if goblets of Alcon and reliefs of Boethus bring no joy,[9] and the Indian Ocean's pearls be of no esteem; yet, with heart free from guile, he oft upon the soft lawn outstretches his body, while blossoming earth, painted with jewelled grasses, in sweet spring marks the fields, picked out with varied hues; and

[9] An Alcon is mentioned in *Eclogues* 5.11. Like Boethus, who is referred to by Pliny (*Natural History* 33.12.55), he was probably a sculptor or engraver in metals.

atque illum calamo laetum recinente palustri
otiaque invidia degentem et fraude remota
pollentemque sibi viridi cum palmite lucens
75 Tmolia pampineo subter coma velat amictu.
illi sunt gratae rorantes lacte capellae
et nemus et fecunda Pales et vallibus intus
semper opaca novis manantia fontibus antra.
    Quis magis optato queat esse beatior aevo
80 quam qui mente procul pura sensuque probando
non avidas agnovit opes nec tristia bella
nec funesta timet validae certamina classis
nec, spoliis dum sancta deum fulgentibus ornet
templa vel evectus finem transcendat habendi,
85 adversum saevis ultro caput hostibus offert?
illi falce deus colitur non arte politus,
ille colit lucos, illi Panchaia tura
floribus agrestes herbae variantibus adsunt,
illi dulcis adest requies et pura voluptas,
90 libera, simplicibus curis: huic imminet, omnis
derigit huc sensus, haec cura est subdita cordi,
quolibet ut requie victu contentus abundet
iucundoque liget languentia corpora somno.
o pecudes, o Panes et o gratissima Tempe,
95 frigus Hamadryadum, quarum non divite cultu
aemulus Ascraeo pastor sibi quisque poetae
securam placido traducit pectore vitam.
    Talibus in studiis baculo dum nixus apricas
pastor agit curas et dum non arte canora
100 compacta solitum modulatur harundine carmen,
tendit inevectus radios Hyperionis ardor

95 frigus *Housman*: fontis Ω

lo! as he delights in the resounding reeds of the marsh, and takes his ease apart from envy and deceit, and is strong in his own strength, the leafage of Tmolus and the sheen of green boughs enwraps him beneath a cloak of vines. His are pleasing goats that drip their milky dew, his the woodland and fruitful Pales, and, deep within the vales, shaded grottoes ever trickling with fresh springs.

Who in a happier age could be more blest than he who, dwelling afar, with pure soul and feelings well tested knows not the greed of wealth, and fears not grim wars or the fatal conflicts of a mighty fleet, nor yet, in order to adorn the gods' holy temples with gleaming spoils, or high uplifted transcend the limits of wealth, wilfully risks his life, confronting savage foes? He reverences a god shaped by pruning knife, not by artist's skill; he reverences the groves; for him the grasses of the field, speckled with flowers, yield Panchaean incense;[10] his are sweet repose and unsullied pleasure, free, with simple cares. This is his goal, toward this he directs every sense; this is the thought lurking within his heart, that, content with any fare, he may be rich in repose, and in pleasant sleep may restrain his weary body. O flocks, O Pans, O lovely vales of Tempe, cool abode of the Hamadryads, in whose humble worship the shepherds, vying each for himself with the bard of Ascra,[11] spend with tranquil hearts a carefree life!

Amid such joys, while leaning on his staff the shepherd rehearses his sunny dreams, and while, with no artful melody, on his joined reeds he attunes the wonted lay, burning Hyperion, mounting aloft, extends his rays, and, parting

[10] Cf. *Georgics* 2.139.
[11] Hesiod.

lucidaque aetherio ponit discrimina mundo,
qua iacit Oceanum flammas in utrumque rapaces.
et iam compellente vagae pastore capellae
105   ima susurrantis repetebant ad vada lymphae
quae subter viridem residebant caerula muscum.
iam medias operum partes evectus erat sol,
cum densas pastor pecudes cogebat in umbras.
ut procul aspexit luco residere virenti,
110   Delia diva, tuo, quo quondam victa furore
venit Nyctelium fugiens Cadmeis Agaue,
infandas scelerata manus e caede cruenta,
quae gelidis bacchata iugis requievit in antro
posterius poenam nati de morte datura—
115   hic etiam viridi ludentes Panes in herba
et Satyri Dryadesque choros egere puellae
Naiadum in coetu. non tantum Oeagrius Hebrum
restantem tenuit ripis silvasque canendo
quantum te, pernix, remorantem, diva, chorea
120   multa tuo laetae fundentes gaudia vultu,
ipsa loci natura domum resonante susurro
quîs dabat et dulci fessas refovebat in umbra.
nam primum prona surgebant valle patentes
aëriae platanus, inter quas impia lotos,
125   impia, quae socios Ithaci maerentis abegit,
hospita dum nimia tenuit dulcedine captos.
at, quibus insigni curru proiectus equorum
ambustus Phaëthon luctu mutaverat artus,

116 choros] chorus (*i.e.* χορούς) Ω
117 Oeagrius *Heinsius*: horridus Ω

midway heaven's vault, there plants his light where into either Ocean he flings his ravenous flames. And now, driven by the shepherd, the straying goats were wending back to the pools of whispering water, which settled dark beneath the verdant moss. Now had the Sun ridden o'er the mid portion of his course, when the shepherd began to gather his flocks within the thick shade. When from a distance he saw them settle in your green grove, O Delian goddess, whither once, smitten with madness, came Cadmus' daughter, Agave, flying from Nyctelius,[12] her cursed hands defiled with blood of slaughter—Agave, who once had revelled on the cold heights, then rested in the cave, doomed to pay later for her son's death. Here, too, Pans sporting upon the green grass, and Satyrs, and Dryad maids with the Naiad throng, once trod their dances. Not so much did Orpheus with his song stay Hebrus, lingering within his banks, or stay the woods, as much as with their dance they keep you tarrying, O fleet goddess, gladly shedding many joys upon your countenance—even they, to whom, of its very nature, the place with its echoing whisper gave a home, refreshing their weary forms in its sweet shade. For first, in the sloping vale, there arose spreading planes, towering high, and among them the wicked lotus—wicked because she seduced the comrades of the sorrowing Ithacan, while she welcomed and held them captive with undue charm.[13] Then they, whose limbs Phaëthon, hurled forth in flames from the resplendent car of the Sun's steeds, had

[12] Bacchus. On recovering her senses, Agave conceived a horror of Bacchus, the god whose rites she was celebrating when she slew Pentheus.

[13] Cf. Homer, *Odyssey* 9.83ff.

Heliades, teneris implexae bracchia truncis,
130 candida fundebant tentis velamina ramis.
posterius cui Demophoon aeterna reliquit
perfidiam lamentanti mala—perfide multis,
perfide Demophoon et nunc deflende puellis.
quam comitabantur, fatalia carmina, quercus,
135 quercus ante datae Cereris quam semina vitae
(illas Triptolemi mutavit sulcus aristis).
hic magnum Argoae navi decus addita pinus
proceros decorat silvas hirsuta per artus
ac petit aëriis contingere motibus astra.
140 ilicis et nigrae species nec laeta cupressus
umbrosaeque manent fagus hederaeque ligantes
bracchia, fraternos plangat ne populus ictus,
ipsaeque ascendunt ad summa cacumina lentae
pinguntque aureolos viridi pallore corymbos.
145 quîs aderat veteris myrtus non nescia fati.
at volucres patulis residentes dulcia ramis
carmina per varios edunt resonantia cantus.
his suberat gelidis manans e fontibus unda,
quae levibus placidum rivis sonat acta liquorem;
150 et quaqua geminas avium vox obstrepit aures,
hac querulae referunt voces quîs nantia limo
corpora lympha fovet; sonitus alit aëris echo,
argutis et cuncta fremunt ardore cicadis.
at circa passim fessae cubuere capellae

133 deflende *Scaliger*: defende Ω   149 acta V: orta Ω

14 Phaëthon's sisters, who were turned into poplars.
15 Phyllis, who at death was changed into an almond tree. She died of grief, supposing that Demophoon had deserted her.

414

through grief transformed—the Heliads,[14] their arms entwining the slender stems—from outstretched branches lavished their white veiling. Next came she,[15] to whom, as she wept over his treachery, Demophoon left unending grief. O cruel Demophoon, breaker of many hearts, whose treachery even now causes girls to weep! Oaks attended her, chanters of the fates,[16] oaks once given for man's sustenance before the grains of Ceres: these oaks the furrow of Triptolemus exchanged for ears of corn.[17] Here the great glory of the Argoan ship, the lofty pine, shaggy in her stately limbs, adorns the woods, and from the soaring mountains essays to reach the stars. Still stand the shapely black ilex, the cypress of grief, shadowy beeches, and ivies binding the poplar's arms, lest, for her brother's[18] sake, she smite herself with blows: themselves, fast clinging, mount to the very tops, and paint their golden clusters with pale green. Hard by these was the myrtle, conscious of her ancient fate.[19] The birds meanwhile, settling on the spreading branches, sing songs resounding in varied melodies. Beneath was water trickling from cold springs, which, tumbling in fine rills, murmurs in its peaceful current; and wherever voice of birds strikes upon both ears, there in querulous tone respond the frogs, whose bodies, afloat in the mire, are nurtured by its moisture. The echoing air swells the sounds, and amid the heat all nature is a-humming with the shrill cicadas. Here and there, round about,

16 Referring to the oracle at Dodona.

17 Cf. *Georgics* 1.19.

18 Phaëthon's.

19 Myrsine, priestess of Venus, was changed into a myrtle.

155 excelsis subter dumis, quos leniter adflans
aura susurrantis poscit confundere venti.
 Pastor, ut ad fontem densa requievit in umbra,
mitem concepit proiectus membra soporem,
anxius insidiis nullis, sed lentus in herbis
160 securo pressos somno mandaverat artus.
stratus humi dulcem capiebat corde quietem,
ni Fors incertos iussisset ducere casus.
nam solitum volvens ad tempus tractibus isdem
immanis vario maculatus corpore serpens,
165 mersus ut in limo magno subsideret aestu,
obvia vibranti carpens, gravis aëre, lingua
squamosos late torquebat motibus orbes:
tollebant irae venientis ad omnia visus.
iam magis atque magis corpus revolubile volvens
170 attollit nitidis pectus fulgoribus, effert
sublimi cervice caput, cui crista superne
edita purpureo lucens maculatur amictu
aspectuque micant flammarum lumina torvo.
metabat sese circum loca, cum videt anguis
175 adversum recubare ducem gregis. acrior instat
lumina diffundens intendere et obvia torvus
saepius arripiens infringere, quod sua quisquam
ad vada venisset. naturae comparat arma:
ardet mente, furit stridoribus, intonat ore,
180 flexibus eversis torquentur corporis orbes,
manant sanguineae per tractus undique guttae,
spiritibus rumpit fauces. cui cuncta parantur,
parvulus hunc prior umoris conterret alumnus
et mortem vitare monet per acumina; namque,

[182] parantur *Housman*: paranti Ω

lay the weary goats beneath the lofty thickets, which a breath of whispering wind, gently blowing thither, seeks to disturb.

As soon as by the spring amid the deep shade the shepherd sought repose with limbs outstretched, he fell into a gentle sleep; troubled by no treachery, but lying at ease upon the grass, he had consigned his exhausted frame to carefree slumber. Prone upon the ground, he was enjoying to the full sweet restfulness—had not Fortune bade him draw perilous lots! For, gliding along at his wonted time in the selfsame course, a monstrous serpent, speckled and mottled in body, with intent to plunge in the mire and seek shelter from the exceeding heat—foul of breath, and snatching with darting tongue at all in its way—in far-circling movements was twisting his scaly coils: as he came on, he raised his eyes in anger to survey the whole scene. Now, rolling more and more his writhing body, he uplifts his breast with gleaming flashes; on his towering neck he rears his head, and his crest rises aloft; his purple coat shines and sparkles, and his blazing eye gleams with savage look. The serpent was surveying the ground round about, when he espies the guardian of the flock lying in his way. More fiercely he rolls his eyes and presses on in his course, and more often does he seize and crush what lies in his path, angered that any man had come to his waters. Nature's weapons he makes ready: he rages in mind, he hisses in wrath; his mouth emits thunder; his body's coils writhe in upheaving curves; all along his course trickle drops of blood: his jaws burst with his panting. The shepherd who is threatened by all this, a tiny nurseling of the marsh alarms in time and warns by its sting to avoid his death. For where

185 qua diducta genas pandebant lumina gemmis,
hac senioris erat naturae pupula telo
icta levi, cum prosiluit furibundus et illum
obtritum morti misit, cui dissitus omnis
spiritus et cessit sensus. tum torva tenentem
190 lumina respexit serpentem comminus; inde
impiger, exanimis, vix compos mente refugit
et validum dextra detraxit ab arbore truncum
(qui casus sociarit opem numenve deorum
prodere sit dubium, valuit sed vincere tales
195 spiras squamosi volventia membra draconis)
atque reluctantis crebris foedeque petentis
ictibus ossa ferit, cingunt qua tempora cristae;
et quod erat tardus somni languore remoti
nec senis aspiciens timor obcaecaverat artus,
200 hoc minus implicuit dira formidine mentem.
quem postquam vidit caesum languescere, sedit.
    Iam quatit et biiuges oriens Erebeis equos Nox
et piger aurata procedit Vesper ab Oeta,
cum grege compulso pastor duplicantibus umbris
205 vadit et in fessos requiem dare comparat artus.
cuius ut intravit levior per corpora somnus
languidaque effuso requierunt membra sopore,
effigies ad eum culicis devenit et illi
tristis ab eventu cecinit convicia mortis.
210 "quîs" inquit "meritis ad quae delatus acerbas
cogor adire vices? tua dum mihi carior ipsa
vita fuit vita, rapior per inania ventis.

195 ‹spiras› *Housman*: horrida Ω
199 nec senis *Hertzberg*: nescius Ω

the eyes are parted and open their lids to reveal their
jewels, there the old man's orb was smitten by the light dart
nature had furnished, whereupon, full of rage, he leaped
forth, and crushed and slew the gnat, whose breath and
life were entirely dispersed and left him. Then, near at
hand, as it fixed its fierce eyes upon him, the shepherd es-
pied the serpent; and thereon with speed and breathless,
scarcely master of his senses, he rushes off and with his
hand tore from a tree a sturdy bough. What chance gave
him aid or what spirit divine, it were hazardous to assert,
but he availed to overcome the gigantic coils which the
scaly serpent managed to contrive. And as it struggles and
attacks in hideous fashion he strikes its bones with multi-
ple strokes where the crest fringes its temples; and since
he was dulled with the drowsiness of the sleep he had
shaken off, and fear at the sight of his foe had not yet be-
numbed his aged limbs, he did not so much confuse his
mind with dread terror; but, when he saw the monster
relax in death, he sat down.

Now Night, arising, was urging on her steeds in the
two-horse car of Erebus,[20] and the evening star was slowly
advancing from golden Oeta, when the shepherd, having
penned his sheep, wended his way in the thickening shad-
ows, and prepared to give rest to his weary frame. As soon
as gentle sleep passed over his body, and his listless limbs,
steeped in slumber, sank to rest, there descended upon
him the ghost of the gnat, and sang him strains of reproach
because of his sad death: "By what deserts and for what de-
nounced am I forced to face this bitter reckoning? While
your life was dearer to me than life itself, I am swept by the

[20] Night is sister and wife of Erebus.

tu lentus refoves iucunda membra quiete
ereptus taetris e cladibus; at mea manes
215 viscera Lethaeas cogunt transnare per undas;
praeda Charonis agor. vidi ut flagrantia taedis
lumina, cum lucent in festis omnia templis!
obvia Tisiphone, serpentibus undique compta,
et flammas et saeva quatit mihi verbera; pone
220 Cerberus est, diris flagrans latratibus ora,
anguibus hinc atque hinc horrent cui colla reflexis
sanguineique micant ardorem luminis orbes.
heu, quid ab officio digressa est gratia, cum te
restitui superis leti iam limine ab ipso?
225 praemia sunt pietatis ubi, pietatis honores?
in vanas abiere vices. et rure recessit
Iustitia et prior illa Fides. instantia vidi
alterius, sine respectu mea fata relinquens.
ad pariles agor eventus: fit poena merenti.
230 poena sit exitium, modo sit dum grata voluntas.
exsistat par officium. feror avia carpens,
avia Cimmerios inter distantia lucos,
quem circa tristes densentur in omnia poenae.
nam vinctus sedet immanis serpentibus Otos,
235 devinctum maestus procul aspiciens Ephialten,
conati quondam cum sint inscendere mundum;
et Tityos, Latona, tuae memor anxius irae
(implacabilis ira nimis) iacet alitis esca.
terreor, a, tantis insistere, terreor, umbris,

---

217 in festis *Housman*: infestis Ω   219 pone *Haupt*:
poenae Ω   220 est *Housman*: et Ω | flagrans *Scaliger*: -ant Ω
227 Iustitia et *Schrader*: Iustitiae Ω
236 inscendere Ω: rescindere V (> *Verg. Aen.* 6.582)

winds through empty space. You, at your ease, are refreshing your limbs in sweet repose, snatched from a horrible death; but my remains the gods below compel to pass over Lethe's waters; I am driven as Charon's spoil. I have seen his eyes burning[21] like torches when the temples are all ablaze with festival. Tisiphone, her locks wreathed on every side with serpents, besets the way and brandishes before me fires and cruel whips; behind her is Cerberus, his mouths inflamed with fearful barking, his necks bristling with twisted snakes this way and that, and his eyes flashing the glow of a blood-red light. Alas, why has no gratitude been shown to my kindness, when even from the very door of death I restored you to the world of the living? Where are the rewards of goodness and the recognition that goodness demands? They have vainly vanished, and Justice and that old-time Religion have fled the land. I saw the fate which threatened another; and disregarding that which threatened me I am driven to a fate like his: punishment falls to the deserving. Let the punishment be death, provided that there be a grateful heart and an equal service rendered. I take my way over pathless regions— pathless regions far away amid Cimmerian groves, and about me throng the woeful penalties for all misdeeds. For, fast bound with serpents, monstrous Otus sits, mournfully gazing at Ephialtes, enchained hard by, for once seeking to mount[22] the sky; and Tityus in distress, mindful, O Latona, of your wrath (wrath too insatiate), is lying there, food for a vulture.[23] I fear, ah! I fear to step near such

---

[21] Cf. *Aeneid* 6.300.

[22] The poet is here following Homer, *Odyssey* 11.308ff.

[23] Cf. *Aeneid* 6.595.

240 ad Stygias revocatus aquas! vix ultimus amni
exstat nectareas divum qui prodidit escas,
gutturis arenti revolutus in omnia sensu.
quid, saxum procul adverso qui monte revolvit,
contempsisse dolor quem numina vincit acerbans?
245 otia quaerentem frustrabitis? ite, puellae,
ite, quibus taedas accendit tristis Erinys.
sicut 'Hymen' praefata dedit conubia Mortis?
247a ⟨iam prope conspicio, vestram quae vertice turbam⟩
atque alias alto densas super eminet umbras,
impietate fera vecordem Colchida matrem,
250 anxia sollicitis meditantem vulnera natis;
iam Pandionia miserandas prole puellas,
quarum vox Ityn edit Ityn, quo Bistonius rex
orbus epops maeret volucres evectus in auras.
at discordantes Cadmeo semine fratres
255 iam truculenta ferunt infestaque lumina corpus
alter in alterius, iamque aversatus uterque,
impia germani manat quod sanguine dextra.
eheu, mutandus numquam labor! auferor ultra
in diversa magis, distantia nomina cerno;
260 Elysiam tranandus agor delatus ad undam.
obvia Persephone comites heroidas urget
adversas praeferre faces. Alcestis ab omni
inviolata vacat cura, quod saeva mariti
in Chalcodoniis Admeti fata morata est.

241 exstat *Heinsius*: restat Ω
245 frustrabitis ite *Housman*: frustra siblite Ω
247a *add. Housman*   248 alto *Housman*: alio Ω
251 Pandionia *Housman*: -as Ω
264 fata *Bembus*: cura (>263) Ω

mighty shades, summoned back to the Stygian waters!
With head scarce rising above the stream, stands he who
betrayed the food of the gods,[24] turning in all directions
with fever-stricken throat. What of him, who rolls a stone
up the mountain afar, whom embittering pain convicts of
having scorned the gods?[25] Will ye thwart me, who seek re-
pose? Depart, ye maidens,[26] for whom the fell Fury kin-
dled the bridal torch. Was it thus, with the announcement
of wedlock, that she brought a marriage fraught with
death? ‹Now close at hand I espy her who overtops with
her tall head your company› and the other dense shades,
the Colchian mother,[27] frenzied with wicked savagery, de-
signing distressful wounds for her frightened children;
now I espy the wretched girls of Pandion's stock[28] whose
voice cries *Itys, Itys*, while, bereft of him, the Thracian
king[29] mourns in his hoopoe shape, wafted to the winged
breezes. Yea, and the quarrelling brothers of Cadmus'
line[30] cast fierce vindictive glances upon each other's per-
son, and now each recoils, for his wicked hand drips with a
brother's blood. Alas, my anguish that will never change! I
am hurried on to far different sights, and in the distance I
espy famous spirits; I must swim across Elysium's waters,
and thither am I borne. In my path Persephone urges the
heroine throng[31] to raise before them their confronting
torches. Alcestis, unscathed, is free from all care, since she
thwarted the cruel death of her husband Admetus among

[24] Tantalus.   [25] Sisyphus.   [26] The Danaids; cf. *Aeneid*
10.497.   [27] Medea.   [28] Philomela and Procne.

[29] Tereus, father of Itys.   [30] Eteocles and Polynices.

[31] A band of women, such as encountered Odysseus in the
lower world; cf. Homer, *Odyssey* 11.225ff.

265 ecce Ithaci coniunx semper decus, Icariotis,
femineum concepta manet, pavet et procul illam
turba ferox iuvenum telis confixa procorum.
quid, misera Eurydice, tanto maerore recesti,
poenaque respectus et nunc manet Orpheos in te?
270 audax ille quidem, qui mitem Cerberon umquam
credidit aut ulli Ditis placabile numen,
nec timuit Phlegethonta furentem ardentibus undis
nec maesta obtenta Ditis ferrugine regna
defossasque domos ac Tartara nocte cruenta
275 obsita nec faciles Ditis sine iudice sedes,
iudice, qui vitae post mortem vindicat acta.
sed Fortuna valens audacem fecerat ante.
iam rapidi steterant amnes et turba ferarum
blanda voce sequax regionem insederat Hebri;
280 iamque imam viridi radicem moverat alte   •
quercus humo, ‹pinusque simul› silvaeque sonorae
sponte sua cantus rapiebant cortice avara.
labentis biiuges etiam per sidera Lunae
pressit equos, et tu currentis, menstrua virgo,
285 auditura lyram tenuisti nocte relicta.
haec eadem potuit, Ditis, te vincere, coniunx,
Eurydicenque ultro ducendam reddere. non fas,
non erat invictae divae exorabile mortis.
illa quidem, nimium Manes experta severos,
290 praeceptum signabat iter nec rettulit intus

266 manet, pavet *Housman*: decus (›265) manet Ω
272 furentem *Bembo*: furens Ω
279 Hebri *Baehrens*: Orphei Ω
281 pinusque simul *suppl. Leo*: steterant amnes (›278) Ω
288 invictae *Haupt*: in vitam Ω

the Chalcodonians. See next the Ithacan's wife,[32] daughter
of Icarius, ever deemed the glory of womankind, and at a
distance there trembles in awe of her that arrogant band of
suitors, pierced with arrows. Why, poor Eurydice, have
you withdrawn in such sorrow, and why even now does the
punishment for Orpheus' backward look await you? Bold
indeed was he, who thought that Cerberus was ever mild,
or that any could appease the godhead of Dis, and who
feared not the blazing waters of Phlegethon, the mourn-
ful waters of Dis, overcast with gloom, the dwellings of
Tartarus, buried deep and beset with cruel night, nor the
abodes of Dis, easy of entry were there not a judge—a
judge who after death passes sentence on the deeds of life.
But Fortune, a mighty supporter of Orpheus in the past,
had made him bold. Earlier, swift rivers had stood still and
the tribe of wild beasts, following the allure of his voice,
had encamped in the valley of the Hebrus; earlier, from
the green ground the oak had moved its deepest roots
aloft, and the pine as well and the rustling woods of their
own free will were snatching his songs with greedy bark.
Even in their gliding course amid the stars he checked the
Moon's two-yoked steeds, which, as they ran, you yourself,
O maiden of the month, held back to hear his lyre, aban-
doning the night. This same lyre possessed the power to
overcome you, too, O bride of Dis, and make you of your
own free will surrender Eurydice to be led away: but the
goddess had no right over invincible death, no right that
would yield to prayer. Eurydice indeed, who had found the
Shades too stern, was following the path prescribed, and

[32] Penelope.

425

lumina nec divae corrupit munera lingua;
sed tu crudelis, crudelis tu magis, Orpheu,
oscula cara petens rupisti iussa deorum.
dignus amor venia, veniam si Tartara nossent.
295 peccatum meminisse grave est. vos sede piorum,
vos manet heroum contra manus. hic et uterque
Aeacides (Peleus namque et Telamonia virtus
per secura patris laetantur numina, quorum
conubiis Venus et Virtus iniunxit honorem:
300 hunc rapuit servata, illum Nereis amavit)
assidet, hic iuvenes, sociatae gloria sortis,
alter in ore ferens expressum a navibus ignis
Argolicis Phrygios torva feritate repulsos—
(o quis non referat talis divortia belli,
305 quae Troiae videre viri videreque Graii,
Teucria cum magno manaret sanguine tellus
et Simois Xanthique liquor, Sigeaque praeter
litora cum Troas saevi ducis Hectoris ira
truderet in classes inimica mente Pelasgas
310 vulnera tela neces ignes inferre paratos?
ipsa vagis namque Ida potens feritatis, ab ipsa
Ida faces altrix cupidis praebebat alumnis,
omnis ut in cineres Rhoetei litoris ora

294 veniam *Baehrens*: gratum Ω
300 servata *Housman*: feritast Ω
301 hic *Baehrens* iuvenes *Housman*: hac iuvenis Ω
302 ore ferens expressum *Housman*: excissum referens Ω
304–321 *placed in parentheses by Housman*
309 truderet *Baehrens*: videre Ω

turned not her eyes to gaze within,[33] nor did she annul the goddess's gifts by speaking. But you, cruel one, you crueller, Orpheus, seeking her dear kisses, violated the commandments of the gods! Your love was worthy of pardon, did the underworld know pardon; but it pains her to remember his mistake. For you, O heroines,[34] over against you in the abode of the righteous, there waits a band of heroes. Here sit side by side the two sons of Aeacus (for Peleus and valiant Telamon rejoice, carefree through their father's divinity[35]—they upon whose nuptials Venus and Valour bestowed glory: Telamon captivated by Hesione whom he saved, Peleus loved by a Nereid). And here sit the youths[36] who share a glorious heroism, the one[37] expressing on his face the Trojan fires thrust back from the Greek ships with wild and savage valour. (O who could not tell of the partings in such a war, which the heroes of Troy and the heroes of Greece experienced, when the Teucrian soil streamed with a deluge of blood, and the Simois and the waters of Xanthus; and when, along the Sigean shores, Hector, stern and angry captain, with vicious intent thrust the Trojans against the Pelasgian ships, ready to inflict wounds and weapons, death and flames? For Ida itself, which fills with ferocity those who roam on it, Ida, their support, furnished brands from itself to its eager nurselings, so that all the coast along the Rhoetean shore might

---

[33] Illogical and meaningless, but the poet could hardly say "look behind," which, though appropriate in regard to Orpheus, did not apply to Eurydice.   [34] The heroine throng mentioned in 261ff.   [35] Peleus and Telamon live among the blest, because their father Aeacus received the gift of immortality.

[36] Ajax and Achilles.   [37] Ajax.

classibus ambustis flamma lacrimante daretur.
315 hinc erat oppositus contra Telamonius heros
obiectoque dabat clipeo certamina, et illinc
Hector erat, Troiae summum decus, acer uterque,
fluminibus veluti fragor ‹est, cum vere vagantur
318a montibus in segetes, sic alter proicit ignes›
tegminibus telisque super, ‹quîs hostibus arma›
320 eriperet reditus, alter Volcania ferro
vulnera protectus depellere navibus instat.)
    "Hos erat Aeacides vultu laetatus honores,
Dardaniaeque alter fuso quod sanguine campis
Hector lustravit devicto corpore Troiam.
325 rursus acerba fremunt, Paris hunc quod letat, et huius
firma dolis Ithaci virtus quod concidit icta.
huic gerit aversos proles Laërtia vultus,
et iam Strymonii Rhesi victorque Dolonis,
Pallade iam laetatur ovans, rursusque tremescit:
330 iam Ciconas iamque horret atrox Laestrygonas ipse.
illum Scylla rapax canibus succincta Molossis,
Aetnaeusque Cyclops, illum metuenda Charybdis
pallentesque lacus et squalida Tartara terrent.
    "Hic et Tantaleae generamen prolis Atrides
335 assidet, Argivum lumen, quo flamma regente
Doris Ericthonias prostravit funditus arces.
reddidit, heu, Graius poenas tibi, Troia, ruenti,
Hellespontiacis obiturus reddidit undis.

318,318a *as restored by Vollmer*: et libet in se Ω   319 *add.*
Vollmer   324 Hector . . . devicto ς: hectora . . . victor de Ω
    330 Laestrygonas ς ipse V: -ne (*last word lost*) Ω
    332 metuenda Ω: Zanclaea V (*interpolated from Ovid, Fasti*
4.499)

be given over to ashes, as the ships were consumed with tear-dropping flames. On one side arrayed against the foe was Telamonian Ajax, offering combat from under his covering shield; and on the other was Hector, chief bulwark of Troy, each eager for the fray. Even as on rivers is heard a roar, when in springtime they descend from the mountains upon the cornfields: so from above the one hurls fire upon shields and darts, that thereby he may rob the foe of weapons of return; the other, defended by his sword, presses on to repel from the ships the assaults of Vulcan.)

"At these successes the face of Telamon brightened, and so did the other's, when Troy was encircled with Hector's vanquished body. Again, they chafe bitterly, because Paris slays the one and the other's stalwart valour falls stricken by the Ithacan's wiles. From him the son of Laertes[38] keeps his countenance averted; and now, as victor over Strymonian Rhesus and over Dolon, and now, as captor of the Palladium, rejoices, then again trembles: he, though dreadful himself, shudders, now at the Cicones, now at the Laestrygonians. He is terrified at ravenous Scylla, girt with her Molossian hounds, at the Cyclops of Etna, at fearsome Charybdis, at the ghastly lakes and foul Tartarus.

"Here too beside him sits the son of Atreus, offspring of the race of Tantalus, the light of Greece, beneath whose rule Doric flame utterly laid low the Erichthonian towers.[39] The Greeks, alas! paid penance to you, O Troy, for your fall—paid it, when doomed to death in Hellespontiac

[38] Ulysses.

[39] I.e. Troy, Erichthonius being the son of Dardanus. Yet in verse 30 above the same expression was used of Athens.

illa vices hominum testata est copia quondam,
340   ne quisquam propriae Fortunae munere dives
iret inevectus caelum super: omne propinquo
frangitur Invidiae telo decus. ibat in altum
vis Argea petens patriam, ditataque praeda
arcis Ericthoniae; comes huic erat aura secunda
345   per placidum cursu pelagus; Nereis ab unda
signa dabat passim flexis super alta carinis,
cum seu caelesti fato seu sideris ortu
undique mutatur caeli nitor, omnia ventis,
omnia turbinibus sunt anxia; iam maris unda
350   sideribus certat consurgere, iamque superne
corripere et soles et sidera cuncta minatur
ac ruere in terras caeli fragor. hic modo laetans
copia nunc miseris circumdatur anxia fatis
immoriturque super fluctus et saxa Capherei,
355   Euboicas aut per cautes Aegaeaque late
litora, cum Phrygiae passim vaga praeda peremptae
omnis in aequoreo fluitat iam naufraga fluctu.
    "Hic alii resident pariles virtutis honore
heroes, mediisque siti sunt sedibus omnes,
360   omnes Roma decus magni quos suspicit orbis.
hic Fabii Deciique, hic est et Horatia virtus,
hic et fama vetus numquam moritura Camilli,
Curtius et, mediis quem quondam sedibus Urbis
devotum livens consumpsit gurges in unda,

    364 livens *Housman:* bellis Ω

waves.[40] That expedition bore witness in its time to human vicissitudes, lest anyone, enriched by his own Fortune's bounty, should rise exalted above the heavens; all glory is shattered by Envy's[41] close-waiting weapon. The Argive host was passing seaward, seeking its homeland, and enriched with spoils from the Erichthonian citadel. A favourable breeze attended its course over a peaceful sea; from the waters a Nereid gave guiding signals to the ships as they steered all over the deep: when lo! either by celestial fate, or through the rising of a star, on all sides the sky's brightness is changed, and everything is thrown into turmoil by blasts and whirlwinds. Now the sea's waves strive to mount to the stars, and now on high the thundering sky threatens to seize all, both suns and stars, and dash them to earth. Here the host—lately triumphant, now reduced to despair—is beset by pitiful calamities, and perishes upon the floods and rocks of Caphereus, or along the Euboean cliffs and broad Aegean shores, while all the prey from plundered Phrygia, drifting far and near, tossed in wreckage upon the ocean waves.

"Here abide others comparable to them in reputation for valour, all heroes, settled in the midst of these abodes, all whom Rome esteems as the glory of the mighty world. Here are the Fabii and the Decii, and here the brave Horatius; here Camillus, whose age-old fame shall never die; and Curtius, whom once in the midst of the City's homes, a willing victim, the sombre flood swallowed up in

[40] "Hellespontiac" is here used of the Aegean as a whole: the Greeks were shipwrecked off Euboea. Cf. *Ciris* 413.

[41] "Envy" here is retribution or Nemesis.

365   Mucius et prudens ardorem corpore passus,
       cui cessit Lydi timefacta potentia regis;
       hic Curius clarae socius virtutis et ille
       Caecilius, devota dedit qui lumina flammae.
       iure igitur talis sedes pietatis honores
370a   instaurat pia ⟨sic meritis. te, Regule, cerno
370b   Scipia⟩dasque duces, quorum devota triumphis
       moenia vepretis Libycae Karthaginis horrent.
         "Illi laude sua vigeant: ego Ditis opacos
       cogor adire lacus viduatos lumine Phoebi
       et vastum Phlegethonta pati, quo, maxime Minos,
375   conscelerata pia discernis vincula sede.
       ergo iam causam mortis, iam dicere vitae
       verberibus saevae cogunt ab iudice Poenae,
       cum mihi tu sis causa mali nec conscius adsis;
       sed tolerabilibus curis haec immemor audis
380   et mane ut vades dimittes omnia ventis.
       digredior numquam rediturus: tu cole fontes
       et viridis nemorum silvas et pascua laetus,
       at mea diffusas rapiantur dicta per auras."
       dixit et extrema tristis cum voce recessit.
385   Hunc ubi sollicitum dimisit inertia vitae

---

368 Caecilius . . . lumina *Loensis:* Flaminius . . . corpora Ω
370 instaurat pia *Housman*: istarum piadasque *B*: Scipiadasque
V: supplement by Housman
373 viduatos *Kershaw*: viduos a Ω

---

42 The legend goes that a huge chasm suddenly appeared in the ancient forum, which, said the soothsayers, could only be filled by casting into it Rome's greatest treasure. Marcus Curtius (a young nobleman), declaring that Rome possessed nothing more

its waters;[42] and wise Mucius,[43] who endured fire upon his body, and to whom the mighty Lydian king yielded in fear. Here is Curius, allied to glorious valour, and Caecilius, who sacrificed his eyes in the flames. Justly therefore the abode of the pious provides such rewards ⟨for the deserving. I behold you, Regulus, and the Scipionic⟩ chiefs, doomed by whose triumphs the walls of Libyan Carthage have become desolate with thickets.

"Let them flourish in their renown: but I am forced to proceed to those shadowy pools of Dis, that are bereft of the light of Phoebus, and to endure waste Phlegethon, whereby, O mighty Minos, you separate the prison of the wicked from the abode of the righteous! So the cruel Fiends with scourges force me to plead my cause, now of death, and now of life, before the judge, while you are the cause of my plight and aid not with your witness, but with lightly borne cares hear these my words, unmindful, and as you go, in spite of all, will abandon everything to the winds. I depart, never to return; do you, rejoicing, haunt the spring, the green forest groves, and the pastures; and for my words, let them be swept aside by the random breezes!" He spoke and with these last words sadly went his way.

Now when that anxious shepherd was released from

valuable than a brave citizen, mounted his horse in full armour and rode into the abyss; upon which the earth closed over it. In another version the hero's name is given as Curtius Mettius.

[43] Gaius Mucius Scaevola, when threatened with torture and death by Porsenna (called Lydian because he was Etruscan), thrust his right hand into the altar flames and held it there until it was consumed.

interius graviter regementem, nec tulit ultra
sensibus infusum culicis de morte dolorem,
quantumcumque sibi vires tribuere seniles
(quîs tamen infestum pugnans devicerat hostem),
390 rivum propter aquae viridi sub fronde latentem
conformare locum capit impiger. hunc et in orbem
destinat ac ferri baculum repetivit in usum,
gramineam ut viridi foderet de caespite terram.
iam memor inceptum peragens sibi cura laborem
395 congestum cumulavit opus, atque aggere multo
telluris tumulus formatum crevit in orbem.
quem circum lapidem levi de marmore formans
conserit, assiduae curae memor. hic et acanthus
et rosa purpureum crescent pudibunda ruborem
400 et violae omne genus; hic est et Spartica myrtus
atque hyacinthus et hic Cilici crocus editus arvo,
laurus item Phoebi decus ingens, hic rhododaphne
liliaque et roris non avia cura marini
herbaque turis opes priscis imitata Sabina
405 chrysanthusque hederaeque nitor pallente corymbo
et bocchus Libyae regis memor, hic amarantus
bumastusque virens et semper florida tinus;
non illinc narcissus abest, cui gloria formae
igne Cupidineo proprios exarsit in artus;
410 et, quoscumque novant vernantia tempora flores,

---

392 baculum *Murgia:* capulum Ω   402 ingens *Housman:*
surgens Ω   407 tinus *Salmasius:* pinus Ω

---

44 I.e. sleep (when he woke up).
45 The savin, *juniperus sabina.*
46 This unknown plant was named from Bocchus, a king of

life's inactive state,[44] from whose breast heavy sighs resounded, and when he could no longer stand the sorrow for the gnat's death that flooded his senses, then to the extent that his aged strength permitted him—wherewith even so he had fought and vanquished his fierce foe—close by the running stream that lurked beneath green leafage, he busily begins to fashion a place, marking it in circular form, and adapting his staff to serve as a spade, to dig up grassy sods from the green turf. And now his mindful care, pursuing the toil begun, heaped up a towering work, and with broad rampart the earthy mound grew into the circle he had traced. Round about this, mindful of constant care, he sets stones, fashioned from polished marble. Here are to grow acanthus and the blushing rose with crimson bloom, and violets of every kind. Here are Spartan myrtle and hyacinth, and here saffron, sprung from Cilician fields, and laurel, the great glory of Phoebus; here are oleander, and lilies, and rosemary, tended in familiar haunts, and the Sabine plant,[45] which for men of old feigned rich frankincense; and marigold, and glistening ivy with pale clusters, and bocchus, commemorative of Libya's king.[46] Here are amaranth, blooming bumastus,[47] and ever-flowering laurestine. Yonder fails not the Narcissus, whose noble beauty kindled with Love's flame for his own limbs;[48] and whatever flowers the season of spring renews, with these

Mauretania, probably the father-in-law of Jugurtha, but possibly a later king of the same name.   [47] Cf. *Georgics* 2.102, and for *tinus,* or laurestine, 4.112 and 141.

[48] The youth Narcissus, falling in love with his own image, as reflected in a fountain, pined away and was changed into the flower that bears his name.

his tumulus super inseritur. tum fronte locatur
elogium, tacita firmat quod littera voce:
PARVE CULEX, PECUDUM CUSTOS TIBI TALE MERENTI
FUNERIS OFFICIUM VITAE PRO MUNERE REDDIT.

the mound is strewn above. Then upon its face is placed an epitaph, which letters thus fashion with silent speech:

O TINY GNAT, A SHEPHERD PAYS YOU, WHO MERIT IT,
RITE OF BURIAL IN RETURN FOR THE GIFT OF LIFE.

COPA

Copa Syrisca, caput Graeca redimita mitella,
    crispum sub crotalo docta movere latus,
ebria fumosa saltat lasciva taberna
    ad cubitum raucos excutiens calamos:

5   "Quid iuvat aestivo defessum pulvere abîsse?
    quam potius bibulo decubuisse toro!
sunt topia et calybae, cyathi, rosa, tibia, chordae,
    et triclia umbrosis frigida harundinibus;
en et Maenalio quae garrit dulce sub antro
10   rustica pastoris fistula more sonat.
est et vappa cado nuper defusa picato,
    est crepitans rauco murmure rivus aquae.
sunt etiam croceo violae de flore corollae
    sertaque purpurea lutea mixta rosa
15 et quae virgineo libata Achelois ab amne
    lilia vimineis attulit in calathis.
sunt et caseoli, quos iuncea fiscina siccat,
    sunt autumnali cerea pruna die
castaneaeque nuces et suave rubentia mala,
20   est hic munda Ceres, est Amor, est Bromius;

mss: Ω = *MSL*   meter: elegiac
5 abisse *Ilgen*: abesse Ω   7 calybae *Scaliger*: calybes Ω

438

COPA

Hostess from Syria with hair caught up in a Greek bandanna, adept in swaying sinuous thighs to the castanet's rhythm, dances in her smoky tavern, tipsily, sexily, tapping against her elbows a noisy tambourine:

"Why go away when you're tired with the heat and the dust? How much better to recline on a couch with a drink! Here are panelled booths and cabins and goblets, roses, flutes, harps, and a pavilion cooled by a shady curtain of reeds. Yes, and here is the sound of country piping, shepherd style, such as sweetly warbles in a glen of Arcady. And there's a house wine freshly broached from its pitch-sealed jar, there's a rivulet of water chattering with noisy splash. There are also garlands of pale violet-blossom and saffron chaplets blended with scarlet roses, and lilies that a water nymph has gathered from a virgin stream and brought in cradles of osier. And there are little cheeses, dried in rush baskets, and waxen plums of autumn's season and chestnuts and sweetly blushing apples: here are loaves of purest bread, here Love, here wine. There are also blood-red

sunt et mora cruenta et lentis uva racemis,
    et pendet iunco caeruleus cucumis.
est tuguri custos armatus falce saligna,
    sed non et vasto est inguine terribilis.

25 "Huic calybita veni: lassus iam sudat asellus;
    parce illi, Vestae delicium est asinus.
nunc cantu crebro rumpunt arbusta cicadae,
    nunc varia in gelida sede lacerta latet:
si sapis, aestivo recubans te prolue vitro,
30   seu vis crystalli ferre novos calices.
hic age pampinea fessus requiesce sub umbra
    et gravidum roseo necte caput strophio,
formosa et tenerae decerpens ora puellae—
    a pereat cui sunt prisca supercilia!
35 quid cineri ingrato servas bene olentia serta?
    anne coronato vis lapide ossa tegi?
pone merum et talos; pereat qui crastina curat:
    Mors aurem vellens 'vivite' ait, 'venio.'"

[26] Vestae *Voss*: vestrae Ω
[29] te ς: nunc Ω
[33] formosa et *Clausen*: formosum Ω
[36] ossa *Ilgen*: ista Ω

mulberries and grapes in thick clusters, and a sea-green cucumber hanging from its stalk. There is the cottage's bodyguard,[1] armed with willow sickle, but for all his gigantic member he is not to be feared.

"Come as his tenant: your weary donkey has long been sweating; spare the little donkey: the donkey is Vesta's darling.[2] Now the incessant song of the cicadas bursts through the thickets, now the spotted lizard lurks in her cool retreat: if you've any sense, you'll lie down and drink deep from summer glass,[3] or maybe you'd prefer a chalice of fresh crystal. Come here and rest your weary limbs beneath the shade of vines, and entwine your drooping head in a coronet of roses, and, kissing the luscious lips of a pretty girl—damn you over there with that prudish frown on your face! Why save fragrant wreaths for ungrateful ashes? D'you want your bones buried under a garlanded tombstone? Set forth the wine and dice! To hell with him who thinks of tomorrow! Death is tweaking my ear and says: 'Live it up now, for I'm coming!'"

[1] Priapus.
[2] Because, according to the story, his braying warned Vesta of an assault by Priapus (cf. Ovid, *Fasti* 6.311ff.).
[3] One of large size.

CIRIS

Etsi me, vario iactatum laudis amore
irritaque expertum fallacis praemia vulgi,
Cecropius suavis exspirans hortulus auras
florentis viridi Sophiae complectitur umbra,
5   mensque, ut quiret eo dignum sibi quaerere carmen,
longe aliud studium inque alios accincta labores,
altius ad magni suspexit sidera mundi
et placitum paucis ausa est ascendere collem:
non tamen absistam coeptum detexere munus,
10   in quo iure meas utinam requiescere musas
et leviter blandum liceat deponere amorem.
    Quod si mirificum decus o Mes‹salla tuorum›,
mirificum saecli, modo sit tibi velle libido,
si mihi iam summas Sapientia panderet arces,
15   quattuor antiquis heredibus edita consors,
unde hominum errores longe lateque per orbem
despicere atque humilis possem contemnere curas,

mss: 1–337 = Z: Ω (338–453) = GZ: Ω (454–497) = GBZ: Ω
(498–541) = BZ   meter: hexameter
  [1] *Cf.* Cat. 65.1ff   [5] mensque ut *Housman*: tum mea
Z | quiret *edd. vett.*: qu(a)eret Z   [6] inque *Housman*: atque Z
    [7] suspexit *Schrader*: suspendit Z
    [12] decus *Salvatore*: genus Z | o Messalla tuorum *Scaliger*:
omnes Z

CIRIS

Tossed though I am, this way and that, by love of
renown, and knowing full well that the fickle throng's re-
wards are vain; though the Attic garden,[1] breathing forth
sweet fragrance, enwraps me in fine-flowering Wisdom's
verdant shade; and though my mind, prepared as she is for
far different tasks and far different toils, has looked aloft to
the stars of the mighty firmament, and has dared to climb
the hill[2] that has found favour with few: nevertheless I shall
not cease to fulfil the task I have begun, wherein I pray that
my Muses may find their due repose, and lightly lay aside
that seductive love.

But if, O Messalla, wondrous glory of your family—
wondrous glory of our age, should you only choose to wish
it—if Wisdom, exalted partner of those four heirs of olden
days,[3] now opened up to me her topmost citadels, whence,
far and wide over the world, I could look down on the
errors of men and despise their lowly cares, I should not be

[1] The garden in Athens where Epicurus used to teach.
[2] The hill of wisdom, or philosophy.
[3] The four philosophers: Plato, Aristotle, Zeno, and Epicurus.

13 saecli ς: sedi Z   14 panderet *Heinsius*: pangeret Z
15 edita *Baehrens*: est data Z

non ego te talem venerarer munere tali,
non equidem (quamvis interdum ludere nobis
20 et gracilem molli libeat pede claudere versum),
sed magno intexens, si fas est dicere, peplo,
qualis Erectheis olim portatur Athenis,
debita cum castae solvuntur vota Minervae
tardaque confecto redeunt quinquennia lustro,
25 cum levis alterno Zephyrus concrebuit Euro
et prono gravidum provexit pondere currum.
felix illa dies, felix et dicitur annus,
felices qui talem annum videre diemque!
ergo Palladiae texuntur in ordine pugnae,
30 magna Giganteis ornantur pepla tropaeis,
horrida sanguineo pinguntur proelia cocco.
additur aurata deiectus cuspide Typhon,
qui prius, Ossaeis consternens aethera saxis,
Emathio celsum duplicabat vertice Olympum.
35   Tale deae velum sollemni tempore portant,
tali te vellem, iuvenum doctissime, ritu
purpureos inter soles et candida lunae
sidera, caeruleis orbem pulsantia bigis,
naturae rerum magnis intexere chartis,
40 aeterno ⟨ut⟩ sophiae coniunctum carmine nomen
nostra tuum senibus loqueretur pagina saeclis.
     Sed quoniam ad tantas nunc primum nascimur artes,

20 libeat *Heyne*: liceat Z
40 aeterno *Heinsius*: -um Z | ut *add. Nic. Loensis*

---

[4] The poem with which the writer would like to honour his patron is compared to the *peplos,* richly embroidered with figures (cf. 29f.), which was offered to Athena at the great Panathenaic

444

honouring you, great as you are, with a gift so slight, no indeed, although at times it is pleasant for us to trifle and cast a slender verse in elegant meter, but I should weave a story into an ample robe,[4] if thus to speak be lawful, such as on occasion is borne in Erechthean Athens, when due vows are paid to chaste Minerva and the fifth-year feast slowly comes round at the lustre's close, as the gentle West Wind waxes strong against his rival of the East propelling the car heavy with its overhanging weight. Happy that day is called, happy that year, and happy they who have lived to behold such a year and day! Thus in due order are inwoven the battles of Pallas, the great robes are adorned with the trophies of the Giants, and grim combats are depicted in blood-red scarlet. There is added he who was hurled down by the golden spear—Typhon, who aforetime, when paving heaven with the rocks of Ossa, sought to double the height of Olympus by piling thereon the Emathian mount.[5]

Such is the goddess's sail, borne at the solemn season, and in such fashion, O most learned youth, should I wish to weave your story amid roseate suns and the moon's white star that makes heaven throb with her celestial chariot into a great poem on Nature, so that unto late ages our page might speak your name, linked eternally in song with wisdom.

But seeing that now for the first time our infant efforts

festival. This was solemnized every five years in the month of Hecatombaeon, the first month of the Attic year. The *peplos*, outstretched like a sail, was carried to the temple on a ship (here called *currus*) which was drawn through the streets of Athens on rollers.　　[5] Pelion, a mountain of Thessaly (Emathia).

nunc primum teneros firmamus robore nervos,
haec tamen interea, quae possumus, in quibus aevi
45 prima rudimenta et iuvenes exegimus annos,
accipe dona meo multum vigilata labore
promissa atque diu iam tandem ⟨reddita vota⟩
impia prodigiis ut quondam exterrita amoris
Scylla novos avium sublimis in aëre coetus
50 viderit et tenui conscendens aethera penna
caeruleis sua tecta super volitaverit alis,
hanc pro purpureo poenam scelerata capillo
pro patria solvens excisa et funditus urbe.
   Complures illam magni, Messalla, poetae
55 (nam verum fateamur: amat Polyhymnia verum)
longe alia perhibent mutatam membra figura
Scyllaeum monstro saxum infestasse voraci;
illam esse, aerumnis quam saepe legamus Ulixi,
candida succinctam latrantibus inguina monstris,
60 Dulichias vexasse rates et gurgite in alto
deprensos nautas canibus lacerasse marinis.
sed neque Maeoniae patiuntur credere chartae
nec malus istorum dubiis erroribus auctor.
namque alias alii vulgo finxere puellas,
65 quae Colophoniaco Scyllae dicantur Homero.
ipse Crataein ait matrem, sed sive Crataeis,
sive illam monstro generavit Echidna biformi,
sive est neutra parens atque hoc in carmine toto

47 *add. Leo*
51 *Cf. Ecl.* 6.81
53 patria *Haupt*: patris Z
59–61 = *Ecl.* 6.75–77

are turned to such high arts,[6] since now first we are
making strong our youthful sinews, nevertheless accept
meanwhile this poem—'tis all we can offer—on which we
have spent life's earliest schooling and the years of our
youth, a gift wrought by me with many a toilsome vigil, a
vow long promised and now at last fulfilled. It is the story
of how, once upon a time, impious Scylla, terrified by love's
portents, saw in the sky aloft strange gatherings of birds,
and, mounting the heavens on slender pinions, hovered on
azure wings above her home, paying this penalty, accursed
one, for the crimson lock, and for the utter uprooting of
her native city.

Many great poets tell us, Messalla (for let us confess the
truth: it is truth that Polyhymnia loves), that she, with
limbs changed to far different form, haunted the rock of
Scylla with her voracious bulk. She it is, they say, of whom
we read in the toils of Ulysses, how that, with howling
monsters girt about her white waist, she often harried the
Ithacan ships and in the swirling depths tore asunder with
her sea dogs the sailors she had clutched. But neither do
Homer's pages[7] suffer us to credit this tale nor does he who
is the pernicious source[8] of those poets' sundry mistakes.
For various writers have commonly substituted various
maidens for the Scylla named by Colophon's Homer. He
himself says[9] that Crataeis was her mother; but whether
Crataeis or Echidna bore that two-formed monster; or
whether neither was her mother, and throughout the poem

---

[6] I.e. Epicurean philosophy.

[7] I.e. in *Odyssey* 12.

[8] Whom the author meant by this is unknown.

[9] *Odyssey* 12.125.

inguinis est vitium et veneris descripta libido;
70 sive etiam iactis speciem mutata venenis
infelix virgo (quid enim commiserat illa?
ipse pater timidam vacua complexus harena
73 coniugium castae violaverat Amphitrites)
80 horribilis circum vidit se existere formas:
81 heu quotiens mirata novos expalluit artus!
82 ipsa suos quotiens heu pertimuit latratus!
74 at tamen exegit longo post tempore poenas,
75 ut, cum cura sui veheretur coniugis alto,
ipsa trucem multo misceret sanguine pontum;
seu vero, ut perhibent, forma cum vinceret omnis
et cupidos quaestu passim populraet amantes,
79 piscibus et canibusque malis vallata repente est
83 ausa quod est mulier numen fraudare deorum
et dictam Veneri votorum avertere poenam,
85 quam mala multiplici iuvenum consaepta caterva
dixerat atque animo meretrix iactata ferarum
(infamem tali merito rumore fuisse
docta Palaepaphiae testatur voce Pachynus):
quidquid et ut quisque est tali de clade locutus,
90 somnia sunt: potius liceat notescere Cirin
atque unam ex multis Scyllam non esse puellis.

---

[72] vacua *Baehrens*: saeva Ω   [73–83] *transpositions by*
Reitzenstein   [75] sui *Loensis*: tuae Ω   [84] avertere *Scaliger*:
vertere Z   [85] consaepta *Sillig*: quod septa Z
[87] merito rumore *Loensis*: meritorum more Ω
[90] somnia *Heinsius*: omnia Z

---

[10] The assumption being that the description of Scylla is alle-
gorical.   [11] This probably refers to the transformation of

she but portrays the sin of lust and love's incontinence;[10] or
whether, transformed through scattered poisons, the luck-
less maiden (luckless, I say, for of what wrong had she been
guilty? Father Neptune himself had embraced the fright-
ened girl on the lonely strand, and broken his conjugal vow
to chaste Amphitrite) beheld awful shapes coming into be-
ing about her: how often, alas! did she marvel and grow
pale at her strange limbs! how often, alas! did she turn in
terror from her own baying! but still, long afterwards, she
exacted a penalty, for when his consort's beloved was
riding upon the deep, she in her turn suffused the savage
sea with a torrent of blood;[11] or whether, as 'tis said, seeing
that she excelled all women in beauty, and in avarice made
wanton havoc of her eager lovers, she of a sudden became
fenced about with dreadful fishes and dogs, because she,
a woman, dared to defraud the powers divine, and to
withhold from Venus the vow-appointed price, even the
payment which a base harlot, surrounded by a thronging
crowd of youths, and stirred with a wild and savage spirit,
had imposed upon her lovers—that by this report she
was with reason defamed, Pachynus has learned and so
bears witness, speaking by the lips of Venus, queen of
Old Paphos[12]—whatever and however each has spoken
of this calamity is sheer moonshine: rather let Ciris be-
come known, and not a Scylla who was but one of many
maidens.[13]

Scylla. The *cura* is Neptune, husband of Amphitrite: so Fair-
clough, but text and interpretation hereabouts are very uncertain.

[12] There seems to have been an inscription about Scylla in the
temple of Venus at Pachynus.   [13] The subject, then, is to be
that Scylla who was transformed into the sea hawk, called Ciris.

Quare, quae cantus meditanti mittere doctos
magna mihi cupido tribuistis praemia, divae
Pierides, quarum castos altaria postis
95   munere saepe meo inficiunt foribusque hyacinthi
deponunt flores aut suave rubens narcissus
aut crocus alterna coniungens lilia caltha
sparsaque liminibus floret rosa, nunc age, divae,
praecipue nostro nunc aspirate labori
100 atque novum aeterno praetexite honore volumen.
Sunt Pandioniis vicinae sedibus urbes
Actaeos inter colles et candida Thesei
purpureis late ridentia litora conchis,
quarum non ulli fama concedere digna
105 stat Megara, Alcathoi quondam murata labore,
Alcathoi Phoebique; deus namque adfuit illi,
unde etiam citharae voces imitatus acutas
saepe lapis recrepat Cyllenia murmura pulsus
et veterem sonitu Phoebi testatur amorem.
110 hanc urbem, ante alios qui tum florebat in armis,
fecerat infestam populator remige Minos,
hospitio quod se Nisi Polyidos avito
Carpathium fugiens et flumina Caeratea
texerat. hunc bello repetens Gortynius heros
115 Attica Cretaea sternebat rura sagitta.
sed neque tum cives neque tum rex ipse veretur

92 doctos *Bergk*: cocos *H*: caecos *AR*
105 Alcathoi *Ribbeck*: act(h)ei *Z* | murata *Ellis*: mutata *Z*
109 amorem *AR*: honorem (*from* 100) *H*
116 *Cf.* Cat. 64.68

14 Athens.

Therefore, ye divine Muses, who, when I essayed to put forth my learned songs, granted me the high rewards I craved—ye, whose pure columns are not seldom stained by the altar offerings I bring; at whose temple doors the hyacinths yield their bloom, or the sweet blushing narcissus, or the crocus and lilies, blended with alternate marigolds, and on whose threshold are scattered blooming roses—now come, ye goddesses, now breathe a special grace upon this toil, and crown this new scroll with glory immortal!

Close to the home of Pandion[14] lie cities between the Attic hills and Theseus' gleaming shores, smiling from afar with their roseate shells;[15] and, worthy to yield to none of these in repute, stands Megara, whose walls were reared by the toil of Alcathous and Phoebus, for the god aided the former; whence too the stones, imitating the lyre's shrill notes, often, when smitten, re-echo Cyllene's murmurs,[16] and in their sound attest the ancient love of Phoebus. This city the prince who in those days was eminent in arms above others, even Minos, had ravaged and laid waste with his fleet, because Polyidos,[17] fleeing from the Carpathian sea and the streams of Caeratus, had taken shelter in the ancestral home of Nisus. Seeking to win him back in war, the Gortynian hero[18] was strewing the land with Cretan arrows. But neither in that hour do the citizens nor in that

---

[15] This is the Megarid, which abounds in white marble, interspersed with shells. Here Theseus founded the Isthmian games.

[16] I.e. the music of the lyre. Mercury, its inventor, was born on Cyllene; cf. *Aeneid* 8.139.   [17] The priest who was said to have once restored Glaucus, son of Minos, to life.

[18] Minos.

infesto ad muros volitantis agmine turmas
deicere et indomitas virtute retundere mentes,
responsum quoniam satis est meminisse deorum.
120 nam capite a summo regis, mirabile dictu,
candida caesaries florebat tempore utroque,
at roseus medio surgebat vertice crinis:
cuius quam servata diu natura fuisset,
tam patriam incolumem Nisi regnumque futurum
125 concordes stabili firmarant numine Parcae.
ergo omnis caro residebat cura capillo,
aurea sollemni comptum quem fibula ritu
Cecropiae tereti nectebat dente cicadae.
　　Nec vero haec urbis custodia vana fuisset
130 (nec fuerat), ni Scylla novo correpta furore,
Scylla, patris miseri patriaeque inventa sepulcrum,
o nimium cupidis Minoa inhiasset ocellis.
sed malus ille puer, quem nec sua flectere mater
iratum potuit, quem nec pater atque avus idem
135 Iuppiter (ille iram Poenos domitare leones
et validas docuit vires mansuescere tigris,
ille etiam divos omnes—sed dicere magnum est),
idem tum tristis acuebat parvulus iras
Iunonis magnae, cuius periura puella
140 olim (sed meminere diu periuria divae)
non ulli licitam violaverat inscia sedem,

---

121 caesarie florebant tempora lauro Z, *corr. Heinsius*
　　122 *Cf.* Cat. 64.309　　125 *Cf. Ecl.* 4.47　　126 caro *ed. Ald.*
1517: cano Z　　128 Cecropiae *Scaliger*: corpsel(la)e Z
　　135 iram *O. Skutsch*: etiam Z　　　　　137 omnes *Heinsius*:
homines Z　　139-140 periuria divae / . . . periura puella Z,
transp. Alton | sed *Ellis*: se Z

hour does the king himself fear to strike down the troops that flock in hostile band to the walls, or valorously to blunt the spirit of the unconquered foe, since it is enough to remember the answer of the gods. For surmounting the king's head (wondrous to tell) sprouted white hair at either temple, while midway on his crown grew a roseate lock. As long as this preserved its nature, so long had the Fates, voicing in unison their fixed will, given assurance that Nisus' country and kingdom would be secure. All their care therefore was centred in that precious hair, which, knotted in customary fashion, a golden buckle bound with an Athenian cicada's shapely clasp.[19]

Nor truly would this defence of the city have been in vain (nor so far had it been), were it not that Scylla, swept away by fresh madness—Scylla, who proved to be the ruin of her luckless father and her fatherland—gaped and gazed upon Minos, ah! with too longing eyes. But that mischievous boy, whom, when angered, neither his mother could sway, nor he who was at once father and father's father, even Jupiter[20] (he taught Punic lions to tame their anger and taught the stout strength of the tiger to soften, and even all the gods—but the theme is too large to expound), that same little boy sharpened the stern wrath of mighty Juno, whose home, forbidden to all, the perjured maid long ago (yet goddesses long remember perjuries) had unwittingly profaned; for, as she was engaging in the

[19] Thucydides (1.6) tells us that in early times Athenian men used to wear the hair on the top of the head in a knot, secured with a pin shaped like a cicada.

[20] Venus, daughter of Jupiter, was by Jupiter mother of Cupid.

dum sacris operata deae lascivit et extra
procedit longe matrum comitumque catervam,
suspensam gaudens in corpore ludere vestem
145   et tumidos agitante sinus Aquilone relaxans.
necdum etiam castos gustaverat ignis honores,
necdum sollemni lympha perfusa sacerdos
pallentis foliis caput exornarat olivae,
cum lapsa e manibus fugit pila, quoque ea lapsa est
150   procurrit virgo. quod uti ne prodita ludo
aureolam gracili solvisses corpore pallam.
omnia quae retinere gradum cursusque morari
possent, o tecum vellem tunc, semper, haberes.
non, numquam violata manu sacraria divae
155   iurando, infelix, nequiquam periurasses.
et, si quis nocuisse tibi periuria credat
156a   ⟨illa nihil numenque Iovis latuisse supremi—⟩
causa pia est: timuit fratri te ostendere Iuno.
at levis ille deus, cui semper ad ulciscendum
quaeritur ex omni verborum iniuria dicto,
160   aurea fulgenti depromens tela pharetra
(heu nimium certo, nimium, ferientia missu)
virginis in tenera defixit acumina mente.
    Quae simul ac venis hausit sitientibus ignem
et validum penitus concepit in ossa furorem,
165   saeva velut gelidis Edonum Bistonis oris
ictave barbarico Cybeles antistita buxo

     [149] quoque *Unger* ea lapsa *Maehly*: cumque relapsa Z
     [151] aureolam *Housman*: aurea iam Z   [153] tunc *Baehrens*:
tua Z   [155] periurasses *Housman*: iure piasses Z
     [156a] *suppl. Housman*   [161] ter(r)et nimium t(h)irintia uisu
Z, *corr. a friend of Schrader's*

goddess's rites, she indulges in a frolic, and goes far beyond the band of matrons and her companions, rejoicing in the ungirdled robe that plays about her body, and throwing loose its swelling folds, as the North Wind tosses it about. Not yet had the fire tasted the holy offerings; not yet had the priestess bathed in the ritual water and adorned her head with pale olive leaves, when the ball slipped away from her hands, and the girl runs after it where it escapes. Would that you had not been beguiled by play, and had not loosened the golden robe on your slender body! O would that you had had with you then and always all your apparel, which might have held back your steps and stayed your course! You would not, unhappy one, by swearing that the goddess's sanctuary was never profaned by your hand, have vainly perjured yourself. And should anyone suppose that that perjury had done you no harm and had escaped the supreme deity of Jupiter, well, there is a righteous reason: Juno feared to show you to her brother.[21] But that fickle god (by whom whatever falsehood lurks in any spoken word is ever marked out for punishment), drawing golden shafts from his gleaming quiver (shafts which, alas, strike home with aim all too sure), had lodged them all in the damsel's tender heart.

As soon as she drank the fire into her thirsty veins, and caught deep within her marrow the potent frenzy, like a fierce Thracian woman in the chill lands of the Edonians, or like a priestess of Cybele, inspired by the barbaric box-

[21] Juno's wrath, which could easily be aroused because of the amorous Jupiter, was feared by Scylla, who therefore swore falsely that she had not exposed her limbs in the temple of the goddess.

infelix virgo tota bacchatur in urbe,
non storace Idaeo fragrantis uncta capillos,
coccina non teneris pedibus Sicyonia servans,
170 non niveo retinens bacata monilia collo.
multum illi incerto trepidant vestigia cursu;
saepe petit patrios ascendere perdita muros,
aëriasque facit causam se visere turris;
saepe etiam tristis volvens in nocte querelas
175 sedibus ex altis tecti speculatur amorem
castraque prospectat crebris lucentia flammis.
nulla colum novit, carum non respicit aurum,
non arguta sonant tenui psalteria chorda,
non Libyco molles plauduntur pectine telae;
180 nullus in ore rubor: ubi enim rubor, obstat amori.
atque ubi nulla malis reperit solacia tantis
tabidulamque videt labi per viscera mortem,
quo vocat ire dolor, subigunt quo tendere fata,
fertur et horribili praeceps impellitur oestro,
185 ut patris, a demens, crinem de vertice sacrum
furtive arguto detonsum mitteret hosti.
namque haec condicio miserae proponitur una,
sive illa ignorans (quis non bonus omnia malit
credere quam tanti sceleris damnare puellam?),
190 heu tamen infelix: quid enim imprudentia prodest?
    Nise pater, cui direpta crudeliter urbe
vix erit una super sedes in turribus altis
fessus ubi exstructo possis considere nido,

168ff *Cf.* Cat. 64.63ff   168 uncta *Heinsius*: picta Z
175 tecti *Heyne*: caeli Z
185 sacrum *Sillig*: serum Z
186 furtive *Goodyear*: furtimque Z

wood flute, the unhappy girl raves throughout the city. No balsam of Ida anoints her fragrant locks, no scarlet shoes of Sicyon protect her tender feet, she wears no collar of pearls upon her snowy neck. Many times her feet hurry to and fro in uncertain course; oft she returns, forlorn one, to climb her father's walls, and makes the plea that she is visiting the lofty towers; oft too at night, when pondering bitter complaints, from her high palace home she watches for her love, and gazes forth to the camp, ablaze with numerous fires. She has no thought for the distaff, she cares naught for precious gold, the tuneful harp rings not with its slender strings, the loom's soft threads are not smitten with the Libyan comb.[22] No blush is on her cheeks; for blushes are obstacles to love. And when she finds no comfort for such suffering, and sees slow-wasting death steal over her frame, she hastens whither anguish summons her, whither the fates compel her to go, and she is driven headlong by awful frenzy, so that she, mad girl, stealthily shearing the sacred lock from her father's head, might send it to the cunning foe. For to the unhappy girl is offered this deal alone[23]—or perhaps she did the deed in ignorance (what good man would not believe anything rather than convict the maid of such a crime?), yet alas! unblest was she: for what does folly avail?

O Nisus, father, who, when your city has been cruelly despoiled, will have scarcely a place left in your lofty castle where in weariness you can settle in your high-built

[22] I.e., of ivory, for elephants were numerous in Libya.
[23] Minos would not return Scylla's love unless she betrayed her father in the manner described.

tu quoque avis metuere: dabit tibi filia poenas.
195   gaudete, o celeres, subnixae nubibus altis,
quae mare, quae viridis silvas lucosque sonantis
incolitis, gaudete, vagae, gaudete, volucres,
vosque adeo, humani mutatae corporis artus,
vos o crudeli fatorum lege, puellae
200   Dauliades, gaudete: venit carissima vobis
cognatos augens reges numerumque suorum
Ciris et ipse pater. vos, o pulcherrima quondam
corpora, caeruleas praevertite in aethera nubes,
qua novus ad superum sedes haliaeetos et qua
205   candida concessos ascendat Ciris honores.
    Iamque adeo dulci devinctus lumina somno
Nisus erat vigilumque procul custodia primis
excubias foribus studio iactabat inani,
cum furtim tacito descendens Scylla cubili
210   auribus arrectis nocturna silentia temptat
et pressis tenuem singultibus aëra captat.
tum suspensa levans digitis vestigia primis
egreditur ferroque manus armata bidenti
evolat. at demptae subita in formidine vires.
215   caeruleas sua furta prius testatur ad umbras:
nam qua se ad patrium tendebat semita limen,
vestibulo in thalami paulum remoratur et alte
suspicit ad celsi nictantia sidera mundi,

194 metuere *G. Hermann*: moriere Z
197 gaudete (2o) *Schwabe*: laudate Z
206 *Cf.* Cat. 64.122
208 *Cf. Ecl.* 2.5
218 celsi nictantia *Scaliger*: celi nutantia Z

nest, as a bird too you will be feared; your daughter will pay you a penalty.[24] Rejoice, you swift creatures that rest upon the heavenly clouds, you that dwell upon the sea, that dwell in green woods and echoing groves, rejoice, you birds that widely roam, rejoice; yes, and you, too, whose human limbs were changed by cruel law of the fates, ye Daulian maids,[25] rejoice; there comes one beloved by you, swelling the ranks of her royal kindred,[26] even Ciris with her father himself. Do ye, O forms once most fair, outstrip the clouds of heaven, and fly to the skies, where the new sea eagle will climb to the abodes of the gods, and the beautiful Ciris to the honours granted her.[27]

And now, even now, the eyes of Nisus were locked in sweet sleep, and at the entrance doors hard by, the sentries on guard were with vain zeal keeping watch, when Scylla, stealthily descending from her silent couch, essays with straining ears the stillness of the night, and checking her sobs, catches at the fine air. Then, poising her feet on tiptoe she passes without and, her hand armed with two-edged shears, hurries forth. But in sudden terror her strength fails her. She first bears witness of her misdeeds to the shades of heaven: for where the path led to her father's threshold, she lingers a moment at the chamber entrance, and glances above at the twinkling stars in the firmament

[24] Scylla, transformed into a sea hawk, will be pursued by Nisus, transformed into a sea eagle; cf. *Georgics* 1.405.

[25] Philomela and Procne, who had also been changed into birds. Procne had married Tereus, king of Daulis.

[26] Philomela and Procne were daughters of the elder Pandion, king of Athens, while Nisus was son of the younger Pandion.

[27] Scylla's transformation is not regarded as a punishment.

non accepta piis promittens munera divis.
220   Quam simul Ogygii Phoenicis filia Carme
surgere sensit anus, sonitum nam fecerat illi
marmoreo aeratus stridens in limine cardo,
corripit extemplo fessam languore puellam
et simul "o nobis sacrum caput" inquit "alumna,
225 non tibi nequiquam viridis per viscera pallor
aegroto tenuis suffundit sanguine venas,
nec levis hoc faceres, neque enim pote, cura subegit,
aut fallor: quod ut o potius, Rhamnusia, fallar.
nam qua te causa nec dulcis pocula Bacchi
230 nec gravidos Cereris dicam contingere fetus;
qua causa ad patrium solam vigilare cubile,
tempore quo fessas mortalia pectora curas,
quo rapidos etiam requiescunt flumina cursus?
dic age nunc miserae saltem, quod saepe petenti
235 iurabas nihil esse mihi, cur maesta parentis
formosos circum virgo remorere capillos.
ei mihi, ne furor ille tuos invaserit artus,
ille, Arabae Myrrhae quondam qui cepit ocellos,
ut scelere infando (quod nec sinat Adrastea)
240 laedere utrumque uno studeas errore parentem!
quod si alio quovis animi iactaris amore
(nam te iactari, non est Amathusia nostri
tam rudis ut nullo possim cognoscere signo),

---

[228] *Cf. Aen.* 10.631

---

[28] Carme, daughter of Phoenix, was loved by Jupiter. Their daughter, Britomartis, being wooed by Minos, fled into the sea. Rescued by Diana, she was worshipped in Crete under the name Dictynna.

on high, promising gifts that win no acceptance with righteous gods.

As soon as aged Carme,[28] daughter of Ogygian Phoenix, was aware of her rising (for she had heard the creaking of the bronze hinge on the marble threshold), straightway she seizes the faint and weary girl, and therewith cries: "O precious foster child, whom we revere, not without reason does a sallow pallor throughout your frame fill your feverish veins with thin blood, nor has some trivial worry forced you—nay, it could not—to this deed, or I am deceived: and, O Rhamnusian maid,[29] rather may I be deceived! For why else am I to say that you touch neither the cups of sweet Bacchus nor the teeming fruits of Ceres? Why do you watch alone by your father's bed at the hour when the hearts of men rest from weary cares, when even rivers stay their rapid course? Come, at least tell your poor nurse that which, oft as I have asked you, you have sworn means naught—why, unhappy girl, you linger near your father's beauteous locks? Ah me! may it not be that that madness has assailed your limbs which once ensnared the eyes of Arabian Myrrha,[30] so that in monstrous sin (which may Adrastea forbid!) you should desire by one folly to wrong both parents! But if you are swayed by some other passionate love (for that you are, not so strange to me is the Amathusian[31] that I cannot learn this by some sign), if a

[29] Nemesis, who was worshipped especially at Rhamnus in Attica.

[30] The story of Myrrha or Smyrna, who was guilty of incest with her father Cinyras and was afterwards transformed into the Arabian myrrh tree, is told in Ovid, *Metamorphoses* 10.298ff.

[31] Venus.

461

si concessus amor noto te macerat igni,
245 per tibi Dictynnae praesentia numina iuro,
prima deum dulcem mihi quae te donat alumnam,
omnia me potius digna atque indigna laborum
milia visuram, quam te tam tristibus istis
sordibus et senio patiar tabescere tali."
250   Haec loquitur, mollique ut se velavit amictu,
frigidulam iniecta circumdat veste puellam,
quae prius in tenui steterat succincta crocota.
dulcia deinde genis rorantibus oscula figens
persequitur miserae causas exquirere tabis;
255 nec tamen ante ullas patitur sibi reddere voces,
marmoreum tremebunda pedem quam rettulit intra.
illa autem "quid <sic> me," inquit, "nutricula, torques?
quid tantum properas nostros novisse furores?
non ego consueto mortalibus uror amore,
260 nec mihi notorum deflectunt lumina vultus,
nec genitor cordi est: ultro namque odimus omnis.
nil amat hic animus, nutrix, quod oportet amari,
in quo falsa tamen lateat pietatis imago,
sed media ex acie, mediis ex hostibus—eheu,
265 quid dicam quove aegra malum hoc exordiar ore?
dicam equidem, quoniam tu me non dicere, nutrix,
non sinis: extremum hoc munus morientis habeto.
ille, vides, nostris qui moenibus assidet hostis,
quem pater ipse deum sceptri donavit honore,
270 cui Parcae tribuere nec ullo vulnere laedi

249 senio *Burman*: seonia *H*: scoria *ρ*: *om. A*: morbo *R*
252 crocota *Scaliger*: corona *Z*
257 sic *add. Leo*
265 aegra *Baehrens*: agam *Z*

lawful love wastes you with familiar flame, I swear to you by the divine presence of Dictynna,[32] who, first of the gods in my eyes, granted me a sweet foster child in you, that sooner shall I face all toils, thousands meet and unmeet, than suffer you to pine away in such sad wretchedness and in such affliction."

Thus she cries, and, clad as she was in a soft gown, she casts her garb about the shivering girl, who before had stood, high-girt, in a thin saffron robe. Then, imprinting sweet kisses on her tear-bedewed cheeks, she earnestly asks the causes of her wasting misery, yet suffers her not to make any reply until, all trembling, she has withdrawn her stone-cold feet within. Then cries the girl: "Why, dear nurse, do you thus torture me? Why so eager to know my madness? It is no love common to mortals that inflames me; it is not the faces of friends that divert my gaze, it is not my father who is thus loved: I rather hate them all. This soul of mine, O nurse, loves naught that should be loved, naught wherein there lurks, however vain, some semblance of natural regard, but loves from amid the ranks of war, from amid our foes. Alas, alas! What can I say? With what speech can I, sorry one, launch forth upon this woe? Yet even so I will speak, since you, nurse, do not permit me to be silent: take this as my last dying gift. Yonder foe, whom you see encamped before our walls, to whom the father of the gods himself has given the glory of kingship, and to whom the Fates have granted that he suffer from no

[32] See note 28.

---

266 tu me non *Baehrens*: tu(m) non Z: tu nunc non *H*²
267 *Cf. Aen.* 8.60

(dicendum est, frustra circumvehor omnia verbis),
ille mea, ille idem oppugnat praecordia Minos.
quod per te divum crebros obtestor amores
perque tuum memori sanctum mihi pectus alumnae,
275 ut me, si servare potes, ne perdere malis;
sin autem optatae spes est incisa salutis,
ne mihi, quam merui, invideas, nutricula, mortem.
nam nisi te nobis malus, o malus, optima Carme,
ante in conspectum casusve deusve tulisset,
280 aut ferro hoc" (aperit ferrum quod veste latebat)
"purpureum patris dempsissem vertice crinem,
aut mihi praesenti peperissem vulnere letum."

Vix haec ediderat, cum clade exterrita tristi
insontes multo deturpat pulvere crines
285 et graviter questu Carme complorat anili:
"o mihi nunc iterum crudelis reddite Minos,
o iterum nostrae Minos inimice senectae,
semper ‹ut› aut olim natae te propter eundem
aut amor insanae luctum portavit alumnae.
290 tene ego tam longe capta atque avecta nequivi,
tam grave servitium, tam duros passa labores,
effugere, o bis iam exitium crudele meorum?
iam iam nec nobis aequo senioribus ullum,
vivere uti cupiam, vivit genus. ut quid ego amens
295 te erepta, o Britomarti, mei spes una sepulcri,
te, Britomarti, diem potui producere vitae?

274 memori sanctum *Sillig*: memoris auctum Z
280 *Cf. Aen.* 6.406   284 insontes *Wakefield*: intonsos Z
288 ut *add. Schrader*   292 o bis iam *Housman*: obsistam Z
293 aequo *Haupt*: ea que Z
294 vivere uti cupiam *Sillig*: vivendi copiam Z

wound (I must speak; vainly with words I travel round the whole story), it is he, it is he, that same Minos, who besieges my heart. I entreat you by the many loves of the gods, and by your heart, revered by me, your mindful foster child, do not, if you can save me, choose to destroy me. But if hope of the salvation I crave be cut off, grudge me not, dear nurse, the death I have deserved. For, good Carme, had not a perverse, yes, a perverse chance or god brought you first before my eyes, then either with this knife" (she reveals the knife hidden in her robe) "I should have cut from my father's head his crimson lock, or with a single stroke before his eyes have accomplished my death."

Scarcely had she uttered these words, when, terrified by the dread disaster, Carme defiles her guiltless locks with a shower of dust, and in aged accents makes grievous lamentation: "O Minos, who now a second time have visited your cruelty upon me! O Minos, in my old age a second time my enemy! how truly through you, and you alone, has Love ever brought grief, either to my child in other days or to my distraught ward! Have I, who was taken captive and carried off to this distant land,[33] who have suffered such grievous servitude and harsh travail, have I failed to escape you, you who are already for the second time the cruel destruction of my loved ones? Now, now, even for me, who am older than is proper, there lives no child to give me desire to live. Why have I, frantic one, when you, Britomartis, you, Britomartis, the sole hope of my shade, were torn from me—why have I been able to prolong my length of

[33] I.e. from Crete to Megara.

atque utinam celeri nec tantum grata Dianae
venatus esses virgo sectata virorum,
Cnosia nec Partho contendens spicula cornu
300 Dictaeas ageres ad gramina nota capellas.
numquam tam obnixe fugiens Minois amores
praeceps aërii specula de montis abisses,
unde alii fugisse ferunt et numen Aphaeae
virginis assignant, alii, quo notior esses,
305 Dictynnam dixere tuo de nomine Lunam.
sint haec vera velim: mihi certe, nata, peristi;
numquam ego te summo volitantem ‹in› vertice ‹montis›
Hyrcanos inter comites agmenque ferarum
conspiciam nec te redeuntem amplexa tenebo.
310   "Verum haec tum non sic gravia atque indigna fuere,
tum, mea alumna, tui cum spes integra maneret,
nam vox ista meas nondum violaverat auris.
tene etiam fortuna mihi crudelis ademit,
tene, o sola meae vivendi causa senectae?
315 saepe tuo dulci nequiquam capta sopore,
cum premeret natura, mori me velle negavi,
ut tibi Corycio glomerarem flammea luto.
quo nunc me, infelix, aut quae me fata reservant?
an nescis, qua lege patris de vertice summo
320 edita candentis praetexat purpura canos,
quae tenui patriae spes sit suspensa capillo?
si nescis, aliquam possum sperare salutem,

302 *Cf. Ecl.* 8.59 | montis abisses *Scaliger*: montibus isses Z
307 *add.* ρ
310 non sic *Sillig*: nobis Z

life? And would that you, maiden so dear to fleet Diana, had neither pursued, a maiden, the hunt that belongs to men, nor, aiming Cretan shafts from Parthian bow, had driven the Dictaean goats to their familiar meadows! Never with such resolve to flee from Minos' passion would you have rushed headlong from the towering mountain crag, whence some relate that you did flee, and assign you the godhead of the virgin Aphaea; but others, so that your fame might be greater,[34] have called the moon Dictynna after your name. May this, I pray, be true: for me at least, my child, you are no more. Never shall I see you speeding on the mountain's highest peak among the Hyrcanian hounds, your comrades, and the wild beast throng, nor on your return shall I hold you in my embrace.

"But this plight was not grievous or shameful, when hope of you, my child, still remained unshattered, and that tale of yours had not yet profaned my ears. Has cruel fortune taken you also from me, you, who alone are for my old age a cause of living? Often, vainly charmed by your sweet slumber, though nature weighed heavy on me, I was loth, I said, to die, for I wished to weave for you a marriage veil of Corycian yellow. For what end, ill-starred one, or by what fate am I preserved? Do you not know by what law the crimson that grows from the crown of your father's head fringes his shining hoary hair, the crimson, hope of your fatherland, that hangs by a slender thread? If you know not, I may hope for some salvation, since in ignorance you

---

[34] The poet implies that the name Dictynna, by which Diana, the Moon goddess, was also known (cf. Tibullus, 1.4.25; Ovid, *Metamorphoses* 2.441, etc.), had been given to Britomartis herself.

inscia quandoquidem scelus es conata nefandum;
sin est quod metuo, per te, mea alumna, tuumque
325   expertum multis miserae mihi rebus amorem,
per te et sacra precor per numina Ilithyiae,
ne tantum in facinus tam nulla mente feraris.
non ego te incepto, fieri quod non pote, conor
flectere amore, nec est cum dis contendere nostrum,
330   sed patris incolumi potius denubere regno
atque aliquos tamen esse velis tibi, alumna, penates;
hoc unum exilio docta atque experta monebo.
quod si non alia poteris ratione parentem
flectere (sed poteris: quid enim non unica possis?),
335   tum potius tandem ista, pio cum iure licebit,
cum facti causam tempusque doloris habebis,
tum potius conata tua atque incepta referto,
meque deosque tibi comites, mea alumna, futuros
polliceor: nihil est, quod texitur ordine, longum."
340   His ubi sollicitos animi relevaverat aestus
vocibus et blanda pectus spe mulserat aegrum,
paulatim tremebunda genis obducere vestem
virginis et placidam tenebris captare quietem,
inverso bibulum restinguens lumen olivo,
345   incipit ad crebrosque insani pectoris ictus
ferre manum, assiduis mulcens praecordia palmis.
noctem illam sic maesta super marcentis alumnae
frigidulos cubito subnixa pependit ocellos.

326 per te . . . sacra *Scaliger* et *add.Curcio*: perdere seva Z
332 exilio *anon.*: exitio Z
335 tandem *Baehrens* ista *Jortin*: tamen ipsa Z
341 mulserat *Gaar*: viserat *H*: iusserat *AR*
347 marcentis *Heinsius*: morientis Z: . . . . entis *G*

have attempted an unspeakable crime. But if it is as I fear, then by yourself, my child, and by your love, of which I, poor wretch, have had many a proof, by yourself and by the sacred power of Ilithyia,[35] do not, I pray, with intent so foolish, pursue this great wickedness. I am not trying to turn you from the love on which you have embarked—that cannot be—nor is it for me to contend with gods; but may it be your wish, my child, to wed when your father's kingdom is safe, and at least to have some home for yourself; this one piece of advice will I give, I who am taught and schooled by exile. But if in no other way you can sway your father (but this you can: for what could you, an only child, not do?) then rather I pray, when moral right will permit you, for you will have reason for action and the proper moment for grievance—then rather renew your endeavours and attempts. The gods and I—I promise you—will stand at your side: no task proves long, which step by step is wrought."

When with these words she had lightened passion's troubled tide, and with cheerful hopes had soothed her lovesick heart, little by little with trembling hands she tries to draw a veil over the maiden's cheeks, and with darkness to woo reposeful calm, tilting up the oil lamp and quenching the thirsty light;[36] then lays her hand upon her mad heart's frequent throbs, soothing her bosom with constant fondling. Thus all that night, sad soul, she hung poised on elbow over the tear-chilled eyes of her drooping foster child.

---

[35] According to *Odyssey* 19.188 this goddess had a cave near Amnisus, in Crete.   [36] The light was extinguished by tilting up the lamp and allowing the oil to cover the burning wick.

     Postera lux ubi laeta diem mortalibus almum
350 et gelida venientem ignem quatiebat ab Oeta,
quem pavidae alternis fugitant optantque puellae
(Hesperium vitant, optant ardescere Eoum),
praeceptis paret virgo nutricis et omnis
undique conquirit nubendi sedula causas.
355 temptantur patriae submissis vocibus aures,
laudanturque bonae pacis bona; multus inepto
virginis insolitae sermo novus errat in ore:
nunc tremere instantis belli certamina dicit
communemque timere deum; nunc regis amicis
360 (namque ipsi verita est) torvum flet maesta parentem,
cum Iove communis qui nolit habere nepotes.
nunc etiam conficta dolo mendacia turpi
invenit et divum terret formidine cives;
nunc alia ex aliis (nec desunt) omina quaerit;
365 quin etiam castos ausa est corrumpere vates,
ut, cum caesa pio cecidisset victima ferro,
essent qui generum Minoa auctoribus extis
iungere et ancipitis suaderent tollere pugnas.
     At nutrix, patula componens sulpura testa,
370 narcissum casiamque herbas incendit olentis
terque novena ligans triplici diversa colore
fila "ter in gremium mecum" inquit "despue, virgo,
despue ter, virgo: numero deus impare gaudet."
inde mago geminata Iovi fert sedula sacra,
375 sacra nec Idaeis anibus nec cognita Grais,

---

361 nolit habere *Ribbeck*: non habuere Ω
370 incendit Ω: contundit (*cf. Ecl.* 2.11) R
371 *Cf. Ecl.* 8.73

As soon as the morrow's dawn was joyously bringing kindly day to mortals, and was scattering on chill Oeta the rays of those advancing fires, which timorous maidens now flee and now desire (the star of Hesperus they shun, they long for Eos to blaze), the girl obeys the bidding of her nurse, and here and there earnestly seeks all manner of pleas for wedlock. In soft accents she assails her father's ears, and praises the blessings of gentle peace; much strange speech flits from the foolish lips of the inexperienced maid: she trembles, she says, at the impending battle strife, and fears the impartial god of war; now to the king's friends (for she is afraid to approach him directly) she sadly weeps over the harshness of her father for refusing to have grandchildren in common with Jove.[37] Now, too, she conceives falsehoods feigned in base deceit, and frightens her fellow citizens with terrors of the gods; now she seeks various omens, from this one and from that, and does not fail to find them. More still; she dared to bribe holy seers, so that, whenever a victim fell, slain by sacred steel, there should be some to prompt the king to join Minos to himself as son-in-law and put an end to the doubtful conflict.

But the nurse, mixing sulphur in a flat bowl, kindles narcissus and cassia, savoury herbs; and thrice tying nine threads, marked with three different hues, she cries: "Spit thrice into your bosom, as I do, maiden; spit thrice, maiden: heaven delights in an uneven number." Then oft paying the Stygian rites to Jupiter Magician, rites unknown to Trojan or Greek witches, and sprinkling the

---

[37] If she became the wife of Minos, Nisus and Jupiter would both be grandfathers to her children.

pergit Amyclaeo spargens altaria thallo
regis Iolciacis animum defigere votis.
verum ubi nulla movet stabilem fallacia Nisum,
nec possunt homines nec possunt flectere divi
380 (tanta est in parvo fiducia crine cavendi),
rursus ad inceptum sociam se adiungit alumnae
purpureumque parat rursus tondere capillum,
tam longo quod iam captat succurrere amori,
non minus illa tamen revehi quod moenia Cretae
385 gaudeat: et cineri patria est iucunda sepulto.
     Ergo iterum capiti Scylla est inimica paterno:
tum coma Sidonio florens deciditur ostro,
tum capitur Megara et divum responsa probantur,
tum suspensa novo ritu de navibus altis
390 per mare caeruleum trahitur Niseia virgo.
complures illam nymphae mirantur in undis,
miratur pater Oceanus et candida Tethys
et cupidas secum rapiens Galatea sorores,
illa etiam iunctis magnum quae piscibus aequor
395 et glauco bipedum curru metitur equorum,
Leucothea parvusque dea cum matre Palaemon,
illi etiam alternas sortiti vivere luces,
cara Iovis suboles, magnum Iovis incrementum,
Tyndaridae niveos mirantur virginis artus.
400 has adeo voces atque haec lamenta per auras
fluctibus in mediis questu volvebat inani,
ad caelum infelix ardentia lumina tendens,
lumina, nam teneras arcebant vincula palmas:
     "Supprimite o paulum turbati flamina venti,

391ff *Cf.* Cat. 64.15*ff*   394–95 *Cf. Georg.* 4.388–89
398 *Cf. Ecl.* 4.49   402f = *Aen.* 2.405–6

altars with Amyclaean branch,[38] she endeavours to snare the king's mind with Thessalian enchantments. Now when no ruse moves steadfast Nisus, and neither men nor gods can sway him (such confidence in warding off peril does he place in his little lock) again she allies herself with her foster child's design, and again makes ready to shear the crimson hair, for now she is eager to satisfy a passion so protracted—yet not less so because of her joy in returning to the towns of Crete; our fatherland is sweet, even to our buried ashes.

Therefore once more Scylla assails her father's head. Then it is that his hair, rich in its Sidonian purple, is cut off; then that Megara is taken and the divine oracles are proved; then that, suspended in strange fashion from lofty ships, the maiden daughter of Nisus is dragged over the blue sea. Many nymphs marvel at her amid the waves; father Neptune marvels, and shining Tethys, and Galatea, carrying off with her her eager sisters. She too marvels, who traverses the mighty main in her azure car, drawn by her team of fishes and two-footed steeds, Leucothea, and little Palaemon with his goddess mother,[39] and they also marvel at the maiden's snowy limbs, the Tyndaridae, who live by lot alternate days, dear offspring of Jupiter, a Jupiter's mighty seed to be. Yea, these cries and these laments she, in the midst of the waves, sent ringing through the air in her fruitless wailing, uplifting to heaven, unhappy one, her blazing eyes—her eyes, for bonds confined her delicate hands.

"Stay, ye wild winds, O stay your blasts for a moment

---

[38] Probably an olive bough; cf. *Aeneid* 6.230.
[39] Ino, daughter of Cadmus.

405   dum queror et divos (quamquam nil testibus illis
       profeci) extrema moriens tamen alloquor hora.
       vos ego, vos adeo, venti, testabor, et aurae,
       vos, vos, humana si qui de gente venitis,
       cernitis? illa ego sum cognato sanguine vobis,
410   Scylla (quod o salva liceat te dicere, Procne),
       illa ego sum Nisi pollentis filia quondam,
       certatim ex omni petiit quam Graecia regno
       qua curvus terras amplectitur Hellespontus;
       illa ego sum, Minos, sacrato foedere coniunx
415   dicta tibi: tamen haec, etsi non accipis, audis.
       vinctane tam magni tranabo gurgitis undas?
       vincta tot assiduas pendebo ex ordine luces?
       non equidem me alio possum contendere dignam
       supplicio, quae sic patriam carosque penates
420   hostibus immitique addixi gnara tyranno.
       verum istaec, Minos, illos scelerata putavi,
       si nostra ante aliqui nudasset foedera casus,
       facturos, quorum direptis moenibus urbis
       o ego crudelis flamma delubra petivi.
425   te vero victore prius vel sidera cursus
       mutatura suos quam te mihi talia captae
       facturum metui. iam iam scelus omnia vicit.
       tene ego plus patrio dilexi perdita regno?
       tene? nec mirum: vultu decepta puella
430   (ut vidi, ut perii, ut me malus abstulit error!)
       non equidem ex isto speravi corpore posse

405f = *Ecl.* 8.19–20
420 gnara *Maehly*: ignara Ω
430 = *Ecl.* 8.41

while I make lament, and to the gods (though their witness has availed me naught) yet as I die, in my last hour, I raise my cry. You, ye winds and breezes, yes you, I will call to witness! And you, if you that meet me are of human stock,[40] do you behold me? I am Scylla, of blood akin to yours (by your leave let me say this, Procne!); I am she who once was daughter of mighty Nisus, she who was wooed in rivalry by Greeks of every realm, wherever the winding sea of Helle[41] embraces land. I am she, O Minos, whom by sacred compact you called wife: this you hear, even if you pay no heed. Shall I in bonds float on the waves of so vast a sea? In bonds shall I be suspended for so many days, each following each? Yet I cannot plead that I deserve a different punishment, I who with my eyes open made over my fatherland and dear home to the enemy and a pitiless tyrant. But, Minos, I thought that it would be my countrymen who would inflict this abominable treatment upon me, if some mischance first revealed our alliance, when their city walls were breached and I, cruel one, attacked their shrines with fire; and if you were victorious, I thought that the stars would sooner change their courses than I feared you would do such things to me, your captive. Now, now it is wickedness that has conquered all.[42] Did I, abandoned one, love you more than my father's realm? Did I love you? And yet it is not strange. A girl, deceived by your looks—the moment I saw you I lost my heart, and a fatal frenzy swept me away!—I did not dream that from that

[40] She is addressing the birds, which have once been human beings.   [41] I.e. the Hellespont, perhaps here standing for the whole Aegean; cf. *Culex* 33.

[42] A variation on *omnia vincit Amor* (*Eclogues* 10.19).

tale malum nasci; forma vel sidera fallas.
    "Me non deliciis commovit regia dives,
curalio fragili aut electro lacrimoso,
435   me non florentes aequali corpore nymphae,
non metus impendens potuit retinere deorum:
omnia vicit amor: quid enim non vinceret ille?
non mihi iam pingui sudabunt tempora myrrha,
pronuba nec castos accendet pinus odores,
440   non Libys Assyrio sternetur lectulus ostro—
parva queror: ne me illa quidem communis alumna
omnibus iniecta tellus tumulabit harena.
mene inter matres ancillarique mitratas
mene avias inter famularum munere fungi,
445   coniugis atque tuae, quaecumque erit illa, beatae
non licuit gravidos penso devolvere fusos?
447   at belli saltem captivam lege necasses.
454   iam tandem casus hominum, iam respice, Minos!
455   sit satis hoc, tantum solam vidisse malorum.
vel fato fuerit nobis haec debita pestis,
vel casu incerto, merita vel denique culpa;
omnia nam potius quam te fecisse putabo."
    Labitur interea resoluta ab litore classis,
460   magna repentino sinuantur lintea Coro,
flectitur in viridi remus sale, languida fessae
virginis in cursu moritur querimonia longo.
deserit angustis inclusum faucibus Isthmon,

432 fallas *Haupt*: fallar *G*: fallor *AR*: falle *H*
434 aut *Nic. Loensis*: et Ω | electro lacrimoso *Scaliger*: l. e. Ω
437 *Cf. Ecl.* 10.69
441 parva *Housman*: magna Ω
442 *Cf. Cat.* 64.153

form of yours such evil could spring; with your beauty you could beguile the stars.

"I was moved not by a palace rich in its delights, frail coral or amber tears; I was moved not by damsels of like youth and beauteous to behold; no fear of the gods with its menace could hold me back: Love conquered all: for what could Love not conquer? No more shall my temples drip with rich myrrh, nor shall the bridal pine kindle its pure fragrance, nor shall the Libyan couch be strewn with Assyrian purple. But these are slight complaints: even yonder earth, that is common to all, will not entomb me, her foster child, with sprinkling of sand! Might I not amid mothers and mitred granddames have discharged the function of a slave, and for your blessed wife, whoever she may be, have unrolled the spindles, weighted with their coils? But would that at least, by the law of war, you had killed me, your captive! Now, pray, now, O Minos, consider the misfortunes of mankind! Be it enough that I, and I alone, have looked upon so much misery! Grant that this disaster has been due to me by fate, or has come by uncertain chance, or, finally, by a guilt that deserves it: I shall believe anything sooner than that you brought it about!"

Meanwhile, casting off from the shore, the fleet glides forth; the great sails swell with the sudden Northwest, the oar bends in the green salt water; the feeble wailing of the exhausted maiden dies away in the long voyage. Behind her she leaves the Isthmus, shut in with its narrow

---

443 mitratas *Housman*: maritas *R*: marinas *GHA*
444 avias *Housman*: alias Ω
448–53 (*after* 447 Ω) *transp. after* 477 *Sudhaus*

Cypselidae et magni florentia regna, Corinthum;
465 praeterit abruptas Scironis protinus arces
infestumque suis dirae testudinis exit
spelaeum multoque cruentas hospite cautes.
iamque adeo tutum longe Piraeea cernit
et notas, eheu frustra, respectat Athenas.
470 iam procul e fluctu Salaminia respicit arva
florentisque videt iam Cycladas: hinc Venus illi
Sunias, hinc statio contra patet Hermionaea.
linquitur ante alias longe gratissima Delos
Nereidum matri et Neptuno Aegaeo;
475 prospicit incinctam spumanti litore Cythnum
marmoreamque Paron viridemque adlapsa Donysam
477 Aeginamque simul salutiferamque Seriphum.
448 iam fesso tandem fugiunt de corpore vires,
et caput inflexa lentum cervice recumbit,
450 marmorea adductis livescunt bracchia nodis.
aequoreae pristes, immania corpora ponti,
undique conveniunt et glauco in gurgite circum
453 verbere caudarum atque oris minitantur hiatu.
478 fertur et incertis iactatur ad omnia ventis,
cumba velut magnas sequitur cum parvula classis
480 Afer et hiberno bacchatur in aequore turbo,
donec tale decus formae vexarier undis
non tulit ac miseros mutavit virginis artus
caeruleo pollens coniunx Neptunia regno.
sed tamen aeternum squamis vestire puellam

472 Sunias *Leo*: sunius *G*: sinius *B*: summus *Z*
474 *Cf. Aen*. 3.74   475 *Cf. Aen*. 3.125f
448 fesso *Schrader*: fessae Ω

43 Periander.   44 The robber Sciron used to throw his vic-

neck, and the rich realm of the great son of Cypselus,[43] Corinth; forthwith she passes Sciron's steep heights, and goes beyond the dread tortoise's cave, so fatal to her fellow citizens, and the cliffs, stained with the blood of many a guest.[44] And at this very moment she sees afar secure Piraeus, and looks back—alas in vain!—upon familiar Athens. Now at a distance, rising from the flood, the fields of Salamis she espies, and now she sees the shining Cyclades: on this side the Venus of Sunium reveals itself, on that, opposite, Hermione's town.[45] Then she leaves Delos, most pleasing beyond all to the mother of the Nereids and to Aegean Neptune; in the distance she sees Cythnus, girt with foaming shore, and draws near to marble-white Paros and green Donysa, with Aegina and health-bringing Seriphus.[46] Now at last the strength flees from her weary frame, her head falls back heavy on her bended neck, her marble-white arms grow livid under the close-drawn knots. Monsters of the sea, giant forms of the deep, throng about her on all sides, and in the grey waters threaten her with lashing tails and gaping mouths. Onward she moves, tossed to and fro by uncertain winds (like a tiny skiff when it follows a great fleet, and an African hurricane riots upon the wintry sea) until Neptune's spouse,[47] queen of the azure realm, suffered it not that such a beauteous form should be harassed by the waves, and transformed the maiden's sorry limbs. But even so she decided not to clothe

---

tims to a tortoise.   [45] The poet incorrectly substitutes Venus (Aphrodite) for Athena, who had a temple on Cape Sunium. Hermione was in the Argolid.   [46] An allusion, probably, to the story of Perseus and Danaë, whose ark was washed up on the coast of Seriphus.   [47] Amphitrite.

485　infidosque inter teneram committere pisces
　　non statuit (nimium est avidum pecus Amphitrites):
　　aëriis potius sublimem sustulit alis,
　　esset ut in terris facti de nomine Ciris,
　　Ciris Amyclaeo formosior ansere Ledae.
490　　　Hic velut in niveo tenera est cum primitus ovo
　　effigies animantis et internodia membris
　　imperfecta novo fluitant concreta calore,
　　sic liquido Scyllae circumfusum aequore corpus
　　semiferi incertis etiam nunc partibus artus
495　undique mutabant atque undique mutabantur.
　　oris honos primum et multis optata labella
　　et patulae frontis species concrescere in unum
　　coepere et gracili mentum producere rostro;
　　tum, qua se medium capitis discrimen agebat,
500　ecce repente, velut patrios imitatus honores,
　　puniceam concussit apex in vertice cristam;
　　at mollis varios intexens pluma colores
　　marmoreum volucri vestivit tegmine corpus
　　lentaque perpetuas fuderunt bracchia pennas;
505　inde alias partes minioque infecta rubenti
　　crura nova macies obduxit squalida pelle
　　et pedibus teneris unguis affixit acutos.
　　et tamen hoc demum miserae succurrere pacto
　　vix fuerat placida Neptuni coniuge dignum.
510　numquam illam post haec oculi videre suorum
　　purpureas flavo retinentem vertice vittas,
　　non thalamus Syrio fragrans accepit amomo,
　　nullae illam sedes: quid enim cum sedibus illi?
　　quae simul ut sese cano de gurgite velox

[511] *Cf.* Cat. 64.63

the gentle maid with scales for ever, or place her amid treacherous fishes (all too greedy is Amphitrite's flock): rather she raised her aloft on airy wings, that she might live on earth as Ciris, named from the deed wrought[48]—Ciris, more beautiful than Leda's Amyclean swan.

Hereupon, as when at first in a snowy egg there is the soft outline of a living thing, and the limbs' imperfect junctures, as they grow together in unwonted heat, float about, yet incomplete; so with Scylla's body, encompassed by the waters of the deep, while the parts were even yet uncertain, the half-human joints were changing it throughout, and throughout were being changed. First, the lovely face and those lips yearned for by many, and the broad brow's charm, began to grow together and to prolong the chin with a slender beak. Then, where on the head the line appeared that parts the hair in equal portions, lo! of a sudden, as if copying her father's glory, on her crown a tuft waved its crimson crest, while soft plumes, blending varied hues, clothed her marble-white body with a covering of wings, and the feeble arms put forth long feathers. Then other parts and the legs, coloured with blushing crimson, a rough leanness overlaid with unfamiliar skin, and to the tender feet fastened sharp nails. And yet to succour the luckless maiden only in this manner was scarcely worthy of Neptune's gentle spouse. Never hereafter did the eyes of her kin behold her tying back her purple headbands upon her golden head; no chamber, fragrant with Syrian spice, no home welcomed her; what, indeed, had she to do with home? And as soon as from the foaming waters with speed

---

[48] Ciris derives from κείρειν, "cut" or "shear."

515   cum sonitu ad caelum stridentibus extulit alis
　　　et multum late dispersit in aequora rorem,
　　　infelix virgo nequiquam a morte recepta
　　　incultum solis in rupibus exigit aevum,
　　　rupibus et scopulis et litoribus desertis.

520   　Nec tamen hoc ipsum poena sine: namque deum rex,
　　　omnia qui imperio terrarum milia versat,
　　　commotus talem ad superos volitare puellam,
　　　cum pater exstinctus caeca sub nocte lateret,
　　　illi pro pietate sua (nam saepe nitentum

525   sanguine taurorum supplex resperserat aras,
　　　saepe deum largo decorarat munere sedes)
　　　reddidit optatam mutato corpore vitam
　　　fecitque in terris haliaeetos ales ut esset:
　　　quippe aquilis semper gaudet deus ille coruscis.

530   huic vero miserae, quoniam damnata deorum
　　　iudicio pactique ea coniugis ante fuisset,
　　　infesti apposuit odium crudele parentis.
　　　namque ut in aetherio signorum limite praestans,
　　　unum quem duplici stellarunt sidere divi,

535   Scorpios alternis clarum fugat Oriona,
　　　sic inter sese tristis haliaeetos iras
　　　et Ciris memori servant ad saecula fato.
　　　quacumque illa levem fugiens secat aethera pennis,
　　　ecce inimicus, atrox, magno stridore per auras

540   insequitur Nisus; qua se fert Nisus ad auras,
　　　illa levem fugiens raptim secat aethera pennis.

---

[524] nitentum *ed.* 1500: videmus Ω   [531] pacti (*Ellis*) que ea
Housman: namque et *B:* natique et *B*[2]
   [533] limite *Housman*: munere Ω
   [534] stellarunt . . . divi *Housman*: stellarum . . . vidi Ω

and uproar she arose to the sky on whirring wings and has scattered a cloud of spray far and wide over the sea, the wretched maid, vainly recovered from death, lives her wild life among the lonely rocks—the rocks and cliffs and deserted shores.

Yet even this drew an extra punishment: for the king of the gods, who with his power sways all regions of the world, dissatisfied that so wicked a girl should be flitting to the world above, while under dark night's cover her father's light should be extinguished, to him because of his piety (for he had oft suppliantly besprinkled the altars with the blood of sleek bulls, and oft with lavish gifts had adorned the homes of the gods) granted under changed form the life he had craved, and suffered him to be on earth a winged sea eagle, for in lightning-swift eagles that god ever delights. But upon that unhappy maid, since she had first been condemned by judgement of the gods and of her plighted husband,[49] he laid an angry father's relentless hate. For even as, foremost in the belt of heaven's constellations, the Scorpion, which alone the gods have enstarred with twofold greatness, puts to rout in alternate strife the brilliant Orion: so the sea eagle and the ciris, with ever remindful fate, maintain the fierceness of mutual wrath from age to age. Wherever she flees, cleaving the light air with her wings, lo! savage and ruthless, with loud whirr Nisus follows through the sky; where Nisus mounts skyward, she flees in haste, cleaving the light air with her wings.

[49] Minos.

538–41 = *Georg.* 1.406–9.

CATALEPTON

I

De qua saepe tibi, venit: sed, Tucca, videre
  non licet: occulitur limine clausa viri.
de qua saepe tibi, non venit adhuc mihi: namque
  si occulitur—longe est, tangere quod nequeas.
5 venerit: audivi. sed iam mihi nuntius iste
  quid prodest? illi dicite cui rediit.

II

Corinthiorum amator iste verborum,
  iste, iste rhetor, namque quatenus totus
Thucydides, tyrannus Atticae febris,
  tau Gallicum, min et sphin ut male illisit,
5 ita omnia ista verba miscuit fratri.

mss: Ω = BZ   I meter: elegiac   6 cui *Heyne*: qui B:
quae Z   II mss = BZ, *codd. Quint.*   meter: choliambic
  4 ut *Wagner*: et Ω

---

[1] Marcus Plotius Tucca is meant, doubtless, to connect the
poem with Virgil; "she" is possibly Plotia Hiereia (*Vit. Don.* 9).

[2] This enigmatic epigram attacks Titus Annius Cimber, a rhet-

484

CATALEPTON

I

She, of whom I have often told you, has come; but, Tucca,[1] one is not allowed to see her. She's kept in hiding, locked inside her husband's door. She, of whom I have often told you, has not yet come, so far as concerns me; for if she's kept in hiding—what you can't touch is miles away. Suppose she has come; so I have heard. but what good is that news to me? Tell it to him for whom she has returned.

II

It's[2] Corinthian[3] words[4] the fellow adores, that sorry rhetorician! For, perfect Thucydides that he is, he is lord of the Attic fever; as he has wickedly pounded up his Gallic *tau*, his *min* and *sphin*, so of all such spells he has mixed a brew for his brother.

orician who affected the style of Thucydides and is said to have murdered his brother (cf. Quintilian 8.3.28 and see Cicero, *Philippics* 11.6.14). Like Quintilian, Ausonius (*Technopaegnion* 15.5 Green) ascribes the piece to Virgil.

[3] Outlandish, exotic.

[4] In this poem *verba* means not only "words" but "spells."

III

Aspice quem valido subnixum Gloria regno
    altius et caeli sedibus extulerat:
terrarum hic bello magnum concusserat orbem,
    hic reges Asiae fregerat, hic populos;
5 hic grave servitium tibi, iam tibi, Roma, ferebat
    (cetera namque viri cuspide conciderant),
cum subito in medio rerum certamine praeceps
    corruit, e patria pulsus in exilium.
tale deae numen: tali mortalia nutu
10   fallax momento temporis hora dedit.

IV

Quocumque ire ferunt variae nos tempora vitae,
    tangere quas terras, quosque videre homines,
dispeream, si te fuerit mihi carior alter
    (alter enim quis te dulcior esse potest?),
5 cui iuveni ante alios divi divumque sorores
    cuncta, neque indigno, Musa, dedere bona,
cuncta quibus gaudet Phoebi chorus ipseque Phoebus;
    doctior o quis te, Musa, fuisse potest?
o quis te in terris loquitur iucundior uno?
10   Clio tam grate candida non loquitur.
quare illud satis est, si te permittis amari:
    nam contra, ut sit amor mutuus, unde mihi?

III meter: elegiac   8 e *AR*: et *BH*   IV meter: elegiac

---

[5] The piece is written as an inscription to a portrait or monument of a famous soldier who in a bid for supreme power was sud-

III

Behold[5] one whom, upborne on mighty authority, Glory had exalted even above the abodes of heaven! Earth's great orb had he shaken in war; Asia's kings and peoples had he crushed; now upon you, even you, Rome, was he bringing grievous slavery, when suddenly, in the midst of his bid for power, he fell headlong, driven from fatherland into exile. Such is the will of Fortune; with such a stroke, in a moment of time, has the deceitful hour dealt out the destiny of mortals.

IV

Wherever the seasons of our varied lives lead us to go, whatever lands to visit, whatever people to see, I'll be damned if anyone else can be more precious to me than you! For who can be dearer than you, O Musa,[6] upon whom in your youth beyond others—and not unworthily— the gods and sisters of the gods[7] have bestowed all blessings, all wherein the choir of Phoebus and Phoebus himself rejoice? O who can have been more skilled than you, O Musa? O who else in all the world speaks with more charm than you? Bright Clio speaks not so charmingly. Therefore it is enough if you allow yourself to be loved; for otherwise, how may I cause that love to be returned?

denly destroyed. Several candidates for identification have been proposed but the only one possible is Pompey the Great.

[6] Octavius Musa, poet and friend of Virgil and Horace (*Sermones* 1.10.82), who is also commemorated in *Catalepton* 11.

[7] I.e. gods and goddesses.

V

Ite hinc, inanes, ite, rhetorum ampullae,
inflata rhoezo non Achaico verba;
et vos, Selique Tarquitique Varroque,
scholasticorum natio madens pingui,
5   ite hinc, inane cymbalon iuventutis;
tuque, o mearum cura, Sexte, curarum,
vale, Sabine; iam valete, formosi.
    Nos ad beatos vela mittimus portus
magni petentes docta dicta Sironis,
10   vitamque ab omni vindicabimus cura.
ite hinc, Camenae, vos quoque ite iam sane,
dulces Camenae (nam fatebimur verum,
dulces fuistis), et tamen meas chartas
revisitote, sed pudenter et raro.

VI

Socer, beate nec tibi nec alteri,
generque Noctuine, putidum caput,
tuone nunc puella talis et tuo
stupore pressa rus abibit? ei mihi,

V meter: choliambic
2 rhoezo (= ῥοίζῳ) *Münscher*: r(h)oso *BH*: *om. AR*
VI meter: pure iambic
3 tuone *Scaliger*: tuoque Ω
4 ei *Haupt*: et Ω

---

8 The poem purports to have been written when Virgil was
giving up his early rhetorical studies in Rome and preparing to

V

Away[8] with you, begone, you empty paint pots of rhetoricians, verbiage inflated with an un-Attic screeching! And you, too, Selius, and Tarquitius, and Varro,[9] a tribe of pedants dripping with fat, begone, you empty cymbals of our youth! Even you, Sextus Sabinus, heart of my heart, farewell! Now fare ye well, my lovely chums!

We are spreading sail for blissful havens, in quest of noble Siro's learned lore, and will free our life from all worries. Away with you, ye Muses! Yes, away even with you, sweet Muses! For let us confess the truth—you have been sweet. Yet even so, revisit my pages, but come modestly[10] and not too often!

VI

O[11] sire-in-law, no blessed good to yourself or the other chap,[12] and son-in-law Noctuinus, you addlepate, must such a fine girl, violated by each of you in drunken stupor, go off to the country?[13] Oh dear! How perfectly that

take up philosophy at Parthenope, a suburb of Naples, under Siro the Epicurean.

[9] The proper names in this paragraph defy precise identification; if Varro (b. 116) is indeed the great Marcus Terentius, the reference will be to his books and fame rather than to a personal relationship.

[10] I.e. inspire me with only virtuous poetry.

[11] The poem is a pendant to *Catalepton* 12, where we learn that the father-in-law's name is Atilius.

[12] Noctuinus.

[13] To conceal the scandal.

5   ut ille versus usquequaque pertinet:
        "gener socerque, perdidistis omnia."

VII

Si licet, hoc sine fraude, Vari dulcissime, dicam:
   "dispeream, nisi me perdidit iste Pothos";
sin autem praecepta vetant me dicere, sane
   non dicam, sed: "me perdidit iste puer."

VIII

Villula, quae Sironis eras, et pauper agelle—
   verum illi domino tu quoque divitiae—
me tibi, et hos una mecum, quos semper amavi,
   si quid de patria tristius audiero,
5 commendo, in primisque patrem. tu nunc eris illi
   Mantua quod fuerat quodque Cremona prius.

IX

Pauca mihi, niveo sed non incognita Phoebo,

VII meter: elegiac   ¹ si licet ς: scilicet Ω
² Pothos *Birt* (πόθος *Spiro*): pot(h)us Ω
VIII meter: elegiac   IX meter: elegiac

---

¹⁴ = Catullus 29.24 (of Caesar and Pompey).

¹⁵ The epigram is written in the persona of Virgil and addressed to his friend Varius, who is represented as objecting to the excessive use of Greek words in Latin verse. Pothos (πόθος, *cupido*, desire) was the name of a handsome young slave of Varius who had set the poet's heart on fire. To meet the imagined objec-

verse applies: "Son-in-law and sire-in-law, you have ruined everything!"[14]

VII

If[15] I may, dear Varius, I shall frankly say: "Damn me, but that Pothos of yours has been the death of me!" Yet if the rules forbid me thus to say, of course I shan't, but "that lad of yours has been the death of me."

VIII

O little villa, once Siro's, and you, poor little farm—yet to such an owner you were wealth—to you, should I hear aught ill of my homeland, I entrust myself and with me these folk, whom I have always loved, my father foremost.[16] You must now be to him what Mantua had been, and ere that Cremona.

IX

A[17] few words, few but not unknown to shining Phoebus,

tion that Pothos is a Greek common noun, the tame but Latin *puer* is substituted. [16] Virgil's father was now blind (Suetonius, *Vita* 14). [17] An extravagant encomium of Marcus Valerius Messalla Corvinus (64 B.C.–A.D. 8), soldier, statesman, and man of letters, patron of Tibullus; originally a Republican, he joined Antony after the defeat at Philippi; disillusioned with him, he went over to Octavian, with whom in 31 he shared the consulship and took part in the battle of Actium; as proconsul he subjugated the Aquitani, for which he was awarded a triumph.

    pauca mihi, doctae, dicite, Pegasides.
victor adest, magni magnum decus ecce triumphi,
    victor, qua terrae quaque patent maria,
5 horrida barbaricae portans insignia pugnae,
    magnus ut Oenides, utque superbus Eryx,
nec minus idcirco vestros expromere cantus
    maximus, et sanctos dignus inire choros.
hoc itaque insuetis iactor magis, optime, curis,
10 quid de te possim scribere, quidve tibi;
namque (fatebor enim) quae maxima deterrendi
    debuit, hortandi maxima causa fuit.

Pauca tua in nostras venerunt carmina chartas,
    carmina cum lingua, tum sale, Cecropia,
15 carmina, quae Phrygium, saeclis accepta futuris,
    carmina, quae Pylium vincere digna senem.
molliter hic viridi patulae sub tegmine quercus
    Moeris pastores et Meliboeus erant,
dulcia iactantes alterno carmina versu,
20 qualia Trinacriae doctus amat iuvenis.
certatim ornabant omnes heroida divi,
    certatim divae munere quoque suo.

Felicem ante alias o te scriptore puellam:
    altera non fama dixerit esse prior—
25 non illa, Hesperidum ni munere capta fuisset,
    quae volucrem cursu vicerat Hippomenen;

14 Cecropia *Wernsdorf*: -io Ω
15 *om. BHM*: Phrygium *Heinsius*: pilium *AR*
21 divi *Dousa pater*: divae Ω

impart to me, ye learned Muses! A conqueror has come—
lo! the mighty glory of a mighty triumph—conqueror he,
wherever lies land and sea, bearing grim spoils of bar-
baric strife, the equal of Oeneus' mighty son,[18] or of proud
Eryx;[19] nor less on that account most mighty in inspiring
your songs and worthy to enter your holy choirs. There-
fore, O noblest of men, I am perplexed all the more by un-
wonted cares, unsure what about you or what for your
fame it is in my power to pen. For (I freely admit it) what
ought to have been the chief deterrent has proved the
strongest incentive.

Few of your poems, songs of Attic speech and wit, appear
in my writings, songs to charm future ages and worthy to
outlive the aged Phrygian and the old man of Pylos.[20] Here
under the green canopy of a spreading oak were the shep-
herds Moeris and Meliboeus[21] at their ease, throwing off in
amoebean verse sweet songs such as the learned young
Sicilian[22] loves. In rivalry all the gods and in rivalry all the
goddesses graced your heroine[23] with their several gifts.

O maiden happy beyond others, having you to record her
charms! No other girl may claim to excel her in fame: not
she[24] who, had she not been tricked by the Hesperides'
gift, had outrun fleet Hippomenes in the race; not the fair

---

[18] Diomedes. [19] An ancient king of Sicily, to whom as to a
hero Aeneas makes sacrifice (*Aeneid* 5.392ff., 772ff.). [20] I.e.
to be remembered longer than Priam or Nestor. [21] A clear
reference to *Eclogues* 1 and 9. [22] Theocritus. [23] The
prima donna of Messalla's poetry, as Cynthia was of Propertius'.

[24] Atalanta.

candida cycneo non edita Tyndaris ovo;
    non supero fulgens Cassiopea polo;
non defensa diu multo certamine equorum,
30   optabant gravidae quam sibi quaeque manus,
saepe animam generi pro qua pater impius hausit,
    saepe rubro pro qua sanguine fluxit humus;
regia non Semele, non Inachis Acrisione,
    immiti expertae fulmine et imbre Iovem;
35   non cŭiŭs ob raptum pulsi liquere penates
    Tarquinii patrios filius atque pater,
illo quo primum dominatus Roma superbos
    mutavit placidis tempore consulibus.

Multa, neque immeritis, donavit praemia alumnis,
40   praemia Messallis maxima Publicolis.
nam quid ego immensi memorem studia ista laboris?
    horrida quid durae tempora militiae?
castra foro, te castra urbi praeponere, castra
    tam procul hoc gnato, tam procul hac patria?
45   immoderata pati iam frigora iamque calores?
    sternere vel dura posse super silice?
saepe trucem adverso perlabi sidere pontum?
    saepe mare audendo vincere, saepe hiemem?

---

29 multo *Némethy*: -um Ω   30 quam *Pomponius Laetus*:
quod Ω   32 pro qua *Sabbadini*: similis Ω (< 33 Semele)
34 immiti *BAR*: immitti *H*   43 te castra *Bücheler*: castra *B*:
solitos *Z*   45 frigora ς: sidera Ω

---

25 Helen.   26 Hippodamia, daughter of Oenomaus.
27 Jove appeared to Semele in the form of lightning, to Danaë,
daughter of Acrisius of Argos, in the form of a shower of gold.

daughter of Tyndareus, born of the swan's egg;[25] not Cassiopea, shining in the heavens above; not she,[26] close-guarded long by the contest of steeds, whom each gift-laden hand craved for its own, for whom her wicked father oft drained the life of him who aspired to be his son, for whom the ground oft flowed with blood incarnadine; not queenly Semele, not the Inachian daughter of Acrisius,[27] they who discovered Jove in the pitiless lightning and in the shower of gold; nor she[28] for whose ravishing the Tarquins, father and son, were driven forth, leaving their fathers' gods, when Rome first changed proud tyranny for peaceful consuls.

Many, and not unearned, are the rewards Rome has bestowed upon her sons, chiefest the rewards bestowed upon Messallas and Publicolas.[29] For why should I recount your tasks of immeasurable toil? Why your grim campaigns of ruthless warfare? How you set the camp before the forum, the camp before the city—the camp that is so far away from this your son, so far from this your home? How you can endure now the extremes of cold, and now the extremes of heat, and can lie down upon flinty rock? How often, under an inclement sky, you glide over the savage deep? How often in your daring you conquer the sea, and

[28] Lucretia.

[29] Publicola (originally Popli-) was a cognomen bestowed upon Publius Valerius, one of the first consuls (Broughton, *Magistrates of the Roman Republic* I p. 2), for his part in popular legislation, and was frequently borne by members of the gens Valeria; but no Valerius ever called himself Messalla Publicola (cf. Pliny, *Natural History* 35.8).

saepe etiam densos immittere corpus in hostes?
50   communem belli non meminisse deum?
nunc celeris Afros, periurae milia gentis,
    aurea nunc rapidi flumina adire Tagi?
nunc aliam ex alia bellando quaerere gentem,
    vincere et Oceani finibus ulterius?

55 Non nostrum est tantas, non, inquam, attingere laudes;
    quin ausim hoc etiam dicere: vix hominum est.
ipsa haec, ipsa ferent rerum monumenta per orbem,
    ipsa sibi egregium facta decus parient;
nos ea quae tecum finxerunt carmina divi,
60   Cynthius et Musae, Bacchus et Aglaie,
si laudi aspirare humili, si adire Cyrenas,
    si patrio Graios carmine adire sales
possumus, optatis plus iam procedimus ipsis.
    hoc satis est: pingui nil mihi cum populo.

X

Sabinus ille, quem videtis, hospites,
ait fuisse mulio celerrimus,
neque ullius volantis impetum cisi
nequisse praeterire, sive Mantuam

61 laudi . . . humili *Sabbadini*: -em . . . -is Ω
X meter: pure iambic

---

30 One of the Graces.
31 The home of Callimachus.
32 A witty parody of Catullus 4, which tells of a wooden model of the yacht that brought the poet home from Bithynia. In

often the storm? And how often you charge upon the serried host, heedless of the common god of war? How you advance upon now the nimble Africans, the swarms of a perjured race, now the gold-bearing waters of the swift Tagus? How in warfare you confront nation after nation, and achieve conquests even beyond Ocean's bounds?

It is not, it is not, I say, for us to attain to such glory; indeed, I should venture to say even this: it is scarcely possible for mortal man. Even of themselves these exploits shall carry their record through the world; of themselves they shall beget their own illustrious renown. As for me, touching those songs which the gods have fashioned in concert with you, even Apollo and the Muses, Bacchus and Aglaia,[30] if we can aspire to modest praise, to approach Cyrene,[31] to approach the wit of Greece in a Roman song, I now advance even beyond my hopes. This is enough: with the stupid rabble I have naught to do.

X

Sabinus[32] yonder, whom you see, my friends, says that he was the fastest of muleteers and never failed to outstrip the speed of any gig on the road, whether he had to race to

Catalepton 10 the model has become one of a muleteer seated in a curule chair: originally named Quinctio he changed his cognomen to Sabinus and in a meteoric career rose to the praetorship. For centuries Sabinus has been identified with Publius Ventidius Bassus (Gellius 15.4), but this is convincingly rejected by Syme (*Latomus* 17 [1958] 73–80 = *RP* I 393ff.), who plausibly suggests another "new man," Gaius Calvisius Sabinus (*PIR*[2] C 352).

5   opus foret volare, sive Brixiam.
       et hoc negat Tryphonis aemuli domum
       negare nobilem insulamve Ceryli,
       ubi iste, post Sabinus, ante Quinctio,
       bidente dicit attodisse forcipe
10   comata colla, ne Cytorio iugo
       premente dura vulnus ederet iuba.

       Cremona frigida, et lutosa Gallia,
       tibi haec fuisse et esse cognitissima,
       ait Sabinus; ultima ex origine
15   tua stetisse dicit in voragine,
       tua in palude deposisse sarcinas,
       et inde tot per orbitosa milia
       iugum tulisse, laeva sive dextera
       strigare mula sive utrumque coeperat
19b   ⟨pecus recalcitrare ferreo pede,⟩
20   neque ulla vota semitalibus deis
       sibi esse facta praeter hoc novissimum:
       paterna lora buxinumque pectinem.

       Sed haec prius fuere: nunc eburnea
       sedetque sede seque dedicat tibi,
25   gemelle Castor, et gemelle Castoris.

XI

"Quis deus, Octavi, te nobis abstulit? an quae
dicunt, a, nimio pocula ducta mero?"

16 deposisse *Scaliger*: deposuisse Ω   19b *lacuna Itali, il-*
lustrative suppl. Birt   22 buxinumque *Salmasius*: proximum-
que Ω   XI meter: elegiac   2 ducta *Heinsius*: dura Ω

Mantua or to Brixia. And this he says is not gainsaid by
the noble house of his rival, Trypho, or the lodging-rooms
of Cerylus,[33] where he, Sabinus-to-be, but before that
Quinctio, tells that with two-bladed shears he once clipped
hairy necks, lest, under the pressure of Cytorian yoke, the
harsh mane might cause some soreness.

O cold Cremona and muddy Gaul, Sabinus says that this
was and is well known to you; he says that from his earliest
origin he stood in your mire, in your marsh unloaded his
packs, and thence over so many miles of rutty roads bore
the yoke, whether the mule on left or on right began to flag
or both ⟨beasts to stamp their iron-shod feet in defiance⟩
and that no offerings to the gods of the byways were made
by him save this at the last—his father's reins and boxwood
currycomb.

But these things belong to the past: now he sits in his ivory
chair and dedicates himself to you, twin Castor and Cas-
tor's twin.

XI

"What[34] god, Octavius, has taken you from us? Or was it, as
they say, cups of potent wine, that you, alas, did quaff?"

---

[33] Presumably Trypho and Cerylus were Sabinus' rivals in the
trade.

[34] Written in dialogue, and in the form of an epitaph, the sub-
ject of which is the Octavius Musa of *Catalepton* 4. Octavius, it
would seem, has been "dead drunk," and so is humorously treated
as if he had died. He is a "son of Bacchus," and Bacchus (i.e. the
wine) had died (was all consumed) before the son. The first four
verses recall an epigram of Callimachus (61 Pf. = *A.P.* 7.725).

"vobiscum, si est culpa, bibi: sua quemque sequuntur
    fata: quid immeriti crimen habent cyathi?"
5 "scripta quidem tua nos multum mirabimur: et te
    raptum et Romanam flebimus historiam.
sed tu nullus eris." perversi, dicite, Manes,
    hunc superesse patri quae fuit invidia?

XII

    Superbe Noctuine, putidum caput,
    datur tibi puella quam petis, datur;
    datur, superbe Noctuine, quam petis.

    Sed, o superbe Noctuine, non vides
5   duas habere filias Atilium?
    duas, et hanc et alteram, tibi dari?

    Adeste nunc, adeste: ducit, ut decet,
    superbus ecce Noctuinus hirneam.
    Thalassio, Thalassio, Thalassio!

XIII

Iacere me, quod alta non possim, putas,
    ut ante, vectari freta,
nec ferre durum frigus aut aestum pati,
    neque arma victoris sequi?

    XII meter: pure iambic
    XIII meter: iambic epodic (trimeter + dimeter)

"With you I drank, if that's a fault. Everyone is pursued by his destiny. Why should the guiltless cups be blamed?"

"We shall much admire your writings and regret that you and your Roman history are lost to us. But still, you yourself shall be no more!" Tell us, ye Spirits perverse, why did ye grudge that he should outlive his father?

XII

Proud Noctuinus,[35] you addlepate, the girl you seek is given you, I say; the girl you seek, proud Noctuinus, is given you.

But don't you see, proud Noctuinus, that Atilius has two daughters, and that two, this and the other, are given you?

Come hither, people, come hither now! Behold, proud Noctuinus weds, as is fitting—a wine jug! Thalassio, Thalassio, Thalassio![36]

XIII

Do you think that I am helpless, because I cannot, as once I could, sail the deep seas or bear the bitter cold or endure summer heat or follow the victor's standard?

[35] See also *Catalepton* 6. Noctuinus is drunk at his wedding; his father-in-law is likewise a toper, and is humorously said to have two daughters, one a wine jug, whom Noctuinus also marries.

[36] Brides had been greeted with this salutation ever since the days of Romulus.

5   Valent, valent mihi ira et antiquus furor
      et lingua qua adsultem tibi,
    seu prostitutae turpe contubernium
      sororis (o quid me incitas,
    quid, impudice et improbande Caesari?),
10   seu furta dicantur tua,
    et helluato sera patrimonio
      in fratre parsimonia,
    vel acta puero cum viris convivia,
      udaeque per somnum nates,
15   et inscio repente clamatum insuper
      "Thalassio, Thalassio."

    Quid palluisti, femina? an ioci dolent?
      an facta cognoscis tua?
    non me vocabis, pulchra, per Cotytia
20   ad feriatos fascinos;
    nec deinde te movere lumbos in stola
      prensis videbo altaribus,
    flavumque propter Thybrim olentis nauticum
      vocare, ubi adpulsae rates
25   caeno retentae sordido stant in vadis
      macraque luctantes aqua;
    neque in culinam et uncta compitalia
      dapesque duces sordidas,
    quibus repletus et salivosis labris
30   obesam ad uxorem redis,
    et aestuantes nocte solvis pantices,
      osusque lambis saviis.

6 adsultem *Ribbeck*: assim *B*: adsim Z
7 seu *Sabbadini*: et Ω

Strong, strong are my wrath and oldtime fury, and my tongue, wherewith to attack you, whether your prostituted sister's vile life within your tent be told—O why do you spur me on, oh why, you shameless one, worthy of Caesar's anger?—or whether your secret crimes be told: your thrift in a late hour at a brother's cost, when your patrimony had been squandered; or the banquets you shared in boyhood with men, your buttocks wet throughout the night, and, over and above, the cry "Thalassio, Thalassio" raised on a sudden by one I know not who.

Why have you turned pale, you pathic?[37] Does jesting hurt you? Or do you recognize your sins? You will not, pretty one, invite me to the phallic merrymaking at the feast of Cotyto,[38] nor shall I see you, with your hands grasping the altar, bestir your loins beneath your woman's robe and, hard by the yellow Tiber, call to the boat-smelling throng, where ships that have reached port stand fast in the shallows, held back by the filthy mud and struggling against the scanty water; nor will you lead me to the kitchen or the greasy crossroads' feast and its mean fare, sated with which and with slobbering lips you go home to your huge wife, to satisfy her passionate desires through the night and, though hating her, smother her with lickings.

37 Literally "woman!"
38 A Thracian goddess of licentiousness.

21 stola *Bücheler*: ratulam *B*: rotulam *Z*
25 stant in vadis caeno retentae sordido Ω, *corr. L. Müller*
29 et *Scriverius*: ut Ω | labris *Haupt*: aquis Ω
31 nocte *Scaliger*: docte *BR*: dote *HA*

Nunc laede, nunc lacesse, si quidquam vales!
　et nomen adscribo tuum,
35　cinaede Lucci. iamne liquerunt opes,
　fameque genuini crepant?
videbo habentem praeter ignavos nihil
　fratres et iratum Iovem
scissumque ventrem et hirneosi patrui
40　pedes inedia turgidos.

XIIIA

Callida imago sub hac (caeli est iniuria!) sede
　antiquis, hospes, non minor ingeniis,
et quo Roma viro doctis certaret Athenis;
　ferrea sed nulli vincere fata datur.

XIV

Si mihi susceptum fuerit decurrere munus,
　o Paphon, o sedes quae colis Idalias,
Troïus Aeneas Romana per oppida digno
　iam tandem ut tecum carmine vectus eat:
5　non ego ture modo aut picta tua templa tabella
　ornabo, et puris serta feram manibus:
corniger hos aries tum dis et maxima taurus
　victima sacrato sparget honore focos,

XIIIA *Verses found only in Z, and there a patent insertion after*
13.16　　meter: elegiac
　1 callida imago *Birt*: callide mage Z | sede *Birt*: secli Z
　XIV meter: elegiac　　　7 tum dis *O. Skutsch*: humilis Ω
　8 sacrato *D. Heinsius*: sacratos Ω

Now attack me, now provoke me, if you can at all! I shall reveal even your name, filthy Luccius. Has your wealth now vanished, and do your back teeth rattle with hunger? I shall yet see you possessed of nothing but worthless brothers and Jove's wrath, split bowels and your ruptured uncle's feet swollen with fasting.

XIIIA

Beneath[39] *this spot, passer-by, lies a scholar's shade—a wrong done by heaven—a man not inferior to the great minds of old, and one with whom Rome could challenge learned Athens: but to none is it given to vanquish iron Fate.*

XIV

If[40] it be granted me to complete the charge I have undertaken, O Lady of Paphos and Idalian groves,[41] and the day shall come at last when, borne with you in worthy song, Trojan Aeneas shall travel through Roman towns: not with incense alone or a painted portrait shall I adorn your temple: then in honour of the gods shall a horned ram and a bull, noblest victim, sprinkle these altars with blood of

[39] Perhaps a humanist's tribute to a fellow scholar who died prematurely, which was then copied into the margin of Z; it can hardly refer to Virgil.   [40] The poem purports to be written by Virgil when he has begun the *Aeneid* and is doubtful whether he will finish it; the last verse implies him to be living in Naples, and "Caesar" must therefore mean Augustus.

[41] Venus.

marmoreusque tibi tum mille coloribus ales
10   in morem picta stabit Amor pharetra.
adsis o Cytherea: tuus te Caesar Olympo
    et Surrentini litoris ara vocat.

XV

Vate Syracosio qui dulcior, Hesiodoque
    maior, Homereo non minor ore fuit,
illius haec quoque sunt divini elementa poetae,
    et rudis in vario carmine Calliope.

9 tum *O. Skutsch*: aut Ω
XV *In the manuscripts these two elegiac couplets follow without a break on 14.12 as if part of the same poem, but are clearly a later editorial addition, designed to assert the young Virgil's authorship of the* Catalepton.

sacrifice; then in your honour shall a marble Love be set up, his quiver painted, as is wont, with iridescent wings of countless hues. Vouchsafe your aid, Cytherea: your Caesar and the altar on Sorrento's shore summon you from Olympus.

XV

To[42] that divine poet who was sweeter than the bard of Syracuse,[43] greater than Hesiod, and not inferior in his diction to Homer—to him also belong these first efforts, even his untutored Muse in various meters.

[42] An editorial epilogue by the collector of the *Catalepton*.
[43] Theocritus.

PRIAPEA

(84 Bücheler)   I

Vere rosa, autumno pomis, aestate frequentor
    spicis: una mihi est horrida pestis hiems;
nam frigus metuo et vereor, ne ligneus ignem
    hic deus ignavis praebeat agricolis.

(85 Bücheler)   II

        Ego haec, ego arte fabricata rustica,
        ego arida, o viator, ecce populus,
        agellulum hunc, sinistra et ante quem vides,
        erique villulam hortulumque pauperis
5   tuor, malaque furis arceo manu.

        Mihi corolla picta vere ponitur,
        mihi rubens arista sole fervido,
        mihi virente dulcis uva pampino,
        mihi gelante oliva cocta frigore.
10   meis capella delicata pascuis
        in urbem adulta lacte portat ubera,

I mss: Ω = *BZ*; meter = elegiac   4 ignavis *Voss*: ignaris Ω
II mss: Ω = *BZ*; meter = pure iambics
9 gelante *Richmond*: glauca Ω

508

PRIAPEA

I

In spring I[1] am covered with roses, in autumn with fruits, in summer with ears of corn: winter alone is to me a horrid time. For I dread the cold, and fear that your god of wood may be used for fuel by rude yokels.

II

I here, O wayfarer, I, made from dry poplar wood with rustic skill, 'tis I that guard this little field you see in front and to the left, with the poor owner's cottage and small garden, I that shield them from the thief's wicked hand.

On me in spring is placed a garland gay; on me in the scorching sun the ruddy corn; on me the luscious grapes with tendrils green; on me the olive hardened by the freezing cold. From my pastures the dainty she-goat bears to town her udders swollen with milk; from my folds comes

---

[1] In the first three poems Priapus himself is the speaker.

meisque pinguis agnus ex ovilibus
gravem domum remittit aere dexteram,
tenerque matre mugiente buculus
15   deum profundit ante templa sanguinem.

Proin, viator, hunc deum vereberis
manumque sursum habebis. hoc tibi expedit;
parata namque trux stat ecce mentula.
"velim pol" inquis? at pol ecce vilicus
20   venit, valente cui revulsa bracchio
fit ista mentula apta clava dexterae.

(86 Bücheler)   III

Hunc ego, o iuvenes, locum
    villulamque palustrem
tectam vimine iunceo
    caricisque maniplis,
quercus arida rustica
    fomitata securi
nutrior: magis et magis
    fit beata quotannis.
5   huius nam domini colunt
    me, deumque salutant
pauperis tuguri pater
    filiusque adulescens,
alter assidua cavens
    diligentia, ut herbae,
aspera ut rubus a meo
    sit remota sacello,
alter parva manu ferens
    saepe munera larga.

the fatted lamb to send home again the money-laden hand; and a young calf, amid its mother's lowing, pours forth its blood before the temples of the gods.

Therefore, O wayfarer, you must revere this god and keep your hands to yourself; this is for your own good; for see! a menacing prick stands ready for you. "By Pollux, I'd like—" you say, but see! by Pollux, here comes the farmer, whose stout arm has snatched up that prick and finds it a cudgel, well fitted to his grasp.

III

This place and cottage in the marsh, my young friends, thatched with osier shoots and handfuls of sedge, I support, I a dried oak chipped into shape by a farmer's axe; year by year, richer and richer it grows. For the owners of this poor hut, a father and his teenage son, honour me and greet me as a god; the one with constant attention ensures that weeds and rough brambles are removed from my shrine, the other frequently brings me humble gifts with lavish hand.

---

14 teneraque . . . vaccula Ω, *corr. Haupt*

18 trux *Voss*: crux Ω

III mss: Ω = *BZ*; meter = priapean

3 fomitata *Voss*: formi- Ω

7 cavens *L. Müller*: colens Ω

9 saepe *Schrader*: semper Ω

10   Florido mihi ponitur
          picta vere corolla,
      primitus tenera virens
          spica mollis arista,
      luteae violae mihi
          lacteumque papaver
      pallentesque cucurbitae et
          suave olentia mala,
      uva pampinea rubens
          educata sub umbra;
15   sanguine haec etiam mihi
          (sed tacebitis) arma
      barbatus linit hirculus
          cornipesque capella.
      pro quîs omnia honoribus
          nunc necesse Priapo est
      praestare, et domini hortulum
          vineamque tueri.

      Quare hinc, o pueri, malas
          abstinete rapinas:
20   vicinus prope dives est
          neglegensque Priapi.
      inde sumite: semita haec
          deinde vos feret ipsa.

(83 Bücheler)   IV

      Quid hoc novi est? quid ira nuntiat deum?
      silente nocte candidus mihi puer
      tepente cum iaceret abditus sinu,
      Venus fuit quieta, nec viriliter

On me in flowery spring is placed a garland gay; on me the
soft ear of corn, when first it is green on the tender stalk, as
well as yellow violets and milky poppy, pale melons and
sweet-smelling apples, and blushing grape clusters, reared
beneath the vine leaves' shade. This weaponry of mine—
but be quiet about this!—a little bearded goat and his
horn-footed sister besmear with their blood. For these of-
ferings Priapus is obliged to render full service by guard-
ing the owner's orchard and vineyard.

So, boys, begone and steal nothing here. Nearby lives a
wealthy neighbour, who shows no respect for his Priapus.
Take from him; this very path will lead you to his place.

IV

What's this about? What means the gods' displeasure? In
the depths of night a beautiful boy lay cuddled in my warm
embrace; but all passion was dead, and betraying its man-

IV mss: Ω = *FGB*; meter = pure iambics

5   iners senile penis extulit caput.

       Placet, Priape, qui sub arboris coma
       soles, sacrum revincte pampino caput,
       ruber sedere cum rubente fascino?
       at, o Triphalle, saepe floribus novis
10   tuas sine arte deligavimus comas,
       abegimusque voce saepe, cum tibi
       senexve corvus impigerve graculus
       sacrum feriret ore corneo caput.
       vale, nefande destitutor inguinum,
15   vale, Priape: debeo tibi nihil.
       iacebis inter arva pallidus situ,
       canisque saeva susque ligneo tibi
       lutosus affricabit oblitum latus.

       At, o sceleste penis, o meum malum,
20   gravi piaque lege noxiam lues.
       licet querare: nec tibi tener puer
       patebit ullus, in tremente qui toro
       iuvante verset arte mobilem natem,
       puella nec iocosa te levi manu
25   fovebit, apprimetve lucidum femur.
       bidens amica Romuli senis memor
       paratur, inter atra cuius inguina
       latet iacente pantice abditus specus
       vagaque pelle tectus, algido gelu
30   araneosus obsidet forem situs.
       tibi haec paratur, ut tuum ter aut quater

     [22] in tremente *Tränkle* (*Heinsius*): imminente *FB*: i . . .
nente *G*

hood my sluggish penis failed to raise its drooping head.

O Priapus, whose favourite place is beneath the tree's foliage, your sacred head garlanded with vine leaves, are you satisfied to sit painted red and your prick red too? Yet we, great phallic god, have oft artlessly bound your hair with fresh flowers, and oft have our shouts frightened away an aged crow or persistent jackdaw who would with horny beak peck at your sacred head. Farewell, you wicked deserter of my genitals! Farewell, Priapus, I owe you nothing. You will be thrown out in the fields, and through neglect you will lose your colour; savage dogs and filthy swine will rub and befoul your wooden skin.

As for you, you accursed cock who are my disgrace, you will be punished according to the severe and rightful terms of law. Well may you weep. No pretty boy will oblige you, and skilfully squeeze his wriggling buttocks on you nor any playful girl encourage you with dainty hand, pressing her lovely thighs against you. Rather there lies ready for you a toothless crone looking like a jade of old Romulus: within her black-haired slit lies a cavern hidden by an overhanging paunch, and, below the flabby skin, a putrid cobweb with its freezing cold blocks entry.[2] Such a drab is waiting for her deep crevice to swallow up thrice or four times your

[2] The precise meaning of this sentence is unclear.

29 vagaque *Scaliger*: vacuaque Ω | algido *Tränkle*: annuo *F*: inguinum *B*: *G missing*

voret profunda fossa lubricum caput.
licebit aeger, angue lentior, cubes,
tereris usque donec, a, miser, miser
35   triplexque quadruplexque compleas specum.
superbia ista proderit nihil, simul
vagum sonante merseris luto caput.

Quid est, iners? pigetne lentitudinis?
licebit hoc inultus auferas semel:
40   sed ille cum redibit aureus puer,
simul sonante senseris iter pede,
rigente nervus excubet libidine,
et inquietus inguina arrigat tumor,
neque incitare cesset, usque dum mihi
45   Venus iocosa molle ruperit latus.

slippery cock. Though you lie indisposed, more sluggish than a snake, she will rub you up, poor devil, until your penis, grown to three or four times its size, is large enough to fill her cavity. Nor will indifference come to your aid, once you have dipped your inconstant prick into that gurgling sink.

What's the matter, lazybones? Aren't you ashamed of your sloth? You may get away with it this time, but when your charming boyfriend returns, as soon as you hear his foot-steps on the way, may your manhood awake with rigid lust and an eager swelling harden the tool and cease not to urge you on, until playful Venus has caused the tender organ to explode!

MORETUM

Iam nox hibernas bis quinque peregerat horas
excubitorque diem cantu praedixerat ales,
Simulus exigui cultor cum rusticus agri,
tristia venturae metuens ieiunia lucis,
5   membra levat vili sensim demissa grabato
sollicitaque manu tenebras explorat inertes
vestigatque focum, laesus quem denique sensit.
parvulus exusto remanebat stipite fomes
et cinis obductae celabat lumina prunae;
10 admovet his pronam summissa fronte lucernam
et producit acu stuppas umore carentis,
excitat et crebris languentem flatibus ignem.
tandem concepto, sed vix, fulgore recedit
oppositaque manu lumen defendit ab aura
15 et reserat casulae, quae pervidet, ostia clavis.
fusus erat terra frumenti pauper acervus:
hinc sibi depromit quantum mensura patebat,
quae bis in octonas excurrit pondere libras.
    Inde abit adsistitque molae, parvaque tabella,
20 quam fixam paries illos servabat in usus,
lumina fida locat; geminos tum veste lacertos

mss: Ω = G; FPDRM (mn); SL   meter: hexameter
8 fomes *Scaliger*: fumus Ω

MORETUM

Now had the winter's night completed its tenth hour, and with his crowing the sentinel cock had proclaimed the advent of day, when Simulus, the rustic tiller of a little farm, fearful of grim hunger on the coming morn, slowly uplifts his limbs from the poor bed on which he had laid them, and with cautious hand feels his way through the lifeless night, and gropes for the hearth, which he at last painfully finds. In a burned-out log there still remained some tiny kindling, while ashes concealed the glow of live coal beneath. Bending low his head, he brings his lamp forward to the embers, draws out with a needle the dried-up wick, and with many a puff wakes up the sluggish fire. Rousing at last a flame, though hard the task, he draws back, and with sheltering hand guards the light from the draught, while his key, peeping through, unlocks the closet door. On the ground was poured a poor heap of corn: from this he helps himself to as much as the measure, which runs to twice eight pounds in weight, would hold.

And now he goes and takes his place at the mill; and on a tiny shelf, firmly fastened on the wall for such needs, he places his trusty lamp. Then he frees both arms from his

---

13 vix *Voss*: lux Ω
15 casulae *DeWitt*: clausae Ω | quae *FSL*: qua *GPDRM*

liberat et cinctus villosae tergore caprae
perverrit cauda silices gremiumque molarum.
advocat inde manus operi, partitus utroque:
25 laeva ministerio, dextra est intenta labori.
haec rotat adsiduum gyris et concitat orbem
(tunsa Ceres silicum rapido decurrit ab ictu),
interdum fessae succedit laeva sorori
alternatque vices. modo rustica carmina cantat
30 agrestique suum solatur voce laborem,
interdum clamat Scybalen. erat unica custos,
Afra genus, tota patriam testante figura,
torta comam labroque tumens et fusca colore,
pectore lata, iacens mammis, compressior alvo,
35 cruribus exilis, spatiosa prodiga planta.
hanc vocat atque arsura focis imponere ligna
imperat et flamma gelidos adolere liquores.
    Postquam implevit opus iustum versatile finem,
transfert inde manu fusas in cribra farinas
40 et quatit; atra manent summo purgamina dorso,
subsidit sincera foraminibusque liquatur
emundata Ceres. levi tum protinus illam
componit tabula, tepidas super ingerit undas,
contrahit admixtos nunc fontes atque farinas,
45 transversat durata manu liquidoque coacta,
interdum grumos spargit sale. iamque subactum
levat opus palmisque suum dilatat in orbem

24 utroque *G*: utri(m)que Ω
40 atra manent *O. Skutsch*: ac remanent Ω
45 coacta *S*: -o Ω

---

[1] In ancient mills, corn was ground by means of two stones, the

garment and girt in a shaggy goatskin he carefully sweeps with its tail the stones and hollow of the mill.[1] Next he summons his hands to the work, which he allots to this side or to that: the left is devoted to supplying the grain, the right to plying the mill. The right hand, in constant circles, turns and drives the wheel (the grain, bruised by the stones' swift blows, runs down); the left, at intervals, relieves her wearied sister and changes places. Now he sings rustic songs, and with rude strains solaces his toil; at times he shouts to Scybale. She was his only help, African by race, her whole appearance proclaiming her native land: her hair curly, her lips swollen, and her complexion dark; she was wide-chested, with breasts hanging low, her belly somewhat pinched, her legs thin, her feet broad and ample. Her he calls, and bids her place fuel on the fire to burn, and over the flame heat cold water.

When the task of grinding has come to its due end, he pours out the meal, transfers it by hand into a sieve and shakes: the black husks remain on the upper side; the flour, clean and pure, sinks down, filtering through the crevices. Then straightway on a smooth table he lays it out, pours warm water on it and packs together the now mingled moisture and meal into lumps which he turns over and over till they are hardened and cohere through the action of hand and liquid, from time to time sprinkling salt thereon. And now he lifts the kneaded mixture and with open palms spreads it out into its rounded shape which he

lower of which, called *meta,* was shaped like a cone. The lower part of the upper stone fitted the *meta* like a cap. Poured into a receptacle above, the corn passed through a small hole above the *meta,* and was ground on the sides of the latter.

521

et notat impressis aequo discrimine quadris.
infert inde foco (Scybale mundaverat aptum
50   ante locum) testisque tegit, super aggerat ignes.
dumque suas peragit Volcanus Vestaque partes,
Simulus interea vacua non cessat in hora,
verum aliam sibi quaerit opem, neu sola palato
sit non grata Ceres, quas iungat comparat escas.
55   non illi suspensa focum carnaria iuxta,
durati sale terga suis truncique vacabant,
traiectus medium sparto sed caseus orbem
et vetus adstricti fascis pendebat anethi:
ergo aliam molitur opem sibi providus heros.
60   Hortus erat iunctus casulae, quem vimina pauca
et calamo rediviva levi munibat harundo,
exiguus spatio, variis sed fertilis herbis.
nil illi deerat quod pauperis exigit usus;
interdum locuples a paupere plura petebat.
65   nec sumptus ullius erat, sed recula curae:
si quando vacuum casula pluviaeve tenebant
festave lux, si forte labor cessabat aratri,
horti opus illud erat. varias disponere plantas
norat et occultae committere semina terrae
70   vicinosque apte circa deducere rivos.
hic holus, hic late fundentes bracchia betae
fecundusque rumex malvaeque inulaeque virebant,
hic siser et nomen capiti debentia porra

65 ullius erat *Kenney*: erat ullius [opus *del. Maehly*] Ω | recula
Ribbeck: regula Ω
70 circa *Bücheler*: cura Ω | deducere *Kenney*: summittere Ω

marks into quadrants, stamped out at equal intervals. Then he puts it in the hearth (Scybale had first cleaned a suitable place) and covers it with tiles, heaping up the fire above. And with heat and hearth playing their part, Simulus meanwhile is not slack in that idle hour, but seeks for himself another resource, and lest bread by itself should displease his palate, he gathers dainties to flavour it. Near his hearth no meatrack hung from the ceiling; backs and sides of bacon cured with salt were lacking; but there was suspended only a round cheese pierced through its middle with a string and some old dill tied up in a bunch. Therefore our provident hero devises for himself another resource.

Adjoining the cottage was a garden, sheltered by a few osiers and the slender stalks of reeds which he used as a fence; it was small in extent, but rich in various herbs. Naught did it lack that a poor man's need demands; at times a wealthy neighbour would turn to the poor man's stock for more. Nor did his little property cost him anything but his labour: if ever rainy weather or a holiday kept him idle in his cottage, if by any chance there was respite from the task of ploughing, that time was given to the garden. He knew how to set out the various plants, to entrust seeds to the hidden soil, and to lead nearby streams as required around the crops. Here flourished cabbage, here beets, their arms far outspread, with sorrel in profusion, mallows, and elecampane; here skirret and leeks, that owe their name to the head,[2] and lettuce that brings pleasing

[2] The *porrum capitatum* as contrasted with the *porrum sectile,* the latter being our chives.

grataque nobilium requies lactuca ciborum,
75 <spinosi asparagi> crescitque in acumina radix,
et gravis in latum dimissa cucurbita ventrem.
verum hic non domini (quis enim contractior illo?)
sed populi proventus erat, nonisque diebus
venalis umero fasces portabat in urbem.
80 inde domum cervice levis, gravis aere redibat
vix umquam urbani comitatus merce macelli:
cepa rubens sectique famem domat area porri
quaeque trahunt acri vultus nasturtia morsu
intibaque et Venerem revocans eruca morantem.
85   Tum quoque tale aliquid meditans intraverat hortum;
ac primum leviter digitis tellure refossa
quattuor educit cum spissis alia fibris,
inde comas apii graciles rutamque rigentem
vellit et exiguo coriandra trementia filo.
90 haec ubi collegit, laetum considit ad ignem
et clara famulam poscit mortaria voce.
singula tum capitum nodoso corpore nudat
et summis spoliat coriis contemptaque passim
spargit humi atque abicit; servatum gramine bulbum
95 tinguit aqua lapidisque cavum demittit in orbem.
his salis inspergit micas, sale durus adeso
caseus adicitur, lectas super ingerit herbas,
et laeva testam saetosa sub inguina fulcit,
dextera pistillo primum fragrantia mollit
100 alia, tum pariter mixto terit omnia suco.
it manus in gyrum: paulatim singula vires
deperdunt proprias, color est e pluribus unus,

---

relief to rich meals:[3] here the roots of spiky asparagus which grow into spearpoints, and the heavy gourd that swells into its broad belly. But this crop was not for the owner (for who more frugal than he?) but for the people; and every ninth day over his neck he would carry his bundles to town for sale. Thence he would return home, with shoulders light but with heavy pockets, and seldom accompanied by purchases from the market. It was red onion that tamed his hunger, and his plot of chives, and watercress which with its sharp taste screws up the face, and rocket which revives a man's flagging potency.

At this hour, too, with some such plan in mind had he entered the garden. At first, lightly digging up the ground with his fingers, he draws out four garlic bulbs with thick fibres, then plucks slender parsley leaves and unbending rue, and coriander, trembling on its scanty stalk. These culled, he sits down by the pleasant fire, and loudly calls to the maid for a mortar. Then he strips the single heads of their rough membranes, and despoils them of the outermost skins, scattering about on the ground the parts rejected and casting them away. The bulb, saved with the leaves, he dips in water, and drops into the mortar's hollow circle. Thereon he sprinkles grains of salt, adds cheese hardened with consuming salt, and heaps on top the herbs he has collected; with his left hand he wedges the mortar between his shaggy thighs, while his right first crushes with a pestle the fragrant garlic, then grinds all evenly in a juicy mixture. Round and round goes his hand: little by little the ingredients lose their peculiar strength; the many

[3] Lettuce was eaten at the close of a feast, though by Martial's time (cf. 13.14) it was taken at the beginning.

nec totus viridis, quia lactea frusta repugnant,
nec de lacte nitens, quia tot variatur ab herbis.
105 saepe viri nares acer iaculatur apertas
spiritus et simo damnat sua prandia vultu,
saepe manu summa lacrimantia lumina terget
immeritoque furens dicit convicia fumo.
     Procedebat opus; nec iam salebrosus, ut ante,
110 sed gravior lentos ibat pistillus in orbis.
ergo Palladii guttas instillat olivi
exiguique super vires infundit aceti
atque iterum commiscet opus mixtumque retractat.
tum demum digitis mortaria tota duobus
115 circuit inque globum distantia contrahit unum,
constet ut effecti species nomenque moreti.
     Eruit interea Scybale quoque sedula panem,
quem laetus recipit manibus, pulsoque timore
iam famis inque diem securus Simulus illam
120 ambit crura ocreis paribus tectusque galero
sub iuga parentis cogit lorata iuvencos
atque agit in segetes et terrae condit aratrum.

colours blend into one, yet neither is this wholly green, for milk-white fragments still resist, nor is it a shining milky-white, being coloured by so many herbs. Often the strong odour stings the man's open nostrils, and with turned-up nose he condemns his breakfast fare, often drawing the back of his hand across his watering eyes, and cursing in anger the innocent smoke.

The work goes on: and the pestle, no longer in uneven pace, as before, but heavier in weight, moves on in slower circles. He therefore pours on it some drops of olive oil, adding a little strong vinegar, then once more stirs up the dish and handles the mixture afresh. Finally he wipes two fingers round all the mortar, and into one ball packs the sundry pieces, so that, in reality as in name, there is fashioned a perfect *moretum*.[4]

Meanwhile Scybale, too, industrious maid, draws forth the bread, which Simulus gladly receives in his hands; now that fear of hunger is driven away, carefree for the day, he wraps his legs in a pair of gaiters, and covered with a cap forces his submissive bullocks under their leather-bound yokes, and drives them to the fields, there in the earth burying his plough.

[4] Thus is designated the rustic dish of herbs, which forms the subject of the poem. Another reference to the *moretum* is found in Ovid, *Fasti* 4.367, where we learn that the mixture was used at the feasts of Cybele. Columella (12.57) gives a prose description.

INDEX

The references are to books and lines in the Latin text. Abbreviations: *A.* = Aeneid; *Ca.* = Catalepton; *Ci.* = Ciris; *Co.* = Copa; *Cu.* = Culex; *D.* = Dirae; *E.* = Eclogues; *G.* = Georgics; *L.* = Lydia; *M.* = Moretum; *P.* = Priapea; also *adj.* = adjective; *fem.* = feminine; *plur.* = plural; *sing.* = singular; *subst.* = substantive.

References to the following names are not given in full on account of their frequency: Achates, Aeneas, Anchises, Apollo, Ascanius, Ausonius, Bacchus, Danai, Dardanius, Dido, Graius, Italia, Italus, Iulus, Iuno, Iuppiter, Latinus, Latium, Laurens, Manes, Mars, Nympha, Pallas (3), Phoebus, Phrygius, Priamus, Romanus, Rutulus, Teucrus, Troia, Troianus, Troïus, Tros, Turnus, Tyrius, Tyrrhenus, Venus.

INDEX

Allia, a branch of the Tiber six miles from Rome, where the Gauls defeated the Romans July 16, 390 B.C., *A.* VII.717

Almo, a Latin, *A.* VII.532, 575

Aloidae, descendants of Aloeus, Otus and Ephialtes, giants, *A.* VI.582

Alpes, the Alps, *G.* I.475; III.474; *A.* X.13

Alphesiboeus, a herdsman, *E.* V.73; VIII.1, 5, 62

Alpheus, river of Elis, which was fabled to reappear in Sicily, *G.* III.19, 180; *A.* III.694; X.179

Alpinus, *adj.* Alpine, *E.* X.47; *A.* IV.442; VI.830; VIII.661

Alsus, a Latin, *A.* XII.304

Amaryllis, a rustic girl, *E.* I.5, 30, 36; II.14, 52; III.81; VIII.77, 78, 101; X.22

Amastrus, a Trojan, *A.* XI.673

Amata, wife of Latinus, *A.* VII.343, 401, 581; IX.737; XII.56, 71

Amathus, a town of Cyprus, *A.* X.51

Amathusia, i.e. Venus, *Ci.* 242

Amazon, *A.* XI.648, 660. Also Amazonides, *A.* I.490; Amazonius, *A.* V.311

Amerinus, *adj.* of Ameria, a town of Umbria, *G.* I.265

Aminaeus, *adj.* of Aminaea, a district of Picenum, *G.* II.97

Amiternus, *adj.* of Amiternum, a Sabine town, *A.* VII.710

Amor, son of Venus, and god of love, Cupid, *E.* VIII.43, 47; X.28, 29, 44, 69; *G.* III.244; *A.* I.663, 689; IV.412; X.188; *Ca.* XIV.10; *Co.* 20

Amphion, king of Thebes, and husband of Niobe, *E.* II.24

Amphitrite, wife of Neptune and goddess of the sea, *Ci.* 73, 486

Amphitryoniades, son or descendant of Amphitryo, i.e. Hercules, *A.* VIII.103, 214

Amphrysius, *adj.* of Amphrysus, *A.* VI.398

Amphrysus, a river of Thessaly, near which Apollo fed the flocks of Admetus, *G.* III.2

Amsanctus, a lake in Samnium, east of Naples, *A.* VII.565

Amyclae: (1) a town of Latium, *A.* X.564; (2) a town of Laconia in Greece, hence Amyclaeus, *adj.*, *G.* III.89, 345; *Ci.* 376, 489

Amycus: (1) a Trojan, *A.* I.221; IX.772; X.704; XII.509; (2) a king of the Thracian Bebryces, *A.* V.373

Amyntas, a shepherd, *E.* II.35, 39; III.66, 74, 83; V.8, 15, 18; X.37, 38, 41

Amythaonius, *adj.* of Amythaon, father of Melampus, and son of Cretheus, *G.* III.550

Anagnia, a town of Latium, *A.* VII.684

Anchemolus, son of Rhoetus, king of the Marsians, *A.* X.389

winds in general; *E.* II.58;
V.82; *G.* I.241, 333, 418, 462;
II.188, 333, 429; III.278, 357;
IV.261; *A.* I.51, 536; II.111,
304; III.61, 70, 357, 481;
V.696, 764; VI.336; VIII.430;
IX.670

Automedon, charioteer of
Achilles, *A.* II.477

Aventinus: (1) a son of Hercules
and Rhea, *A.* VII.657; (2) the
Aventine, one of Rome's
seven hills, *A.* VII.659;
VIII.231

Avernus, *adj.* of Avernus, a lake
near Cumae in Campania, in
a volcanic crater; it was said
that birds flying over were
killed by the fumes, and pop-
ular etymology connected the
name with ἄορνος, birdless
(see *A.* VI.242); tradition
placed near this an entrance
to the lower world, hence the
word is used of the lower
world itself, *G.* II.164; IV.493;
A. III.442; IV.512; V.732, 813;
VI.118, 126, 201, 564, 898;
VII.91

Baccheius, *adj.* of Bacchus, *G.*
II.454

Bacchus, son of Jupiter and
Semele, god of wine and of
poets; also used figuratively
of the vine and of wine; *E.*
V.69; *G.* II.113, 380, etc.

Bactra, capital of Bactriana, a
remote district between
Hindu Kush and the Oxus, *G.*
II.138; *A.* VIII.688

Baiae, a town of Campania, a
favourite seaside resort of the
Romans, *A.* IX.710

Balearis, *adj.* Balearic, of the
Balearic Islands Majorca and
Minorca, whose people were
famous for the use of the
sling, *G.* I.309

Barcaei, Barcaeans, or people of
Barce, in Libya, *A.* IV.43

Battarus, *D.* 1, 14, 30, 54, 64,
71, 97

Batulum, a town of Campania,
A. VII.739

Bavius, a poetaster, contempo-
rary with Virgil, *E.* III.90

Bebrycius, *adj.* of Bebrycia or
Bithynia, a province of Asia
Minor, *A.* V.373

Belgicus, *adj.* Belgian, or of the
Belgae, a Gallic tribe which
used war chariots, *G.* III.204

Belides, son of Belus, or de-
scended from Belus, *A.* II.82

Bellona, sister of Mars, and
goddess of war, *A.* VII.319;
VIII.703

Belus: (1) founder of Dido's
royal line, *A.* I.729, 730; (2)
father of Dido, *A.* I.621

Benacus, one of the Italian
lakes, near Verona, now Lago
di Garda, *G.* II.160; *A.* X.205

Berecyntius, *adj.* of Berecyntus,
a mountain in Phrygia, sacred
to Cybele, *A.* VI.784; IX.82,
619

Etruria, the country of the Etruscans, in Italy, *G.* II.533; *A.* VIII.494; XII.232

Etruscus, *adj.* Etruscan, *A.* VIII.480, 503; IX.150, 521; X.148, 180, 238, 429; XI.598

Euadne, wife of Capaneus, who burned herself on her husband's funeral pyre, *A.* VI.447

Euandrus or Euander, the king of Pallanteum who welcomed Aeneas, *A.* VIII.52, 100, 119, 185, 313, 360, 455, 545, 558; IX.9; X.148, 370, 420, 492, 515, 780; XI.26, 31, 45, 55, 140, 148, 394, 835; XII.184, 551; with Euandrius, *adj.* used of Evander's son, Pallas, *A.* X.394

Euanthes, a Phrygian in the Trojan force, *A.* X.702

Euboicus, *adj.* of Euboea, the island east of Attica and Boeotia, *A.* VI.2, 42; IX.710; XI.260; *Cu.* 355

Euiades, Bacchants, *A.* IV.469

Eumedes, a Trojan, *A.* XII.346

Eumelus, a Trojan, *A.* V.665

Eumenides, the Furies, *G.* I.278; IV.483; VI.250, 280, 375

Euneus, a Trojan, *A.* XI.666

Euphrates, a river of Asia, used also of the peoples near it, *G.* I.509; IV.561; *A.* VIII.726

Europa, Europe, *A.* I.385; VII.224; X.91

Eurōtas, a river of Lacedaemon, flowing by Sparta, *E.* VI.83; *A.* I.498

Eurus, the southeast wind; used also of wind in general, *G.* I.371, 453; II.107, 339, 441; III.277, 382; IV.29, 192; *A.* I.85, 110, 131, 140, 317, 383; II.418; VIII.223; XII.733; *Ci.* 25; *D.* 38; with Eurōus, *adj.* Eastern, *A.* III.533

Euryalus, a Trojan, friend of Nisus, *A.* V.294, 295, 322, 323, 334, 337, 343; IX.179, 185, 198, 231, 281, 320, 342, 359, 373, 384, 390, 396, 424, 433, 467, 475, 481

Eurydice, wife of Orpheus, *G.* IV.486, 490, 519, 525, 526, 527, 547; *Cu.* 268, 287

Eurypylus, a Greek, *A.* II.114

Eurystheus, a king of Mycenae, the enemy of Hercules, *G.* III.4; *A.* VIII.292

Eurytides, son of Eurytus, i.e. Clonus, *A.* X.499

Eurytion, a Trojan, *A.* V.495, 514, 541

Fabaris, a tributary of the Tiber, *A.* VII.715

Fabius, a famous name in Roman history; especially of Q. Fabius Maximus, general opposed to Hannibal, *A.* VI.845; *Cu.* 361

Fabricius, the conqueror of Pyrrhus, *A.* VI.844

Fadus, a Rutulian, *A.* IX.344

Falernus, *adj.* Falernian, of the

tains of the Ida range in
Mysia, *G.* I.103; III.269

Gela, a city by a river of the
same name, on the south
coast of Sicily, *A.* III.702;
with Gelōus, *adj.* Geloan, *A.*
III.701

Gelōnus, one of the Geloni, a
Scythian people, *G.* III.461;
plur. G. II.115; *A.* VIII.725

Germania, Germany, *E.* I.62; *G.*
I.474, 509

Geryon, and Geryones, Geryon,
a mythic three-bodied mon-
ster in Spain, whose oxen
were carried off by Hercules,
A. VI.662; VIII.202

Getae, a Thracian tribe on the
Danube, *G.* III.462; IV.463;
A. VII.604; with Geticus, *adj.*
Getic, *A.* III.35

Giganteus, *adj.* of the Giants,
sons of Earth and Tartarus,
struck by the bolts of Jupiter,
Ci. 30; *Cu.* 28

Glaucus: (1) a sea deity, *G.*
I.437; *A.* V.823; VI.36; (2) a
son of Antenor, *A.* VI.483; (3)
a son of Imbrasus, *A.* XII.343

Gorgo, a snaky-haired daughter
of Phorcus, one of three sis-
ters, the chief being Medusa,
A. II.616; VI.289; VIII.438;
with Gorgoneus, *adj., A.*
VII.341 (where *venena* refers
to the venom of the snakes)

Gortynius, *adj.* of Gortyna, a
city of Crete, *E.* VI.60; *A.*
XI.773; *Ci.* 114

Gracchus, a Roman family of
the Sempronian *gens,* espe-
cially Tiberius and Gaius, the
reformers, *A.* VI.842

Gradivus, the strider, a name of
Mars, *A.* III.35; X.542

Graecia, Greece, *G.* I.38; III.20;
A. XI.287; *Ci.* 412; *Cu.* 34;
with Graecus, *adj.* Greek, *Co.* 1

Graiugena, one born a Greek,
A. III.550; VIII.127

Graius, *adj.* Greek, *G.* II.16,
etc. (36 instances)

Graviscae, a town of Etruria, *A.*
X.184

Gryneus, *adj.* of Grynia, a town
of Aeolis where Apollo was
worshipped, *E.* VI.72; *A.*
IV.345

Gyaros, an island of the Aegean,
A. III.76

Gyas: (1) a Trojan, *A.* I.222,
612; V.118, 152, 160, 167,
169, 184, 223; XII.460; (2) a
Latin, *A.* X.318

Gyges, a Trojan, *A.* IX.762

Gylippus, an Arcadian, *A.*
XII.272

Hadriacus, *adj.* of the Adriatic,
A. XI.405 (where the refer-
ence is to a river flowing back
to its source, a perversion of
nature)

Haemon, a Rutulian, *A.* IX.685;
with Haemonides, son of
Haemon, *A.* X.537

Haemus, a Thracian mountain
range, *G.* I.492; II.488

INDEX

Hyades, the Hyades, "daughters of rain," seven stars in Taurus, *G.* I.138; *A.* I.744; III.516

Hybla, a mountain in Sicily, *E.* VII.37; with Hyblaeus, *adj.,* *E.* I.54

Hydaspes: (1) a river of India, *G.* IV.211; (2) a Trojan, *A.* X.747

Hydra: (1) a fifty-headed monster in the lower world, *A.* VI.576; (2) a seven-headed snake, killed by Hercules, *A.* VII.658

Hylaeus, a Centaur, *G.* II.457; *A.* VIII.294

Hylas, a companion of Hercules in the Argonautic expedition, who was carried away by fountain nymphs, *E.* VI.43, 44; *G.* III.6

Hylax, name of a dog, *E.* VIII.107

Hyllus, a Trojan, *A.* XII.535

Hymen, god of marriage *Cu.* 247

Hypanis: (1) a river of Scythia, now the Bug, *G.* IV.369; (2) a Trojan, *A.* II.340, 428

Hyperboreus, *adj.* of the far North, *G.* III.381; IV.517

Hyperīon, a Titan, father of the Sun, then the Sun himself, *Cu.* 101

Hyrcānus, *adj.* of the Hyrcani, a people of Asia near the Caspian Sea, *A.* IV.367; VII.605; *Ci.* 308

Hyrtacides, son of Hyrtacus: (1) Hippocoon, *A.* V.492, 503; (2) Nisus, *A.* IX.177, 234, 319, 492, 503

Hyrtacus, a Trojan, *A.* IX.406

Iacchus, a name of Bacchus, *E.* VII.61; *G.* I.166; also of wine, *E.* VI.15

Iaera, a wood nymph, *A.* IX.673

Ianiculum, the Janiculum, a hill at Rome on the west side of the Tiber, *A.* VIII.358

Ianus, Janus, a two-faced Italian deity, *A.* VII.180, 610; VIII.357; XII.198

Iapetus, one of the Titans, *G.* I.279

Iapys, *adj.* of the Iapydes, an Illyrian people, at the head of the Adriatic, *G.* III.475

Iapyx, *adj.* Iapygian, or Apulian, *A.* XI.247, 678; as *subst.* (1) Iapyx, a wind blowing from Iapygia toward Greece, *A.* VIII.710; (2) son of Iasus, *A.* XII.391, 420, 485

Iarbas, a Gaetulian king, son of Jupiter Hammon, *A.* IV.36, 196, 326

Iasides, son of Iasus, *A.* V.843; XII.392

Iasius, brother of Dardanus, and son-in-law of Teucer, *A.* III.168

Icariotis, daughter of Icarus, the son of Oebalus, king of Sparta, i.e. Penelope, *Cu.* 265

Icarus, son of Daedalus, who,

INDEX

INDEX

Machāon, a Greek physician, son of Aesculapius, *A.* II.263

Maeander, a river of Lydia noted for its windings; hence, a winding border, *A.* V.241

Maecenas, patron of Virgil, friend of Augustus, *G.* I.2; II.41; III.41; IV.2

Maenalus, or Maenala, a mountain of Arcadia, *E.* VIII.22; X.15, 55; *G.* I.7; with Maenalius, *adj.* of Maenalus, Arcadian, *E.* VIII.21, 25, 31, 36, 42, 46, 51, 57, 61; *Co.* 9

Maeon, a Rutulian, *A.* X.337

Maeonia, old name of Lydia, and therefore used for Etruria, *A.* VIII.499

Maeonidae, Lydians or Etruscans, *A.* XI.759

Maeonius, *adj.* Maeonian or Lydian, *G.* IV.380; *A.* IV.216; IX.546; X.141; *Ci.* 62

Maeōtius, *adj.* of the Maeotians, a Scythian people, dwelling about Lake Maeotis, now Sea of Azov, *G.* III.349; *A.* VI.799

Magus, a Rutulian, *A.* X.521

Maia, mother of Mercury and daughter of Atlas, one of the Pleiades, *G.* I.225; *A.* I.297; VIII.138, 140

Malea, a promontory at the southeast of the Peloponnesus, *A.* V.193

Mānes, the spirits of the departed, the gods below, or the lower world in general, *G.* I.243; *A.* III.63; VI.896; *Ca.* XI.7; *Cu.* 214, etc. (30 instances in Virgil)

Manlius, i.e. M. Manlius Capitolinus, who saved the Capitol from the Gauls, *A.* VIII.652

Manto, a prophetess, wedded to the Tiber, *A.* X.199

Mantua, a city of Gallia Transpadana, near Virgil's birthplace, *E.* IX.27, 28; *G.* II.198; III.12; *Ca.* VIII.6; X.4

Marcellus, a family name in the Claudian *gens;* especially, M. Claudius Marcellus, who opposed Hannibal and conquered Syracuse, and M. Marcellus, nephew and adopted son of Augustus, who died in 23 B.C., *A.* VI.855, 883

Mareotis, *adj.* of Mareotis, a district of Egypt, *G.* II.91

Marīca, a nymph, *A.* VII.47

Marius, conqueror of the Cimbri and Jugurtha; in *plur.* men of his stamp, *A.* II.169

Marpesius *adj.* of Marpesus, a mountain of the island Paros, *A.* VI.471

Marruvius, *adj.* of Marruvium, a city of Latium, capital of the Marsi, *A.* VII.750

Mars, the god of war, *E.* X.44; *G.* I.511; *A.* I.274, etc. (42 instances); with Martius, *adj.* of Mars, warlike, *E.* IX.12; *G.* IV.71; *A.* VII.182; IX.566; XI.661

INDEX

Marsus, *adj.* of the Marsi, a Sabellian tribe in Italy, *A.* VII.758; *plur. subst.* Marsi, the Marsians, *G.* II.167; *A.* X.544

Massicus: (1) *adj.* of Mt. Massicus, a mountain on the borders of Latium and Campania, *G.* II.143; III.526; *A.* VII.726; (2) an Etruscan, *A.* X.166

Massȳlus, *adj.* of the Massyli, a people of North Africa, *A.* IV.132, 483; *plur. subst.* the people themselves, *A.* VI.60

Maurusius, *adj.* of the Mauri, Moorish, *A.* IV.206

Mavors, another name of Mars, *A.* VI.872; VIII.630, 700; X.755; XI.389; XII.179, 332; *L.* 69; with Mavortius, *adj.* of Mars, martial, *G.* IV.462; *A.* I.276; III.13; VI.777; IX.685

Maximus, i.e. Q. Fabius Maximus, *A.* VI.845

Media, a country of Asia, south of the Caspian, *G.* II.126; with Medus, *adj.* Median, *A.* IV.211; *plur. subst.* Medi, Medes, *G.* II.134, 136; also Medicus, *adj.* Median, *G.* I.215

Medon, a Trojan, *A.* VI.483

Megaera, one of the Furies, *A.* XII.846

Megara, chief city of the Megarid, a district of the Isthmus between the Saronic and Corinthian Gulfs, *Ci.* 105, 388

Megarus, *adj.* of Megara (in Sicily), *A.* III.689

Melampus: (1) a seer and physician, *G.* III.550; (2) a Latin, *A.* X.320

Meliboeus: (1) a shepherd, *E.* I.6, 19, 42, 73; III.1; V.87; VII.9; *Ca.* IX.18; (2) *adj.* of Meliboea, a town of Thessaly, home of Philoctetes, *A.* III.401; V.251

Melicerta, son of Ino and Athamas, changed into a sea god, *G.* I.437

Melite, a sea nymph, *A.* V.825

Mella, a river of Cisalpine Gaul flowing through Brescia, *A.* IV.278

Memmius, a Roman gentile name, *A.* V.117 (where Virgil seems to assume that Μνησθεύς was assimilated to the Latin *meminisse,* and so became *Memmius*)

Memnon, son of Tithonus and Aurora and king of the Ethiopians; his armour was made by Vulcan, *A.* I.489

Menalcas, a shepherd, *E.* II.15; III.13, 58; V.4, 64, 90; IX.10, 16, 18, 55; X.20

Menelaus, son of Atreus, brother of Agamemnon and husband of Helen, *A.* II.264; VI.525; XI.262

Menestheus, a Trojan, *A.* X.129

INDEX

Menoetes: (1) a Trojan, *A.* V.161, 164, 166, 173, 179; (2) an Arcadian, *A.* XII.517

Mercurius, Mercury, son of Jupiter and Maia and messenger of the gods, *A.* IV.222, 558; VIII.138

Meropes, a Trojan, *A.* IX.702

Messalla, a Roman surname; especially M. Valerius Messalla Corvinus, patron and friend of Tibullus, *Ca.* IX.40; *Ci.* 54

Messapus, the eponymous hero of Messapia or Iapygia (at the heel of Italy), represented by Virgil as leading a force from southern Etruria, *A.* VII.691; VIII.6; IX.27, 124, 160, 351, 365, 458, 523; X.354, 749; XI.429, 464, 518, 520, 603; XII.128, 289, 294, 488, 550, 661

Metabus, a Volscian, father of Camilla, *A.* XI.540, 564

Methymnaeus, *adj.* of Methymna, a city of Lesbos, *G.* II.90

Metiscus, a Rutulian, charioteer of Turnus, *A.* XII.469, 472, 623, 737, 784

Mettus, i.e. Mettus Fufetius, dictator of Alba, who for his treachery was torn asunder by horses, *A.* VIII.642

Metus, Fear, Dread (personification), *G.* III.552; *A.* VI.276

Mevius, a poet hostile to Virgil, *E.* III.90

Mezentius, an Etruscan king, *A.* VII.648, 654; VIII.7, 482, 501, 569; IX.522, 586; X.150, 204, 689, 714, 729, 742, 762, 768, 897; XI.7, 16

Micon, a shepherd, *E.* III.10; VII.30

Milesius, *adj.* of Miletus, a city of Ionia in Asia Minor, *G.* III.306; IV.334

Mimas, a Trojan, *A.* X.702, 706

Mincius, now the Mincio, a river of Cisalpine Gaul, *E.* VII.13; *G.* III.15; *A.* X.206

Minerva, a Roman goddess, patroness of arts, handicrafts, and science, identified with Athene, *G.* I.18; IV.246; *A.* II.31, 189, 404; III.531; V.284; VI.840; VII.805; VIII.409, 699; XI.259; *Ci.* 23

Minio, a river of Etruria, *A.* X.183

Minos, a king of Crete; after death a judge in the lower world, *A.* VI.432; *Ci.* 111, 132, 272, 286, 287, 301, 367, 414, 421, 454; *Cu.* 374. Hence Minois, daughter of Minos, *i.e.* Ariadne, *L.* 49; and Minoius, *adj.* of Minos, *A.* VI.14

Minotaurus, Minotaur, the man-bull killed by Theseus, *A.* VI.26

Misenus: (1) a Trojan, trum-

Passero, *A.* III.429, 699;
VII.289; *Ci.* 88

Pactōlus, a river of Lydia, *A.*
X.142

Padus, the river Po, north Italy,
G. II.452; *A.* IX.680

Padusa, one of the mouths of
the Po, *A.* XI.457

Paeonius, *adj.* of Paeon (god
of medicine); hence medical
or healing, *A.* VII.769;
XII.401

Paestum, a city of Lucania, *G.*
IV.119

Pagasus, an Etruscan, *A.* XI.670

Palaemon: (1) son of Athamas
and Ino, changed to a sea
god, *A.* V.823; *Ci.* 396; (2) a
shepherd, *E.* III.50, 53

Palaepaphius, *adj.* of Old
Paphos, referring to Venus,
who had a famous temple in
Paphos, *Ci.* 88

Palamedes, a Greek hero, *A.*
II.82

Palatium, the Palatine hill, on
which Augustus had his resi-
dence, *G.* I.499; hence
Palatīnus, *adj.* of the Palatine,
A. IX.9

Pales, a shepherd goddess, *E.*
V.35; *G.* III.1, 294; *Cu.* 20,
77

Palīcus, the name of twin sons
of Zeus (Jupiter) by Thalia,
worshipped in Sicily, *A.*
IX.585

Palinurus, the Trojan pilot of
Aeneas, *A.* III.202, 513, 562;

V.12, 833, 840, 843, 847, 871;
VI.337, 341, 373, 381

Palladium, a statue of Pallas, es-
pecially that stolen from Troy
by Ulysses and Diomedes, *A.*
II.166, 183; IX.151

Palladius, *adj.* of Pallas, i.e.
Athene or Minerva, *G.*
II.181; *Ci.* 29; *M.* 111

Pallantēus, *adj.* of Pallas (2), *A.*
IX.196, 241; *neuter,* as *subst.*
Pallantēum, the city built by
Evander, *A.* VIII.54, 341

Pallas: (1) an epithet of the
Greek goddess Athene (= Mi-
nerva), *E.* II.61; *A.* I.39, 479;
II.15, 163, 615; III.544;
V.704; VII.154; VIII.435;
XI.477; *Cu.* 329; (2) an an-
cient king of Arcadia, fore-
father of Evander, *A.* VIII.51,
54; (3) son of Evander, killed
by Turnus, *A.* VIII.104, 110,
etc. (41 instances)

Pallene, a peninsula of Macedo-
nia, on the Thermaic Gulf, *G.*
IV.391

Palmus, an Etruscan, slain by
Mezentius, *A.* X.697, 699

Pan, a son of Mercury, and god
of woods and of shepherds; in
plur. gods resembling Pan, *E.*
II.31, 32, 33; IV.58, 59; V.59;
VIII.24; X.26; *G.* I.17; II.494;
III.392; *A.* VIII.344; *Cu.* 94,
115

Panchaia, an island or district of
Arabia famous for frankin-
cense, *G.* II.139; hence

itself, *A*. I.466, 651; II.177, 291, 375, 556, [571]; III.87, 336, 350; IV.344, 426; VI.516; VII.322; VIII.37, 374; X.58; XI.280; hence, Pergameus, *adj*. Trojan, *A*. III.110, 476; V.744; VI.63

Pergamea, the name given by Aeneas to his city in Crete, *A*. III.133

Peridĭa, mother of Onites, *A*. XII.515

Periphas, a Greek, *A*. II.476

Permessus, a river of Boeotia flowing from Helicon, a haunt of the Muses, *E*. VI.64

Persae, the Persians, *Cu*. 34

Persephone, the Greek form of the name Proserpina, *Cu*. 261

Persis, Persia (used loosely by Virgil to include Arabia and Syria), *G*. IV.290

Petella, a town of the Bruttii, *A*. III.402

Phaeăces, the Phaeacians, mythic inhabitants of Corcyra (the Scheria of the *Odyssey*), *A*. III.291

Phaedra, wife of Theseus and daughter of Minos, *A*. VI.445

Phaëthon: (1) Helios, the sun god, *A*. V.105; (2) more commonly, a son of Helios, who attempted to drive his father's steeds but losing control of them was destroyed by Jove's thunderbolt, *A*. X.189; *Cu*. 128

Phaëthontiades, the sisters of Phaëthon, who when mourning their brother's fate were changed into alders (or, according to some, poplars), *E*. VI.62

Phanaeus, *adj*. of Phanae, a promontory of Chios, noted for its wine, *G*. II.98

Pharus, a Rutulian, *A*. X.322

Phasis, a river of Colchis, emptying into the Euxine, *G*. IV.367

Phegeus, a Trojan, *A*. V.263; IX.765; XII.371

Pheneus, a town of Arcadia, *A*. VIII.165

Pheres, a Trojan, *A*. X.413

Philippi, a town of Macedonia where Brutus and Cassius were defeated by Octavius and Antony, *G*. I.490

Phillyrides, son of Phillyra, nymph beloved by Saturn; i.e. the centaur Chiron, *G*. III.550

Philoctetes, son of Poeas, king of Meliboea, in Thessaly; from Hercules he inherited the poisoned arrows without which Troy could not be taken, and with which he slew Paris; after the war he founded Petelia in Italy, *A*. III.402

Philomela, daughter of Pandion, and sister of Procne; Tereus, the latter's husband, violated Philomela and then cut out her tongue,

583

INDEX

Tellus, Earth (personification), A. IV.166; VII.137

Telon, a king of the Teleboae, A. VII.734

Tempe, a valley in Thessaly, famous for its beauty, G. II.469; IV.317; Cu. 94

Tempestates, goddesses of the weather or storm, Tempests, A. V.772

Tenedos, an island in the Aegean, near the Troad, A. II.21, 203, 255

Tereus: (1) a king of Thrace, husband of Procne the sister of Philomela, and father of Itys, E. VI.78; (2) a Trojan, A. XI.675

Terra, Earth (personification), E. VIII.93; G. I.278; A. IV.178; VI.580, 595; XII.176, 778

Tethys, a sea goddess, wife of Oceanus, and mother of all waters, G. I.31; Ci. 392

Tetrica, a mountain in the Sabine territory, A. VII.713

Teucer and Teucrus: (1) first king of Troy, father of Batea, who married Dardanus, A. I.235; III.108; IV.230; VI.500, 648; hence Teucri, subst. the Teucrians or Trojans, A. I.38, 89; II.252, etc. (130 instances); also Teucrius, adj. Teucrian or Trojan, Cu. 306, with Teucria, subst. the Teucrian or Trojan land, A.

II.26; (2) a son of Telamon and Hesione, half-brother of Ajax, and founder of Salamis in Cyprus, A. I.619

Teuthras, an Arcadian, A. X.402

Teutonicus, adj. of the Teutones, a tribe of Germany, A. VII.741

Thaemon, a Lycian, A. X.126

Thalassio, salutation to a bride at her wedding, possibly of Etruscan origin, Ca. XII.9; XIII.16

Thalia: (1) a Muse (also Thalea), usually assigned to Comedy, E. VI.2; Cu. 1; (2) a sea nymph, A. V.826

Thamyrus, a Trojan, A. XII.341

Thapsus, a city and peninsula on the eastern coast of Sicily, A. III.689

Thasius, adj. of Thasos, an island in the north Aegean, G. II.91

Thaumantias, fem. subst. daughter of Thaumas, i.e. Iris, A. IX.5

Theano, a Trojan woman, A. X.703

Thebae, Thebes, capital of Boeotia, where the scene of the Bacchae of Euripides is laid, A. IV.469; hence Thebanus, adj. Theban, A. IX.697

Themillas, a Rutulian, A. IX.576

Thermodon, a river of Pontus,

584

Composed in ZephGreek and ZephText by
Technologies 'N Typography, Merrimac, Massachusetts.
Printed in Great Britain by St Edmundsbury Press Ltd,
Bury St Edmunds, Suffolk, on acid-free paper.
Bound by Hunter & Foulis Ltd, Edinburgh, Scotland.